Praise for Michael Robotham and

THE
SECRETS
SHE KEEPS

"A can't-put-down mama drama . . . Each woman reveals her tale in riveting alternating chapters that merge into a series of chilling twists. . . . A premium delivery."

—*People*

"I love this guy's books."

—Lee Child

"An insightful psychological thriller about the joys and fears of impending motherhood."

—Marilyn Stasio, *The New York Times Book Review*

"Robotham's book is well-paced and his lead characters are compelling."

—*USA Today*

"Michael Robotham is the real deal."

—David Baldacci

"Impressively compelling . . . Robotham is stealthy."

—*Bookreporter*

ALSO BY MICHAEL ROBOTHAM

THE SECRETS SHE KEEPS

— A Novel —

MICHAEL ROBOTHAM

POCKET BOOKS

New York   London   Toronto   Sydney   New Delhi

Pocket Books
An Imprint of Simon & Schuster, Inc.
1230 Avenue of the Americas
New York, NY 10020

This book is a work of fiction. Any references to historical events, real people, or real places are used fictitiously. Other names, characters, places, and events are products of the author's imagination, and any resemblance to actual events or places or persons, living or dead, is entirely coincidental.

First Pocket Books paperback edition May 2020

POCKET and colophon are registered trademarks of Simon & Schuster, Inc.

For information about special discounts for bulk purchases, please contact Simon & Schuster Special Sales at 1-866-506-1949 or business@simonandschuster.com.

The Simon & Schuster Speakers Bureau can bring authors to your live event. For more information or to book an event, contact the Simon & Schuster Speakers Bureau at 1-866-248-3049 or visit our website at www.simonspeakers.com.

Manufactured in the United States of America

10 9 8 7 6 5 4 3 2 1

ISBN 978-1-9821-4900-0
ISBN 978-1-5011-7033-1 (ebook)

For Sara and Mark

I'm hurt, hurt and humiliated beyond endurance, seeing the wheat ripening, the fountains never ceasing to give water, the sheep bearing hundreds of lambs, the she-dogs too; until it seems that the whole countryside rises to show me its tender sleeping young, while I feel two hammer-blows here, instead of the mouth of my child.

—Federico García Lorca, *Yerma* (1934)

Translated by James Graham-Lujan and Richard L. O'Connell

PART ONE

AGATHA

I am not the most important person in this story. That honor belongs to Meg, who is married to Jack, and they are the perfect parents of two perfect children, a boy and a girl, blond and blue-eyed and sweeter than honey cakes. Meg is pregnant again and I couldn't be more excited because I'm having a baby too.

Leaning my forehead against the glass, I look in both directions along the pavement, past the green-grocer and hairdressing salon and fashion boutique. Meg is running late. Normally she has dropped Lucy at primary school and Lachlan at his preschool by now and has joined her friends at the café on the corner. Her mothers' group meets every Friday morning, sitting at an outdoor table, jostling prams into place like eighteen-wheelers on the vehicle deck of a ferry. One skinny cappuccino, one chai latte, and a pot of herbal tea . . .

A red bus goes past and blocks my view of Barnes Green, which is opposite. When it pulls away again I see Meg on the far side of the road. She's dressed in her stretch jeans and a baggy sweater, and carrying a colorful three-wheeled scooter. Lachlan must have insisted on riding to his preschool, which would have slowed her down. He will also have stopped to look at the ducks and at the exercise class and at the old people doing tai chi who move so slowly they could almost be stop-motion puppets.

Meg doesn't appear pregnant from this angle. It's only when she turns side-on that the bump becomes a basketball, neat and round, getting lower by the day. I heard her complaining last week about swollen ankles and a sore back. I know how she feels. My extra pounds have turned climbing stairs into a workout and my bladder is the size of a walnut.

Glancing both ways, she crosses Church Road and mouths the word "sorry" to her friends, double-kissing their cheeks and cooing at their babies. All babies are cute, people say, and I guess that's true. I have peered into prams at Gollum-like creatures with sticky-out eyes and two strands of hair, yet always found something to love because they're so newly minted and innocent.

I'm supposed to be stocking the shelves in aisle three. This part of the supermarket is usually a safe place to slack off, because the manager, Mr. Patel, has a problem with feminine hygiene products. He won't use words like "tampons" or "sanitary pads"—calling them "ladies' things" or simply pointing to the boxes that he wants unpacked.

I work four days a week, early morning to three, unless one of the other part-timers calls in sick. Mostly I stock shelves and sticker prices. Mr. Patel won't let me work the cash register because he says I break things. *That happened one time and it wasn't my fault.*

With a name like Mr. Patel, I thought he'd be Pakistani or Indian, but he turned out to be Welsher than a daffodil, with a shock of red hair and a truncated mustache that makes him look like Adolf Hitler's ginger love child.

Mr. Patel doesn't like me very much and he's been itching to get rid of me ever since I told him I was pregnant.

"Don't expect any maternity leave—you're not full-time."

"I don't expect any."

"And doctor's appointments are on your own time."

"Sure."

"And if you can't lift boxes you'll have to stop working."

"I can lift boxes."

Mr. Patel has a wife and four kids at home, but it hasn't made him any more sympathetic to my pregnancy. I don't think he likes women very much. I don't mean he's gay. When I first started working at the supermarket he was all over me like a rash—finding any excuse to brush up against me in the storeroom or when I was mopping the floor.

"Oops!" he'd say, pressing his hard-on against my buttocks. "Just parking my bike."

Pervert!

I go back to my stock cart and pick up the price gun, careful to check the settings. Last week I put the wrong price on the canned peaches and Mr. Patel docked me eight quid.

"What are you doing?" barks a voice. Mr. Patel has crept up behind me.

"Restocking the tampons," I stutter.

"You were staring out the window. Your forehead made that greasy mark on the glass."

"No, Mr. Patel."

"Do I pay you to daydream?"

"No, sir." I point to the shelf. "We're out of the Tampax Super Plus—the one with the applicator."

Mr. Patel looks queasy. "Well, look in the storeroom." He's backing away. "There's a spill in aisle two. Mop it up."

"Yes, Mr. Patel."

"Then you can go home."

"But I'm working until three."

"Devyani will cover for you. She can climb the step-ladder."

What he means is that she's not pregnant or afraid of heights, and that she'll let him "park his bike" without going all feminist on his arse. I should sue him for sexual harassment, but I like this job. It gives me an excuse to be in Barnes and nearer to Meg.

In the rear storeroom I fill a bucket with hot soapy water and choose a sponge mop that hasn't worn away to the metal frame. Aisle two is closer to the registers. I get a good view of the café and the outside tables. I take my time cleaning the floor, staying clear of Mr. Patel. Meg and her friends are finishing up. Cheeks are kissed. Phones are checked. Babies are strapped into prams and pushchairs. Meg makes some final remark and laughs, tossing her fair hair. Almost unconsciously, I toss mine. It doesn't work. That's the problem with curls—they don't toss, they bounce.

Meg's hairdresser, Jonathan, warned me that I couldn't get away with the same cut that she has, but I wouldn't listen to him.

Meg is standing outside the café, texting someone on her phone. It's probably Jack. They'll be discussing what to have for dinner, or making plans for the weekend. I like her maternity jeans. I need a pair like that—something with an elasticized waist. I wonder where she bought them.

Although I see Meg most days, I've only ever spoken to her once. She asked if we had any more bran flakes, but we had sold out. I wish I could have said yes. I wish I could have gone back through the swinging plastic doors and returned with a box of bran flakes just for her.

That was in early May. I suspected she was pregnant even then. A fortnight later she picked up a pregnancy test from the pharmacy aisle and my suspicions were confirmed. Now we're both in our third trimester with only six weeks to go and Meg has become my role model because she makes marriage and motherhood look so easy. For starters, she's drop-dead gorgeous. I bet she could easily have been a model—not the bulimic catwalk kind, or the Page Three stunner kind, but a wholesome and sexy girl-next-door type; the ones who advertise laundry detergent or home insurance and are always running across flowery meadows or along a beach with a Labrador.

I'm none of the above. I'm not particularly pretty, nor am I plain. "Unthreatening" is probably the right word. I'm the less attractive friend that all pretty girls need because I won't steal their limelight and will happily take their leftovers (food and boyfriends).

One of the sad truths of retailing is that people don't notice shelf-stockers. I'm like a vagrant sleeping in a doorway or a beggar holding up a cardboard sign— invisible. Occasionally someone will ask me a question, but they never look at my face when I'm answering. If there was a bomb scare at the supermarket and everyone was evacuated except me, the police would ask, "Did you see anyone else in the shop?"

"No," they'd say.

"What about the shelf-stocker?"

"Who?"

"The person stocking the shelves."

"I didn't take much notice of him."

"It was a woman."

"Really?"

That's me—unseen, inappreciable, a shelf-stocker.

I glance outside. Meg is walking towards the supermarket. The automatic doors open. She picks up a plastic shopping basket and wanders along aisle one—fruit and veg. When she gets to the end she'll turn and head this way. I follow her progress and catch a glimpse of her when she passes the pasta and canned tomatoes.

She turns into my aisle. I push the bucket to one side and step back, wondering if I should nonchalantly lean on my mop or shoulder it like a wooden rifle.

"Careful, the floor is wet," I say, sounding like I'm talking to a two-year-old.

My voice surprises her. She mumbles thank you and slides by, her belly almost touching mine.

"When are you due?" I ask.

Meg stops and turns. "Early December." She notices that I'm pregnant. "How about you?"

"The same."

"What day?" she asks.

"December fifth, but it could be sooner."

"A boy or a girl?"

"I don't know. How about you?"

"A boy."

She's carrying Lachlan's scooter. "You already have one," I say.

"Two," she replies.

"Wow!"

I'm staring at her. I tell myself to look away. I glance at my feet, then the bucket, the condensed milk, the custard powder. I should say something else. I can't think.

Meg's basket is heavy. "Well, good luck."

"You too," I say.

She's gone, heading towards the checkout. Suddenly, I think of all the things I could have said. I could have asked where she was having the baby. What sort of birth? I could have commented on her stretch jeans. Asked her where she bought them.

Meg has joined the queue at the register, flicking

through the gossip magazines as she waits her turn. The new *Vogue* isn't out, but she settles for *Tatler* and a copy of *Private Eye*.

Mr. Patel begins scanning her items: eggs, milk, potatoes, mayonnaise, arugula, and Parmesan. You can tell a lot about a person from the contents of a shopping cart; the vegetarians, vegans, alcoholics, chocaholics, weight watchers, cat lovers, dog owners, dope smokers, celiacs, the lactose intolerant and those with dandruff, diabetes, vitamin deficiencies, constipation, or ingrown toenails.

That's how I know so much about Meg. I know she's a lapsed vegetarian who started eating red meat again when she fell pregnant, most likely because of the iron. She likes tomato-based sauces, fresh pasta, cottage cheese, dark chocolate, and those shortbread biscuits that come in tins.

I've spoken to her properly now. We've made a connection. We're going to be friends, Meg and I, and I'll be just like her. I'll make a lovely home and keep my man happy. We'll do yoga classes and swap recipes and meet for coffee every Friday morning with our mothers' group.

MEGHAN

Another Friday. I am counting them down, crossing them off the calendar, scratching tally marks on the wall. This pregnancy seems to be longer than my other two. It's almost as though my body has rebelled against the idea, demanding to know why it wasn't consulted.

Last night I thought I was having a heart attack, but it was only heartburn. Chicken Madras was a big mistake. I drank a whole bottle of Mylanta, which tastes like liquid chalk and makes me burp like a trucker. This baby is going to come out looking like Andy Warhol.

Now I need to pee. I should have gone at the café, but it didn't seem necessary then. My pelvic floor muscles are working overtime as I hurry across the park, cursing every time Lachlan's scooter bashes me in the shins.

Please don't pee. Please don't pee.

An exercise class has taken over one corner of the park. Elsewhere there are personal trainers standing over clients, telling them to do one more push-up or sit-up. Maybe I'll get one of those when this is all over. Jack has started making cracks about my size. He knows I'm bigger this time because I didn't lose my baby weight after Lachlan.

I shouldn't be made to feel guilty. Pregnant women should be able to eat chocolate and wear sensible pajamas and make love with the lights off. Not that there's much of that nowadays. Jack hasn't touched me in weeks. I think he has this strange aversion to sleeping with a woman who is carrying his child, viewing me as some sort of virginal Madonna figure who can't be soiled.

"It's not because you're fat," he said the other night.

"I'm not fat, I'm pregnant."

"Of course, that's what I meant."

I called him a bastard. He referred to me as Meghan. He does that when we're having an argument. I hate the long form of my name. I like Meg because it reminds me of nutmeg—an exotic spice that men and countries have fought wars over.

Jack and I have skirmishes rather than battles. We are like Cold War diplomats who say nice things to each other while secretly stockpiling ammunition. When do couples run out of things to say, I wonder. When does the passion wane? When do the conversations become dull-witted and boring? When do iPhones make it to the dinner table? When do mothers' groups graduate from talking about their babies to bitching about their husbands? When does the house-training of a man become proof of love? When does the gap between every woman's dream husband and every man's dream wife become a journey from pole to pole?

Ooh, this stuff is good. I should be writing it down for my blog.

No, I can't do that. When I married Jack I promised I wouldn't be one of those wives who tried to change him into something he wasn't. I fell in love with him as is, off-the-rack, straight out of the box, no customizing necessary. I am happy with my choices and refuse to waste time contemplating alternate lives.

Our marriage isn't so bad. It's a partnership, a meeting of minds and kindred spirits. Only up close do the flaws become apparent, like a delicate vase that has been dropped and pasted back together. Nobody else seems to notice, but I nurse that vase in my mind, hoping it still holds water, telling myself that midlife humps are like speed bumps that make us slow down and smell the roses.

Jack and I didn't plan to have another child. This one is our "oops" baby, accidental, unscripted, but not unwanted—not by me, anyway. We took a rare weekend away for a friend's fortieth birthday party. My mother offered to look after Lucy and Lachlan. Jack and I drank too much. Danced. Fell into bed. Made love in the morning. Jack had forgotten the condoms. We took a chance. Why wouldn't we, when you consider the number of times we had risked a quick shag only to be interrupted midcoitus by "Mummy, I'm thirsty," or "Mummy, I can't find Bunny," or "Mummy, I've wet the bed."

My other pregnancies were arranged like military campaigns, but this one was literally a shot in the dark.

"If it's a girl, we should call her Roulette," Jack said, when the shock wore off.

"We're not calling her Roulette."

"OK."

These jokes came after the arguments and the recriminations, which have stopped now but are likely to surface when Jack is angry or stressed.

He's a sports reporter for one of the cable channels, doing live football feeds from Premier League games and a full-time wrap-up of the goals and scorers. During the summer he covers a mixture of sports including the Tour de France, but never Wimbledon or the Open. His star is on the rise, meaning bigger games, more airtime, and a higher profile.

Jack loves being recognized. Normally it's by people who have some vague notion they've met him before.

"Aren't you someone?" they ask when they interrupt our conversation, gushing over Jack and ignoring me. I look at the backs of their heads and want to say, "Hello, I'm chopped liver." Instead I smile and let them have their moment.

Jack apologizes afterwards. I love that he's ambitious and successful, but sometimes wish he'd give me and the kids more of the public "Jack the Lad" rather than the stressed version who comes home late or leaves early.

"Maybe if you went back to work," he said last night, which is another sore point. Jack resents me "not having a job." *His words, not mine.*

"Who would look after the children?" I asked.

"Other women go to work."

"They have nannies or au pairs."

"Lucy is at school and Lachlan is in child care."

"Half days."

"And now you're pregnant again."

These arguments cover the same old ground as we lob grenades from opposite trenches.

"I have my blog," I say.

"What good is that?"

"It earned two hundred pounds last month."

"One hundred and sixty-eight," he replied. "I do the accounts."

"Look at all the free stuff I get sent. Clothes. Baby food. Nappies. That new pram is top of the line."

"We wouldn't need a new pram if you weren't pregnant."

I rolled my eyes and tried a different tack. "If I went back to work, we'd spend my entire wage on child care. And unlike you, Jack, I don't clock in and clock out. When was the last time you woke up for a nightmare or to fetch a glass of water?"

"You're right," he said sarcastically. "That's because I get up and go to work so I pay for this lovely house and our two cars and those clothes in your wardrobe . . . and the holidays, school fees, gym membership . . ."

I should have kept my mouth shut.

Jack belittles my blog, but I have over six thousand followers and last month *Mucky Kids* was named by a parenting magazine as one of the five best mummy blogs in Britain. I should have hit Jack with that fact, but by then he'd gone to have a shower. He came downstairs wearing nothing but his short dressing gown, which always makes me laugh. After apologizing, he offered to rub my feet. I arched an eyebrow. "What are you going to rub them on?"

We settled for a cup of tea in the kitchen and began discussing getting a nanny, trotting out the same cases for and against. I love the idea in theory—the me time, added sleep, and extra energy for sex—but then I picture a tight-bodied Polish girl bending over to fill the dishwasher or wrapped in a loosely tied towel as she leaves the bathroom. *Am I paranoid?* Maybe. *Sensible?* Absolutely.

I met Jack at the Beijing Olympics. I had a job in the media center looking after the accredited journalists. Jack was working for Eurosport. He was still quite junior, learning the ropes, watching how it was done.

Both of us were too busy in Beijing to notice each other, but when it was over the host broadcaster threw a party for all the affiliated media. By then I knew a lot of the journalists, some of whom were quite famous, but most were boring, always talking shop. Jack seemed different. He was funny. Cool. Sexy. I liked everything about him, including the name Jack, which made him seem like a regular Tom, Dick, or Harry. He also had a great smile and film-star hair. I watched him from across the room and made the mistake of plotting our entire relationship in the course of sixty seconds. I had us marrying in London, honeymooning in Barbados, and having at least four children, a dog, a cat, and a big house in Richmond.

The party was winding down. I thought of something clever to say and made my way through the crowd. But before I could reach Jack he was waylaid by a female reporter from Sky Italia. Big hair. Voluptuous. Faces close. Shouting to be heard. Twenty minutes later I watched him walk off with the Italian job and I immediately felt cheated upon. I found a dozen reasons why I didn't like Jack. He was cocky. He put highlights in his hair. He whitened his teeth. I told myself that he wasn't my type because I didn't go for pretty men. *This might not have been a conscious choice. Pretty men didn't usually go for me.*

It was two years before we met again. The International Olympic Committee held a reception for delegates who were in London to inspect venues for the 2012 Games. I saw Jack arguing with a woman in the hotel foyer. He was animated and adamant about something. She was crying. Later I saw him alone at the bar, drinking the free booze and hijacking plates of canapés from passing waiters.

I pushed my way between bodies and said hello. Smiled. *Was it wrong to catch him on the rebound?*

We chatted. Laughed. Drank. I tried hard not to try too hard.

"I need some fresh air," Jack said, almost falling off the stool. "Fancy a walk?"

"Sure."

It was nice to be outside, walking in step, leaning close. He knew a coffee place in Covent Garden that stayed open till late. We talked until they threw us out.

Jack escorted me home and walked me to my front door.

"Will you go out with me?" he asked.

"On a date?"

"Is that OK?"

"Sure."

"How about breakfast?"

"It's two thirty in the morning."

"Brunch, then."

"Are you angling to spend the night?"

"No, I just want to make sure I see you tomorrow."

"You mean today?"

"Yes."

"We could do lunch."

"I don't know if I can wait that long."

"You're sounding needy."

"I am."

"Why did you fight with that woman I saw you with?"

"She broke up with me."

"Why?"

"She said I was too ambitious."

"Are you?"

"Yes."

"Is that it?"

"She also said I killed her fish."

"Her fish?"

"She keeps tropical fish. I was supposed to be looking after them and I accidentally turned off the water heater."

"When you were living with her?"

"We weren't exactly living together. I had a drawer. It's where she kept my balls."

"She was crying."

"She's a good actress."

"Did you love her?"

"No. Are you always like this?"

"Like what?"

"Interrogating."

"I'm interested."

He laughed.

Our first proper date was a lunch at Covent Garden, close to where we both worked. He took me to the Opera Terrace. Afterwards we watched the street performers and buskers and living statues. Jack was easy company, curious and attentive; one good story led to another.

We went out again the next evening and shared a cab home. It was past midnight. We both had to work the next day. Jack didn't ask to come inside, but I took his hand and led him up the stairs.

I fell in love. Madly. Deeply. Hopelessly. It should happen to everyone once—*even if love should never be hopeless*. I adored everything about Jack—his smile, his laugh, his looks, the way he kissed. He was like an everlasting packet of chocolate biscuits. I knew that I'd eat too many and make myself sick, but I ate them anyway.

Six months later we were married. Jack's career blossomed, then stalled for a while, but now it's moving again. I fell pregnant with Lucy and turned down a promotion that would have taken me to New York. Lachlan arrived two years later and I quit my job to become a stay-at-home mum. My parents helped us buy the house in Barnes. I wanted to go farther south and have a smaller mortgage. Jack wanted the postcode as well as the lifestyle.

So here we are—the perfect nuclear family—with an oops baby on the way and the doubts and arguments of the middle years starting to surface. I love my children. I love my husband. Yet sometimes I rake my memory to find moments that make me truly happy.

The man I fell in love with—the one who said that he loved me first—has changed. The happy-go-lucky, easygoing Jack has turned into a brittle man whose emotions are wrapped so tightly in barbed wire that I cannot hope to unloop them. I'm not focusing on his failings or tallying his shortcomings. I still love him. I do. I only wish he wouldn't fixate so much on himself or question why our family isn't more like the Disney Channel variety where everyone is happy, healthy, and witty and there are unicorns tethered in the garden.

AGATHA

My shift finishes and I get changed in the stockroom, rolling my smock and name tag into a ball and shoving them behind the tins of olive oil and cans of tomatoes. Mr. Patel expects employees to take their uniforms home, but I'm not doing his laundry.

Shrugging on my winter coat, I slip out the rear door, skirting the rubbish bins and discarded cardboard boxes. Pulling my hood over my head, I imagine I look like Meryl Streep in *The French Lieutenant's Woman*. She was a whore abandoned by a French ship's officer, who spent her life staring out to sea, waiting for him to return. My sailor is coming home to me and I'm giving him a baby.

On the eastern edge of Putney Common I catch the number 22 double-decker bus along Lower Richmond Road to Putney Bridge. In the early part of my pregnancy people weren't sure whether to congratulate me or buy me a gym membership, but now I get offered seats on buses and crowded trains. I love being pregnant, feeling my baby inside me, stretching, yawning, hiccuping, and kicking. It's like I'm never alone anymore. I have someone to keep me company and listen to my stories.

A businessman sits opposite me, dressed in a suit and tie. In his midforties, with hair the color of mushroom soup. His eyes travel over my baby bump and he smiles, finding me attractive. Fertile. Fecund. Isn't that a good word? I only learned it the other day. *Fe-cund*. You have to put the accent on the *un* sound and punch out the *d*.

Mr. Businessman is checking out my rock-star cleavage. I wonder if I could seduce him. Some men get off on sleeping with pregnant women. I could take him home, tie him down, and say, "Let me do the touching." I would never do it, of course, but Hayden has been away for seven months and a girl has needs.

My sailor boy is a communications technician in the Royal Navy, although I don't really know what that means. It's something to do with computers and intelligence and briefing senior officers—which sounded very important when Hayden tried to explain it to me. Right now he's on HMS *Sutherland* chasing Somali pirates somewhere in the Indian Ocean. It's an eight-month deployment and he won't be home until Christmas.

We met last New Year's Eve at a nightclub in Soho. Hot and noisy, with overpriced drinks and strobing lights. I was ready to go home well before midnight. Most of the guys were drunk, checking out the teenage girls in their crotch-defying dresses and fuck-me heels. *I feel sorry for hookers these days—how do they stand out anymore?*

Occasionally some guy would summon up enough courage to ask a girl to dance, only to be dismissed with a flick of her hair or the curl of a painted lip. I was different. I said hello. I showed interest. I let Hayden press his body against me and yell into my ear. We kissed. He grabbed my arse. He assumed he was in.

I was probably the oldest woman in the place, but a hell of a lot classier than the rest of them. Admittedly, gravity has made some inroads on my arse, but I have a nice face when I paint it properly, and I can hide my muffin top with the right clothes. All-importantly, I have great boobs, have done since I was eleven or twelve, when I first noticed people staring at my bust—men, boys, husbands, teachers, and family friends. I ignored them at first—my boobs, I mean. Later I tried to diet them away and strap them down, but they wouldn't be easily squashed or flattened or diminished.

Hayden is a boob man. I could tell from the first time he set eyes on me (or them). Men are so obvious. I could see him thinking, *Are they natural?*

You bet they are, buster!

At first I thought he might be too young for me. He still had pimples on his chin and looked a little scrawny, but he had lovely dark wavy hair, which I always think is wasted on a boy.

I brought him home and he shagged me like a man who thought he might not get laid for another eight months, which was probably right, although I don't know what sailors get up to on shore leave.

Like a lot of my boyfriends, he preferred me on top so my boobs hung down around his face while I bucked and moaned. Afterwards I cleaned myself up in the bathroom and half expected Hayden to get dressed and leave. Instead he snuggled deep under the covers and wrapped his arms around me.

In the morning he was still there. I cooked him breakfast. We went back to bed. We had lunch and went back to bed. That was pretty much the story for the next two weeks. Eventually we ventured out and he treated me like his girlfriend. On our first proper date he took me to the National Maritime Museum in Greenwich. We caught the River Bus from Bankside Pier and Hayden pointed out landmarks along the way, like HMS *Belfast*, a museum ship near Tower Bridge. Hayden knew the whole history—how she'd been damaged by a German mine in World War II and later took part in the Normandy landings.

At the Maritime Museum he continued my education, telling me about Lord Nelson and his battles against Napoleon.

One particular painting caught my eye. Called *Tahiti Revisited*, it showed an island in the South Pacific with rocky peaks, lush forests, palm trees, and voluptuous women bathing in a river. As I stared at the scene, I could feel the warmth of the sand beneath my toes and smell the frangipani blossoms and feel the salt water drying on my skin.

"Have you ever been to Tahiti?" I asked Hayden.

"Not yet," he said, "but I'll go one day."

"Will you take me?"

He laughed and said that I looked seasick on the River Bus.

On another date we went to the Imperial War Museum in South London and I learned that more than fifty thousand sailors died in World War II. It made me frightened for Hayden, but he said the last British warship to be lost at sea was the HMS *Coventry* during the Falklands War, which was before Hayden was even born.

We had three months together before Hayden had to rejoin his ship. I know that doesn't seem like long, but I felt married during that time, like I was part of something bigger than both of us. I know that he loves me. He told me so. And even though he's nine years younger than me, he's old enough to settle down. We're good together. I make him laugh and the sex is great.

Hayden doesn't know that I'm pregnant. The silly boy thinks we broke up before he left. He caught me going through his emails and text messages and completely overreacted, calling me paranoid and crazy.

Things were said that I'm sure both of us regret. Hayden stormed out of my flat and didn't come back until after midnight. Drunk. I pretended to be asleep. He fumbled with his clothes, pulling off his jeans, falling on his arse. I could tell he was still angry.

In the morning I let him sleep and went out to the shops to buy bacon and eggs for breakfast. I left him a note. Love. Kisses. When I returned, he was already gone. My note was balled up on the floor.

I tried to call him. He didn't answer. I went to the bus stop and to the train station but I knew he'd gone. I left messages saying I was sorry, begging him to call me, but he hasn't answered any of my emails or texts and he unfriended me on Facebook.

Hayden doesn't realize that I was trying to protect us. I know lots of women who will happily steal someone's boyfriend or husband. You take his ex, Bronte Flynn, a right slag, notorious for "doing a Britney" (going commando). Hayden still follows her on Facebook and Instagram, posting comments on her slutty selfies. She's the reason I looked at his phone—out of love, not jealousy.

Anyway, we're pregnant now and I don't want to break the news to Hayden in an email. It has to be face-to-face, but that can't happen unless he agrees to talk to me. Navy personnel are allowed twenty minutes of satellite calls a week when they're away at sea, but recipients must be on a list. Hayden needs to register me as his girlfriend or partner and give the navy my number.

Last week I talked to the Royal Navy welfare office and told them I was pregnant. A nice woman took down my details and was very sympathetic. They'll make Hayden call me now. The captain will give him a direct order. That's why I've been home every evening, waiting by the phone.

MEGHAN

My father is turning sixty-five and retiring this month after forty-two years with the same finance company. Tonight is his birthday dinner and Jack is running late. He promised to be home at five thirty and it's after six. I won't call him because he'll accuse me of nagging.

He finally arrives and blames the traffic. We have an argument in the car, conducted in whispers while Lucy and Lachlan are strapped into their seats listening to the soundtrack from *Frozen*.

Jack accelerates through a changing light.

"You're driving too fast."

"You said we were late."

"So now you're going to kill us?"

"Don't be ridiculous."

"You should have left earlier."

"You're right. I should have come home at midday. We could have painted our nails together."

"Fuck you!"

The words just slip out. Lucy's head shoots up. Jack gives me a look that says, *Really? In front of the children?*

"You said a bad word," says Lucy.

"No, I didn't. I said 'duck soup.' We might be having that for dinner."

She screws up her face.

"I don't like duck soup. It's yucky," says Lachlan, who shouts rather than talks.

"You've never had it before."

"Yucky, yucky, duck soup," he sings, louder than before.

"OK, we'll have something else," I say.

We drive in silence, edging through traffic towards Chiswick Bridge. Quietly fuming, I think of all the meals that have been spoiled by Jack turning up late. I hate him when he derides and belittles what I do. We reach my parents' house at seven. The kids run inside.

"You can be such a shit sometimes," I say as I grab the salads and Jack picks up the traveling cot.

My sister comes out to help. Grace is six years younger than me, happily single but always accompanied by an attractive, successful man who seems to worship the ground she walks upon, even when she's walking all over him.

"How's Daddy?" I ask.

"Holding court." We hug. "He's fired up the barbecue. We're going to be eating charred sausages and kebabs again."

Grace and I don't exactly look like sisters. I'm prettier, but she has more personality, I've heard people say, which I thought was a compliment when I was fourteen, but now I know different.

Jack sets up the traveling cot in one of the spare bedrooms before joining the men in the garden, where they are standing around the barbecue—that great leveler of legends, where any man can be king if he's holding the tongs. His first two beers go down in a matter of minutes. He gets a third. When did I start counting?

Mum needs help in the kitchen. We dress the salads and butter the potatoes. Grace is playing with Lucy and Lachlan, keeping them amused until dinner. She says she loves kids, but I suspect that's only *other* people's children, who can be handed back when they're over-tired or emotional.

I hear laughter outside. Jack has cracked everyone up with one of his stories. They love him. He's the life and soul of every party—the TV star who is full of gossip about transfers and signings. A lot of guys are knowledgeable about football, but they all defer to Jack on the subject because they imagine he has some added insight or inside knowledge.

"You're lucky with that one," my mother says.

"Pardon?"

"Jack."

I smile and nod, still looking into the garden, where flames are leaping from the barbecue.

"I have no idea what I'm going to do with him," says my mother, referring to Daddy's retirement.

"He has plans."

"Golf and gardening? He'll be bored silly within a month."

"You could always travel."

"He keeps wanting to go back to places we've been before. They're like pilgrimages."

She reminds me of when they went back to the hotel in Greece where they spent their honeymoon. They were woken at three in the morning by a Russian waving money around and demanding sex.

"The place had become a brothel."

"Sounds like an adventure," I say.

"I'm too old for *that* kind of adventure."

When the meat is suitably cremated we sit down to eat. Lachlan and Lucy have their own little table, but I finish up sitting with them, coaxing food into Lucy and stopping Lachlan from drowning his sausage in ketchup.

There are toasts and speeches. Daddy gets maudlin and thick-voiced when he talks about how much his family means to him. Jack keeps making wisecracks, but it's not the time or the place.

At ten o'clock we each carry a sleeping child to the car and make our farewells. I drive. Jack dozes. I wake him at home and we repeat the kid shuffle, carrying them to their beds. I'm exhausted and it's not even eleven.

Jack wants a nightcap.

"Haven't you had enough?" I say, wanting to reclaim the words as soon as they come out.

"What did you say?"

"Nothing."

"No, I heard you."

"I'm sorry. I didn't mean it."

"Yes, you did."

"Let's not fight. I'm tired."

"You're always tired."

Too tired for sex is what he means.

"I wanted to have sex all week, but you weren't interested," I counter, which technically isn't true.

"Can you blame me?" asks Jack.

"What does that mean?"

He doesn't answer, but I know he's saying that he doesn't find me attractive right now and that he didn't want another baby. Two is enough—a boy and a girl—all bases covered.

"I didn't do it on purpose," I say. "It was an accident."

"And you decided to keep it."

"We agreed."

"No, you *decided*."

"Really? Is that what you tell your mates at the pub—that you're so pussy-whipped that I bully you into having children?"

Jack's fist tightens on his glass and his eyes shut, as though he's counting to ten. He takes his drink into the garden and lights a cigarette from the packet he keeps on a high shelf beside the kitchen clock. He knows I hate him smoking. He also knows I won't complain.

Our fights are like this. We snipe rather than throw plates. We go for those tender spots, the weaknesses and embarrassments that we have each learned how to find in the course of a marriage.

Once we made a point of never going to sleep angry at each other. I don't know when that changed. I keep telling myself that everything will be fine when the baby is born. I'll have more energy. His doubts will disappear. We'll be happy again.

AGATHA

Sometimes I feel as though my past ticks inside me like a phantom clock telling me what dates must be acknowledged and what sins need to be atoned for. Today is such a date—the 1st of November—an anniversary of sorts, which is why I'm traveling north under a bleak gray sky on a National Express coach that hugs the inner lane of the motorway.

Rolling my forehead against the glass, I watch cars and trucks overtake us, their wheels spitting water and wipers swaying back and forth. The rain seems particularly apt. My childhood memories do not involve endless summers, long twilights, and crickets chirruping in the grass. The Leeds of my youth was eternally gray, cold, and drizzling.

My family home is gone, bulldozed to make way for a bulk-goods warehouse. My mother bought again—a small terrace not far from our old house—using money my stepfather left her. He died on a golf course, having sliced his drive into a pond—a heart attack. *Who knew he had one?* My mother rang to tell me the news, asking if I would come to the funeral, but I told her I'd rather gloat from a distance.

I won't be seeing my mother today. She's "wintering in Spain" as she likes to call it, which means roasting like a chicken beside a swimming pool in Marbella, drinking sangria, and being rude about the locals. She's not rich, simply racist.

From Leeds coach station I head to the nearest florist and have her make three small crowns of baby's breath and greenery. She wraps them in tissue paper and puts them in a polished paper box that I tuck into my shoulder bag. Afterwards, I buy myself a sandwich and a drink before catching a minicab along the A65 as far as Kirkstall, where it crosses the River Aire. The minicab drops me near Broadlea Hill, where I climb over a stile and follow a muddy path through the forest.

I can name most of the trees and shrubs, as well as the birds, thanks to Nicky, my ex-husband. He thought I wasn't listening when he pointed things out to me, but I loved listening to his stories and marveling at how much he knew.

I met Nicky a month after my thirtieth birthday— just when I thought time was running out to meet Mr. Right or Mr. Wrong, or any old Mister. Most of my friends were married or engaged or in long-term relationships by then. Some were pregnant for the second or third time, wanting big families or more welfare or not planning at all.

Living in London, I worked for a temp agency doing short-term secretarial placements, mainly for women on maternity leave. I had a bedsit in Camden above a kebab shop that served up fights and doner kebabs when the pubs shut their doors at night.

It was Halloween. Gangs of witches, goblins, and ghosts knocking on my door, holding out sacks and baskets. Having made another donation to British dentistry, I found myself standing barefoot in the kitchen, feeling like a container of milk that had been left for too long in the fridge.

My laptop was open on the kitchen table. On either side were piles of typewritten pages. For three months I'd been transcribing tapes for a writer called Nicholas

David Fyfle, who penned biographies of famous soldiers and war histories. He would courier me tapes and I would send back the transcripts. Our only other contact came via the quirky notes he wrote in the margins if he wanted me to retype certain sections.

I wondered if he was flirting with me. I wondered what he looked like. I pictured a quiet, tortured artist creating beautiful prose in his garret, or a wild-haired, hard-drinking war correspondent living life on the edge. I knew him only from his notes and his voice on the tapes, which sounded gentle and kind, with a slight stutter at certain syllables and a nervous laugh when he lost his place.

I made a decision. Instead of posting the transcripts, I delivered them by hand, knocking on the door of his house in Highgate. Nicky looked surprised, but also pleased. He invited me inside and made tea. He wasn't as handsome as I'd hoped, but he had a nice enough face and a skinny body that seemed to be growing into his clothes.

I asked him about his books. He showed me his library. "Do you read?"

"I used to read a lot when I was little," I said. "Nowadays I struggle to choose."

"What sort of stories do you like?"

"I like happy endings."

"We all like those," he said with a laugh.

I suggested I transcribe the tapes at his house to save on the cost of couriers and speed up the process. I would arrive every day at 9 a.m. and work in his dining room, breaking occasionally to make us tea or microwave something to eat. It took weeks of flirting before Nicky kissed me. He was a virgin, I think. Tender and considerate, attentive, but not skillful. I wanted him to moan or cry out when we made love, but he was always silent.

Around his friends he acted like a typical lad, enjoying a pint and a punt on the horses, but with me he was different. He took me on long walks in the countryside, investigating ruined castles and spotting woodland birds. Nicky proposed to me on one of our "expeditions" and I said yes.

"When am I going to meet your parents?" he asked.

"You're not."

"But they'll come to the wedding, won't they?"

"No."

"They're your *parents*."

"I don't care. We have plenty of other guests."

Even after we were married, Nicky kept trying to negotiate a reconciliation. "You can't just stop talking to them," he said. But I could and I did. It was like any relationship—if both parties cease to make an effort it will wither and die.

The ground slopes gently away from me as I follow a riding path dotted with puddles. Periodically I look over my shoulder. Nobody is following. My pregnancy is hidden beneath an overcoat, but I can feel the weight of the baby in my hip joints and the pressure in my pelvis. Clumsily, I climb an embankment, using saplings as handholds. Twigs and dead leaves snap and crumble beneath my boots. I come to a ditch and jump across with all the grace of a leaping hippo.

The sun has steadily strengthened and I'm warmer now, sweating beneath the coat. Following a zigzagging track, I reach a clump of trees next to the ruins of a farmhouse. I hear water falling into a deep pond at the base of a weir that is farther down the slope.

Kneeling on the damp earth, I clear away vines and weeds, pulling out clumps of vegetation and clods of earth. Slowly, I reveal three small pyramids of stones, spaced at equal intervals around the clearing. When

I'm satisfied, I take off my coat and lay it on the ground as a makeshift picnic blanket, leaning my back against the crumbling wall of the farmhouse.

I found this place long before I met Nicky. I must have been eleven or twelve when I rode my bicycle along the towpath past Kirkstall Abbey and the forge towards Horsforth. Pedaling in my cotton dress and sandals, I remember waving at the canal boats being maneuvered through the locks. As I turned a corner I glimpsed the remains of a chimney just visible through the trees. Fighting my way through brambles and vines, I found the ruined farmhouse, which felt almost enchanted, like a fairy-tale castle that had been put to sleep a thousand years ago.

Much later I brought Nicky here and he fell in love with it too. I said we should buy the land and rebuild the house; he could write and we'd have lots of children. Nicky laughed and told me to hold my horses, but I was already trying to get pregnant.

Unprotected sex was like buying a scratch-lotto card every twenty-eight days, waiting to win a prize. I won nothing. We visited doctors and fertility clinics and alternative healers. I tried hormone injections, vitamins, drugs, acupuncture, hypnotherapy, Chinese herbs, and special diets. IVF was the obvious step. We tried four times, using up our savings, and each failure became another heartbreak. A marriage of hope had turned to desperation.

Nicky didn't want to try again, but did it for me. On our last throw of the dice one embryo clung to my womb like a limpet on a rocky shore. Nicky called it our "miracle baby." I worried every day because I didn't believe in miracles.

Weeks passed. Months. I grew bigger. We dared to choose names (Chloe for a girl and Jacob for a boy). I was thirty-two weeks when I stopped feeling the baby moving. I went straight to the hospital. One of the midwives hooked me up to a machine and couldn't find a heartbeat. She said it was probably just in a weird spot, but I knew something was wrong. A doctor came. He did another ultrasound and couldn't find any blood flow or heartbeat.

I had a dead baby inside me, he said. Not a life. A corpse.

Nicky and I cried for the longest time, grieving together. Later that day they induced the birth. I went through the pain and the pushing, but there were no baby cries, no joy. Handed a bundle, I stared into the eyes of a still-warm baby girl who didn't live long enough to take a breath or grow into her name.

This is where we brought her ashes, Nicky and I, burying Chloe beside the crumbling farmhouse, above the weir, our special place. We promised to come back here every year on Chloe's birthday—which is today—but Nicky could never bring himself to visit. He told me we had to "move forward," which is a term that I've never understood. The planet turns. Time passes. We move forward even when we're standing still.

Our marriage didn't survive the fallout. Within a year we had separated—my fault, not his. My love for a child will be greater than my love for an adult because it is a singular love that isn't based on physical attraction, or shared experiences, or the pleasures of intimacy, or time together. It is unconditional, immeasurable, unshakeable.

The divorce was simple and clean. Five years of marriage ended with the stroke of a pen. Nicky moved away from London. Last I heard, he was living with a schoolteacher in Newcastle, a divorcée with two teenage boys—an instant family, just add water and stir.

Taking out the roast beef sandwich and soft drink, I open the plastic triangle and eat slowly, collecting the crumbs in my cupped hand. A robin hops between the spindly branches of a shrub and perches on the top of Chloe's cairn, pivoting from side to side. I toss the crumbs onto the grass. The robin jumps down and pecks at my offering, occasionally cocking his head to look at me.

Today is Chloe's birthday, but I mourn all of my babies—the ones I've lost and the ones I couldn't save. I mourn them because somebody must take responsibility.

Before I leave the clearing, I unzip my backpack and take out the small floral crowns, trying not to crush the petals, and place one on each of the cairns, saying their names.

"I am having another baby," I tell them, "but that doesn't mean I will love you less."

MEGHAN

I've been painting the baby's room and putting stencils on the walls. I'm not very adventurous when it comes to home decorating. I blame my parents, who didn't believe in allowing children freedom of expression. Trees had to be green and roses red.

I'm also trying to keep one eye on Lachlan, who has already put handprints on the door and a paintbrush in the wrong tin. It's all good material for my blog, I think as I clean his hands in the laundry-room sink.

Lachlan isn't exactly thrilled about me having another baby. It's not about sibling rivalry or being usurped as the youngest. He wants someone his own age to play with—either that or a puppy.

"Why can't the baby be four, like me?"

"Because he wouldn't fit inside my tummy," I explain.

"Can't you shrink him?"

"Not really."

"You could grow bigger."

"I think Mummy is big enough."

"Daddy says you're fat."

"He's only teasing." *The arsehole!*

Speaking of Jack, he phoned earlier, saying that he'd be home tonight instead of taking the train to Manchester. He sounded in a good mood. For months he's been fleshing out ideas for a new TV show where big-name stars discuss the hot-button issues in sports. Jack wants to be the anchor. He's written a pitch but is waiting for the right time to approach the "powers that be."

"Make sure you stay up," he said.

"Why?"

"I have news."

I decide to make us something nice for dinner—steak, new potatoes, and an endive salad. Typical French. I'll even open a bottle of red wine and let it breathe. I've been rather lazy in the kitchen since I fell pregnant. I couldn't ever think of food for the first trimester.

I go upstairs and shower, catching a glimpse of myself in the mirror. Turning side-on, I examine my butt and boobs, ignoring the stretch marks. Leaning toward the mirror, I notice a strange curly hair corkscrewing out of my left temple. I look more closely.

Oh my God, I have a gray hair! I take a pair of tweezers and pull out the alien strand, examining it, hoping it might be paint. No, it's definitely gray. Another indignity. I pen a blog piece.

I found a gray hair today and freaked out a little. This particular hair was devoid of color and wiry near the tip. I've always been kind of smug about the fact that I didn't have any silver (yet) when others I know have been plucking and dyeing since they were twenty-one.

Now the ravages of time are beginning to show. What next? Wrinkles? Varicose veins? Menopause? I refuse to panic. I have friends my age who are living in complete denial, refusing to contemplate turning forty, telling everyone, "Nothing to see here! Move along!"

I used to laugh at them, but now I have a gray hair. I want to put it down to the stress

*of pregnancy, but according to Google there is
no evidence that stress causes gray hair. Nor
does trauma or spending too long in the sun.
The good news is that I can pluck it out without fear of three more growing in its place.
The bad news is that I now have roughly ten
years before gray becomes my natural color.*

Yeah. Right. Over my dead body.

When I've posted the piece, I begin reading some
of the recent comments. Most of them are nice and
supportive, but occasionally I get trolled by people
who don't like my "mindless babbling" or tell me to
get off my "mummy high horse." I've been called a
skank, a whore, a whinger, and a slut. Worse still, I'm
a bad mother for putting Lachlan into child care and
I'm guilty of "lording it over" women who can't have
children and I'm personally responsible for global over-
population because I'm having a third child.

Last week someone wrote, "I love the sound you
make when you shut the fuck up." Another said, "Your
husband must like waking up with fleas." I delete the
abusive comments, but I don't touch the negative ones
because apparently everybody is entitled to an opinion,
even the ignorant and foul-mouthed.

Jack arrives home after nine. By then I'm asleep on the
sofa. He bends and kisses me on the forehead.

"Sorry," I say, reaching up and kissing him properly.

He helps me stand. I pour him a glass of wine. "How
was your day?"

"Great. The best." He sits at the kitchen bench,
looking pleased with himself.

"Do I have to guess?"

"I'll tell you over dinner."

He can't wait that long and tells all as I'm dressing the salad.

"I pitched the idea for the new show today. They love it—Bailey, Turnbull, the whole team got excited. They're going to put it in the spring schedule."

"Are you going to host?"

"I'm sure I'll get it. I mean—it was my idea."

I feel a pang of concern, but I don't want to spoil Jack's mood. "When will you know?"

"In the next few weeks." He nuzzles my neck and gives my bottom a squeeze. I playfully push him away and tell him to wash his hands. It's ages since I've heard him sound so upbeat. Maybe things are looking up. A new job, more money, and a baby—there are so many ways to move forward and only one way to stand still.

AGATHA

On Saturdays Jack gets up early and goes for a run along the river. Afterwards he takes the kids to a café in Barnes for babyccinos and muffins, meeting up with other dads who drink coffee, read newspapers, and ogle the au pairs and yummy mummies.

Gail's is the newest place to be seen in Barnes. On weekends it is full of dads and their kids and weekend road warriors dressed in Lycra who chain racing bikes to the railings while they fuel up for the ride home.

This area of London is a leafy village trapped in a bend in the river between Putney and Chiswick—an oasis of calm full of overpriced houses, boutique shops, and cafés. The locals are mostly company directors, stockbrokers, diplomats, bankers, actors, and sports stars. I saw Stanley Tucci walking across Barnes Bridge the other day. And I once spotted Gary Lineker at the farmers' market. He played football for England and now works as a sports commentator just like Jack.

Have you ever noticed that TV presenters have big heads? I don't mean they're conceited or up themselves, although some of them probably are. I'm talking very literally. I've seen Jeremy Clarkson and his head was humongous. It was like a poorly inflated beach ball, all jowly and pale. They don't tell you that in the gossip magazines—about the big heads—and it's not like you can inflate your head on purpose if you want a job on TV. You either have one or you don't. Jack has one—a big head and great hair and whiter-than-white teeth. His chin is a little on the weak side, but he keeps it tilted up when he's on camera.

Now he's on his second coffee. I like the way he licks his forefinger before he turns the pages of a newspaper. He's good with the kids. He picks up crayons when they drop them and carries their drawings home to show "Mummy."

I first saw Meg not a hundred yards from this very spot. She was in the park with Lucy and Lachlan, who were playing with a bubble wand, chasing after the soapy orbs. Meg wore a simple white shirt and jeans. I pictured her working for a fashion magazine as a photographer or a stylist—which wasn't far from the truth. I thought she'd have a stockbroker husband and a holiday villa in the South of France where they went for long weekends. They invited friends, all of whom were attractive and successful, and they'd eat French cheese and drink French wine; and Meg would complain that baguettes were "the work of the devil" because they went straight to her hips.

I love making up stories like this. I imagine whole lives for people, giving them names and careers, inventing their backstories and populating their families with black sheep and terrible secrets. Maybe it comes from reading so many books as a child. I grew up with *Anne of Green Gables*, spied with Harriet, wrote plays with Jo March, and explored Narnia with Lucy, Peter, Edmund, and Susan.

It didn't matter that I sat alone at lunchtimes and rarely got invited to parties. My fictional friends were just as real, and when I closed a book at night I knew they would still be there in the morning.

I still love reading, but nowadays I search the Internet for information about pregnancy and childbirth and

looking after babies. That's how I discovered that Meg
has her own blog: a site called *Mucky Kids* where she
writes about motherhood and the funny weird stuff
that happens in her daily life—like the time Lucy wrote
a letter to the Tooth Fairy and argued that two pounds
was "too little for a front tooth," or when Lachlan broke
a full bottle of blue nail polish and created a "Smurf
murder scene."

The website has several photographs of Meg, but
she doesn't use any real names. Jack is called "Hail Caesar." Lachlan is Augustus and Lucy is Julia (Caesar had
a daughter). Meg is Cleopatra, of course.

If you read her blog posts, you can tell that she used
to be a journalist. She wrote for a women's magazine
and some of her articles are still online, including an
interview with Jude Law, whom she called "sex on legs"
and admitted to flirting with over oysters and champagne at the Savoy Hotel.

Across the road at the café, Jack is packing up the
kids, strapping Lachlan into a pushchair and holding
Lucy's hand. As they cross the park, Lucy has to touch
the trunk of every tree, while leaves fall in their wake
like confetti at a wedding.

I follow from a distance, across the green, past the
pond, turning left and right until we reach Cleveland
Gardens, a pretty road lined with Victorian semi-
detached houses and neatly trimmed hedges.

During the Blitz a German bomb flattened three
houses at the far end of the road. A block of flats
replaced them, which the locals call "Divorce Towers"
because so many straying husbands (and the occasional
wife) have finished up there in the aftermath of an affair.
Some eventually go home. Others move on.

Directly behind Jack and Meg's house is a railway
line—the Hounslow Loop—which gets about four

trains an hour during the week and less on weekends. The trains aren't so noisy—not like the planes, which line up from first light and sweep overhead, a mile apart, descending towards Heathrow.

Crossing the road, I cut through Beverley Path until I come to the pedestrian underpass. The wire fence has partially collapsed, making it easy to climb over. Checking that the coast is clear, I walk along the railway tracks, stumbling over the broken scree, counting the back gardens. A very angry Alsatian hurls itself at one of the fences as I pass. My heart leaps. I snarl back at him.

When I near the right house, I crawl through the undergrowth and climb onto a fallen tree, which is my favorite vantage point. From here I can look across a narrow garden that runs fifty feet past a playhouse and a children's swing set and a rear shed that Jack has turned into a home office, which he never uses.

I hear little girls giggling. Lucy has a friend over for a play date. They're in the playhouse, pretending to make cups of tea. Lachlan is sitting in the sand pit, moving mini-mountains with a bulldozer. The French doors are open and Meg is in the kitchen cutting up fruit for a morning snack.

Leaning back against a large branch, I take a can of soft drink from my coat pocket and pull the tab, sipping the spillage. I also have a chocolate bar that I'm saving for later.

I can sit for hours and watch Meg and Jack and the children. I've watched them having summer barbecues and afternoon tea, or playing games in the garden. One day I saw Meg and Jack lying on a blanket. Meg had her head resting on Jack's thigh while she read a book. She looked like Julia Roberts in that scene in *Notting Hill*, lying with her head in Hugh Grant's lap. I love that movie.

Every fifteen minutes a train rattles past. I turn to see the carriages lit from within; the passengers captivated by mobile phones, or newspapers, or leaning their heads against the glass. One or two are looking at me as they pass. Being seen doesn't worry me. I don't look like a burglar or a peeping tom.

When it begins to grow dark, I follow Meg's path through the house as she turns on lights. Children are bathed, teeth are brushed, and bedtime stories are read.

Cold and hungry, I don't stay to see Jack arrive home, but I picture him coming through the door, shrugging off his coat, loosening his tie, and grabbing Meg around the waist. She shoos him away and pours him a glass of wine, listening to him talk about his day. After they've eaten, they'll pack the dishwasher and curl up together on the sofa, their faces painted with flickering light from the TV. And later they will lead each other upstairs and make love in their king-sized bed.

It's easy to imagine these things because I have been inside the house. It was before Meg and Jack moved in, when the place was up for sale. House hunting is one of my hobbies and I arranged a viewing. The estate agent, a bottle blonde with a figure-hugging wardrobe, showed me round, pointing out the important features, calling it "characterful" and "priced to sell."

I could see how she operated, flirting with the husbands and charming the wives, but never within earshot of each other. She acted like a co-conspirator, convincing each spouse that she would help sway his or her partner. She tried the same thing with me, asking questions about my husband and whether he'd be coming along. I pretended to be talking to him on the phone.

"Yes, I think it's big enough, but I'm a little worried about the train noise . . . You'll hear them in the summer with the windows open."

Walking from room to room, I examined the oven and the self-closing drawers and ran my finger over the stainless steel appliances and marble worktops. I tested the water pressure and flicked the gas rings on and off. The estate agent took my name and details—not the real ones, of course. I have lots of favorite names—Jessica or Sienna or Keira.

I didn't realize that Meg and Jack had bought the house until I followed Meg home that first time. Now I can picture them in every room—Lucy in the back bedroom, Lachlan in the middle one, and the nursery immediately above the stairs.

I have left it too late and it's grown too dark to see the path. Feeling my way forward, I stumble over roots and feel brambles tugging at my clothes. The railway tracks shine silver in the ambient light and I move tentatively over the broken rocks and cross ties. The crickets fall silent and the rails begin to hum: a train coming. Stumbling to one side, I turn to be blinded by a bright light. The engine blasts past me in a roar of noise and rushing air that shakes the ground and sends dead leaves dancing around my legs.

I hold my belly, protecting my baby, telling him I'll keep him safe.

MEGHAN

Maybe I'm not cut out for motherhood. In the first trimester I worried about miscarriage. Later I fretted about premature labor, birth complications, medical negligence, and myriad other disasters. After he's born I'll be anxious about SIDS, influenza, infections, meningitis, bumps, bruises, rashes, and high temperatures. Every cough, sniffle, or sneeze will have me on edge. When he learns to walk and run and climb, I will worry about falls, broken bones, open drawers, hot plates, and domestic poisons. This will never change, regardless of his age. When he's eighteen I'll worry about drunk drivers, drug dealers, bullies, unemployment, student debt, and girls that break his heart.

I write about these doubts and insecurities in my blog and readers think I'm joking. They expect me to be an expert, having practiced on Lucy and Lachlan, but I simply find new mistakes to make and new fears to keep me awake at night.

I had a scan today. An ultrasound technician smeared gel over my belly and gave me a running commentary, pointing out all the bits. My little passenger has two arms, two legs, and the requisite number of chambers in his heart, which is beating like the wings of a hummingbird.

My doctor says everything is fine—my blood pressure, my urine, my iron levels, etc. I've put on thirty-eight pounds and that's OK too, although I feel clumsy and uncoordinated because I keep bumping into things. My belly is like an airbag.

Home again, I'm looking at the unfinished nursery. The curtains must be measured and ordered, and Lachlan's old baby clothes are in boxes in the attic. I started with great plans for a perfect little boy's room, but nothing has turned out like I imagined. The truth is I don't care, as long as he's healthy and happy and treats me nicely.

As if reading my mind, he chooses that moment to kick me hard in the kidneys.

"Hey! What was that for?"

He kicks me again.

"Do that again and you're never borrowing the car."

I picture him sometimes—my unborn son—as the world's smallest assassin, a fetal torturer who is punishing me for what I did to Jack. Every kick and elbow and head-butt is retribution, and every scan a reminder of my eternal shame. The other memory aid plays tennis with my husband every week. His name is Simon Kidd and he and Jack are best friends.

They met at Exeter University and were thick as thieves, sharing a house, going to the same parties, and playing wingman when they were "on the pull," which they reminisce about constantly. Lucy once asked them what they were "pulling" and I waggled my little finger at Jack.

I've always thought them an odd pair of friends. Simon was the sort of undergraduate who couldn't leave a drug or a girl untried, while Jack was far more studious, dependable, and health conscious.

Although Jack doesn't know it (and never will), I had a brief fling with Simon years before I met and married Jack. I was working for a magazine and Simon was trying to get funding for a film project. He invited

me to lunch, hoping I'd write a story, and we were
in bed within two hours. Simon had a house share in
Brook Green, which was full of secondhand film equip-
ment and second-rate flunkies. I broke it off after four
months because I couldn't handle the sweat-soaked
sheets and his itinerant druggie friends.

By then I was well aware of Simon's effect on
women, how they hung on his every word or went gig-
gly if he smiled at them. Is he handsome? Yes, but not
ruggedly so. He's almost too pretty, with his high cheekbones and piercing gray eyes. I have learned how to
look at him and be unaffected, which is a bit like viewing a partial eclipse of the sun—never straight on or
you risk going blind.

Even after we stopped seeing each other, I would
run into Simon occasionally at film premieres and
short-film festivals. He was always very flirty and attentive, asking if I was seeing anyone. Later he moved to
America, and then Hong Kong. We lost touch.

When I met Jack he sometimes mentioned a friend
called Simon, but I didn't put two and two together
because they had nicknames for each other. It wasn't
until our wedding eve that I realized. Jack had arranged
to pick Simon up from Heathrow and I did a double
take when I saw him. Caught by surprise, I made a
spur-of-the-moment decision not to say anything to
Jack, and Simon played along. It seems silly now, but I
was getting married the next day and I knew how jealous and competitive Jack can be. I didn't want to spend
my last night being quizzed about old boyfriends and
what we did together.

Later, in the kitchen of Jack's flat, I whispered to
Simon, "You remember me?"

"Of course."

"I thought maybe you were so . . ."

"Out of it?"

"Yes."

"I stopped all that. It's strange, being lucid all the time. Boring, but I'll live longer."

All of Simon's neurotic energy had gone. He was still snobbish and sarcastic, but more fun to be around. Women remained easy prey—most of them deathly pale model types with cheekbones instead of breasts, who were "serious girlfriends" until he announced otherwise.

After I married Jack, Simon became a regular visitor at our first house and then this one. He and Jack play regular games of tennis and golf at the Roehampton Club. Jack helped Simon get his job at the network, where he's proved a hit with viewers, having just the right combination of gravitas and cheeky charm.

Apart from being Jack's best man, Simon is Lucy's godfather, which he finds hilarious, because he's so utterly godless and he says he can't wait until Lucy turns eighteen when he can get her stoned or pissed or both. I know that he's joking, but not completely. My own relationship with him was fine until eight months ago, and he hasn't been to the house since. Jack keeps inviting him, but Simon makes excuses.

"I can't understand what's happened," Jack told me. "Did you guys have a fight?"

"No."

"Well, he seems to be avoiding you."

I changed the subject and tried not to mention Simon. In truth, I can't think about him without wanting to curl up in a corner and sob. I can't think of him without remembering a night in mid-March when Jack and I had a blazing row about money, which was merely the trigger. It began when I reversed the car into a lamppost, denting the rear hatch. It was my fault.

I should have admitted my mistake, but I pushed back when Jack accused me of being careless. We fought. My mother once told me that someone had to be soft in a marriage or it wasn't going to work. Not me, I thought. Not this time.

Jack has a similar stubborn streak, charging into every argument, wielding accusations like a bayonet. Wounded, I went low, almost begging him to overreact. He did. He raised his fist. I cringed. He didn't strike, but I saw it in his eyes. "I don't know why I married you!" he roared. "If it weren't for the kids, I'd be long gone."

Silently, I packed Lucy and Lachlan into the car and dropped them at my parents' place. My mother wanted to know what had happened. I couldn't talk to her. I drove to Simon's flat, struggling to see the road through splintered tears. I wanted to ask him why Jack was so unhappy. Had he said anything? Was it over?

I was a mess. Simon poured me some wine. I talked. He listened. A lot of men fail to realize how attractive that is to a woman: listening. Not interrupting. Not judging. He let me sob on his shoulder. He wiped away my tears with his thumb. He whispered that things would all work out.

I was too drunk to drive home. Simon offered to call me a cab. I stood and stumbled. He caught me. Our lips were close. We kissed. I clung to him. We tumbled backwards onto the sofa, kissing again and again, taking off our clothes, kicking off boots and popping buttons. I lifted my hips. He spread my knees. He lowered his head and used his tongue. I shouted and it didn't sound like me. Afterwards I drew him inside me, urging him to fuck me harder. I knew it was wrong, but I didn't want him to stop. I wanted to feel something other than anger and disappointment. I wanted to have hot, raw, unadulterated sex and fuck the consequences.

Afterwards we lay on Simon's Pashtun rug catching our breath. I saw the silhouette of branches thrown by the streetlights against the blinds and recognized a different world from the one that had existed only a few moments ago. The lust and anger had seeped away, leaving behind a terrible numbness and an emptiness that felt violent. Where did it come from? Was I *really* so unhappy?

I retrieved my knickers and pulled them on under my skirt, smoothing my blouse. I was in shock. What had I done? After six years of blissful (OK, reasonably happy) marriage, out of the clear blue sky, I had shagged my husband's best friend.

What was I thinking? *Clearly, I wasn't.*

There are no excuses. I am a terrible person. I am the sort of crass, shameless slag who should be humiliated by Jeremy Kyle or Dr. Phil. Yes, Jack raised his hand, but he didn't hit me. He said he didn't love me, but he was angry. Lashing out.

Every relationship goes through rocky patches. We had been through worse and always bounced back. Normally, all it takes is a weekend away, or a great night out, or a moment of intimacy to remind us why we fell in love.

In the days that followed I was convinced that people could see my guilt. I felt it was tattooed on my forehead or sticking out like a forgotten label on a new pair of jeans. Jack apologized for scaring me and agreed to see a marriage counselor. He wasn't particularly open about his feelings at our therapy sessions, but he made an effort, which is more than I did. My secret crippled me. It isn't simply about the betrayal—it is the shameful memory of how good the sex was; how hot and urgent and desperate. Each time the details flood back to me my thighs want to open and close. I have to squeeze them together, hating myself even more.

Anyone who says that honesty is the best policy is living in la-la land. Either that or they have never been married or had children. Parents lie to their kids all the time—about sex, drugs, death, and a hundred other things. We lie to those we love to protect their feelings. We lie because that's what love means, whereas unfettered honesty is cruel and the height of self-indulgence.

Then came our weekend away and the madly impulsive hotel sex. I missed my periods in April and May. I panicked. I couldn't remember if Simon had used a condom. I rang him. In the background I could hear people laughing and drinking in a noisy bar. Simon told me yes.

"Why?" he asked, shouting.

"No reason."

"I thought we were never going to speak about that night."

"We're not. Ever."

"I'll take it to my grave."

"Good."

AGATHA

We had a robbery at the supermarket today. A jittery-looking dodo in a hoodie and sunglasses was hanging around near the freezer section, muttering and shaking his head. He didn't have a shopping basket and he kept glancing at the CCTV cameras above the aisles.

"What can't you find?" I asked, trying to be helpful.

He ignored me completely and walked away, heading towards the doors. I was going to say something to Mr. Patel, who was at the registers, but I thought the guy was leaving. At the last moment he turned back and pulled a knife.

Mr. Patel's eyes snapped open like they were spring-loaded. I think I might have screamed.

The guy told him, "Empty the register or I'll cut your throat." He spun around and waved the knife at me. "Get on the floor!"

I pointed to myself as if to say, *Who, me?* and dropped to my knees.

"All the way down," he said. "On your stomach."

"Really?"

He noticed I was pregnant and said I could stay on all fours.

Mr. Patel was trying to open the register. He kept pressing the No Sale button, but the key was on the wrong setting and the cash drawer wouldn't open.

The robber told him to hurry up.

"You have to buy something," said Mr. Patel.

"What?"

"I can't open the drawer unless you buy something."

The robber looked at him incredulously. "I don't think you know how this works."

"Right," said Mr. Patel, nodding furiously.

I was in the process of moving away, crawling backwards towards the end of the aisle, but I could see Mr. Patel was panicking. I called out, "Scan the cigarettes."

Mr. Patel took his eyes off the knife and looked at me.

"The cigarettes—scan them," I said. "The register will open."

That solved the problem and the drawer opened. Mr. Patel gave him the cash.

"Where's the rest of it?"

"That's all."

The knifeman pointed to the drawer below the register. It's where Mr. Patel keeps the daily cash float and any large bills. It's also where he has a loaded gun, which he shows to all the new employees—particularly the college girls who work weekends and he hopes might be impressed.

Great plan, I thought. He'll make a citizen's arrest, or shoot the guy if necessary. But Mr. Patel didn't go for the gun. He handed over the cash float and said to the knifeman, "Can I get you anything else?"

Why not join our loyalty program? How about some lotto tickets?

Later Mr. Patel told the police he was trying to protect me, which was bollocks because I saved his arse. We both had to give statements and look at mug shots on a computer, but I'm terrible at remembering faces. The knife I could have picked out of any lineup.

The police wanted to have a doctor examine me because of my pregnancy but I told them I was fine and just wanted to go home. They gave me a taxi voucher and said I should take tomorrow off work, which didn't impress Mr. Patel.

The cab drops me outside my flat and I step over junk mail as I shoulder open the large front door. I'm tired now that the adrenaline has evaporated, and the stairs seem steeper than before.

My flat is on the second floor. Mrs. Brindle, my landlady, lives downstairs with her two sons, Gary and Dave, who are both forty-something and in no hurry to leave home. Gary, the older one, is on a disability pension, while Dave drives a minicab. I suspect half the reason Mrs. Brindle charges me so little rent is because she's hoping I might take one of them off her hands.

A door opens behind me.

"Hello, princess."

"Go away, Dave."

"Need a hand?"

"No."

He positions himself at the bottom of the stairs so he can look up my dress. I move closer to the wall.

"Don't be like that," he says. "You have great legs, Agatha, what time do they open?"

"Drop dead."

I keep climbing. He shouts after me. "Just remember, I've got a condom with your name on it."

"What? Durex Extra Small?"

"That's a good one," he says with a laugh, "but I'll be gentle with you."

Flopping onto the sofa, I kick off my shoes and rub my feet, which ache from standing up all day. The buttons on my blouse are stretched so tightly across my belly they could pop and take out an eye. I loosen them and glance at the mess around me, wishing I had cleaned up last night, or yesterday. Unwashed dishes are piled up in the sink and the dining table is covered in brochures and catalogues for baby clothes.

Farther along the hallway is a bathroom with a tub, and my bedroom, which is really nice because I can make it dark and sleep until noon when I don't have work. My double bed is a rickety affair with a varnished headboard and a boggy soft mattress. At night I like turning off the lights and listening to the trains pulling into Putney Bridge station.

My best friend, Jules, lives upstairs with her husband, Kevin, and their little boy, Leo, who is four and a real cutie. I sometimes babysit Leo when Jules nips out to the shops or the Laundromat or to get her hair done.

Jules is pregnant again and we've been inseparable these past months, shopping and having manicures and treating ourselves to chocolate milkshakes, which are the best cure for morning sickness ever invented.

Having caught my breath, I retrieve three envelopes from the doormat: a gas bill, a telephone bill, and a letter from my mother. I recognize her handwriting and the Spanish stamps.

What does she want? I should throw it away. Something makes me tear at the flap and unfold the single perfumed page.

Dear Agatha,

Please don't be angry with me for writing to you again. I'm not even sure I have the right address. I tried to call, but you must have changed your number.

I miss you. I've been dreadfully lonely and you're the last family I have left. I know a lot has happened between us but I'm hoping that you can forgive me.

Marbella is sunny, but not as warm as it was last year. I'm renting the same apartment, which is next door to Mr. and Mrs. Hopgood (I mentioned them in my past letters). He's a bit of a bore, but Maggie is nice. We play bingo together and have cocktails at the yacht club.

You should come and visit. I could send you money for the airfare. We could spend Christmas together. They do a lovely spread at the yacht club—with roast turkey and a free bottle of wine on every table.

Please write back to me.

With all my love,

Mum
xxoo

I tear the letter into little pieces and put them in the kitchen bin, which is so full of rubbish that the scraps fall on the floor. My mother doesn't know I'm pregnant. She'd only mess things up.

Someone knocks on the door.

"Piss off, Dave," I shout.

"It's me," answers Jules.

Shit!

"OK. Give me a minute."

I straighten my clothes and button my blouse, checking myself in the mirror before unlocking the door.

"What took you so long?" asks Jules. She waddles past me and throws herself onto the sofa with a grunt. "You left me waiting out there forever."

Half German and half Scottish with an explosion

of steel-wool hair and legs like tree stumps, Jules is a striking-looking woman and I envy her clear skin and doe-brown eyes. Big even before she got pregnant, she loves to flaunt her size because Kevin likes her that way. He's not a "feeder" or a "fatty lover" but he definitely plumps for the plump.

I tell her about the robbery and she hangs on every word, wanting to know if I was frightened.

"He was probably an ice addict," she says. "Those guys are mega-scary. They eat people's faces."

"Really?"

She nods. "That stuff causes holes in your brain and makes your teeth fall out."

"This robber had all his teeth."

"For now."

Suddenly she remembers why she's come downstairs. "Hey, do you want to come with me to an acupuncturist? I got a two-for-one offer."

"Nobody is sticking needles in my baby," I say.

"They don't stick needles in the baby," she replies, waving a brochure. "This says acupuncture helps pregnant women get over nausea, fluid retention, tiredness, cramps, and heartburn."

"Even so."

"What about a bikini wax?"

"I'm not bothering at the moment."

"Lucky for some," she sniffs. "I got a full seventies triangle growing down there. Kevin needs a machete to find my grotto."

"You're disgusting."

"At least I'm getting some," says Jules. "Upon which subject—have you heard from Sailor Boy?"

"I haven't checked."

My laptop is hidden under magazines. I open it up and wait for the wireless to find a signal. Two emails pop into my inbox. One of them is spam. The other is from Hayden. My heart trembles.

"He's going to call me tonight," I whisper, blinking at her in shock.

"What else does it say?" she asks excitedly.

"That's all."

MEGHAN

Lucy has a friend over this afternoon. Her name is Madeleine and she's a grumpy little madam who ignores my fruit platter and asks for chocolate biscuits and crisps.

I tell her, "We don't have those in our house," and Madeleine looks at me as though I'm something nasty on her shoe. They're playing outside now. I think Lachlan is getting a cold so I give him a bath and some paracetamol and let him watch the Disney Channel.

I glance at the clock. Madeleine is getting picked up at six. I want to fast-forward and have everyone in bed, so I can crawl beneath the covers and sleep. Jack is away tonight. He's been in a good mood all week. I'd say "back to normal" but I don't know what "normal" is anymore. No, that's not true. I love it when Jack teases me and flirts and randomly touches me, brushing my backside, or cupping my waist, or stealing a quick snog when we pass on the stairs.

Lachlan is laughing at something. I sit next to him on the sofa and put my arm around him, sniffing his fresh-out-of-the-bath little-boy smell.

"Is Daddy coming home?"

"Not until tomorrow."

"Where is he?"

"Working."

"Is he going to be on TV?"

"Uh-huh."

Later I make Lachlan a boiled egg for dinner and

line up toast soldiers on either side of his eggcup. He's a hungry child in all senses, desperate to grow up; a wrecker of games, a hoarder of toys, and a monopolizer of attention. Lucy appears tolerant, but recently I have noticed scratches and pinch marks on Lachlan's arms. His favorite truck disappeared a week ago, triggering howls of outrage. Lucy watched from the corner, denying all knowledge. I found the truck beneath her bed a few days later.

Lucy and Madeleine have macaroni and cheese, which Lucy normally loves, but today she turns up her nose, mimicking Madeleine. Why do children choose the most inappropriate friends? I'll probably write about this tonight—changing the names, of course. My blog is like a hungry beast that has to be fed with more and more content.

At university I dreamed of being a serious journalist—the next Marie Colvin or Kate Adie, reporting from the rubble-strewn streets of Baghdad or teeming refugee camps in North Africa. I don't know when that ambition died. In truth, I have always been someone who matched expectations rather than exceeded them.

When I began writing my blog I wanted to make it edgy and funny—maybe even controversial. I thought with my background in marketing and public relations, I could influence opinions and build a brand, but in reality I spend my time writing quirky stories about my imperfect family and oh-so-happy marriage.

I read the other day that the average mummy blogger is thirty-seven, has two children, is left-leaning and socially conscious and buys eco-friendly products. That's me! I am a cliché. My blog sums up my existence—safe, uncontentious, and shallow.

I clean up the kitchen and the bathroom before making my own dinner—leftovers from the children.

Jack calls me from Old Trafford, where Manchester United are playing Tottenham at home. "It's one of the games of the round," he says, sounding excited. "I think the new talk show is in the bag."

"Don't say that. You could jinx it."

He laughs and needs a favor. He left a business card in his other jacket. Can I find it for him?

I carry the phone upstairs and go through his wardrobe. Jack spends more money on clothes than I do. He has three Paul Smith suits and two dozen shirts. Searching through the pockets, I come across a folded sheet of paper. It's a mobile phone number, written in longhand, but someone has placed a lipstick kiss next to the number. No name.

I keep searching the pockets until I find a business card.

"Is this the one you wanted?" I ask, reciting the number to Jack.

"Thanks, babe."

"I found another number. It's on a piece of paper . . . the one with a lipstick kiss. No name."

"Oh, that," he says, not missing a beat. "Some woman put that in my pocket in the pub. She recognized me. I think she thought I was a famous footballer."

"And you kept her number?"

"I didn't *keep* her number—I forgot it was even there. Are you jealous?"

"No."

He starts teasing me. "You should be. She was all of twenty-five."

"Dirty old man."

"She wanted a job in TV."

"Don't they all."

He laughs and sends hugs and kisses before hanging

up. I look at the slip of paper, crumple it up, and toss it into the bin.

I don't mind that Jack treats me like a girlfriend sometimes, because that can be exciting. We used to have date nights where we each pretended to be someone else. He'd be a pilot and I'd be a weathergirl and we'd meet in a bar where one of us would take the lead and chat the other one up. Once I pretended to be a crazed fan.

"Oh my God, you're Jack Shaughnessy, aren't you?"

"Ah, yeah," he'd replied.

"You're on TV. I love your voice. Say something sexy."

"Like what?"

"That's it. Ooh, I could just melt. Jack Shaughnessy, blimey. What are you doing here?"

We chatted for about twenty minutes and left arm-in-arm, a textbook pull. The bar staff were stunned.

I used to love our date nights and how Jack would write me lovely notes, leaving them in random places such as the microwave, or a coat pocket, or tucked into my Wellingtons. *Dearest wife, your boobs are the best*, he'd write, or: *This coupon is good for one extra-special foot massage.* Yes, he had an ulterior motive, but he didn't have to be so thoughtful.

Memories like this make me feel grateful as well as angry. How dare I doubt Jack! I'm the one who broke our vow.

AGATHA

The satellite image is fuzzy and breaking up, but Hayden's voice comes through clearly. He's dressed in blue overalls, sitting in a small room with charts and maps on the wall. Is that a beard? *Ugh!*

"Can you see me?" I ask, hoping he might comment on my new dress, or the effort I've made on my makeup.

"Yeah," he replies, not bothering to look at the screen. "What's this about you being pregnant?"

"Isn't it wonderful!"

"How did it happen?"

"You must know that, silly."

"I mean, when did you find out?"

"I knew I was late, but my periods are generally all over the shop. Then I went and peed on the stick. Want to see it? I kept it." I wave the stick in front of the screen. "The pink line means I'm pregnant."

"How pregnant?"

"I'm due in early December."

"Is it mine?"

"What?"

"The baby—is it mine?"

"Of course it is—I love you."

"I've been at sea for seven months."

"I'm eight months pregnant. It happened when you were here in London. We were going at it like rabbits."

"You said you were on the pill."

"I also asked you to use a condom because I'd missed a few days. You said you didn't like them."

"Why didn't you tell me sooner?"

"I tried, but you wouldn't answer my messages. I sent emails and letters. I posted Facebook messages. You didn't answer."

"You said nothing about a baby."

"I wasn't going to just blurt it out. It's a private thing. I have the ultrasound pictures. Do you want to see them?"

Hayden takes a deep breath and sighs, staring at the ceiling as though looking for a celestial sign or hoping for heavenly intervention.

"What do you want me to do?" he asks.

"I'm not expecting you to marry me or anything daft like that."

"Why tell me at all?"

"I thought you should know. If you don't want anything to do with me, I'll accept that, but this is *your* baby as much as mine."

He looks at the screen and shakes his head. "I don't want a baby."

"Well, it's a bit late for that now." I stand up and turn sideways, running my hands over my tummy. "This is really happening."

He looks away again.

"I know you think I'm springing this on you," I say, "but I did try to tell you. I wrote almost every day, but you were angry with me and wanted a break."

"We weren't on a break! We broke up!"

"I did a foolish thing, going through your emails, but don't you see—I must have been pregnant when I did that. My hormones were all over the place."

"And that's your excuse."

"It's the truth."

Hayden pushes away from the screen. "Christ to hell, I can't deal with this!"

"We can talk when you get home."

"No! I want you to stay away from me."

"What about the baby?"

"You want it—you have it!"

"Please, Hayden, don't be cruel."

"I didn't sign up for this. You should have got rid of it."

"What?"

"Had an abortion."

"No!"

"Don't contact me again. Understand?"

The screen goes blank. I tap the keyboard but can't bring him back.

Refusing to cry, I tell myself that Hayden can change his mind. Right now, he thinks I'm a "battalion bike" or "base bunny" who hangs around navy barracks hoping to snare a man in uniform. He's wrong. I love him. I'm going to show him what a great mother I can be. And before long he'll be down on one knee, begging to marry me, and thirty years from now we'll laugh about this and be talking about our grandkids.

Jules knocks. She's probably been waiting outside, busting to know what Hayden said. I let her in. She looks at me hopefully, ready to commiserate.

"So? What happened? Was he excited?"

"Over the moon."

"I told you he would be." She laughs and dances around the room, shaking her curves.

"He asked me to marry him," I say.

"Get away!"

"Yeah."

"Why didn't he answer your messages?"

"He said he was scared of falling in love with me."

"That's so sweet. So what did you tell him?"

"I said I'd have to think about it."

"You're a daft cow! Why didn't you say yes?"

"He made me wait. Now I'll make him wait."

Jules wants to hear all the details—what I said, what he said. I have to make up the conversation, but she doesn't question any of my explanations.

"Where is Hayden now?"

"They're sailing to Cape Town."

"Maybe he'll buy you an engagement ring in South Africa. They have the best diamonds."

"I don't want a diamond ring."

"Yes you do. All girls love diamonds. Is he coming home for the birth?"

"No."

"But he should be with you."

"That's OK. I'm going to have the baby in Leeds."

"You *hate* your mother."

I shrug. "We've had our ups and downs, but I need a birth partner and she's offering."

"Shame I can't do it," says Jules, "but I have one small problem." She points to her bump.

I give her a hug. "I could always borrow Kevin."

"He's useless—believe me. When will you go up north?"

"Closer to the time."

Jules knows about my family. Not the whole story, but enough for her to understand my love/hate relationship with my mother. She says I should reach out and build bridges, but I think certain bridges are meant to burn and it's a shame some people can't be on them when it happens.

MEGHAN

The house is quiet. The kids are asleep. I have spent the past hour doing the ironing in front of the TV, producing a pile of neatly folded linen and a collection of sweet-smelling shirts hanging from the doorknob. I like the regimen and skill involved with ironing, which makes me feel in some small, domestic way that I am keeping the chaos at bay.

Occasionally, I glance up the stairs and listen for a cry or a summons. Lucy sleeps with the light on. She doesn't have nightmares or fear the dark, but she likes to know where she is in the world when she wakes at night.

Jack still isn't home. He normally calls if he's running late. I've tried his mobile and his office said he left hours ago. The new show has been preying on his mind. They have a name: *Shoot!* but he still hasn't heard who is going to be the host. Other presenters are being auditioned—not just anyone: Simon Kidd, the man I slept with, the one I'm desperately trying to forget. Jack and Simon have always been competitive, but that hardly matters when they're on a tennis court or golf course or playing Trivial Pursuit. This is important. If Simon were to get the nod, I don't know how Jack would react.

I try his mobile again. It goes straight to messages. I leave another one:

"Jack. It's me. Where are you? I'm worried. Please call."

I'm in bed when he arrives home. I hear the car keys hitting the side table and his shoes being kicked off. The fridge door opens. He's getting himself a beer. A part of me wants to turn off the light and pretend to be asleep.

Instead I go downstairs. He is in the garden, sitting on Lucy's swing, nursing the beer. I take the swing next to him, rocking back and forth in my slippers.

"Did you drive home?"

"No." He has loosened his tie and half pulled out his shirt. "I didn't get the job."

"Did they give it to Simon?"

"No."

"Who?"

"Becky Kellerman—she works on one of the lifestyle channels."

"Does she know anything about sports?"

"She looks good on camera."

"That's so unfair."

His forehead creases. "The whole show was my bloody idea. I came up with the concept, the name. I even came up with the promo line: 'Straight from the lip.'"

"At least it wasn't Simon," I say.

"Why do you say that?"

"I know how competitive you two are."

"What makes you think we're competitive?"

"Nothing. Forget I said anything."

We sit in silence for a while. I want to ask him what he's thinking, but I'm afraid of what he might say. There was a time when we talked a lot, sharing our thoughts, but now Jack communicates more by his silences.

"I wish I could do something to help," I say, reaching out and taking his hand. "And I know it's no consolation, but I think you're brilliant and they're mad not to give you the hosting job."

Jack turns over my hand and kisses the palm. "Do you ever worry about things?"

"Like what?"

"Money."

"We're not poor."

"We're going to need a bigger car and another bedroom."

"This house is big enough."

"What if three children are too many? What if we have no time for each other?"

This one catches me by surprise and my tongue suddenly feels too thick for my mouth.

"I don't want to lose you ever," he whispers.

"So don't go anywhere," I reply softly, hoping it sounds convincing.

He gives me a reproachful look. "I envy you."

"Why?"

"You can make the best of any situation. You don't get depressed. You don't have doubts."

"Everybody has doubts."

"And you have this weird kind of honesty. You don't hide things. You show everybody exactly who you are—and they love you back."

I hear the catch in my voice as I change the subject. "Are you hungry?"

Jack shakes his head.

I stand and pull my dressing gown tighter around me. "I'm going to bed. Are you coming?"

"Not yet."

"Don't stay up too late."

Sliding under the duvet, I close my eyes but cannot sleep. Lying awake, I try to understand Jack's sadness. I know he's crazy about Lucy and Lachlan and I still think he's crazy about me, but we approach life differently. Jack anticipates problems in advance and prepares for the worst, marshaling the resources to handle things. I take problems as they come, bending rather than breaking.

If Jack reacts like this to losing a job opportunity, how would he handle knowing that I slept with Simon? He can never know. *Never.*

AGATHA

Hayden's parents live in Colindale, North London, in one of those postwar cottages with a pebble-dashed façade and a small front garden. Two stories. Bay window. Neat flower beds. The climbing roses are blooming late.

Mr. and Mrs. Cole know that I'm coming. I phoned ahead and Mr. Cole offered to pick me up from the station, but I said I could walk. I'm wearing one of my nicest dresses—a cute A-line from Mothercare with cap sleeves and a round neckline. It's a little short and flouncy for meeting the parents, but I want them to see me as a future daughter-in-law, not someone auditioning for Amish life.

I find the house. Ring the bell. The door opens instantly. Mrs. Cole is beaming at me. She looks like a fifties austerity bride who sews and bakes and organizes street parties on royal occasions. Her husband is in the hallway behind her, his bald dome shining under a miniature chandelier. I didn't picture Hayden losing his hair, which is a little worrying.

Mr. Cole works for the Royal Mail and has some fancy-sounding title but I think he sorts parcels or stamps letters. Hayden's mum is a teacher at a deaf school and can do sign language. That's because Hayden's younger brother is deaf. He might also be dumb, although I don't think people use that term anymore. Hayden's older sister is married and living in Norfolk. I can't remember if she has kids.

After the introductions, I'm shown into the room they call "the parlor," where I perch on the edge of the sofa, knees together. Everything in the room seems to match, with the same floral pattern on the curtains, the cushions, and the wastepaper basket. Tea and cake are served. I'm starving, but I'm on crumb watch.

"Are you sure you won't have a piece?" asks Mrs. Cole.

"No, thank you."

They've both noticed that I'm pregnant, but I haven't referenced the fact. Instead we talk about the weather and the train journey and how much we like lemon cake.

"I don't know if Hayden has told you much about me," I say when the conversation begins to falter.

"Very little," replies Mrs. Cole, glancing at her husband.

"Well, he and I began a relationship when he was on shore leave in January. You might have wondered why he didn't come home on many of those nights. He was staying at my place."

They are still perched forward on their armchairs, not reacting.

What do I have to do—draw them a diagram?

I take a tissue from my coat pocket and blow my nose. "This is very difficult," I say. "Normally I wouldn't have bothered you, but Hayden has given me little choice. He won't answer my emails. I talked to him a week ago and he . . . he . . ." I can't get the words out.

Mrs. Cole puts her hand on my knee. "Are you having Hayden's baby?"

I nod and cry even harder.

There is a beat of silence. Mr. Cole looks like he would rather be having a prostate exam than sitting in the parlor talking to me. I'm crying softly. I apologize and smear mascara across my cheeks.

Mrs. Cole sits next to me on the sofa and puts her arm around my shoulders.

"What did Hayden say?"

"He said he wants nothing to do with me, or the baby. He said I should have an abortion, but it's too late and it's against my religion. I have no one else to turn to. My real mum is dead."

"Dead?"

"To me," I blurt, catching my mistake. "She's dead to me. We rarely speak."

"You poor thing," says Mrs. Cole. "More tissues, Gerald."

He jumps to attention and turns in a complete circle before heading into the kitchen. Once the tissues are found I blow my nose again and wipe my eyes. Mrs. Cole has been asking the obvious questions about when the baby is due and whether I've visited a doctor. I show her the ultrasound pictures.

"Oh, look, Gerald. You can see everything. Fingers. Toes."

"He's very healthy," I say.

"Are you having a boy?"

"Yes."

Within twenty minutes we're talking like a mother and daughter-in-law, discussing hospitals, morning sickness, and pain relief. Soon she's bringing out the family photo albums and showing me pictures of Hayden as a baby.

"He was a big lump. Nine pounds," she says. "I needed stitches."

I flinch and she pats my knee. "Don't you worry. You look like you're built to have babies. I was a mere slip of a thing, wasn't I, Gerald?"

Mr. Cole doesn't answer.

She asks where I'm living and how I'm coping. I tell her about Jules and my lovely mothers' group that meets every Friday morning for coffee opposite Barnes Green. Soon I'm looking at photographs of Hayden as a toddler and starting school and as a spotty teenager. I get the guided tour of his bedroom and a recap on how he won each of his sporting trophies.

It grows dark. Mrs. Cole insists I stay for dinner, sitting me at the head of the table. Clearly this is a big deal, their first grandchild. Hayden's sister "hasn't been blessed," says Mrs. Cole, who gives me extra helpings of everything.

The deaf son, Regan, has been hiding in his bedroom all afternoon. He stares at me through dinner, signing questions to his mother, who signs back. I get the impression they're discussing me, which is unnerving. I've heard that people who lose a particular sense like their sight or hearing sometimes develop heightened abilities in other areas. What if Regan can read my mind?

The plates are cleared away and we return to the parlor, where Mr. Cole lights the gas fire and sits next to me on the sofa. I think he's warming to me, or it could be the third sherry I saw him pouring when Mrs. Cole wasn't watching.

"Where are you planning to have the baby?" he asks.

"My mother lives in Leeds."

"You said she was dead to you."

"Yes, but I'm going to make things right. Today— coming here—has been a big step for me, and you've been so nice and welcoming that I know I can patch things up with my mum."

"So you'll go up north?"

"Uh-huh. I did hope that Hayden would be with me . . ."

I leave the statement hanging. Mr. Cole pats me on the knee. "You did the right thing, coming to see us. Don't you worry about our Hayden. I'll see he does right by you."

I wipe away another tear. They come so easily.

"I hate the idea that he thinks I'm having this baby to make him stay, or to make him love me. It's not like I'm asking him to marry me."

I take Mr. Cole's hand and hold it against my belly. "Can you feel that?"

He nods uncertainly. "Does he move a lot?"

"All the time."

Mrs. Cole joins us with more tea and lemon cake.

"Hayden still has some growing up to do," she says, cutting me a slice. "But he's a good boy. I'm sure that, once I've had a quiet word with him, he'll be far more understanding. In the meantime, is there anything you need, Agatha?"

I shake my head tentatively.

"Are you sure?"

"Well, I've been quite sick and I've missed a lot of shifts at work. My rent is due, and . . ."

"How much do you owe?"

"You don't have to, really."

"How much?"

"A few hundred."

"Is that enough?"

"If I had five hundred I could cover all my bills— the electricity and the gas."

"I'm sure we can find it," says Mr. Cole. "And

don't you worry about our Hayden. We'll set him straight."

Hayden calls me that night. I expect him to be angry with me for going behind his back, but he is sweet as can be. I act a little hurt and don't accept his apology. The satellite image is clearer than last time. He keeps saying he's sorry and he didn't mean to hurt me. Slowly I soften my tone, but I wonder if he's being nice to me under sufferance.

"I know you're still getting used to the idea," I say, "but you're going to be a great dad."

He flinches around his eyes. "Listen, Agatha—"

"Call me Aggy."

"Right, Aggy." He rocks forward. "I accept that I'm probably the father—"

"You are."

"And I respect your decision to have the baby."

"Thank you."

"But I'm not going to marry you."

"I didn't ask you to marry me. I haven't asked you for anything."

"I know, I know. I talked to my folks. They made me realize that I've said all the wrong things. I mean, it came as a shock—the baby."

"You're telling me," I reply, giggling nervously.

"I've had time to think and make some decisions."

"I'm happy to raise this baby on my own, if that's what you decide, but if you did want to play a part—I think you should have that right. I mean, how horrible would it be if you really wanted a baby and I didn't tell you that you were a father?"

He nods in grim acceptance. The silence stretches out.

"Your mum and dad are nice," I say.

"They don't have any grandchildren."

"I'm happy to let them help me. It's not about the money, but I am going to struggle to pay the rent when the baby is born. Then there are expenses . . ."

"How much do you need?"

"If I tell the government, they'll make you pay child support."

"How much?"

"A hundred quid a week."

His eyes squeeze shut. "Fine. So when are you due?"

"Early December, but it could be earlier."

"I'm not home until Christmas."

"That's OK. My mother is going to be my birth partner." I hold up an ultrasound picture. "Can you see it?" Hayden leans closer to the screen. "That's his head and there are his little arms and legs. He's all curled up."

"Is it a boy?"

"Uh-huh. Hey! Do you want to see me?" I stand up and turn side-on to the webcam, holding my dress down and running my hands over my stomach. "Pretty big bump, huh? You should see my rock-star boobs." I cup them and sit down again.

"Shame I'm not there to play with them," says Hayden.

"Cheeky sod," I say. My hands slide higher. "They are pretty big."

"They were always pretty big."

"Do you want to see them?"

He glances over his shoulder. "Someone might see."

"A quick peek?"

I pull down the top of my dress and the cups of my bra. His eyes go wide.

"My nipples are extra sensitive. I can feel the fabric rubbing back and forth over them. Makes me horny."

"You'd better cover up," he says, his voice growing thicker.

I push my chair back from the screen and slide my dress a little higher, rocking my legs open and closed. Hayden looks ready to crawl through the screen.

"I'm not wearing knickers."

His breath catches. He utters a groan. Poor boy. He's been at sea for seven months. He adjusts something in his lap.

"Are you touching yourself?" I ask, grinning at him. "I wish I was there. I'd do it for you. I've been ever so lonely. If I were there, I'd run my fingers along your thighs, inching them closer and closer, bit by bit. Ooh, yes, would you like that?"

His breathing has grown ragged.

"Say it."

"Yes."

"Yes, what?"

"I'd like that."

I slide my hands beneath my dress. "Ooh, I wish you were here right now. I'd let you fuck another baby into me." I open my thighs wider. "I can feel you. I can feel you inside me. So big. So hard . . . oh, yes, yes, harder . . . I need you to touch me. Please, please, Hayden. Fill me up. Fuck me . . . yes . . . yes . . . Harder."

I hear a different groan and the sound of a man dying a little death.

Hayden's eyes are glazed and heavy-lidded. He looks at his lap, horrified.

"Let's talk again soon, lover," I say.

He doesn't answer.

MEGHAN

I'm upstairs going through old baby clothes in the attic, wishing I had put labels on the boxes instead of just throwing everything inside.

I should put some of this stuff on eBay. I have the full DVD collections of *Sex and the City* and *The West Wing*, which may be worth something. Do people buy DVDs anymore? What about secondhand ski boots?

The doorbell sounds. Why do people always ring when I'm upstairs? Navigating the lumps of Play-Doh and odd bits of Lego on the stairs, I reach the front door. This had better not be a salesman.

I turn the latch. Simon Kidd smiles at me from behind a huge bunch of roses that have lost petals on the journey.

"Hello, Megs."

I don't answer, but my heart feels like a taiko drum.

"I bought you these," he says, slurring his words.

"Are you drunk?"

"I had a long lunch."

"Jack isn't here."

"I know. We need to talk."

"No! We have nothing to say to each other."

"It's about the baby."

My heart lurches. I try to close the door, but he steps forward and braces his palm against it.

"You rang me and asked me whether we used a condom that night."

"It doesn't matter."

"The condom broke."

"What?"

"It broke. I didn't tell you because . . . I didn't think it was . . ." He is staring into my eyes as though hoping I might finish the statement.

I'm shocked, but won't let him see it. "You're right—it's not important. Please go away."

"I've been thinking about you."

"What?"

"About that night."

"Christ, Simon! It was sex. A one-night stand. Not even that. A mistake. An embarrassment."

He looks miserable. "It was more than that for me."

"What does that mean?"

Simon lowers his eyes, looking at the flowers, whispering, "What if the baby is mine?"

"It's not."

"You don't know if it's Jack's."

"Yes I do."

"If you knew that, you wouldn't have asked me if we used a condom."

"It's Jack's baby, OK? I don't want to mention this ever again. We agreed."

"I need to know if it's mine."

"What?"

"I need to know." Simon gives me his lost-puppy look.

I make a strange unworldly gurgle in my throat. "Why would you risk my marriage, your friendship with Jack . . . ?"

"I want . . . I want you . . ." He doesn't finish. "I want to be a father."

"Fine. Ask Gina to marry you. Get her knocked up. Leave me out of this."

"You don't understand."

My voice is getting louder. "No! *You* don't understand! This is my home. This is my family. I am having Jack's baby. You have no right to come here and ask me these questions."

I'm crying now—tears of frustration and anger. I want to hit Simon. I want to hurt him. But mostly I want to make him go away. He steps back and I slam the door, turning the key in the deadlock and bracing my back against the heavy wood. Sliding to the floor, I sit on the inner doormat, my shoulders shaking, frightened of what I've done. We don't have extramarital affairs in my family. We don't have one-night stands or wild flings. Braced against the cold door, my knees bunched up, I stare at the polished floorboards of the hallway.

What if Jack finds out? What if the baby is Simon's?

I've been stupid, but I don't deserve this grief. I've been a good wife. I love Jack. I shouldn't be punished for one mistake.

AGATHA

I haven't seen Meg in almost a week. She didn't meet up with her mothers' group this morning and hasn't come into the supermarket. Her last blog post went up ten days ago and none of the comments have been liked or acknowledged.

I wanted to wait outside Lachlan's preschool this afternoon, but Mr. Patel kept me back because we had a delivery. I had to take an inventory of every box because he's convinced our suppliers are shorting us.

Finally, he lets me go. Unclipping my name tag, I take off my smock and stash it and the tag in the usual place before hurrying across Barnes Green, past the pond and the church, turning left and right through the streets until I reach Cleveland Gardens.

Meg's car is parked outside the house. The front curtains are open, but I can't see anyone inside. I cut through to Beverley Path and walk as far as the railway underpass before climbing the fence and following the train tracks. When I reach the right house, I crawl through the undergrowth and climb onto my favorite fallen tree. There are toys outside the playhouse, but the French doors are shut up and there's no sign of anyone downstairs.

I contemplate calling the home phone. What would I say? I could hang up if Meg answered. At least I'd know she was there. I take out my mobile and look for the number. My thumb hovers over the green button. I glance again at the house and notice a shadow moving behind a curtain upstairs. I wait, watching, hoping she might reappear.

There she is! I feel a surge of relief. She's healthy. Pregnant. Perfect. She's in the kitchen, opening the fridge door, taking out ingredients. I relax and lean back against the trunk of the tree, happy again, able to breathe comfortably and dream.

My biggest flaw is my attraction to people. I find somebody new and attach myself, desperate for a friend. That's why I've been so careful around Meg, watching from a distance rather than getting too close. I know her timetable, her friends, her habits, and the rhythm of her life. I know where she shops for groceries. I know her favorite coffee shops, her family GP, her hairdresser, her younger sister, and where her parents live—all the connections and intersections, the geography and topography of her life.

I think I'd make a good spy because I'm gloriously bland, as adaptable as water, able to flow into spaces and settle into cracks, becoming so smooth and still that I reflect my surroundings. I learned how to do that as a child, when I was rarely seen and less often heard. I tell people I grew up in foster care, but that's only partially true. When it comes to my past, people get *some* of the truth *some* of the time.

My real father disappeared on the day I was born. He dropped my mother at the hospital, went home, packed his things, and cleaned out her bank account. Who says chivalry is dead?

It was just the two of us, Mum and me, until I was four. That's when she started going to Bible studies and became a Jehovah's Witness. I had to become one too. No more holidays, no more birthdays, no more Christmases or Easters. I didn't mind. It didn't matter which religion I chose to reject later, but my mother embraced it wholeheartedly because it offered her a community.

We went to weekly services at Kingdom Hall, which were called "meetings," and sang Kingdom songs, praising Jehovah. I had scripture classes that taught me about "The Truth" and how the rest of society was morally corrupt and under the influence of Satan.

Within a year my mother married one of the elders from the church. She became a trophy wife, sailing through life in her Hermès scarf, faultlessly charming, always reaching for the next rung on the social ladder. I have no doubt that she loved my stepfather, who did tax returns from a small office above a furniture store in Leeds. She was ambitious for him, prodding and cajoling and networking until his business grew and we moved into a bigger house.

Elijah was born when I was six. I loved him and he loved me. I became his second mother, pushing him around in his pram and spoon-feeding him in his high chair. Later I would dress him up and we "married" under the willow tree in the back garden.

At age three he became sick and spent two months in hospital. My mother and stepfather took turns sleeping by his bed and barely saw each other as they passed in the night and the day. Elijah got better. Life carried on. But my parents watched him more closely after that, letting their anxiety show in dozens of small ways.

I grew older. Elijah kept pace. He was like a shadow, following me around, asking me endless questions that I couldn't possibly answer. "What if whales could walk?" "Are there dinosaurs in heaven?" "Where does the light go when you turn it off?"

Usually I made stuff up and his little face would beam with pleasure when he learned something new, even complete bollocks. Occasionally, he made me angry and I yelled. Elijah's mouth would turn down in a perfect frown and tears would pool in his eyes. I hated myself for that.

He turned five and started school. I had to walk with him every day, holding his hand at intersections as he bounced up and down in his new shoes, wanting to run ahead. My friends thought he was cute. I thought he was embarrassing.

On show-and-tell day, Elijah brought a castle that he'd made from shoeboxes and toilet paper rolls. He needed both hands to carry it and could barely see over the tops of the turrets.

"Hurry up. Hurry up," he said, excited to get to school.

He waited at each intersection, knowing I was supposed to hold his hand. Once we'd crossed, he ran ahead, the turrets swaying above his head. Nobody saw exactly what happened next. I heard the high-pitched squeal of tires against tarmac and turned my head as Elijah bent against the hood of the car and sprang back again. He turned in midair and for a moment seemed to be looking directly at me. The cardboard castle disintegrated against the windscreen. Elijah landed on the road and his head snapped in a different direction. He came to rest on his back with one leg twisted beneath him at a strange angle. I could see a bone poking out through a ripped hole in his trousers.

Like an explosion in reverse, people were sucked inwards, appearing from nearby buildings and cars. I cradled Elijah's head in the crook of my arm. He lay, looking up at me, a scattering of freckles across his nose and cheeks and a cold fog clouding his eyes.

"What happened to his shoe?" I asked someone. "He can't lose a shoe. They're brand new. My mum will be angry."

The driver, Mrs. McNeil, had a daughter in my class. We found out later it was Mrs. McNeil's birthday. She hit Elijah at thirty-five miles per hour—fifteen over the speed limit in a school zone—but was never charged.

The paramedics came but they didn't take Elijah away. They put curtains around him and left him lying in the street for hours, taking photographs and interviewing witnesses. People assured me it wasn't my fault and that Elijah had run out onto the road.

My parents arrived. My stepfather took off his glasses so he could sob into his cupped hands. Meanwhile, my mother kept asking, "Where were you, Aggy? Why weren't you holding his hand?"

"He was carrying his castle," I said, but that was no excuse.

Later, whenever a therapist asked me what I most wanted from our sessions, I told them, "To be normal."

"What makes you think you're not normal?"

"I killed my brother."

"That was an accident."

"I should have held his hand."

From the day Elijah died it was clear to me that God or fate had made the wrong choice. If my mother and stepfather were going to lose a child, why couldn't it have been me? That might sound melodramatic or self-loathing, but the truth cuts deeper than the lie. Elijah's death stole all the oxygen in our family and nothing I did would ever allow my parents to breathe easily again. I could have aced my exams, helped old ladies across the street, rescued cats from trees, and cured cancer, but none of it would have mattered. Dead or alive, my half brother could do no wrong, while I could do no right.

I could understand my stepfather loving me less than Elijah, but not my mother. Why did she mourn

Elijah and ignore me? I wanted to scream at her. I wanted to bite and scratch and pinch to generate some emotion or recognition that I counted too.

Although I didn't realize it yet, Jehovah had turned his back on me long before I turned my back on Him.

MEGHAN

I wake with a start, my heart pounding and panic filling my throat with cotton wool. I dreamed my baby came out looking exactly like Simon, with smoky gray eyes, sharp cheekbones, and dark hair parted on the left. He was wearing a rumpled linen jacket and brogues—baby-sized—and had a designer stubble shading his jawline.

What sort of wife sleeps with her husband's best friend? I'm not some sixteen-year-old groupie at a rock concert, throwing myself at the drummer because the lead singer is already taken. I'm not a sex-starved housewife who flirts with tradesmen or answers the door naked under her housecoat. I don't even own a housecoat.

Jack rolls over and puts his hand across my chest. His fingers cup my right breast. My heart slows. I breathe. Close my eyes. Drift off. His hand drifts lower, over the rising slope of my belly and down the other side between my thighs. He snuggles closer. I feel his erection. That's more like it.

I raise my hips and he pulls off my knickers. His boxer shorts go twirling through the air.

"What is Daddy doing?" asks Lucy, who is standing with one hand on the doorknob and the other holding a bunny.

"Nothing," says Jack, covering up.

"Go back to bed," I tell her.

"I'm not sleepy."

"Go downstairs and watch cartoons."

"Lachlan wet the bed."

"How do you know?"

"The smell." She wrinkles her nose and waits for me to do something. I pull down my nightdress and swing my legs out of bed. Jack groans. I lean over and kiss his cheek, whispering, "Wait here."

"I can't," he says. "I'm being picked up at seven."

"When will you be home?"

"Not until late."

By the time I get back to the bedroom he's showered and shaved and is answering emails on his phone. The car arrives. He kisses each of the children. I get the same peck, but no words of encouragement or secret squeeze. I envy him going off to work, talking to adults about grown-up things. OK, I don't regard sports as being a grown-up subject, but it beats the hell out of discussing tantrums, toddler recipes, and teething trouble with a group of mothers who subtly try to one-up each other, complaining about their precocious offspring, calling them "too clever for their own good," by which they mean cleverer than other children.

Neither of my kids is a budding Einstein. Lachlan once shoved a raisin up his nose and we spent four hours in Accident and Emergency; and Lucy swallowed a pound coin, which meant squeezing her stools for a week to make sure it passed.

This morning they're being particularly obstreperous. Clothes are rejected, breakfast orders are rescinded, negotiations are undertaken, and squabbles are nipped in the bud. Lachlan wants to wear his Wellingtons and Lucy insists her space buns are crooked and make her look lopsided. I blame Jack for showing her *Star Wars*.

Leaving the house late, I rush across the green, dragging them along while they complain and bicker. As I near the pond, I notice someone standing between the trees. I recognize her from somewhere but can't think of where or why.

I kiss Lucy at the school gates and drop Lachlan at his preschool. Today he decides to latch on to my leg, begging me not to leave. One of the staff distracts him long enough for me to slip away.

As I'm folding up the pushchair, I catch sight of two mothers whispering and stealing glances at me. They look away guiltily.

"Is something wrong?" I ask.

"No, nothing," says one of them, curling her top lip. I hear them laughing as I leave. I want to know what they're saying, but it's not worth the effort. I have a whole five hours in which to cook, clean, shop, wash, and iron before I get to have some Meg time.

First I have an appointment to see an obstetrician, Dr. Phillips, who has consulting rooms on the lower floor of a large Victorian house near the river. My GP made the referral because of complications when I had Lucy and Lachlan. Nothing particularly serious. Their heads were too big. My pelvis was too small. Something had to give.

Dr. Phillips has a waiting room covered with testimonials, photographs, and cards from satisfied patients, thanking him for delivering their "precious gift," as though he'd personally arranged the conception, pregnancy, and birth. Reassuringly middle-aged, he has John Lennon spectacles and a slight overbite that makes his mouth the most interesting feature on his face. I wonder if he's married. If so, what does his wife think about this part of his job—looking at other women's bits? I can imagine him getting home and not

wanting to look at another vagina. This sets me giggling
and I can't stop even when he's palpating my womb.

"He's almost crowning," he tells me. "Not long now."

"Thank God," I mumble.

He goes to his desk and types notes on his computer. I pull down my dress and take a seat opposite.

"We do need to discuss the birth," he says, clasping
his fingers on his small potbelly. "I know you were hoping to have another natural birth, but you tore in both
previous deliveries."

"Maybe I won't tear this time."

"That's highly unlikely, and stitching you again will
be more difficult. I think you should seriously consider
a cesarean."

I'm struggling with this—not because of political
correctness or the idea that I'll be judged by other mothers as being "too posh to push." Twice before I've done
things the old-fashioned way, which hurt like hell but
gave me a tremendous sense of satisfaction.

"How long would I have to stay in hospital?" I ask.

"Without complications, you're looking at three to
four days."

"And that's what you recommend?"

"Absolutely." Dr. Phillips opens his calendar on-
screen. "We can bring you into hospital early on Thursday, December seventh, and operate first thing."

I want to argue, but I know he's right.

"Talk to your husband. If there's a problem with that
date, give my office a call. Otherwise I'll see you then."

AGATHA

At thirteen I was baptized as a Jehovah's Witness. It meant I could go door-to-door and help others repent their sins and live in peace on earth. In the months leading up to the baptism I attended scripture classes. My teacher, Mr. Bowler, was a church elder with a moon face and a bowl haircut that made his name seem very apt. He talked a lot about God's Kingdom and Armageddon, who I thought must be an apostle because the scriptures kept saying, "Armageddon is coming."

Mr. Bowler had four daughters and owned a clothing store in Leeds. His youngest daughter, Bernie, was a year above me at school, but we weren't really friends.

After my baptism, I continued going to Kingdom Hall twice a week, where Mr. Bowler helped me with my maths and science homework. He also read my English texts in advance and helped me write essays.

One day he asked me if I would go door-to-door with him, distributing the *Watchtower*, which was the church's magazine. I wanted to be the best Jehovah's Witness I could be, so we walked the streets and stood on doorsteps, telling people they could live forever in paradise if they woke up to the truth. Most of them were annoyed but didn't say anything nasty because I was so young.

It grew dark and started to rain. We had to run. I laughed. Mr. Bowler bought fish and chips. We ate them in the basement of Kingdom Hall, licking salt and vinegar from our fingers.

I shivered.

"You're cold," he said. "You should take off those wet clothes."

He tried to unbutton my blouse. I told him no. He tickled me, pressing me down. He kissed me on the lips. He said he loved me. I said I loved him too. It was true. I did. He had been nicer to me than anyone I had ever known. I wanted him to be my father, but he had his own daughters.

I remember the musty smell of the sofa and the rough fabric of the upholstery itching my skin. My dress had ridden up to the top of my thighs. His fingernails were scrabbling at my knickers. I pushed his hand away.

He said that when two people love each other they did more than kiss. They took off their clothes. They touched. He kissed me again. I didn't like the fat wetness of his tongue, which tasted of cod and vinegar.

I knew what he wanted. I had heard girls talking. He took my hand and moved it up and down. He sighed. He shook. I wiped it off with his handkerchief. *This will be our secret*, he said. Nobody else would understand.

Why must it always be a secret?

The next time we went door-knocking he gave me a bracelet engraved with a message: *There is no cure.*

"To what?" I asked.

"To love," he replied.

Afterwards we went back to the basement at Kingdom Hall. We sat on the sofa. He pushed the same fat wet tongue into my mouth and forced his knee between my thighs. I didn't like the kissing. I didn't like his weight or the pain or the shame, so I burrowed inside myself and hid in the shadows.

"Open your eyes, princess," he said. "I want you to look at me."

Please don't do that.

"Isn't this nice?"

No, you're hurting me.

"You're a proper woman now."

Can't we go back to the way it was before?

I vomited the fish and chips. He reared back as though scalded, swearing at the mess on his clothes. Marching me into the small stark bathroom, he made me undress. I stood naked on the freezing floor and noticed the semen and blood on my thighs. I cried. He said he was sorry. I felt sad for him.

In the weeks and months that followed, we knocked on many more doors without saving any souls. We had sex in the basement afterwards and Mr. Bowler said that when I turned seventeen we were going to run away together and live in a house by the sea. He showed me photographs of pretty cottages covered in wisteria or ivy. In the meantime, we had to keep our love secret because he was married.

That summer Mr. Bowler took his family to Cornwall for a holiday. I thought I'd be relieved, but instead I missed him and couldn't wait for him to come home. He brought me another present—a fossil of a snail that was millions of years old—and he said our love would last that long. I knew that wasn't true.

I grew more silent as the weeks passed. "Where's that pretty smile?" he'd ask, and I would try to smile. "You like this, don't you?" he'd say as his hot breath puffed against my face. "Tell me you like it."

One day he asked me if his youngest daughter, Bernie, had a boyfriend or if any boys had shown an interest in her. I didn't know. He became quite agitated at the thought of some "grubby teenager pawing her" and asked me to spy on her and report back to him. I recognized the hypocrisy. He thought it was OK to have sex with me, but his daughter had to remain pure. I watched Bernie in the playground, chatting and laughing with her friends. She was pretty and popular and excited to be alive. I knew I would never be like that again, never clean or happy.

Mr. Bowler had sex with me for another year, never using a condom, always withdrawing from me at the last second. When he finished, he buckled his belt and told me to clean up before he took me home.

One evening, as he seesawed into me, I felt my mind separate from my body and float upwards, looking down on the room. I could see Mr. Bowler's white buttocks and the corduroy trousers around his ankles and the sleeveless sweater his wife had knitted him. I opened my mouth to scream but no sound came out. Instead I felt a creature slide down my spine and slither between my organs until it curled around my heart, stopping it from breaking.

I came to with Mr. Bowler slapping my cheek and calling my name. I didn't want to wake.

"You must have blacked out," he said, zipping up his fly. "You made a strange sound, as though you were talking to someone, but it wasn't your voice. I hope you don't talk in your sleep at home."

Mr. Bowler no longer helped me with my homework or asked me to go door-knocking. And as the weeks passed, he found more and more things to criticize about me. My skin. My weight. My smell. He didn't kiss me anymore or tell me he loved me.

The creature woke and slept and slithered inside me, whispering advice, scribbling spidery words on the pages of my diary, laughing at my feeble attempts to express my feelings.

Nobody cares what you think.

Mr. Bowler cares.

He doesn't love you. He thinks you're getting fat.

No.

That's why he pinches the rolls of fat above your hips. He finds you disgusting.

He loves me.

He doesn't kiss you. He doesn't buy you presents. He doesn't take you door-knocking.

I turned fifteen. There was no birthday celebration. My mother asked me about my last period. She gasped when the doctor confirmed I was pregnant. My stepfather demanded to know the name of the father. I shook my head. He looped my hair around his closed fist and lifted me off my feet.

I remember the look on their faces. Shock. Disbelief. I was sent to my room, where I sat on the bed and listened to them arguing. My mother wanted to call the police, but my stepfather said the elders would know what to do. I scratched at the *Little Mermaid* stencil on my headboard, slowly peeling it away. The notion that I was carrying a baby seemed ridiculous. I still had a dollhouse and a dress-up box.

The following day my parents received a phone call and I heard my stepfather ask, "Is it a judicial committee hearing?"

I didn't hear the answer.

I was taken to Kingdom Hall and interviewed by three elders whom I had known since I was a child. Brother Wendell ran a carpet-cleaning business, Brother Watson installed blinds, and Brother Brookfield worked as a gardener for the local council.

They asked me questions. When did I have sex? Where? How often? Was Mr. Bowler circumcised? (I didn't know what that meant.)

"How far were your legs apart?" asked Brother Brookfield, who had a face like a tomato.

"Pardon?"

"Show us how far your legs were apart."

I was sitting on a hard wooden chair, wearing a knee-length dress. The elders were lined up along a long table. I opened my knees. They leaned forward.

"She must be lying," said Brother Wendell. "How could she be raped with her legs like that?"

"Why didn't you tell your parents?" asked Brother Watson.

"Mr. Bowler said he loved me."

Brother Wendell scoffed. "So you willingly had sex with him?"

"No. Yes. I didn't enjoy it. Not the sex."

"Did you tell anyone else?" asked Brother Watson.

"No."

"Did anyone see this happen?"

"We kept it a secret. Mr. Bowler said when I was seventeen we would run away together and live in a house by the sea. He showed me pictures."

I thought they might laugh.

"When was the first time?" asked Brother Brookfield.

"I don't remember the exact date."

"Were you a virgin?"

"Yes."

"Surely you must remember the date," said Brother Wendell. "The week . . . the month?"

I struggled to think, eventually guessing a date. "Around Easter."

"You don't sound very sure."

"I think it was around then, but I'm not sure."

The elders left me alone. I wanted to go to the bathroom but I was too scared to ask. Instead I crossed my legs, squeezing everything shut. Soon I heard Mr. Bowler shouting in another room, accusing me of telling lies. A little bit of wee came out.

When the elders came back they had my parents with them. Mr. Bowler entered through a separate door. Before it closed I saw his daughter Bernie standing behind him. She was holding her mother's hand.

The judicial committee took their seats at a long table. My stepfather sat behind me and my mother stood just inside the main doors, looking bewildered.

Brother Wendell spoke first.

"Very serious allegations have been made against Brother Bowler, a senior member of our flock. Sister Agatha is pregnant. She claims that on more than one occasion, Brother Bowler fornicated with her and made her perform other sexual acts. Brother Bowler denies any wrongdoing and has made a countercomplaint against Sister Agatha, accusing her of slander. He has asked for permission to question his accuser."

I thought I was going to vomit.

Mr. Bowler crossed the room and stood directly in front of me. He wore familiar corduroy trousers and a sleeveless sweater. Smiling kindly, he said hello, telling me he was sorry to see me in such circumstances.

"Do you have a boyfriend?"

"No."

"So you haven't had sex with a worldly boy from your school."

"No."

"You are lying, Sister."

"No."

"You came to me and confessed to me six weeks ago. I told you that the *Watchtower* forbids such acts. I counseled you. I warned you to stay away from this boy, but you failed to listen."

"No!" I looked at my mother. "It's not true."

"My daughter Bernie has confirmed it," said Mr. Bowler. "You admitted it to her."

I was shaking my head, trying to think clearly. Why would Bernie say I had a boyfriend?

"Do you know what a lie is, Agatha?" asked Mr. Bowler.

"Yes."

"You told your parents you were going door-to-door with me, was that a lie?"

"Yes."

"So you lie when it's convenient for you?"

"No. Yes. I don't know."

"You told the judicial committee that I first had sex with you at Easter two years ago. I have my diary here, which shows that I was away at a trade fair for a week over Easter."

My mouth opened and closed. "I couldn't remember the date."

"So were you lying about that?"

"No, I mean, I wasn't sure."

"So when you're not sure about something, you tell a lie."

"No."

"Were you lying to the committee, or are you lying to me?"

"That's enough!" yelled a voice from the back of the hall. My mother marched down the center aisle, gripping her handbag. Normally so meek and submissive, she fixed her gaze on the elders and declared, "Agatha has answered your questions. Make a decision so I can take her home."

Nobody tried to argue, not even Mr. Bowler.

The committee retired to consider its verdict. I went to the bathroom and washed out my knickers, holding them under the hand-dryer.

An hour passed. The committee returned. I was

told to stand but I didn't think my legs could hold me. My mother and stepfather remained in their seats.

Brother Wendell had a Bible with him. He didn't look at me.

"The scriptures say in Timothy 5:19, 'Do not admit an accusation against an older man, except only on the evidence of two or three witnesses.' In the case before us, Sister Agatha is the only witness against Brother Bowler. This is not to say that she is lying or that Brother Bowler is lying, but the *Watchtower* policy states that two witnesses or a confession are necessary to prove allegations of this nature. Since none of these rules of evidence have been met, the judicial committee will take no further action and the matter is left in Jehovah's hands."

Mr. Bowler stood and announced himself unsatisfied.

"I am an esteemed elder of this church and Sister Agatha has grievously wronged me. She is a false accuser who has had sexual relations outside of marriage with a worldly boy. She is unrepentant. I demand an apology and ask for Sister Agatha to be disfellowshipped."

I heard the intake of breath and felt my mother's body stiffen at the word. I knew what it meant. I had seen other Jehovah's Witnesses thrown out for much lesser crimes than being a "false accuser."

"Will you apologize to Brother Bowler?" asked Brother Wendell.

I shook my head.

"Will you repent?"

"No."

My mother clutched my arm. "Do as they say, Agatha. Tell him you're sorry."

"I didn't lie."

"It doesn't matter."

"I'll go to the police."

"Then you will be condemned by God," rumbled Brother Wendell. "And you will be lost to Satan forever."

My stepfather put his hand on my shoulder. I could feel his fingers digging into the flesh on either side of my collarbone.

"Tell the man you're sorry, Agatha."

The pain shot down my arm and my fingers tingled.

"No."

The judicial committee glanced at one another and nodded. The hearing was over. A week later I received a letter with my name, date of birth, and congregation number. It didn't specify the precise offense but the meaning was clear. I had been ostracized from the church. I could no longer participate in Bible studies or group prayer or freely associate with other members. As a minor, I could remain living under the same roof as my parents, who would take care of my physical needs, but nothing more. My mother could not comfort me if I was crying, or offer guidance or emotional support.

My stepfather said to me, "I love you, Agatha, and I'll be waiting for you on the day you come back. I will welcome you with open arms and I will say, just as the father said of his prodigal son, 'This daughter of mine was dead, but now has returned to life. She was lost, but now is found.' But until that day you are alone because you have chosen to turn your back on God."

MEGHAN

Jack has taken the day off work because he thinks he's coming down with something. He's saying the flu, but I'm calling it a cold until proven otherwise. All morning I've been up and down the stairs.

"Megs?" he bawls from his sickbed.

"What is it?"

"Sorry to be a bother."

"You're not a bother."

"Can I have a cup of tea?"

"I'll put the kettle on."

I retrace my steps, making him tea and adding a few biscuits, anticipating his next request.

"What are you doing?" he asks when I bring it upstairs.

"Vacuuming."

"Have you seen the newspaper?"

"It didn't get delivered."

"You couldn't pick one up for me, could you?"

"Sure."

"And some throat lozenges—the lemon ones with cough suppressant, not the cherry-flavored ones that taste like medicine."

"It *is* medicine."

"You know what I mean. And can I have some soup for lunch?"

"What sort of soup?"

"Pea and ham . . . with croutons."

Who was your slave yesterday?

The wind has an Arctic bite today, tugging at my coattails and sending fallen leaves skittering across the grass on Barnes Green. I pick up Lachlan from preschool because he does half days on Tuesdays. He runs ahead of me, his mittens dangling from the sleeves of his jacket and his sneakers lighting up at the heels with every stride.

The supermarket doors slide open and Lachlan stops to look at the coloring books at the far end of the aisle. I study the different cough medicines and lozenges. An employee wearing a brown smock appears at the end of the aisle. I talked to her a few weeks ago. She's pregnant. I look at her name badge.

"Do you know anything about cough suppressants?"

Agatha glances at me nervously and looks away. "Is it for you?"

"No, my husband."

"Does he have a temperature?"

"To be honest, I don't think it's that bad."

Agatha moves products aside, looking at the back of the shelf.

"He wants the lemon flavor," I say. "When are you due? You did tell me, but I've forgotten."

"Early December."

"We're both having Sagittarians. Should we be worried?"

"I don't know much about Sagittarians," says Agatha.

"They've very strong-willed, highly sexed, and virile, according to my husband."

"Let me guess, he's a Sagittarian?"

"Exactly."

We both laugh. She has a pretty smile.

"What does your husband do?" Agatha asks.

"He's a TV journalist."

"Would I know him?"

"Not unless you follow sports—he works for one of the satellite channels."

The manager of the supermarket interrupts us. "Is everything all right?" he asks, brushing down his short mustache with two fingers.

"Perfectly fine," I say.

"Is there something I can help you with?"

"No, I'm being helped already, thank you."

He hesitates. I match his stare. He looks away and leaves.

"Is that your boss?" I ask.

"Uh-huh. He's a creep." Agatha covers her mouth. "I'm sorry. I shouldn't have said that."

"Every woman has had a boss like that," I say, looking for a wedding ring.

She notices and covers her hand. "I'm engaged."

"I didn't mean to pry."

"I know. My fiancé is in the navy. He's on deployment in the Indian Ocean, but he's going to buy me a ring when he's in Cape Town. That's the best place for diamonds."

"Will he be home for the birth?"

"Not unless the navy give him the time off."

I glance behind me, searching for Lachlan. He's no longer looking at the coloring books. He might be reading the comics near the checkout. Excusing myself, I go in search, calling his name. I call again, louder this time. No answer.

"Don't you hide from me, Lachlan. It's not funny."

I'm moving quickly, running down the aisle, yelling for him, suddenly aware of a sinkhole that has opened in my stomach.

Agatha helps me search. We spy each other at the different ends of the aisles as we cover the width of the supermarket. Lachlan isn't here. Running back to the main doors, I ask shoppers if they've seen a little boy. The manager suggests I calm down because I'm upsetting the customers. The girl at the checkout looks frightened of me.

"Did you see him leave?"

She shakes her head.

"Oh my God. LACHLAN! LACHLAN!"

On the pavement I look in both directions along the road and into the park. I'm trembling. Dizzy. A man walks past.

"Have you seen a little boy? He's about yea high, with blond hair. He's wearing a blue parka. His shoes light up."

The man shakes his head. Unwittingly, I've grabbed hold of his arm, squeezing it tightly. He pulls free and hustles away.

A bus has stopped across the road. The doors open. What if Lachlan gets on board? He loves buses. I yell to the driver, waving my arms, crossing the street without looking. A car brakes and the horn sounds. The bus driver opens his side window.

"My little boy, did he get on?"

He shakes his head.

"Are you sure? Can you check?"

The driver walks down through the bus, peering under the seats. Meanwhile I'm scanning the park, fighting against my panic. There are two people with dogs. A frazzled-looking mother sits on a picnic blanket beside a pram. An old man shuffles along the path. The sophisticated parts of my brain are shutting down. I run, calling Lachlan's name, my heart convinced that someone has taken him. My beautiful boy. Gone. Lachlan Shaughnessy. Aged four. With a floppy fringe of hair and perfect little white teeth and a fierce look of concentration when he plays games or makes believe he's a knight, or a soldier, or a cowboy.

I glance across the expanse of grass towards the pond. What if Lachlan went to look at the ducks? He might have fallen in. I'm moving again, yelling his name, terrified that I'll see his little body floating face-down in the water.

Scrabbling through drifts of dead leaves, I reach the edge. Ducks explode into flight, their wings beating at the air. Lachlan isn't there. The turgid brown water ripples in the breeze. He could have gone back to the preschool or tried to walk home by himself. He asked for a chocolate at the supermarket but I told him to wait. He could be at the café, looking at the cakes in the window. I run back, but Lachlan isn't at the café. Could he have gone to Lucy's school? He's always saying he wants to start school now rather than wait until next year. I start running again, studying every passing car and van and truck, fighting the rising panic. Names pop into my head. Missing children. Murdered children. What am I going to tell Jack? How will I explain it to Lucy? My vision is fragmented and blurred by tears. I can't find him. I must.

My name is being called.

"Mrs. Shaughnessy!"

I twice turn full-circle before I see Agatha. She's holding Lachlan's hand. I run to them, scooping Lachlan into my arms, squeezing him so tightly that he complains.

"You're hurting me, Mummy."

Relief is like a valve being opened or a balloon deflating.

"He was in the storeroom," explains Agatha. "I don't know how he got in there."

"Thank you so much," I say, wanting to hug her as well.

Lachlan wriggles out of my arms. "Why is you crying, Mummy?"

"Never run away like that again," I tell him.

"I didn't run away. The door shut."

"What door?"

"It must have locked behind him," says Agatha.

"Well, you shouldn't have wandered off," I say to Lachlan. "I was frightened. I thought I'd lost you."

"I'm not lost. I'm here."

I've left my shopping at the supermarket. Lachlan takes hold of Agatha's hand as well as mine, swinging between us. Now that the fear has gone I feel exhausted and ready to curl up and sleep.

Agatha helps me pack my groceries and we chat about pregnancy and the responsibility of raising children. At first glance I thought she was younger than me, but now I see we're about the same age. She is a little on the plump side—a size fourteen to my twelve, with gray-blue eyes and a nervous smile. I like her quaint northern accent and that she doesn't have any airs and graces—not like some women around here, who can be quite cliquey and standoffish. She makes fun of herself. She laughs. She makes me feel better.

I should invite Agatha along to my mothers' group. She'd be like a breath of fresh air. But in the same heartbeat I consider how snobbish my friends can be. Most of them went to private schools and on to university and speak in identical tones. They are socially confident, attractive, and capable of passing muster at any country house weekend or garden party. Could Agatha do the same? How would I introduce her?

"We should have coffee one day," I suggest, meaning it.

"Really?"

"What's your number?" I take out my mobile. "I'm Meghan, by the way. You can call me Meg."

"And I'm Agatha."

"I know." I point to her badge. "We spoke a few weeks ago—you warned me about the wet floor."

She looks surprised. "You remember?"

"Of course, why?"

"It doesn't matter."

AGATHA

"Tours are usually arranged by a midwife," says the maternity nurse, who is dressed in dark blue trousers and a navy blouse with white piping around the collar. Barely five feet tall, she looks Italian, with thick eyebrows that almost join above her nose.

"When are you due?" she asks.

"Early December."

"You've left it very late."

"I have other options," I say, brushing my hands over my belly. "My sister had a home birth and swears by them."

"It can be a very positive experience if you're healthy with no complications," she says, leading me along the corridor in her sensible rubber-soled shoes. "Is this your first?"

"Yes."

I make a note of how she's secured her ponytail with a simple black hairband and the small watch pinned to her breast pocket. A cheap ballpoint pen is tucked behind her right ear.

"If we can't accommodate you, I can recommend some community and hospital clinics. Will you be going private?"

"Possibly."

"Who is your obstetrician?"

"Dr. Phillips."

She stops at a door and glances through a small glass

viewing window. "I might not be able to show you all
the birthing suites. Some of them are occupied. You
can take a virtual tour on our website."

The corridors are white and clean and bright. Pastel-
colored. Calming. We pass a woman wearing slippers
and a hospital gown being supported by her husband.

"We deliver five thousand babies a year at the
Churchill. Visiting hours are at set times for friends and
family, but partners can come and go," says the nurse,
who shows me a delivery suite with a water-birthing
pool.

"This is the postnatal ward. We have a limited number of private rooms, but it's first in, best dressed."

The tour finishes at the reception desk, where I'm
given a self-referral form. "Your doctor can also submit
an application," she says, "but don't leave it too long."

I thank her and take a seat in the patient lounge,
looking over the form as I watch the passing parade of
expectant mothers and nervous fathers emerging from
the lifts. Others are going home—the babies in infant
car seats or carriers; the mothers holding bunches of
flowers and soft toys.

When I'm ready to leave, I follow the exit signs,
making a note of the corridors and stairwells. People
nod and smile as they pass because pregnant women
are cute and glowing and we waddle like penguins.
What isn't there to like!

There's a note under my door when I get home: *Come
upstairs!*

I knock on Jules's door. She answers, swinging it
open with a flourish. I see Hayden's mother standing
behind her in a tweed twinset, beaming like she's won
the lottery.

"I hope you don't mind," she says, giving me a hug. She smells exactly like her house—fabric softener and lemon cake. I have to stop myself stiffening in her arms.

"How did you know where I live?" I ask nervously.

"Hayden told me. Have you spoken to him?"

"Not since Saturday."

"He has big news."

She breaks the clinch. Jules must know already because she's grinning at me like a court jester. I look from face to face, wondering if I'm supposed to guess.

"Hayden is coming home for the birth," Mrs. Cole announces.

I stare at her openmouthed.

"He spoke to the family liaison department and explained the situation. The navy don't normally allow personnel to interrupt a tour of duty, but they gave him permission. Isn't that wonderful?"

My legs wobble. Jules takes hold of my arm and makes me sit.

"Oh, dear, I'm so sorry," says Mrs. Cole. "It's the shock. I should have realized."

"When?" I ask.

"Pardon?"

"When is he coming home?"

"He docks in Cape Town two weeks from today. Then he'll catch a flight to Heathrow and should be home just in time."

My stomach lurches and I taste vomit in my mouth before swallowing hard. Jules suggests a cup of tea and goes to put the kettle on. Her little boy, Leo, is watching TV with the sound turned down, occasionally looking at us as though we're invading his territory.

"Hayden is over the moon," says Mrs. Cole, all fluttering hands and smiles. "I know it took him a while to come around but he's fully on board. He wants to be with you, if that's OK."

I feel like Alice in Wonderland sliding down the rabbit hole, trying to stop myself falling into a parallel world.

"He can't," I say.

Mrs. Cole stops in midsentence. Jules looks from the teapot. They're waiting for me to explain.

"I mean, he's doing important work . . . catching pirates. What if the pirates seize another ship? I saw that movie—you know—the one with Tom Hanks where the captain was taken hostage."

Mrs. Cole laughs. "They can stop pirates without Hayden." She points to her shopping bags. "I've brought you a few things. We'll look at them later." *I don't want there to be a later.* "I hope you don't mind me coming over. I didn't know Hayden had proposed."

"Who told you?"

"Your friend Julie—she's so lovely. It's nice that you have each other."

"Each other?"

"Being pregnant together."

I nod, still trying to come to terms with her news.

Jules carries a tray to the sitting room. She hands me a mug of tea. "Two sugars." I sip and take a deep breath. I must stop this. I can't have Hayden coming home for the birth.

"Are you sure it's OK? I don't want to put the navy to any trouble."

"It's perfectly fine."

"My mother is going to be with me."

"I understand," says Mrs. Cole. "But now you have two birth partners. I don't expect Hayden will be much use, but I've never seen him so excited about anything."

She doesn't understand. I can't explain. I *want* to

be Hayden's wife and I *want* him to take care of me. A month from now he can sail into Portsmouth like a Viking warrior home from sacking cities, but not now, not yet.

"Are you all right, Aggy?" asks Jules. "You look very pale."

"It's the shock," says Mrs. Cole. "You should lie down."

Mrs. Cole follows me downstairs to my flat, waiting as I unlock the door. The place is a mess. I apologize.

"Nonsense. You've been on your own."

She makes me sit down and put my feet up as she begins cleaning. The dishwasher is unpacked and repacked. Worktops are wiped. Bins are emptied. Out-of-date food is discarded. She asks if I have a bucket and mop.

"Please don't clean the floor."

"Just the kitchen."

I watch her from the sofa.

"You should eat more fresh fruit and vegetables," she says, commenting on the contents of the fridge. "Are you a good cook?"

"Not really."

"I can show you how to make some of Hayden's favorites."

"Great."

She tackles the bathroom next, yelling questions, asking about my family—where I'm from and where I went to school. I try to remember what I told her the last time.

"Is your mother excited about being a grand-mother?"

"Not really."

"Why not?"

"I think the label 'granny' rather bothers her."

"It does tend to age a woman."

Mrs. Cole won't let me see what she's brought me until the cleaning is finished. Pulling off her rubber gloves, she brushes hair from her eyes and takes a seat on the sofa, opening each bag in turn. The first has a dressing gown and nightdress. "Something to wear to the hospital," she explains. The next bag contains a baby's blanket, cardigans, socks, and knitted hats. "I wasn't sure if you were going with blue for a boy so I went for neutral colors. Boys are lovely. So are girls, but it's always nice to get a boy first up."

Mrs. Cole finds nice things to say about my flat and asks where the baby will sleep.

"I thought I'd buy a Moses basket."

"Good idea," she declares. "I can take you shopping. What about a pram?" she asks.

"I'm borrowing one."

"I could get you a new one."

"It's not right that you pay."

"Of course it is. We want to help."

Fully settled in, she continues to talk about the birth, telling me not to worry about the money. I wish she'd leave. I need to think about Hayden and what I'm going to do. I have fourteen days before he arrives home. He'll want to see me. He'll want proof that he's the father.

Sometimes it's best not to know how babies are made.

MEGHAN

Grace wants to throw me a baby shower, which I think is tacky third time around. We're sitting in the kitchen watching Lachlan's attempts to fly a homemade kite in the garden. He fashioned it out of a pizza box and it has less chance of getting airborne than our lawn flamingo.

"Don't be such a spoilsport," says Grace. "Every baby should be celebrated."

"What if I don't feel like a party?"

"That would make you a grouch."

For a brief moment, perhaps craving her sympathy, I contemplate telling her about Simon, but I instantly dismiss the notion.

"No gifts," I stipulate.

"What about baby clothes?"

"I have boxes of clothes in the attic."

"Secondhand stuff!" She pouts. "Please don't make him wear hand-me-downs. That's what happened to me. I had to wear your old stuff. Secondhand school uniforms, hand-me-down shoes, tennis rackets, ski jackets . . . I remember one Christmas—I was nine— Mum and Dad bought me a pair of boots. They were the first *new* shoes I'd ever owned."

I want to laugh and make some wisecrack about first-world problems, but I can see she's being serious. Grace has always resented being the second child. She doesn't accept that being the youngest has any benefit. Maybe she has a point. Everybody celebrates a first baby. When Lucy was born there were cards, flowers, and toys from friends, family, and colleagues. Lachlan didn't get even half that number. And when I look through our photographs, there are far more of Lucy than Lachlan.

"You had Mum and Dad to yourself," Grace says. "When I came along, I had half their time."

"You had *three* people loving you. You had me."

"You weren't very nice to me. Remember that time you pushed me off a box in the garden and I broke my arm?"

"Oh my God, that was *one* time!"

"Very caring."

"I signed your cast."

"Big whoop!"

Grace knows I'm teasing her.

"If you're so keen to have a baby shower, have your own baby," I say.

"A husband might come in handy."

"What about Darcy?" Her latest.

"He's on the way out."

"You've only just introduced him to the family."

"I think that's my problem—once my family likes a guy, I go right off him."

"Darcy is lovely."

"He reminds me too much of Dad."

"Is that a bad thing?"

"Yes!" She pulls a face. "The whole idea of getting married and having children terrifies me. What if becoming a parent doesn't make me grow up? It could be just a cheap disguise."

"It's not cheap."

"True."

AGATHA

My memories are ruthless with the details of my life. I cannot edit or alter or delete moments, or rewrite the endings. I see my babies—the ones I lost or gave away—and I imagine different lives and better times but cannot change what happened.

Now I have another problem. Hayden will be home in ten days. The creature is coiled around my lungs, making it hard to breathe. It is goading me—sometimes in a whisper, sometimes a shriek. I block my ears, telling it to go away.

Foolish! Foolish!

It's not my fault.

You'll never be a mother.

I will.

Getting out of bed, I shuffle to the wardrobe and dress in yesterday's clothes. The first gray hint of dawn brightens the eastern sky, revealing a rainy day after a soggy night. I'm not working today. Normally I'd stay in bed, but the creature won't let me rest.

Turning on the TV, I watch the news headlines, followed by a perky weathergirl who is paid to find rainbows on miserable mornings like this. At nine o'clock there's a knock on the door.

"Who is it?" I ask.

"It's me," says Jules.

She's dressed to go out, holding Leo's hand.

"Have you been crying?" she asks.

"No."

"Your eyes are red."

"It must be hay fever."

"At this time of year?"

She ushers Leo into the flat. He's dressed in baggy jeans and a sweatshirt featuring Thomas the Tank Engine.

"You said you'd look after him this morning," says Jules. "I have a doctor's appointment. Did you forget?"

"No, it's OK. You go."

Leo is hiding under her baby bump, holding onto her legs. Jules hands me a bag full of coloring books, crayons, and DVDs.

"Come on, little man," I say. "Let's watch some cartoons."

Jules leaves quickly before Leo can grow anxious. Sitting on the sofa, we watch TV until he grows bored. "Why don't you draw me a picture?" I say, getting the crayons and paper. Twenty minutes later he's running around the flat wearing a cardboard box on his head, pretending to be an astronaut. He runs into a wall. Cries. Kisses are dispensed.

"I could just eat you up," I say.

He looks alarmed. "You can't eat me!"

"Why not?"

"I'm a boy."

"But boys are so yummy." I chase him into the bedroom and catch him on the bed, blowing raspberries into his soft white tummy.

Later I get him a biscuit and he cuddles up to me on the sofa.

"Do you want some more milk?"

He nods.

I stand up and Leo points to the back of my denim skirt. "You spilled."

I look over my shoulder and see the patch of blood. The sofa has a smaller stain. Something small and fragile breaks inside me—as though I've run through a single strand of spider's web. My whole body cramps. I stare at the blood. My knees are shaking.

Stumbling to the bathroom, I take off my skirt and knickers. Standing over the sink, I scrub at the stained fabric with soap and my bare hands, lathering and rinsing. The water grows pink. My hands are sore.

I'm losing my baby!

You were never pregnant.

Shut up! Shut up!

I told you so.

I weep and pull at my hair, enjoying the pain. I rail at the unfairness, hating myself, wanting to do violence. I want to shove my fist inside myself and stop the flow of blood. Sitting on the edge of the bathtub, I hiccup and sob, letting my sodden skirt drip onto my socked feet.

I hear a creak and glance up. Leo is watching me through a narrow gap in the door. I quickly grab a towel and try to cover myself, but he has pushed his way inside.

"What's that?" he asks, pointing at my stomach.

"It's where babies come from."

"My mummy doesn't have one of those."

"Her baby is coming from somewhere else."

I glance at the mirror and see a sad, half-naked clown wearing a ridiculous-looking silicone belly that is wrapped around my back. What a wretch I am. What a pathetic, pitiable excuse for a human being. I am a joke. I am an echo. I am a failure.

The creature is right. What is the point of a barren woman?

Leo reaches out and touches the prosthetic. "Do you have a baby in there?"

"That's right."

"How did he get in there?"

"God put him there."

Leo frowns.

"What's wrong?" I ask.

"My daddy put a baby in Mummy's tummy," says Leo. "Did he put a baby in you too?"

I shake my head, wiping my eyes. "Go back to the TV."

"I'm thirsty."

"I won't be long."

When he's gone, I wash my thighs and take a tampon from the bathroom cabinet. I dress in fresh clothes, moving slowly, like an accident victim, testing for bruises or broken bones.

I fetch Leo a drink of milk and join him on the sofa. He puts his hand on my belly, still curious.

The boy knows.

He's done nothing wrong.

He could tell someone.

Nobody will believe him.

Foolish girl.

Jules arrives home at midday, shaking out her umbrella. "It's horrible out there," she says, giving Leo a hug.

"Was everything all right at the doctor's?"

"Fine."

She turns to Leo. "What do you say?"

The little boy looks at me shyly. "Thank you for looking after me, Auntie Agatha."

"Any time," I reply.

I hear them climbing the stairs, unlocking the door, Leo running across the sitting room. Jules goes to the bathroom. The toilet flushes. The cistern refills. Water sighs and gurgles down pipes in the walls. I envy Jules, feeling her baby grow inside her, listening to the heart-beat, watching the scans.

I am not impetuous or impulsive by nature, nor am I a monster, but there are nights when I have lain awake, staring at the ceiling, contemplating how to drug my best friend and cut the baby from her womb.

I would not do it. I could not do it. But I *want* to do it.

I feel claustrophobic. I cannot breathe. Shrugging on my coat, I go downstairs, raising my hood against the spitting rain. My uterus cramps. My heart aches. My body is mocking me. The creature cackles.

I told you so. I told you so. I told you so.

I sing to myself, drowning out the voice, and keep walking, past the shops in the King's Road and Sloane Square, north towards Kensington and Marble Arch. London has an ominous gravity that makes every step seem heavier, like I'm climbing to the gallows.

At an intersection I spy a line of preschoolers in matching raincoats, lined up two by two, holding hands, waiting for the lights to change. Their teacher chaperones stand in front and behind. I think of Elijah, my baby brother—my first loss.

At Kingdom Hall I learned that envy is one of the seven deadly sins, but I am guilty of it on a daily basis. I envy the good-looking, the wealthy, the happy, the suc-cessful, the connected, and the married. But more than anything else, I envy the new mothers. I follow them into shops. I watch them in parks. I gaze longingly into their prams.

My biological clock is broken and cannot be fixed. Twelve fertility clinics turned me away over the past four years. I've had my turn, they said. One specialist at Hammersmith Hospital told me not to give up hope. I wanted to slap him and yell, *Hope? Hope doesn't make you pregnant. Hope whispers, "One more time," but still disappoints. "Hope is a good breakfast but a bad supper," my grandmother used to say.*

A psychotherapist said my desire for a baby was some sort of metaphor for something else missing in my life.

"What do you mean?" I asked.

"The birth is metaphorical. There is something that wants to be born that is not really a baby."

"Not a baby."

"Yes."

This is bullshit, I thought. A baby isn't a metaphor. A baby is my reason for being born a woman. Why else was I given a womb and made to bleed every month? Why else do I feel so empty inside? Why else do I mourn the babies I've lost and the one I surrendered?

People who have children seem to regard infertility as being an outdated condition, like smallpox or the plague. They think it was cured long ago by IVF and surrogacy and that anyone settling for childlessness is weak-willed and ignoble. They're wrong. Science offers no safety net. Only one in four fertility treatments results in a live birth, and once a woman reaches thirty-five the odds get even worse.

I have blown those odds. I have tricked boyfriends, fucked strangers, stolen sperm, and undergone five rounds of IVF, but still my womb refuses to grow a mini-me. I have advertised for donor eggs, investigated adoption, and given up on international surrogacy because I could never afford the fees being asked by brokers, lawyers, and surrogates.

I have tried to avoid baby showers, children's birthday parties, playgrounds, and school gates. It's not that seeing babies and children makes me unhappy. I love watching them. What makes me sad is listening to mothers sitting around, swapping stories, complaining about their sleepless nights, or teething troubles, or the expenses, or the germs, or the tantrums. How dare they complain? They are blessed. Chosen. Lucky.

My desire for a child is like a missing piece that cannot be substituted or replaced. It hurts, this hollow feeling, this empty womb; this baby-sized hole inside me. I feel it when I glimpse a baby, or read a magazine, or watch TV. I want a happy marriage, a house, and a dog, but I will forgo all of these for the chance to have and hold a child, to love, to cherish, to own, to raise, to belong.

It's midafternoon and the light is already fading. Somehow I have reached the river near Westminster with no recollection of what roads I took or what corners I turned. Big Ben strikes the hour. Sitting on a painted wooden bench with a cast-iron base, I can smell the dampness on me. Light rain is still falling. A church bell rings. A bus passes. A jackhammer shudders. Gulls wheel above my head. London has no time for silence. It does not reflect upon its past.

A barge passes me slowly, edging forward against the tide. A schoolboy stops and asks if I have a light. A soggy cigarette clings to his lips. He leaves. I stand. Numb with cold, I walk forward and peer at the river, frothing and boiling around the pylons. The world is enormous and I am a tiny unmemorable speck within it, easily lost, quickly forgotten.

The creature uncoils inside me.

You could jump.

I'd probably fail.

You could slip beneath the surface and disappear.

My prosthetic would keep me afloat like a lifejacket. I would bob along until someone pulled me out.

You could take it off.

Confusion creeps over me. I brace my hands against the stonework and lean over and out, rising onto my toes. I stare at the swirling water, wondering how cold it would be. At that moment a Labrador puts its paws on the wall next to me, standing on its hind legs to peer at the same water. Wagging its tail and trembling with joy, it turns to me excitedly, as though asking me what I'm looking at.

"Hello," I say. "Where did you come from?"

"I'm so sorry," says a voice. An elderly man shuffles into view. He's carrying a dog leash and puffing. "She got away from me. Get down, Betty, leave the nice lady alone."

Betty licks at my hand.

"She won't bite," he says. "Is everything all right?"

I don't answer him.

"You're upset. Can I do anything?"

"No, please just go."

He clips the leash on Betty's collar and turns away. He doesn't go far. I see him speaking on his phone, looking at me. Meanwhile a seagull has settled on the wall. It's an ugly fat thing with beady eyes and webbed feet and a hooked beak.

I stare at the evil-looking bird, aware that the old man and his dog are still watching me. A police car pulls up behind them. A constable gets out, puts on his hat, and approaches me.

"Good afternoon," he says, cheerfully. I half expect him to add, "Lovely day."

"That bird is evil," I say, motioning to the seagull.

"Pardon?"

"It's staring at me."

He looks at the seagull, not understanding.

Betty barks. "I was the one who called," says the man. "I was worried about her."

The officer steps nearer and puts his gloved hands on mine. "What's your name?"

"Agatha."

"Are you cold, Agatha?"

"Yes."

"How about we get you a cup of tea?"

"That's all right. I have to go home."

"Where is home?"

I point west along the river.

"Have you been crying?"

"It's the rain."

"When is your baby due?" asks the constable.

"In two weeks."

The officer nods. He is younger than I first thought. A silver wedding band glints on his ring finger.

"What are you doing out here?" he asks.

"I went for a walk."

"It's raining."

"I like the rain."

I must look a mess. I must sound crazy.

"Do you have some form of identification?"

"I left my wallet in the car."

"Where is your car?"

"Around the corner."

"OK, let's go to your car."

The plot holes are apparent even as I come up with the plot. "Sorry, I made a mistake. I don't have a car. I walked." I glance around me. "I have to go. I'm due home."

"Maybe you should let me take you," he says, brushing raindrops off the shoulders of his jacket.

"No!"

He's waiting for me to say something more, but I can't begin to explain the misery of today. Turning his back, he talks into a shoulder radio. I hear the words "agitated" and "doctor."

Growing anxious, I look both ways along the pavement, but there's nowhere to run. I am such a wretched weakling, so easily thrown into turmoil, so quickly frightened and panicked. The creature laughs.

You're in trouble now.

"Shut up!"

The constable turns. "Did you say something?"

"No."

"I think you should come with me."

"Where?"

"To the hospital."

"I'm not sick."

"I want the doctors to check out your baby."

He leads me to the police car. "Mind your head."

The last time I sat in a police car was when Elijah died. My mother sat next to me and we waited for the coroner to finish looking at his body.

"My name is Hobson," he says, glancing at me in the mirror. He asks for my full name. I invent one. "Agatha Baker." It sounds fake. I should have chosen a different one.

"Where exactly do you live, Agatha?" he asks.

"In Leeds," I say. Another lie. "I'm visiting my sister."

"Where does she live?"

"Richmond."

"What were you doing beside the river?"

"Nothing."

"Has something upset you?"

"No. I'm fine."

The police car pulls up in an ambulance bay at Chelsea and Westminster Hospital. The A&E department is on the ground floor. The waiting room is newly refurbished with polished wooden benches and bright green splashes of color. The seats are taken by the walking wounded, the bandaged, broken-limbed, and burned.

"They look very busy," I say. "I could come back later."

"We're here now," says Constable Hobson, ushering me to the reception desk.

I fill out a form using my fake name and address. A triage nurse looks into my eyes with a pencil light.

"How many weeks?"

"Thirty-eight."

"What's your GP's name?"

"Dr. Higgins . . . he's in Leeds."

"You seem to be carrying quite low." The nurse reaches for my stomach and I pull away. She frowns and tells me to pop into the next cubicle and slip on a gown. A doctor will be along soon.

Constable Hobson looks relieved. "Is there someone I can call—your husband perhaps?"

"He's away at sea. He's in the Royal Navy."

"How about your sister?"

"She'll be at work. I'll call her. You don't have to stay."

I disappear behind the curtain. The examination room has a trolley bed and shelves full of disposable gloves, antiseptic wipes, and bandages. I can't stay here. I can't let them examine me.

Before I can move, a doctor appears. He looks young and tired and clever.

"You're not undressed," he says.

"Sorry, I misunderstood."

He puts on a pair of surgical gloves and glances at his notes. "Agatha?"

I nod.

"Do you know what you're having?"

"A boy."

"When did you last feel him moving?"

"Just now—he's right as rain."

"Any blood or spotting?"

I flinch. "No."

"Contractions?"

"Twinges."

The trick to lying is not to add superfluous details. Keep it simple. Don't elaborate or decorate. "Are you going to touch me?"

"I'm going to check the baby's position. Then I'll hook you up to a fetal monitor and we'll listen to his heartbeat."

"Is that necessary?"

"Definitely."

"I need to use the loo."

He sighs impatiently. "It's down the corridor. Third door on the left."

"Won't be long."

Taking my overcoat, I slip past him, along the corridor. Reaching the ladies', I duck inside a cubicle and try to steady my breathing. I can't go back. I can't let him touch me or see me naked.

Easing open the door, I lean out and scan the busy corridor. Turning away from the A&E, I walk purposefully past random nurses and white-coated doctors, who don't appear to notice me. The corridor hits a junction. I turn right and then left. I pass a cleaner and a patient being wheeled by two orderlies. Reaching a dead end, I turn back.

A nurse asks, "Are you lost?"

I jump, startled. "I'm looking for the maternity ward."

"You're on the wrong floor."

"Of course. My sense of direction is hopeless."

She shows me to the lifts. I press the button and wait, glancing over my shoulder to make sure she's gone. The doors open. A middle-aged woman is standing inside.

"Are you getting in?" she asks.

"No. Sorry."

The doors close and I peel away, following the exit signs to the main entrance. Crossing the foyer, I keep waiting for someone to yell, "Stop!"

The creature twists inside me, enjoying this.

Run!

I haven't done anything wrong.

You've faked a pregnancy.

That's not against the law.

They'll investigate. They'll find out about the others.

As I near the main doors I notice an overweight security guard in a gray uniform. He's pressing a walkie-talkie to his mouth. I keep my head down, not making eye contact. The automatic doors open. I turn along Fulham Road, shivering from the shock and the sweat and my rain-dampened clothes.

The creature is still talking.

They'll come looking for you.

I gave them a fake name and address.

They'll find you anyway.

There is no Dr. Higgins in Leeds and I don't have a sister in Richmond.

What about the CCTV cameras?

A bus is coming. I raise my arm and step on board, sliding down into a seat, below the windowsill. I edge upwards and glimpse the police car still parked outside the hospital.

Stupid! Stupid! Stupid!

MEGHAN

Simon has sent me another bunch of flowers, tulips this time, along with a card apologizing for his behavior.

> *Please forgive me, Meg, you're the last person in the world I would ever want to hurt. I hope you'll think about what I said. I love you, Meg, and I love Jack, but some things are more important than friendship.*

I tell Jack the flowers came from a PR company that wants me to review a client's baby products on my blog. I should have thrown them away because they keep reminding me of Simon and what he said to me. In a bad mood, I pick a fight with Jack, which is completely unfair because he's done nothing wrong. I complain about the nursery not being finished.

"You promised to help."

"I've been busy."

"You said that last week."

"I was busy then."

"Right, so shall I push the baby back? Tell him to wait until you're less busy?"

"I'll do it on the weekend."

"You're away this weekend."

"On Sunday."

Why is he being so reasonable? I want to yell, *Don't take my crap! Stand up for yourself!*

Finally, I make some comment about Simon, saying, "At least he has a backbone."

"What does that mean?" Jack asks.

"Nothing. I don't want to talk about Simon."

"What has Simon done? You used to be friends."

"He makes me feel uncomfortable."

"How?"

"Forget it."

"Did he touch you?"

"No." I feel my body betraying me, blushing from my ankles to the top of my head. "It's the way he looks at me."

"How does he look at you?"

"I take it back. I shouldn't have said anything."

"You can't just take it back. He's Lucy's godfather. He's my oldest friend."

I stop talking, which finally makes Jack angry. He goes into the garden, where he plucks leaves from a bush and throws them into the air as though wishing they were rocks.

I feel guilty because I'm the one who deserves to be punished. I should be marched to the stocks or stoned like some biblical whore.

After Jack leaves for work, I wallow in self-pity, listening to an interview on *Woman's Hour*. A mother whose baby girl disappeared five years ago is recounting what happened, her voice stripped bare and scoured by grief.

I checked on Emily when I went to bed and she was sleeping in her cot. Jeremy came home late and also looked in. She was still there. It was a hot night in August. We left the window open to catch the breeze. When I woke it was almost six. I thought Emily had finally slept through. I went to check on her, but the Moses basket was empty.

We have never given up hope of finding her alive, but we have to face the reality that with each passing year our chances are fading. But I'm asking again for information. Appealing for someone to come forward. With your help, we can end the torment of our uncertainty.

Lachlan has come into the kitchen. "Why is you crying, Mummy?"

"I'm not crying."

"Your eyes are leaking."

I touch my wet cheeks.

"Did the baby make you cry?" he asks.

"No."

I hug him, burying my face into his neck. He hugs me back as hard as he can.

"Careful, you'll hurt the baby," I say.

"Can he feel me?"

"And he can hear you. Would you like to tell him something?"

Lachlan frowns in concentration and puts his face down, pressing it against my swollen belly.

"Don't make Mummy cry."

AGATHA

There is no baby inside me. I am carrying an idea. I am nursing a dream. Many things can be stolen—ideas, moments, kisses, and hearts, to name just a few. I am going to steal a baby. I am going to take what I am owed because others have more than enough. I am going to live the life I was meant to live—with a husband and a child.

I can't remember the exact moment when I made the decision to fake a pregnancy. The idea seemed to germinate in darkness and grow slowly towards the light. I read a magazine story about a surrogacy arrangement where the new mother wore a prosthetic belly hoping to "share the experience" with the birth mother. Not for the first time, I shoved a pillow under my pajama top and stood in front of the mirror, turning from side to side, smoothing my bump, imagining myself pregnant.

I enjoyed the fantasy and began repeating it, adding more details each time. Going online, I discovered a website called My Fake Pregnancy, which sold three different sizes of prosthetic bumps, covering each trimester. Made from "high-grade medical silicone," the bellies were supposed to look and feel like real skin. I read the testimonials from couples who used the prosthetics because they were adopting babies and wanted people to believe they were having their own.

It took a week for my order to arrive. I began wearing the prosthetics around the flat, never outside. I bought maternity clothes and played dress-up, feeding my fantasy with more and more real-world details, looking at nursery furniture and baby catalogues. At first I simply wanted to *feel* pregnant and imagine a baby growing inside me. Later, I wanted people to look at me differently. I wanted to be blessed. Special. Doted upon.

When I met Hayden I hid the prosthetic bumps away and hoped he might fall in love with me. He was kind and considerate and just handsome enough not to stray too far. I could imagine being his wife and having his child.

Jules fell pregnant and I celebrated even as I cried inside. I envied her swollen ankles and her sticky-out navel and her bliss. Hayden had gone back to his ship. I found the fake bellies in the back of the wardrobe and strapped on the largest size. Was that when I decided? Perhaps. Not all ideas come fully formed or from a single source. Often there are no lightbulb moments or crashes of thunder.

Faking a pregnancy isn't difficult. It helped having Jules living so close. First I drained the water from my toilet and sabotaged the cistern so it wouldn't flush. Then I invited Jules downstairs and plied her with cups of tea until she had to use my bathroom.

"Your toilet is broken," she said. "It won't flush."

"It's being temperamental."

"Do you want Kevin to look at it?"

"No, Mrs. Brindle should call a plumber."

After Jules had gone, I dipped a jar into the toilet bowl—a little icky, I know, but when needs must. The next day I went to see an out-of-area GP and sat in his waiting room amid coughing infants and crumbling old people, rehearsing a story in my head.

Dr. Bailey ushered me into a consulting room that smelled of alcohol swabs and handsoap. He had thinning hair and bushy eyebrows that made his forehead seem enormous. I wondered if his brain expanded to fill the space, or if it rattled around like a walnut in a saucepan.

"So this is your first visit," he said, looking at his notes. "How do I pronounce your surname?"

"Fyfle."

"And what can I do for you, Ms. Fyfle?"

"I think I might be pregnant."

"How late are you?"

"Four weeks."

"Have you taken a test?"

"I didn't know how accurate they were."

"Very." He rolled his chair across the floor to a small bank of drawers, producing a syringe in sealed plastic. "I can do a blood test."

"No, no, not a needle," I said, covering my arms. "I faint at needles—ever since I was a little girl."

He reached into a different drawer and handed me a jar. "The women's room is just down the hall. Fill this up for me and I'll do a pregnancy test."

Inside the toilet cubicle I opened my bag and pulled out the bottle containing the sample I collected from Jules. After transferring the contents, I washed my hands and went back to Dr. Bailey's office.

"Well, you're definitely pregnant," he said, showing me the stick. "You won't see a pinker line than that one."

"You're sure?"

"These tests are never wrong."

He signed a letter confirming that I was pregnant and told me to see my own GP, who would schedule an ultrasound and give me my dates. I took the letter home and pinned it to the fridge. Later I showed it to the girls at the supermarket, who were all excited for me, maybe even a little jealous, which I could understand.

I have been very diligent since then. No alcohol or soft cheeses, or sushi or mayonnaise, and I've put the bungee-jumping and skydiving on hold. If anyone lights up a cigarette nearby, I glare at them and hold my swollen belly.

In that first trimester I complained of morning sickness until the nausea seemed real and I slipped away to the staff toilet, retching into the bowl. Abigail held back my hair and fetched me water, telling me to sip it slowly.

Mr. Patel grumbled that I was avoiding the heavy jobs and disappearing to the toilet whenever he had a chore. I tried to explain to him about increased blood supply to the pelvic area and pressure on the bladder creating the urge to pee, but he covered his ears and retreated.

When I first wore a prosthetic belly outside—the smallest size—I felt self-conscious, but now it has become part of me. I wear tight-fitting dresses and proudly arch my back as I walk along the street, letting the world know that I am with child.

At twenty weeks I downloaded ultrasound pictures from the Internet. I doctored them up with my name and National Insurance number, making them look official. I showed them around work and stuck them on the fridge beside my favorite photograph of Hayden. By then I was so confident I wore my fake belly with summer dresses and silk blouses. Days and weeks went by when I lost myself in the dream. I felt the baby growing inside me. He kicked and hiccuped and rolled while I stroked my belly and spoke to him.

I'm on the biggest size now—the third-trimester version—and I love the looks I get from random strangers who smile at me as though I'm their favorite niece or daughter-in-law.

For months I told myself I could stop at any time. I could "miscarry" or move away from London, beginning my life somewhere else. But a small, irrational part of me hoped I could keep the deception going forever. Impossible, I know. A clock has been set running inside me—an hourglass with trickling sand. I have less than two weeks to go. Come that time I will have to *lose* my baby . . . or find one.

MEGHAN

I'm at a yoga class for pregnant women at a studio beneath Barnes Bridge station. I know most of the women, although each week we lose a few mothers as their babies arrive. The instructress is also pregnant, wearing a leotard so sheer and tight I can see her outie belly button. Her tank top has a cartoon drawing of a scowling pregnant woman and the caption: *The word you're looking for is "radiant."*

Speaking with breathless fervor, she exhorts us to "Inhaaaaale. Exhaaaaale. Inhaaaaaale. Exhaaaaaale. Start to find your breath, becoming more conscious of it. Inhaaaaaaale. Exhaaaaaale. Use my voice as a guide . . ."

I look past her at my reflection in the mirror. The only time I see my toes is at these yoga classes.

"Now take one hand to your precious baby, the other hand to your heart. Allow your lungs to expand and gently draw your baby towards you like you're giving him or her a hug."

I like these sessions—the stretching bits and meditation, not the new-age babble about self-exploration, emotional balance, or surrendering to a higher being. The trick, I've decided, is to add the science and subtract the spiritual.

"Inhaaaaaaaale. Exhaaaaaaale. Two more breaths . . . that's right . . . now come back to center and get on all fours for a prenatal sun salutation."

On my hands and knees, I feel more like a cow than ever. I look past my bump and notice Agatha at the back of the class. I give her a little wave. She smiles nervously.

"One arm to the leg, the other behind you. Innnhaaaling and exxxhaaaaling. Keep moving with the breath. Your body is bedding down your baby and creating a beautiful home."

I roll my eyes and Agatha copies me.

I look for her after the class. She's brushing her hair and pulling it into a ponytail.

"I haven't seen you here before," I say.

"I try to hide at the back," she replies.

We're both wearing the same brand of leggings and sports top. "We could be twins," I say.

"Except I do yoga like a hippo."

She's funny. "How about that coffee?" I ask.

"Me?"

"Sure. My treat. It's the least I can do after you found Lachlan."

"He was never really missing," Agatha says. "He was always safe . . . in the storeroom."

"I know, but I still don't understand how the door locked behind him."

"No," says Agatha, who changes the subject. "Let's have coffee at Gail's—unless you want to go somewhere else." She looks at me hopefully.

"No, I love Gail's."

We grab our bags and push through the swinging doors. Clusters of women are chatting on the footpath, dangling keys from manicured fingers. Across the road the river smells of low tide and fat-bottomed boats are marooned on the mud, canted drunkenly sideways. Turning onto Barnes High Street, we pass rows of specialty shops, boutiques, and property agencies. The butcher waves to me. A school mother smiles and nods.

"You seem to know everyone," says Agatha.

"It's a village," I say, "but there isn't much privacy."

At the café we decide to sit inside, out of the cold wind. Automatically, the conversation turns to babies. What else is there when we're both so near? Pregnancy. Prenatal classes. Obstetricians. Pain relief.

"I'm booked in for a cesarean," I say. "Otherwise I'll tear again."

"Tear?"

"Down there." I motion to my lap. "Lucy and Lachlan had big heads and I have a small pelvis."

Agatha grimaces.

"You'll be fine. It's amazing how far we women can stretch."

"Did it hurt?"

"Christ, yes! But you forget about that afterwards. That's why we do it all over again."

"So you know the day?"

"December seventh."

"How long will you be in hospital?"

"Four or five days." I pour my peppermint tea. "Where are you having yours? Wait! You told me. Leeds."

"My mother lives there. She's going to be with me."

"So there's no chance your fiancé can get home?"

Agatha shakes her head. "I'll make sure there are lots of photographs."

"It's not the same thing though, is it?" I say. "When Lucy was born, Jack said he wanted to stay at the top of the bed, holding my hand because he didn't want to see the 'business end,' but when push came to shove—and I mean that literally—he was down there, giving me a blow-by-blow account. He called it like a penalty shoot-out at the World Cup."

Agatha laughs. She has a pretty face and a bashful smile, as though embarrassed or fearful of making a mistake. She asks me how I met Jack and how long we've been married. Like everyone else, she seems impressed that he works on TV.

"It's not as glamorous as you think," I say. "He's away most weekends and he missed our last two wedding anniversaries because of European Cup qualifiers. My birthday falls during the Tour de France, so he misses that as well."

"How long does he go away?"

"Three weeks for the tour. I get boozy telephone calls from French bars or bistros every night."

"Men have no idea," says Agatha, whose sweater is covered in pastry crumbs. "Do you ever worry about him being away from home—all the temptation?"

"I used to," I say, "but he's a keeper."

I sound confident, but occasionally I have pictured Jack partying with those skimpily clad models in Lycra shorts and sponsors' T-shirts who stand on the podium with the stage winners. I don't say this to Agatha (I've never said it to Jack), but I know he loves me.

"Is he excited about the baby?" asks Agatha.

"It took him a while."

"Why?"

"This is our oops baby. We hadn't planned on having another one."

"Really?"

Agatha seems surprised by the news. We order more drinks and keep talking.

"How about you?" I ask. "Where did you go to school?"

"Leeds, mainly," she says, "but really all over the place. I ran away from home when I was fifteen."

"Why?"

"I didn't get on with my stepfather."

"Did you go back?"

"I went into foster care."

"But your mother . . . ?"

"We're friends now."

"What about after school?"

"I went to secretarial college," says Agatha, making it sound very underwhelming. "But I did once do a course to become a makeup artist. Mostly I did weddings and parties."

"Anyone famous?"

"God, no! I've never met anyone famous—not like you."

"What makes you think I've met famous people?"

Agatha's mouth opens, but no sound comes out. There is an awkward pause.

"Jack works in TV . . . I just assumed," she mumbles.

I laugh, hoping she might relax. "I used to work for a magazine. I once interviewed Jude Law."

"What was he like?" asks Agatha.

"Very handsome and very cheeky."

"Did he flirt with you?"

"I think maybe he did."

"He fancied you?"

"He wouldn't look twice at me now."

AGATHA

I marvel at how Meg can transform herself from a ponytailed, Lycra-clad gym bunny into a sophisticated, modern wife and mother. Next to her I feel as clumsy and frumpy as a pantomime horse. Meg ordered the peppermint tea and a fruit salad—the healthy choice. I chose a large cappuccino and a chocolate éclair that has flaked all over my sweater, which is knitted from such wiry wool that it foils any attempt to brush the crumbs away.

"It's so nice to see someone enjoy her food," says Meg, not meaning to tease me.

"I'm such a klutz."

"So am I."

"No you're not."

"You would be amazed at how much baby food I managed to get in my hair."

"Yes, but that's not your fault."

A trio of teenage schoolgirls pass the café wearing lip gloss and eyeliner and their skirts rolled up an inch or two, showing off their legs.

"I used to have a body like that," says Meg, sounding mournful.

"Lucky you."

"Shush. I think pregnancy suits you," she says.

"That's because I've grown into my body," I reply. "Right now I feel decidedly unsexy and un-lusted after."

"I don't think un-lusted is a word."

"You know what I mean."

Meg keeps asking me questions and I swing between the truth and lies, rarely answering her directly. Lying comes very naturally to me, while the truth is awkward and uncomfortable, like ill-fitting shoes. It's not that I set out to be manipulative or cunning, and the lies I tell others are nothing compared to the ones I tell myself.

Meg talks about growing up in Fulham and going to a private girls' school in Hammersmith.

"Any brothers or sisters?" I ask.

"A sister—Grace. How about you?"

"I did have a half brother, but he died when he was five."

"What happened?"

"He was killed in a car accident."

"That's terrible. How old were you?"

"Eleven."

Meg tells me more about Grace, making her out to be a rebel. I'm expected to disclose similar intimacies about my upbringing. Why do casual conversations inevitably turn to childhood? I know that friends share memories like this, but why should I have to reveal details of siblings, punishments, pets, holidays, hijinks, broken bones or broken hearts or who has the craziest mother?

"What about you, Agatha?" she asks. "What do you do in your spare time?"

I laugh nervously. "My life is boring."

"People who say that always have the best stories."

"Not me."

I try to deflect her again. Meg notices. I don't want her thinking I'm secretive.

"I was married once," I say, and begin telling her about Nicky. "It lasted five years but didn't work out."

"Are you still friends?"

"He sends me a Christmas card every year."

"And you didn't have children?"

My eyes swim and the café blurs. I lower my head, unable to get the words out.

"I've upset you," says Meg. "I'm sorry."

"No, it's my fault," I say. "I thought after all this time . . ." I don't finish. Start again. "We lost a baby—a little girl—I miscarried at five months."

"That's awful."

"It shouldn't still affect me, but it does."

"You didn't try again?" she asks. Something instantly comes alert inside me. I've revealed too much. Shared truths that will make it harder.

Meg seems to sense my disquiet. "Well, that's all in the past. Now you have a fiancé and a baby on the way." She smiles. "Have you set a date for the wedding?"

"Not yet. Maybe next summer."

"Perfect."

"We're thinking of honeymooning in Tahiti," I add, hoping to impress her.

"I hear the South Pacific is beautiful."

"We're going to get a bungalow on the beach and live like natives."

"How romantic," says Meg. "Lucky you." Her face suddenly lights up as though she's had a brilliant idea. "What are you doing now?"

"What?"

"Right now."

"Nothing."

"You should come home with me. I have boxes and boxes of baby clothes to sort through—far more than I need. Please take some."

"I don't need clothes."

"At least have a look. Some of them are brand new. I get free samples because of my blog."

"What blog?"

"I write a little mummy blog about being pregnant and bringing up kids. Come back to the house. I'll make lunch. You can help me decide what to keep."

Outside the sky has darkened and the wind picked up, snapping at the canvas awnings and rattling windows. Fat drops begin dotting the pavement.

"I don't have an umbrella," says Meg.

"Neither do I."

"We'll have to run for it."

I laugh. "Are you serious? We're in no condition to run."

"Waddle, then."

Meg runs ahead of me, holding her gym bag over her head as the rain gets heavier, falling in sheets. Shoppers are sheltering in doorways and unfurling umbrellas.

Laughing and splashing through puddles, she yells, "The house isn't far."

If I run too quickly I'm worried my belly will slip or the elastic backing will stretch.

By the time I arrive at the house, Meg has unlocked the front door and kicked off her shoes. She gets two large towels from the linen cupboard. Giggling like schoolgirls, we dry our hair. Meg looks like a fair-haired Andie MacDowell in *Four Weddings and a Funeral*. I look like Janet Leigh in *Psycho* before the knife starts shredding the shower curtain.

I pull off my sodden sweater and notice my long-sleeved top is clinging to me like a second skin, revealing the outline of the prosthetic belly where it wraps around my back. A breath catches in my throat. I hold the towel against me.

"Do you have any dry clothes I could borrow?"

"You bet. Come upstairs."

I let Meg go first. I don't want her seeing me from behind. I know the layout of the house. The main bedroom is on the second floor, overlooking Cleveland Gardens. Meg opens her wardrobe and collects leggings and sweaters. Without a moment's hesitation she peels off her gym top. Her swollen belly is silhouetted in the light from the window. She unhooks her sports bra and turns towards me. I notice her *linea nigra*, the slight discoloration of her skin that runs from above her navel to her pubic bone. Her nipples are the same color.

"Get changed before you die of cold," she says.

"Can I use the bathroom?"

She points to the bathroom. I scoop up the dry clothes and shut the door behind me.

Meg calls out. "I'm sorry, Agatha, I should have asked. I'm always getting my kit off in front of other women at the gym."

"That's all right," I reply.

"It's almost like I want to show off," she says. "God knows why."

"I'm the opposite," I say, yelling through the closed door. I take off my wet clothes, trying not to look at myself in the mirror. I quickly get dressed, making sure the prosthetic is fitted properly. I'm taking too long.

"Is everything OK?" asks Meg.

"Fine."

"Do you need a hairdryer?" she yells.

"No. I'm OK."

"Well, I'm just going up to the attic to get the baby clothes. I'll meet you downstairs."

Once she's gone, I open the bathroom cabinet and look through Meg's moisturizer and night creams, making a mental note of the brands. She and Jack have matching electric toothbrushes. Back in the main bedroom, I open drawers, looking at Meg's lingerie and underclothes. Tucked at the very back of her knicker drawer, I discover a small pink vibrator in a velvet pouch. Cute. Sexy. Modern.

Wandering along the landing, I come to the nursery, which smells of fresh paint. Admiring the furnishings and stencils, I sit in the rocking chair and pivot back and forth, imagining that I'm nursing my baby.

Meg calls me to come downstairs. She is warming a quiche in the oven and has made a salad. Once we've eaten, we spend two hours sorting through boxes of clothes, styling baby outfits and mentally playing dress-up. Meg talks about making friends and choosing the right day nursery and primary school.

"Does Lucy like St. Osmund's?" I ask.

"How do you know she's going there?"

"I've seen her school uniform."

"You've seen Lucy." Meg frowns.

"I've been working at the supermarket, remember? I've seen you coming and going with Lucy and Lachlan. I didn't know their names, of course. But if I'm right, Lachlan has a brightly colored scooter and Lucy likes her hair in space buns."

"She wants to be Princess Leia."

"Who?"

"Didn't you ever watch *Star Wars*?"

"A long while ago."

Meg looks at her mobile. "Speak of the little devils—I have to pick them up."

The rain has stopped. My wet clothes have been tumble-dried. Baby clothes are neatly folded in polished paper bags. Meg walks me to the front door.

"When are you going up north?"

"Next week."

"Will I see you before then?"

"I don't know."

"You have my phone number. Here's my email." She writes her address on a scrap of paper.

We hug. Our bellies bump.

"If I don't see you—best of luck," Meg says.

"You too."

"Send me pictures."

"OK."

She stands at the door and waves good-bye. I walk along the road, not looking back but wanting to. I knew Meg and I would be friends. I kept picturing us together, playing tennis and organizing picnics and discussing what schools the kids should attend.

At the same time, I have to be careful because nothing is sewn up, or surefire, or open and shut. It's not over until the fat lady has a baby.

MEGHAN

"I made a friend today," I say.

Jack is sitting on the bed, lacing up his tennis shoes. He and Simon have booked a court at the Roehampton Club.

"Someone in my yoga class."

"So she's pregnant."

"Obviously."

"You're like the mummy whisperer." Jack chuckles. "You attract them with that blog of yours."

"They're not friends—they're followers."

"Disciples, you mean."

Jack has no idea about social media and the difference between friends, followers, "likes," and subscribers. He checks the grip of his tennis racket and practices his forehand.

"So who is she?"

"She works at the supermarket."

He looks surprised.

"What's wrong with that?"

"Your usual friends don't work in supermarkets."

"Agatha is refreshingly down-to-earth and she makes me laugh. I thought I might introduce her to my mothers' group."

"The coven?"

"Very funny. This is her first baby and her fiancé is away at sea."

"Is he a fisherman?"

"In the Royal Navy."

"Ah, a sailor."

"Why do you say it like that?"

"You know what they say about sailors?"

"What?"

"There was this one sailor who was away six months at sea. When he finally reached port he visited a brothel, put down two hundred quid, and said, 'Give me your ugliest woman and a grilled cheese sandwich.' The brothel madam replied, 'Sir, for that sort of money you could have our prettiest girl and a three-course meal.' The sailor said, 'Listen, lady, I'm not horny—I'm homesick.'"

Jack snorts with laughter.

"That's terrible," I say.

"The best ones are." He pecks me on the lips. "I thought I might invite Simon back for dinner. Gina's away so he's looking after himself."

I feel something shift inside me as though a tremor has set off an alarm that jangles in my ears.

"Did he invite himself?" I ask, struggling to hear my words above the internal noise.

"No, but he's always asking about you."

"Me?"

"About your pregnancy—maybe he's angling to be godfather again. Can he do that?"

I don't answer. Jack is almost at the front door.

"We're only having leftovers. You should eat at the club," I say.

"Nonsense. Simon wants to see you. We'll order takeaway. Whatever happened between you two has to be sorted out."

I say nothing. The front door closes. My heart beats like a blown tire. I told Simon he wasn't welcome. Why is he doing this? Opening the fridge, I spy a half-drunk bottle of white wine. I contemplate pouring myself a glass—a huge one. I want to get drunk. I want to leave home. Mostly I want to avoid Simon.

For the next two hours I am on edge. I snap at Lachlan for spilling a drink and make Lucy cry when I'm brushing knots out of her hair. It's not fair to them. It's not fair to me.

I hear Jack and Simon arriving home. They talk more loudly when they're with each other, like people who shout into mobile phones. They're not drunk, but they're each carrying an open beer and a six-pack.

I don't look at Simon. He tries to hug me, but I turn my face away and arch my back.

"What's the matter?" he asks. "I had a shower."

"Dinner won't be long," I say, changing the subject.

Jack begins telling me about their game, talking about his great comeback from five games down to win the deciding set. I glance at Simon and realize that he let Jack win. Others wouldn't be able to tell, but I know him too well.

It's put Jack in a good mood because he doesn't win often enough—not since "I married and got fat," he says, patting his stomach—a remark aimed more at me, because Jack is the same weight as when I met him.

Simon finishes his beer and Jack gets him another. They sit on stools at the kitchen counter, watching me dress a salad and set the table.

"You look great," Simon says.

"Radiant," I reply, not hiding my sarcasm.

"When are you due?"

"December the seventh," says Jack.

Maybe I'm paranoid, but I sense Simon doing the calculations in his head, counting backwards, plotting the date of conception.

Jack is still talking. "Simon has been telling me that

he wants to be a father. I told him he should get Gina pregnant, but he might want to put a ring on her finger first."

I don't reply. Both of them sense the tension, but Jack doesn't understand why.

"So when did you decide you wanted a third?" asks Simon, directing the question at me.

"It wasn't exactly planned," says Jack.

"Weren't you taking precautions?"

"Do you remember Heston's fortieth?"

"In Hampshire."

"We had a bit of morning delight and played Russian roulette."

Again I sense Simon doing the mental arithmetic. The silence stretches out.

"So how are the kids?" he asks. "I thought I might see them."

"Lachlan is in bed. Lucy is watching TV in our room," I reply. I touch Jack's shoulder. "She wants you to say good night to her."

"I'll do it now."

Jack swallows the last of his beer, putting his tongue inside the bottle as though searching for the last drop.

Alone with Simon, I begin wiping worktops that are already clean. Simon picks at the label of his beer with a thumbnail.

"You can't keep freezing me out, Megs. I'm Jack's best friend. I'm *your* friend."

"Why are you doing this?"

"We played tennis. I'm having a few beers. I've always been welcome in this house. You're like my second family."

"We're not."

He stands and moves towards me. I step away, keeping the island worktop between us.

"Why are you asking questions about my due date?"

"It's what people do—they ask about each other. Imagine if I stayed away. Jack would want to know why. What do I tell him?"

"Nothing."

"You're punishing me for your mistake."

"It was *our* mistake."

"Sure, I cheated on Gina, but we're not married. So if we're going to start assigning blame, I think I know where most of it lies."

He's right, of course, which is all the more infuriating.

"So for your sake—and Jack's—I suggest you calm down and begin treating me nicely."

I start clearing away the empty bottles. Simon moves closer. "You should worry about staying healthy and looking after that baby."

"Why do you care?"

He smiles. "You know the answer."

"This is *not* your baby."

"Prove it."

AGATHA

My mother has written another letter. This one has a red wine stain where she rested her glass.

Dear Agatha,

Have you been thinking about coming to Spain for Christmas? We could get a car and drive along the coast, and I could introduce you to all my new friends. They're not all old like me—and the Spanish men are very handsome. The yacht club has a lifeguard who you'll be "drowning" to meet.

If you don't want to see me, I'll understand. I've always depended upon strangers in life, so it shouldn't be any different now that my time is running out.

My mother loves playing the death card on me but she's healthy as an ox, and she's not going to guilt me into being the dutiful daughter. When my stepfather died, she tried to "reconnect"—that's the word she used, making it sound like one of us had accidently kicked a plug out of the wall.

I continue reading.

I forgot to tell you before now, but Mr. Bowler passed away recently. I know that you had your differences, but I hope you can find it in your heart to forgive him—just as I pray that you'll forgive me.

She has included a torn newspaper clipping from the *Yorkshire Evening Post.*

BOWLER Charles Stewart

Passed away peacefully on 18 October in St. Anne's Hospice, aged 68. Mr. Bowler joyfully served as one of the Jehovah's Witnesses along with his wife, Elizabeth, and children, Helen, Nancy, Margaret, and Bernice.

He found great joy in glorifying the word of Jehovah, our Creator, by teaching the "Good News" of the now-established heavenly kingdom to "those rightly disposed to everlasting life" (Acts 13:48; Matthew 24:14), and learning about all of God's wonderful creations.

A service will be held on Monday, 23 October, at 11:40 a.m. at the Kingdom Hall of Jehovah's Witnesses, 103 Silvermere Road, Leeds.

Elizabeth requests that all guests wear bright colors, please. Family flowers only. Donations in lieu to St. Anne's Hospice.

I picture the funeral—the coffin being lowered while his wife and children weep, wearing bright colors, celebrating a life that brought so much pain to me. I see the elders lining up to sing his praises, talking about Brother Bowler's kindness and godliness.

My hands are shaking as I open my laptop and search for more evidence, wanting to be sure. I discover Bernie's Facebook page and remember her giving evidence against me at the judicial committee hearing. She has posted a picture of her father, calling him "my rock and guardian." Dozens of her friends have commented, sending their condolences. I want to add a comment calling him an evil pervert, but I'm too scared.

You'd think after more than twenty years I'd be free of Mr. Bowler, but I still wake some nights with the smell of fish and chips in my nostrils and a voice telling me to open my eyes. I keep them closed. I don't want to see his face.

I could never explain to my therapists or social workers how society misuses words like "horror" and "monster." For me, horror is something that infects me like a disease, and my "monster" can be conjured up by the smell of vinegar on chips.

I don't want to be a victim, which is why I downplay what happened, telling myself that I slept with my abuser only a handful of times and that Mr. Bowler truly loved me, but I'm arguing against my own memories, detoxing details, trying to convince myself it was less awful or that I'm untouched by what happened when in reality it has poisoned everything.

I was pregnant and fifteen and my church and family had disowned me. As we drove home from Kingdom Hall that evening my mother quietly sobbed and my stepfather gripped the steering wheel with white-knuckled intensity. Later, lying in my bed, I listened to them arguing while the creature inside me whispered.

I told you not to tell. I told you not to tell.

The next morning the sun rose unexpectedly because I did not believe that any day could follow the previous one. My stepfather told me I wasn't going to school. Instead he drove me to a large Victorian house on a quiet street on the outskirts of Newcastle. I looked at the bay windows and soot-stained walls and wondered if it might be an orphanage or a children's home.

"What is this place?"

"It's a clinic," he said.

"I'm not sick."

A group of protesters were on the opposite side of the road, holding banners and posters. One of the placards read A PERSON IS A PERSON NO MATTER HOW SMALL. They were singing a hymn: "Amazing Grace."

"I want to keep my baby," I said.

My stepfather spoke softly, holding my hand. "Maybe if you were older."

"I'm nearly sixteen."

"You're barely fifteen. This way you'll get to finish school and go to college and have a career. One day you'll get married and have a family."

"I didn't lie to the elders."

"I know."

"Mr. Bowler is the father."

"We let Jehovah decide these things."

Two security doors had to be unlocked before we reached the reception area. My hands were shaking so much that my stepfather had to fill out the forms. A nurse came to fetch me, a smiley woman with skin so black it almost shone purple under the fluorescent lights. Her braided hair was threaded with brightly colored beads that clacked as she walked.

"I need to speak to Agatha alone," she said to my stepfather.

He tried to argue. She told him to be quiet and sit down. I don't think I'd ever heard any woman speak to him like that.

"Remember what we decided," he said as the nurse led me away. She took me to an examination room with a low bed, a desk, and an ultrasound machine. I wondered if this was where it happened—the termination. Jehovah doesn't condone abortion. Mr. Bowler taught me that in our scripture classes at Kingdom Hall, which would have seemed ironic if I weren't so frightened.

"Hello, Agatha, my name is Janice," said the nurse. "Why are you here today?"

"I'm pregnant."

"I see. And why have you come here?"

"I'm too young to have a baby."

"How old are you, Agatha?"

"Fifteen."

"How long have you been having sex?"

"Since I was thirteen."

"Were you raped?"

"No. I mean, it wasn't rape. We did it, you know. We both decided."

I glanced anxiously at the door.

"The man in the waiting room—is he your father?"

"My stepfather."

"Is he the father of your baby?"

"No."

Janice asked me to hop up on the bed and lie down. "I'm going to do an ultrasound to confirm the pregnancy and see how advanced it is. Then I'll take a blood test and a medical history."

She pulled up my blouse and smeared gel on my stomach. "I'm sorry if it's cold."

"That's OK."

"Would you like to see the fetus?"

"No." I paused. "Thank you for asking."

"You look about twelve weeks. Does that sound right?"

I nodded.

She wiped down my stomach with a paper towel and told me to button my blouse.

"Have you told the father?"

"Yes."

"How old is he?"

"I don't know."

"Is he your age?"

I shook my head.

"Is he much older than you?"

I didn't answer.

"Have you considered talking to the police?"

"I can't do that."

"Why not?"

Again I said nothing.

Janice didn't get angry or make me feel ashamed. She gave me a drink of apple juice in a box with a straw and held my hand, speaking in a gentle voice. I almost told her about Mr. Bowler. I almost said, *Help me.*

"Agatha, I need to be sure that you're not being pressured or rushed into making this decision. It's important that you're sure. You're safe here. Nobody can hurt you. Was it your decision to come here?"

"My parents want this."

"What do you want?"

"I don't know."

"Agatha, there are rules about terminations. Unless you give me the right reasons, it cannot happen."

"What reasons?"

"I can't put those words in your mouth."

"I don't know what to do."

"Have you considered giving the baby up for adoption?"

"Is that possible?"

"Yes. My advice is to talk to your parents. They might be disappointed, but I'm sure they love you and will support whatever decision you make."

We walked in silence back to my stepfather's car. He held the door open for me. As I passed him, he slapped me in the face. Pain washed up and down in my eyes. He raised his hand but didn't hit me again.

       ✦   ✦   ✦

I put on forty-eight pounds during the pregnancy and haven't worn a bikini since. At school I sat by myself like a leper whose condition might be infectious. It didn't matter that other girls were having sex—*I* was having a baby.

One lunch hour I arrived at the canteen to find that every girl had shoved a jumper up her blouse and was standing in the queue, backs arched and legs bowed, waddling forward to collect her tray. The boys were laughing and hooting, enjoying the spectacle. Keeping my head down, I ate my food, determined not to cry. Afterwards I walked home through flurries of snow that made me miss Elijah because he loved the snow. He was lucky to be dead, I thought, because he didn't have to experience such cruelty.

I stopped going to school and stayed home for the last two months, watching TV and eating too much, waiting for my baby to be born. I didn't go to meetings at Kingdom Hall and I didn't talk to my stepfather. My mother acted as though everything were normal, ignoring my pregnancy and treating me like a child.

My water broke in the middle of the night and I was taken to a maternity hospital. My voice, strangely detached, roared and groaned and whimpered for twelve hours as my baby fought to come out and my body fought to keep it inside.

She was born at 2:24 p.m. on March 24, weighing five pounds, nine ounces. The midwife put her on my stomach while she cut the cord. Such a tiny baby, with a wrinkled, mucky face and fine wispy hair. Her eyes were closed in concentration, as though she were making a wish.

I studied every feature of her, every wrinkle, curve, hollow, and hue. The rise and fall of her chest. The curling of her fingers. The softness of her skin. Her smell, her touch, her warmth, her beauty. I imprinted her onto my brain, creating a template that is just as vivid today.

The adoptive parents were waiting outside. I had met them once for a few minutes. They were awkward and nervous, but seemed nice enough. A social worker came to my bedside. "I'm here to collect her," she said, not making eye contact with me.

All through the pregnancy I had refused to envision this moment, forcing it out of my mind, telling myself I was doing the right thing. Now everything changed. I had created a tiny, fragile, perfect human being—someone who belonged to me, my flesh and blood, my baby, who would love me and I would love her back.

"I'm not giving her away," I whispered.

My mother answered. "You can't do that, Aggy."

"Why? She's mine."

"You signed a paper."

"Tear it up."

The social worker reached for the baby.

I tightened my grip. "I've changed my mind. Don't take her! She's mine!"

"I don't want to get physical," the social worker said, grabbing at my wrists. I kicked at her. She cursed.

Two male orderlies held me down, peeling back my fingers and forcing my arms down, pulling my baby away. My mother hugged me. I fought against her arms. I cried. I begged.

"Please, please, give her back!"

The social worker carried my baby away, while I went on screaming. I screamed to wake the sleeping and rattle the air and lift birds from the trees. I screamed for someone—anyone—to help me, but nobody came, nobody listened. A needle slid into my arm. My brain grew foggy.

I will never forgive my mother for what she did. Mr. Bowler may have robbed me of my childhood, but my mother and stepfather stole my future. Two weeks later, I ran away from home. They brought me back. I ran away again. A series of foster homes followed.

When I turned eighteen I asked the adoption agency about my daughter. That's when I discovered my mother's ultimate act of betrayal. She had tricked me into signing a document saying that I would seek no future contact with my child. With one flick of the pen, in my childish handwriting, I had condemned myself to a lifetime of wondering. Wondering if I did the right thing. Wondering if she's happy. Wondering if she ever thinks of me.

Every mother who gives up a baby has these questions, but for me they echo loudest because I have no other children to ease the pain. My daughter will be twenty-three now. She could be at university. She could live a few streets away. She could be strolling down King's Road in Chelsea, hips swinging and handbag swaying, checking her reflection in the shop windows.

I have no legal right to search for her, but now that she's over eighteen my daughter can look for me. That is my hope, my dream, my prayer to the God who turned his back on me. I hope that one day I will open the door and she will be standing on the step. I will tell her that I didn't abandon her and that I have loved and cherished her for twenty-three years. My daughter . . . my first child . . . the one who survived . . .

MEGHAN

Simon has left me a dozen text messages, all of them the same. He wants to see me. I've turned off my mobile and chosen to ignore him. In the meantime, I try to cheer myself up with some retail therapy.

John Lewis has a babywear and nursery department on the third floor, as well as a maternity section and gift service. My "fashion adviser," Caitlin, is annoyingly perky and clearly has never had a muffin, let alone a baby. I let her show me outfits and sell me spa treatments. One particular dress catches my eye. It's black and elegant and I have nothing in my wardrobe even half as beautiful.

"Sadly, we don't have it in your size," says Caitlin.

I don't like her tone. I don't like her skinny waist and her flat stomach and her high cheekbones. I take the black dress and head for the changing rooms, where I strip down to my bra and maternity knickers. Unzipping the black dress, I lift it over my head. The layers of silk begin to slide over my shoulders and then they don't. I tug, squirm and pull, slowly working the dress down over my breasts and my bump.

I look at myself in the mirror. It's horrible! The once sleek dress balloons out from under my bust like an empire-waist ball gown. Pop a bonnet on my head and I could audition for *Pride and Prejudice—The Mourning Years*.

Seizing the hem, I pull it over my head, forgetting

to unzip the side. Halfway up, my arms lock. I'm stuck. I can't get my arms back down and I can't get the dress over my head.

I glimpse myself through the sweetheart neckline and see a strange, misshapen black-and-white creature whose stomach bulges over the top of grandma knickers. I don't look pregnant. I look like I ate all the pies.

"Is everything all right?" asks Caitlin, speaking from the other side of the door.

"I'm having a small problem with the dress."

"I'll get the manager."

"No, that's OK."

I heave at the dress, huffing and puffing. The manager has arrived, talking through the door. "What seems to be the problem?"

"Nothing."

I curse some more. The lock rattles. The door swings open. I cannot lower my arms to cover my bits.

The manager and Caitlin and three shoppers are witness to my retailing horror, seeing my purple veins, stretch marks, and dimples of cellulite.

"You're stuck," says Caitlin, stating the obvious. "I told you it wasn't your size."

Bitch!

"It fit me just fine. I forgot to unzip it, that's all."

The manager and Caitlin have to pull the dress off me, almost costing me an ear.

"Would you like to try something else on?" asks the manager.

"No. Thank you. This one is fine."

I get dressed, my face on fire and static electricity having made my hair fly around my head. I pay for the dress and walk out of John Lewis, picturing the staff laughing at me. I can never go back. I blame Simon. If I weren't so worried, I would never have tried on that dress.

Arriving home, I discover more messages on the answering machine. What if Jack had picked them up first? I have to stop this. The phone rings again. I don't recognize the number.

"If you hang up on me, I'll come to the house," says Simon.

My finger is paused over the button to disconnect. "Please leave me alone."

"We have to sort this out."

"No! Stop texting me. Stop calling. I don't want to see you again."

"You have no choice."

"I'll call the police."

"Fine. Call them."

I want to kill the arrogant fuck, but there's nothing I can do. I can't involve the police or take out a restraining order without Jack finding out. Simon knows I'll do anything to protect my marriage and family.

"I don't want to hurt anyone," he says quietly. "Meet me. Let me explain."

At high tide on the Thames path at Kew the water has breached the banks in places, trickling across the towpath, turning into puddles and muddy pools. I wait on a bench, watching a rowing eight skate across the river, creating ripples that angle like a feathered arrow.

"Sorry I'm late," says Simon.

"We're both early," I reply, standing to meet him, not hiding my anger.

He's come straight from the office, wearing a rumpled suit and loosened tie, the picture of studied nonchalance. Sunglasses are propped on his head. He leans close, as though expecting an embrace, but I step back and away.

"What is it, Simon? I have to get home."

We begin walking along the path beneath the trees where the last of the leaves have turned, yet cling stubbornly to the branches.

Simon clears his throat. "When the baby is born, I want a paternity test done."

The gasp of breath is mine, but sounds like it comes from behind me. "What?"

"You heard me."

I stop walking and step to the side of the path. A jogger passes, nodding hello. My fingernails are cutting into my balled fists.

"You have to stop this. Jack is your best friend. He's my husband. What happened between us was wrong. We admitted that. We promised never to speak of it again."

"That was before."

"Before?"

"I want to be a father."

"This baby *has* a father."

"You don't understand."

"Explain it to me."

He takes in a deep breath, as though the story is like a balloon that needs inflating.

"I don't have a father. I have only vague memories. He's a man in a photograph, standing next to a VW Beetle in the driveway of a house. He's someone banging on the door, begging my mother to let him come inside, his voice getting louder. Angrier. My brother and I were cringing in the darkness. My mother threatened to call the police.

"A few years later my brother saw a man standing opposite our school. He followed my brother home but never crossed the road. My mother called the police, but the man had gone when they arrived.

"For years I told myself that I didn't care about not having a dad. Loads of kids come from broken homes. Some are better off than if their fathers had stuck around. When I turned fourteen I began asking questions. My mother wouldn't answer them. I went searching among her things and found the photograph—the one of him standing next to the VW. I asked her if it was him, but she snatched the picture away and accused me of stealing. I never saw it again."

I don't know why Simon is telling me this. I want him to get to the point because my feet ache and I need to pee.

"A year after I finished school, I visited my grandmother in Scotland, whose mind had started to scatter. She told me my father was a master of get-rich-quick schemes that always seemed to fail, leading to bankruptcy and bailiffs knocking on his door. Even as she told me the story, I remembered my mother in tears, watching our furniture being carried out of the house and loaded into a truck.

"After I graduated I was living with my mother. A water main burst and flooded her basement, where she kept old letters and postcards. Most were water-damaged. I began throwing things away. In one of the boxes I came across dozens of unopened letters. They were addressed to my brother and me. There were birthday and Christmas cards dating back to when we were children . . . all sent by our father. He didn't abandon us. He had tried to stay in touch."

"If he'd really wanted—"

"Please let me finish," says Simon, grimacing and apologizing for his tone. "I started searching for my father. I tried the usual channels—phone books and electoral rolls. I hired a private investigator. It took six months and most of my savings. An email arrived with two attachments: a death certificate and the findings of a coroner's inquest. My father had died of a drug overdose in Morocco. He was forty-seven."

Simon looks at me, pain etched into his forehead, and I feel a flutter of sympathy.

"I know what you're thinking," he says. "The guy was a loser and we were better off without him. But I have mourned the absence of that man for my entire life. It probably seems ridiculous to miss someone I barely met, but I've always wondered if his absence was the cause of my problems with women. Is that why I can't commit to a relationship? I also wonder if it's easier for children who lose a father they have grown to love. They can mourn an absence or try to fill the space that was once taken. I have no space to fill, but I still feel empty. Maybe the separation wasn't worse on him than me. Did he worry about me? Did he mourn for me? Is that why he turned to drugs?"

"That's a big leap," I say.

"Maybe"—he shrugs—"but I don't want to be like him, Meg. I don't want to waste any part of my life, and that includes being a father."

He delivers this last statement as though pleading with me. I fight the urge to prick his grandiosity. I have seen Simon snort more coke than Charlie Sheen and change women more often than his designer ties. I hold my tongue and stay calm.

"There is a difference here, Simon," I say, speaking softly. "You grew up without a father. My children have one."

"But is Jack the right father?"

"He is the *only* father."

"I want to be in my son's life."

"He is not your son. He has *nothing* to do with you."

"I have a right to know if he's mine."

"You have no rights."

"I talked to a lawyer. He said I could have a case. He said a judge might order a paternity test."

I raise my eyes skywards. "Christ, Simon, have you any idea . . . this will destroy my family."

He goes quiet. Inhales. Whispers. "Please understand, I don't want to upset you, but I've thought about this. I've thought about you . . ."

"What does that mean?"

Simon's face seems to be shapeshifting in the dappled light. "Do you ever think about our time together—back before you met Jack?"

"No."

The answer seems to sting him.

"I was devastated when you left me."

"You were stoned most of the time."

"I was in love with you."

"Rubbish!"

"I told you so."

"You told every girl you loved her—it was part of your foreplay."

"You're wrong." He touches my arm and makes me turn to face him. "I have said those words to two women in my life. One of them was my mother. The other is you."

I study his face, looking for some sign that he's lying.

"Are you saying . . . ?"

"Yes."

"You're still . . . ?"

"In love with you."

He seems to hold his breath, waiting for me to answer. I can't. He fills the silence—giving me a history lesson, recounting our first date and our first weekend away and our trip to Paris for Easter. He remembers everything, right down to what I was wearing when he first saw me.

"I've tried to forget you. I went to live in America and then Hong Kong. I dated loads of other women, hoping that one of them would make me forget you. I can't tell you how it felt when I came back to London for Jack's wedding and discovered that he was marrying you. I was happy for him. I carried on. I pretended it didn't matter. I told myself that I'd meet someone, fall in love, and forget that I ever felt this way." He hesitates. "That night when you fought with Jack and came to see me . . . I hate myself for saying this, but a small part of me hoped, wanted, wished I could tell you how I felt. I know what we did was wrong, but I can't deny my feelings anymore. And if that night led to this . . ." He points to my pregnancy. "If you're carrying *our* child, I want to play a part. I love you, Megs. Always have. Always will."

His arms close around me, but I do not soften. My body grows hard like a mannequin and I push him away. My mind is racing. All these years . . . the dinners . . . the barbecues . . . the tennis and golf games . . . the Christmases and christenings. Did I give Simon false hope? Am I a terrible person?

"I have to go," I mumble, looking around me, suddenly lost. How could I have missed this? I've known Simon for years. I know he's prone to wheedling self-pity and sodden promises, but not love. Does he expect me to choose between him and Jack?

"I'm sorry, Megs," Simon says. "I wish I could do this without hurting anyone, but I can't live with the thought that a child came into the world not knowing his true father."

"It happens all the time."

"And it's wrong."

"Is this about me or the baby?"

"Both of you."

The glibness of his answer triggers something inside me. I spin around and slap him hard across the face. It stings my hand. I have never hit anyone before.

"You truly are a selfish prick."

"I love you."

"No! Don't you dare say that! If you loved me, you would never have told me. If you loved me, you would have sent me away that night instead of getting me drunk."

Simon starts to protest. I interrupt him.

"If you go through with this—if you insist on a paternity test—I will make sure that you never see this child. You will never hold him in your arms. You will never again enter our house. You will be dead to me."

AGATHA

This is my last day at the supermarket. I asked Mr. Patel if he could write me a reference but he said he didn't know me well enough.

What an arsehole!

Consequently, I don't feel guilty about stealing a Snickers bar and a can of Coca-Cola when I sneak outside on my break. Abigail joins me, lighting up a cigarette and waving the smoke away from me. We've perched our buttocks on a low brick wall behind the bins beneath an ivy-covered trellis.

"I won't be staying long," she says. "I've applied for a job at the new Apple store in Regent Street. They give you free T-shirts."

"What about discounts?"

"Yeah. I need a new iPhone."

She shows me her broken screen.

I like Abigail because she's unapologetically loud and is far more adventurous than I am. She once hitch-hiked across Europe and spent a month traveling in Turkey by herself. On top of that she rides a motorbike and has no interest in getting married, but that could be because her boyfriend has a wife and two kids.

Mr. Patel whistles out the back door. We've had our fifteen minutes. He wants me to mop the floor in the produce section, which is always the dirtiest spot. I fill a bucket with hot water and wheel it out of the store-room.

"Excuse me," says a male voice.

I step to one side and mumble an apology. It's not until he's gone past me that I realize who it is. Jack is scanning the shelves in the pharmacy section. He doesn't have a basket or cart. It's a quick purchase, something forgotten perhaps. He picks up condoms and reads the packet, trying to decide which brand or size to buy. Having made a decision, he goes to the checkout. Abigail has a little smirk on her lips as she rings up the sale.

Something about the scene makes me uncomfortable. Why would Jack be buying condoms? I set down the mop and walk to the front window. A car is double-parked out front—a black BMW convertible with a woman driver. I recognize her. It's the estate agent who showed me around the house in Cleveland Gardens that Jack and Meg eventually bought. I watch as Jack gets into the passenger seat.

"What's wrong?" asks Abigail.

"Nothing."

"Do you know him?"

"No."

I return to mopping the floor, sloshing water angrily. It's obvious what's happening. Jack is cheating on Meg. He's sleeping with that stiletto-wearing, Botox-frozen, painted whore of an estate agent. How dare she break up my perfect family? What if Jack leaves Meg? What if she kicks him out?

At three o'clock I collect my last pay slip and say good-bye to Abigail and the other girls. Having changed into my winter coat, I walk along the back lane, heading into Barnes village. Pausing outside the estate agent's window, I look at the glossy photographs of flats and houses for sale. Below the specs for each property there is contact information and a photograph of the agent. Rhea Bowden—that's her name. I remember her fawning over me when I looked at the house and asking if my husband wanted a private viewing.

There is a pay phone at the pub. I call the estate agency. A receptionist answers, young and plummy.

"Can I speak to Rhea Bowden?" I ask.

"She's not in the office this afternoon. Can I take a message?"

"I'm calling from Homebase. One of our drivers is trying to deliver bathroom tiles but can't find her house. We must have the wrong address."

"Bathroom tiles?"

"I tried her mobile number. No answer. I think she has a tiler waiting for them."

I hear her tapping at her keyboard. "It's 34 Milgarth Avenue, Barnes."

"Right road, wrong number," I say. "Thanks for your help."

The address is less than half a mile away. Detouring slightly, I stop at the Barnes Fish Shop and buy two pounds of cooked prawns. The fishmonger is full of banter about fish being good for pregnant ladies.

"You know why fish are so smart?" he chirps.

"They swim in schools," I reply.

"You've heard that one."

"Noah heard that one."

Rhea Bowden lives in a pretty detached cottage on a street with lots of trees and builder's skips. There are two types of cars in places like this—the stockbroker brands like Mercedes, BMWs, or Audis, and the cool cars like Mini Coopers, Aston Martins, or original Beetles. Jack's car is parked across the road behind the BMW convertible.

Slipping through the main gate, I take the narrow side path past a rusting bicycle chained to a post. As I pass each window, I crouch to avoid casting a shadow on the curtains.

At the rear of the house, I hear music and voices. Stepping in a flower bed, I stand on tiptoes and peer through a window, seeing the corner of a bed and a discarded pair of trousers on the floor . . . a shoe . . . a shirt . . . a blouse.

Holding the window ledge, I scrabble upwards, lifting my chin higher. This time I see Rhea Bowden dressed in black lingerie. She's straddling Jack, bracing her hands on his chest and rapidly jerking her hips. Her belly is jiggling and Jack reaches up and massages her breasts beneath the camisole. She's talking dirty to him, grinding her hips and moaning like a porn star.

A part of me is disgusted and another part wants to keep watching. I contemplate interrupting them. I could ring Rhea's doorbell or set off her car alarm. No, that's too childish.

Retreating along the path, I walk to Jack's car and tear a page from a notepad in my handbag. I picture Jack inside having a postcoital cigarette while Rhea douches in the bidet. She's the sort of woman who will have a bidet because it makes her feel more European and sophisticated.

Dear Jack,

I know you're having an affair. I know where and when. I have photographs of you and Rhea Bowden together. I also know your wife is pregnant. End the affair now or I'm going to tell Meg. You don't deserve her. Arsehole!

Yours honestly,
A friend

Folding the page in half, I tuck it beneath the wiper blades of Jack's car.

Checking the street again, I wander along to Rhea's BMW and crouch by the passenger-side tire. Unwrapping the prawns, I begin cramming them into the hubcap, moving from wheel to wheel and then the air vents and grille. Some of the heads break off, but I shove them through the gaps.

It will take a few days for the prawns to rot. At first Rhea will wonder where the stench is coming from and blame the neighbors, but slowly she'll narrow it down because the smell will keep following her around.

Satisfied with my work, I wash my hands under a nearby tap. Hopefully I've done enough to teach Jack a lesson. If not, I'll send the next letter to him at home. I need him to stay married to Meg and be faithful and raise Lucy and Lachlan. I might not be the most moral person, but I will not let them break up. Soon they're going to need each other.

MEGHAN

What am I going to do about Simon? I am trapped by his demands, caught between my infidelity and his misguided declarations of love; a rock and a hard place, the frying pan and the fire. Memories of our night together keep popping into my head, creating waves of shame and emotions that swing between murderous rage and my complete surrender.

What if I were to tell Jack and beg for forgiveness?

"It was just sex," I'd say. "It meant nothing." How pathetically trite. "Just sex" is what every unfaithful spouse says, as though putting *just* in front of a word minimizes the betrayal.

Do I also tell Jack that Simon is in love with me and I once had a relationship with him? Surely it makes everything worse because I've kept it hidden. I should have told Jack from the very beginning, but it was the night before our wedding.

This is Simon's fault. He professes to love me, but I don't think he's capable of loving anyone other than himself. He's an opportunist and a dilettante. You can see it in the girlfriends he chooses, who are dull-witted and earnest and never his intellectual equal. Underneath his charm and lavish good looks is a man lacking in emotional conviction or depth. He has no idea what it takes to hold a family together or to maintain a relationship. And the only reason he wants a child is because it would make him more interesting.

Grace wants to take me for a girls' day out because I quashed her plans for a baby shower. She has booked us into a day spa just off Sloane Square and insisted on driving.

"I hope they have a whale wash," I say, but she ignores me and says self-pity is proof that I need pampering.

The spa is hidden discreetly behind a heavy wooden door. The décor has a Southern Asian feel, like some idyllic Malaysian oasis with teak carvings, marble floors, and sandalwood scents. Grace won't let me look at the price list.

"This is my treat," she says, sipping on her first glass of champagne. "Three hours from now we're going to feel like new women."

She's not wrong. Soon I'm being pummeled, rubbed, stroked, stretched, and perfumed until I fall asleep and drool on my towel. A couple of the male masseurs keep vying to get their hands on Grace, who has that effect on men and boys, straight or gay.

We were so different growing up. Grace was rebellious and headstrong while I was timid and eager to please. Each time I won new freedoms because of my maturity, Grace would get hers taken away. "Give that girl an inch and she thinks she's a ruler," my father would say.

I studied English at Edinburgh—choosing a university as far away from home as I could find. I passed my exams, graduated with honors, all the while watching Grace talk her way into nightclubs at sixteen, get drunk, chain-smoke, wear miniskirts, and run away to Europe for two years, pretending to be a hippie. Eventually she came home and went to university, somehow passing her exams. I suspect she slept with some of her tutors, but that's my jealousy showing.

For most of that time I thought we had nothing in

common, but we're closer now. She's easy company—never trying too hard to impress or make me laugh.

"How about lunch?" she says as we're leaving.

"Only if you let me pay."

Her car is parked on a side street. We walk arm in arm, still drowsy from the spa.

"You've been quiet all morning. Is everything all right?" she asks. "Is it Jack?"

"No."

"The kids?"

"They're great." I take a deep breath. My voice shudders. "I'm in trouble."

"Bit late now." She laughs, looking at my bump. Her smile vanishes because I'm not joining in.

"I can't tell anyone. I can't tell you."

"Sure you can. We tell each other everything."

"Not this."

Tears are hovering. I wipe them away angrily.

Across the street, I notice a removal van with its back doors propped open. Two men are carrying a sofa from a house and hauling it up the ramp. I imagine that it's my home and Jack is divorcing me.

"Come on, Megs, don't cry, it can't be that bad."

"I fucked up. I did something truly stupid." My voice trembles. "It only happened once. I was drunk. Angry." I stop. Sigh. Steel myself.

Grace frowns. "What are you talking about?"

"I slept with Simon."

Grace doesn't react. She can barely speak.

"Jack and I had a fight. He said some hurtful things . . . he said . . . he said he wanted out of the marriage. I went to Simon's house. I wanted to know if Jack had said anything to him. Did he still love me? Simon poured me a drink. We talked. I cried. He put his arm around me. It was really stupid."

"You had an affair!"

"It was one time."

"You? Miss Goody Two-Shoes."

"Please don't."

"I mean, I know it happens all the time, but not to you."

"I know, I know."

"Didn't you have a fling with him—before you met Jack?"

"Yes."

She sucks air between her teeth, making a whistling sound. We've reached her car. She unlocks the doors and we sit in silence, staring out the windscreen.

I bite my bottom lip. "Say something."

"I'm shocked."

"Is that all?"

"I feel a little vindicated."

"Why?"

"You were always Little Miss Perfect—the favorite daughter. You could do no wrong."

"I wasn't the favorite. Compared to you, I was sensible."

"Until now."

Why are we arguing about this?

Grace has both her hands on the wheel. I wonder how much she's had to drink. There is an edge to her voice. "Get over it, sister."

"What?"

"You're feeling guilty. Get over it. Move on."

"It's not that. There's more. Simon thinks the baby is his."

This time her mouth opens and shuts without a sound emerging. She tries again. "Is it?"

"No. Definitely not." I'm shaking my head adamantly, trying to appear confident.

"So why does he think it is?"

"He has this stupid idea . . . because . . . you see, I asked him about whether he used a condom, so he thought . . ."

"So it could be Simon's baby?"

"He said he used a condom."

"You don't remember?"

I shake my head. Grace laughs.

"It's not funny."

"It's a nervous laugh, OK? But why does any of this matter? If you both keep quiet, nobody will ever know."

"Simon wants to know. He's demanding I take a paternity test after the baby is born."

"Tell him no."

"I told him."

Grace is finally fully engaged and cognizant of my problem. She is angry, which is good. She has a first-class mind and third-class morals, which is exactly what I need right now if I'm going to stop Simon.

"I'll talk to him," says Grace.

"It won't do any good."

"I can be very persuasive."

"You're not going to . . . ?"

"What?"

"Nothing."

Her eyes narrow and create twin creases that concertina on her forehead. "No, Meg, I'm not going to sleep with him. Contrary to your perception of me, that's not my answer to everything."

"Sorry."

"We need something on him."

"Like what?"

"Dirt."

"That won't work."

"Didn't he used to take a lot of drugs?"

"So did lots of people."

"Did he deal in them?"

"Yes . . . a little."

"Maybe we can blackmail the blackmailer to guarantee his silence. I'm sure his bosses won't be impressed by employing a former drug dealer."

Grace is on a roll, enjoying this a little too much.

"No! We're not going to blackmail him. I don't want anyone getting hurt."

"Hey! This is war, big sister. We have to fight fire with fire—or in this case, dirt with dirt." She squeezes my hand. "If this doesn't work out—you might have to tell Jack."

"I know."

"What will he do?"

"I wish I knew."

AGATHA

Jules went into hospital yesterday and had her baby in the early hours. I heard the news from Kevin, who came home this morning to shower and change.

"A little girl," he said breathlessly when I met him on the stairs.

"How is Jules?"

"Brilliant. No dramas. It was textbook, according to the midwife. They'll be home later today."

"So soon?"

"Jules doesn't want to stay in hospital. I'm off to pick up Leo from her mum's so he can meet his baby sister."

"If you need any help," I said, but Kevin was already skipping down the stairs. I imagine Hayden being like that when he becomes a father. He'll be bouncing around the place like an Irish setter puppy. He'll be clumsy, of course. I'll have to teach him how to hold a baby and change a nappy, but he'll soon get the hang of things.

Later that afternoon I hear Jules arriving home. Kevin is carrying the baby in a car seat while Jules struggles with her overnight bag and two bunches of flowers—one of them from me.

"I got a new sister," brags Leo as he climbs past me on the stairs.

Taking the flowers from Jules, I give her a hug and follow her up to their flat, where I make a cup of tea and put water in vases, arranging the bouquets on the table.

Kevin wants to go out with his mates and celebrate the old-fashioned way with beer and cigars. "To wet the baby's head," he says. "But if you want me to stay . . . ?"

"No, you go," says Jules. "Say hello to the boys from me. And don't get too pissed."

"I won't." He peers into the crib. "A little girl."

"Have you decided on a name?" I ask.

"We're thinking of Violet," says Jules.

"That's pretty."

Kevin grabs his coat and kisses her on the forehead, calling her a clever girl. I hear him jogging down the stairs, taking them two at a time and swinging across each landing.

"So how was it really?" I ask. "I want all the gory details."

She smiles tiredly. "Easier than last time."

"Great."

"You'll be fine."

I listen as Jules describes her labor and the delivery. She has photographs on her phone. Some of them show Violet in the minutes after her birth, being cleaned and weighed by a midwife.

"Kevin was really good. You'll be glad that Hayden is with you," she says wearily. Her words are beginning to lose shape.

Leo has come to peer into the crib. He looks at me. "When is your baby coming out?"

"Soon."

"Are you still bleeding?"

"No." I laugh nervously and ruffle his hair.

"What do you mean, sweetie?" asks Jules. She's looking at Leo.

"Nothing," I say, my heart hammering. "I spilled something on my skirt. Leo thought it was blood."

Leo wants to say something else. I interrupt him and tell him Mummy needs to rest.

"I'll look after Leo. You have a nap."

"Are you sure?"

"Absolutely."

I tuck Jules into bed and she's asleep within moments. Leo has gone to the sitting room, where he's watching TV. I sit next to him and make him look at me.

"I didn't bleed."

"But I saw."

"I spilled something."

He nods, more interested in the TV.

"Listen to me," I say, squeezing his upper arm. "You shouldn't tell lies."

He tries to pull away.

He knows. He knows.

He's a child.

What if he tells someone?

Nobody will believe him.

Stupid! Stupid!

Leaving Leo, I return to the bedroom, quietly opening the door, making sure that Jules is sleeping. Tiptoeing across the floor, I take a nightdress from the dresser drawer before going to the small painted crib and gently lifting Violet into my arms. I carry her out of the room, shielding her from Leo's gaze when he turns and looks at me reproachfully. He goes back to watching TV.

Slipping into Leo's bedroom, I lay Violet on the floor between two pillows and quickly remake the bed, pulling back the SpongeBob duvet and taking plain sheets from the linen cupboard. Retrieving two bunches of flowers from the kitchen, I arrange them on either side of the bed. The only other furniture in the room is a chest of drawers with a tilting beveled mirror on top. Using books and soft toys, I prop my phone next to the mirror and turn on the camera, adjusting the angle to put the bed in the center of the frame. Some of Leo's drawings have been stuck on the wall above the bed. I pull them off gently, trying not to tear the corners.

Once I'm satisfied, I take off my clothes and the prosthetic bump, before slipping the nightgown over my head. I dampen my hair using Leo's water bottle, plastering strands on my forehead and splashing water on my face before picking up Violet, who is still swaddled in a crocheted woolen blanket. Half sitting up in bed, I hold her in the crook of my arm so that only part of her face can be seen. She smells so beautiful, so clean and new.

Using the timer, I take multiple photographs, checking the composition after each one. Satisfied, I unhook my bra and press Violet's face into my breast, smiling tiredly at the camera. This time I'm recording.

"Hello, everyone, this is Rory. I would love to show you his face, but he's pretty hungry right now. I'm exhausted, but so, so happy."

Violet has woken. She snuffles and opens her mouth, searching for my nipple. I set her down and stop the recording before quickly rearranging the room and remaking the bed. Violet is now fully awake and her cries are getting louder. I pull off the nightdress and begin fastening my prosthetic. I hear a sound from the main bedroom. Jules is awake.

"Where's Violet?" she asks, panic straining her voice.

"She's with me," I reply, wrestling with my clothes. Jules is in the hallway . . . at the door.

She appears. I'm breathless.

"What were you doing?"

"Violet was restless. I didn't want her waking you."

"How long did I sleep?"

"Not long. I think she might be hungry."

Jules picks Violet up from the bed and points to my blouse. "Your buttons aren't done up properly."

"Oh. Silly me . . . I'd forget my head . . ."

"Are you OK?"

"Fine."

I make Jules go back to her bedroom and prop pillows behind her back. Once she's breast-feeding, I put Leo's drawings back on the wall, but I can't quite remember the sequence. Hopefully Jules won't remember either.

I'm returning the flowers to the kitchen when I spy Violet's PCHR booklet. The personal health record is given to every newborn, listing details of the birth—weight, length, and head circumference, as well as the name of the midwife and family doctor. I'm going to need a booklet like this.

I begin photographing the pages. Jules appears. "What are you doing?"

"Nothing. I mean—I'm just looking. How's Violet?"

"Full as a fat lady's socks."

"Cup of tea?"

"No."

"How about a piece of toast?"

"Two."

I get bread from the freezer and fill the slots of the toaster. "I didn't get a picture of Violet," I say. "Can I have one of yours?"

"Sure."

Jules unlocks her phone and hands it to me. I scroll through the images and find one that I want. It shows the midwife weighing Violet. I send the picture to my phone, which chirrups in my pocket.

"Is there anything else I can do?" I ask. "I could make dinner for Leo."

"No, you've been wonderful. I'll be fine."

"Well, I'm going downstairs to tell Hayden. He's due to call me tonight."

"Where is he now?"

"Eight days out of Cape Town. He'll be home a week from Wednesday."

"Well, tell him to hurry. He doesn't want to miss this."

MEGHAN

Today I phoned an old friend who works for a law firm in the City. Jocelyn made partner this year. I'm not really sure what that means, but she celebrated by throwing a party at the Savoy Grill, so I figured a lot more money.

She returns my call, shouting to be heard above the noise of traffic. "Sorry, Megs, I'm just out of court. Have you had the baby?"

"Not yet."

"I want to see pictures."

"You will."

She whistles for a taxi. I hold the phone away from my ear.

Jocelyn and I were at school together—inseparable from the age of ten, doing all the usual stuff, graduating from hopscotch and jumping rope to dripping black eye makeup and stalking Oasis. Later her hobby was bulimia, while I became fixated on self-help books. We both pulled through.

She's found a black cab and some silence. "What's with the mysterious phone message?"

"I need some legal advice."

"Are you in trouble?"

"No, I'm calling for a friend."

"Mmmm," says Jocelyn, choosing her words carefully. "Because if this was about you, Megs, I would be obliged to warn you not to make any admissions or confessions of guilt to me because I cannot mislead a court. At the same time, I have a duty to keep whatever you tell me a secret."

"Oh my God, I haven't killed anyone!"

She laughs and I realize that she's joking.

"I have a hypothetical situation for you."

"Hypothetical."

"Yes."

This was a bad idea. I should hang up.

"Can a court order a woman to have a paternity test on her new baby?"

"That depends on the circumstances," says Jocelyn.

"What if she's happily married?"

"Is her husband demanding the test?"

"No."

"Who then?"

"A third party."

"Someone who thinks he might be the father?"

"Yes."

"Fuck, Megs, what have you done?"

"Nothing. This isn't about me."

Why am I still talking?

Jocelyn begins thinking out loud. "I practice commercial law, so I'm not an expert in this area. Most paternity suits are filed to establish financial or moral responsibility. The mother wants money, or a father wants visitation rights. If both husband and wife agree they're the parents, I doubt whether any court would order a test."

"What if the husband doesn't know there's a question mark over the paternity?"

"He would have to be told."

"Even if it puts the marriage in jeopardy?"

"The wife put the marriage in jeopardy the moment she slept with someone else."

"What if she *knows* the baby is her husband's?"

"So you're saying this third party is making a completely baseless accusation?"

"Yes."

"There was no affair?"

I hesitate. "No."

"Why would he do that?"

"I don't know—spite, jealousy, cruelty."

"Are you being blackmailed?"

"This is not about me."

"Right, of course. Well, my advice to your *friend* would be to come clean and tell her husband."

"There's no other way—no restraining orders or letters?"

"Not really."

I can hear Jocelyn breathing down the phone. "Are you all right, Megs?"

"I'm fine. Forget I called."

I hang up and take a deep breath, biting my bottom lip to stop myself from screaming. I am trapped. My past mistake is growing inside me, ticking like a time bomb that will go off unless I can stop Simon.

It doesn't help that Jack is being so nice to me. He bought me flowers on Friday—arum lilies, which are my favorite—and he stayed home all weekend.

On Monday morning I wrote a blog piece:

Reflections

I had an ordinary Sunday. I don't mean ordinary in terms of boring, but it was normal. I woke to the sound of two little people talking and giggling, having crawled into each other's beds to read books. They played happily for almost an hour, letting me doze next to Hail Caesar.

Sunday morning means BBC Radio 2, plunger coffee, bacon and eggs, and the newspapers, of course. This was followed by swimming lessons—which I prefer to call "controlled not-drowning"—then lunch at the pub, before a long walk along the river, a bath, a cuddle, and a DVD (Frozen—again!).

Sunday is curry night and the house still reeks of chicken korma, no matter how many windows I open. Caesar drank half a bottle of wine. I fell asleep in front of a BBC costume drama. And at midnight I was ironing school clothes because I forgot to do it earlier.

It was an ordinary Sunday—except that Caesar said he loved me more than once. A more mistrustful wife might have been suspicious that he doth protest too much, but I'm not the skeptical type.

Men are so funny when it comes to understanding women. Caesar thinks my dream scenario for romance is a five-star hotel, a massage, champagne, a great dinner, fantastic sex, and falling asleep after an hour of him telling me how wonderful I am. In truth, I would settle for a Sunday like yesterday— a sleep-in, a cooked breakfast, a day with the kids, clumsy sex, and loads of voluntary cuddles and compliments.

Life doesn't get much better than that.

AGATHA

At Euston I walk across the cavernous station concourse and wait in line to buy a ticket to Leeds. I'm wearing my best maternity dress with low black heels and a patent leather handbag over my shoulder. I make a point of messing up my request. The tickets are reprinted. I want people to see me. I want them to remember.

My train is on time. Pulling my suitcase along the platform, I ask a porter to help me lift it up the stairs and store it in the luggage bay. I find my seat. A businessman is sitting next to me, tapping on his laptop. I apologize for taking up so much room, using the royal "we," pointing to my pregnancy.

"When are you due?"

"Any day now—that's why I'm going home."

"Home?"

"Leeds." I notice his wedding ring. "Do you have children?"

"Two girls—six and four."

"You're a lucky man."

"Yes, I am."

He's looking for my wedding ring. Not seeing one, he won't ask. When the conductor comes along to check on my ticket, I make a fuss about looking for it, growing anxious and apologetic.

"Take your time," he says. "I can come back."

I search my handbag and the pockets of my coat, sighing in relief when I find the ticket.

The businessman relaxes. The conductor makes light of the delay. Both will commit me to memory.

The train rattles through the Midlands into the north of England, past plowed fields and pastures dotted with wheels of hay covered in plastic. Beads of melting sleet run slantwise across the fogged windows. My stomach rumbles. I should have brought something to eat before I left Euston.

Arriving in Leeds, I drag my suitcase to the cab rank and give the driver an address in Holbeck. He takes New Station Street, Wellington, and Whitehall Road, skirting warehouses and railway yards that look abandoned in the gloom.

The cab drops me outside Ingram Road Primary School, where lights burn brightly from within. The windows are draped in Christmas decorations and little heads on hunched shoulders face the front of the class. A bell sounds and children stampede for the doors, filling the corridors with laughter and shouted good-byes.

I grew up five streets away from here. I walked to school every day from age seven to twelve, dodging cracks and playing hopscotch on the footpath. The intersection where Elijah died is three blocks ahead, but I take a different route because I don't want to be reminded of the accident. Instead, I quicken my pace, splashing through puddles, dragging my suitcase.

In Colenso Grove every redbrick terrace looks identical, with matching satellite dishes bolted to the walls. The front doors have been painted different colors—blue, red, yellow, or green—which could be a sign of self-expression or suburban anarchy.

Reaching my mother's house, I retrieve the spare key from beneath a loose brick at the side of the steps. Letting myself inside, I throw open the windows and pull drop cloths from the furniture. The beds have been stripped of bedding and the wardrobes are full of my mother's clothes. I have never lived in this house and visited only once before, but my mother seems to inhabit every room. She has no photographs of my childhood displayed on the mantelpiece or hanging on the walls, nothing to show that I played a part.

I look at my watch. The courier company told me four o'clock. It's after that now. I get changed into my work clothes and begin cleaning the house, dusting, polishing, and mopping the floors.

The truck pulls up just after five, when the sky is winter dark. The bearded driver is on his last delivery. He carries in a large box containing the birthing pool, inflation pump, pool liner, hose, tap adapters, floor sheet, submersible water pump, and thermometer.

Am I having a baby or cutting up a body?

The water-birthing kit is rented because I didn't see the point of shelling out for a new one. I wonder how many babies have been delivered in the pool and how they disinfect it afterwards.

The driver has gone back to his van. This time he brings my super-absorbent bed pads, sanitary towels, lip balm, lavender oil, flannels, and raspberry-leaf tea.

"Do you need a hand putting up the pool?" he asks.

"No, I'll be fine."

He's looking around for signs of my husband.

"My mother will be home soon," I explain. "She's at work."

He taps his forehead in a casual salute and jogs to his truck. I sort through the paperwork that came with the delivery. There is a maternity certificate that must be signed by a registered midwife or GP, with a space for the patient's name and details of the birth.

This is one of the gaps in my plan. I can forge a signature and registration number, but it won't survive a check of the records or a phone call. Two thousand babies are born in Britain every day—that's one every forty seconds—popping out, drawing breath, bawling. Surely records must occasionally get lost or misplaced. Parents forget. Infants die. Their births are never recorded. My baby will be overlooked. Time will hide him.

Going to the back garden, I light the incinerator, piling on progressively bigger logs until the heat forces me back. I burn my prosthetic pregnancy, watching as the silicone bubbles and melts, sending up plumes of thick black smoke that make the night seem darker.

Research is the key to good planning. I have gathered intelligence and studied my options until I'm confident that I can cover most contingencies apart from the unforeseen or the unforeseeable. I may not succeed, but I will limit the risk. Whatever happens, I don't want to hurt Meg, but I reserve the right to use whatever means . . .

I go to my mother's bedroom and open my suitcase. Inside I have a set of men's overalls, work boots, and a baseball cap, along with several wigs that I've purchased over the past few months from eBay and a uniform shop. I pack these into an upright trolley, covered in a tartan fabric, with twin wheels and a U-shaped handle to pull it along.

Having checked everything twice, I go over the timetable, committing it to memory. Finally, I stand under the shower, washing away the soot and sweat and anxiety before stretching out on a bare mattress, wrapped in a blanket, waiting for sleep to steal my thoughts away.

MEGHAN

I recognize the woman on the doorstep, but it takes me a moment to place her. She's the estate agent who sold us the house. I've seen her since, driving around Barnes in a BMW convertible, wearing her big sunglasses and silk scarves.

Handing me her business card, she gives me a practiced smile, all teeth no gums, calling me Mrs. Shaughnessy. Perfume seems to be lifting off her skin—the smell of overripe apricots and lime.

I look at the card. *Rhea Bowden.*

"I'm sorry to trouble you," she says. "I was in the neighborhood and I thought I'd drop by."

Her hair is tousled in an expensive, undeniably sexy way and brings to mind a former beauty queen ten years past her prime. *Is that cruel? Probably.*

"I'm checking to make sure you're completely happy with the house."

"Is this some sort of after-sales service?"

She smiles again. "That's right. I normally contact people on the anniversary they moved in. It helps keep the channels open."

"The channels?"

"It makes good business sense. Property prices have been rising. You're probably not considering selling, but if you did want a valuation, I could give you one."

"We're not planning on selling."

"Good. So you're happy?"

"Yes."

"How is Jack? Your husband, I mean. I tried to call him earlier to say I'd be dropping by."

"He's at work."

"And is he also happy with the house?"

"We're both happy."

"Excellent." She hesitates and looks past me along the hallway as though wanting to be invited inside. "Well, if you ever do contemplate selling, I hope you consider listing the property with me."

"OK."

"Right, then. Very good."

I watch her saunter down the path and wrestle with the stiff latch on the gate. Cursing, she looks at her fingernail and sucks her finger. I wonder what that was about. Maybe nothing, but Rhea Bowden is the sort of woman who makes my protective senses hum. In the same breath I dismiss the notion because I have no right to be suspicious of Jack—not after what I've done.

Crumpling up the business card, I toss it in the rubbish and go back to packing my suitcase for the hospital. I have done it three times already because I keep changing my mind.

AGATHA

I wake up shivering, cocooned in a single blanket. The central heating hasn't triggered and I can see my breath when I exhale. Dressing quickly, putting on layers, I go downstairs to the kitchen and hold my hands above the spout of the kettle as it boils.

There is nothing to eat in the cupboards so I make myself a black tea with extra sugar and wrap my hands around the mug, soaking up the warmth. My body feels lighter now that I'm not wearing a prosthetic, but I miss how secure and worthwhile it made me feel . . . as though I had a purpose.

Leaving the house, I raise the hood of my coat and walk to the nearest bus stop. Two old women with wrinkled faces are waiting, complaining about the cold. The traffic gasps and stops at the roundabout, never confident. Across the road I see a little boy holding his mother's hand and begin to ache inside.

Having caught the No. 49 towards Bramley, I get off at Kirkstall Bridge Inn and walk across the River Aire and the railway line. A quarter mile farther on, I take the steps down to the towpath alongside the Leeds to the Bradford canal.

The creature has woken fully now, humming faintly, sensing where I'm going, telling me where to leave the path and when to stay hidden. Reaching a three-tier lock, I cross to the opposite side of the canal through open fields with bright green grass. I pass a man throwing a stick for his two dogs. The bigger dog always wins the race, but the smaller dog doesn't seem to mind. A farmer on a red tractor is pulling a plow, turning the earth in neat rows.

When I reach a second lock I am deep in the forest, which smells of damp and ancient secrets. The ruined farmhouse is almost completely hidden by vines, apart from the brick chimney, which is darkened by moss and lichen. I'm close now.

I reach the clearing. The stone pyramids are visible in a carpet of dead leaves. The floral crowns are brittle and dry. I should have brought new flowers. I loosen my coat and crouch beside each cairn, putting my fingertips on the rocks, letting each baby know that I haven't forgotten her. Chloe, Lizzie, and Emily.

I mourn all of them equally, the dead and the unborn and the one I gave away. Lizzie was my second baby. I was eighteen when I took her from outside a betting shop in Bradford. The father only went inside for a few minutes to place a bet on a horse running in the three thirty at Doncaster. The horse was called Baby Lizzie, which he thought was a good sign, so he put ten pounds on the nose. I know these details from the news coverage, which condemned him in the days that followed. The columnists asked, what sort of man leaves a baby outside a betting shop? The same sort of parent who leaves a five-year-old home alone, or locked in a hot car, or who feeds their entire wage into slot machines, or lets a baby lie in a filthy nappy while they're smoking crack or shooting up. People like that don't deserve to be parents, according to the *Daily Mail*.

Lizzie was tiny, only a few weeks old, with dark hollows under her eyes like she might have been born prematurely or "not quite cooked," as my mother used to say. She had a small pinched face and reddish skin and skinny little limbs like a chimpanzee.

I loved Lizzie, but she didn't take to the baby formula. She wouldn't suck hard enough. I made bigger holes in the teats, but she swallowed too much and coughed it up again. At least she was quiet. She had the softest cry.

I let her sleep in my bed. I lay with my cheek against her small head, feeling the soft fontanelles where the plates in her skull were still forming. I woke the third night and she was burning up with fever. I sponged her down with a damp towel and gave her paracetamol and prayed to Mary, the mother of Jesus, asking her what to do.

The fever broke during the night. I fell asleep. Exhausted.

When I woke the sun was streaming through the window, painting patterns on the rug. I felt Lizzie next to me. She was pale. Peaceful. Cold. I cried and rocked her in my arms and said I was sorry. It was my fault.

I put Lizzie's body in a heavy cotton supermarket bag and caught the bus from Bradford to Leeds. I dug her grave with my bare hands because I had forgotten to bring any tools. I collected the stones and made the small cairn. I reach out and touch it now, listening to the stillness of this sacred place, where water falls and grass grows and seasons pass and my children sleep.

"My new baby comes in two more days," I whisper. "I'm going to try much harder this time."

MEGHAN

An email message pings into my inbox. I look at the subject line: *A Little Boy*.

There are two photographs attached and a multimedia file. One image shows Agatha sitting up in bed holding her baby, looking exhausted but happy. The second shows a midwife cleaning and weighing the newborn, whose eyes are barely open.

I click on the media file and Agatha appears onscreen. She's sitting up in bed, breast-feeding.

"Hello, everyone, this is Rory. I would love to show you his face, but he's hungry right now. I'm exhausted, but so, so happy."

I type a reply:

> *Congratulations. He's beautiful. I want all the details. How was the labor? Did Hayden make it home? Call me when you get a chance.*

AGATHA

I contemplate phoning Meg straightaway, but it's too noisy to hear anything above the diarrheal labors of the coffee machine. Every table in the café is taken with students hunched over laptops or thumbing messages on their phones. I chose this place because of the free Wi-Fi and the anonymity it affords.

So far I've sent emails and photographs to old school friends and former colleagues, some that I haven't seen in years, telling them my wonderful news. Those who live in London are being told that I've had the baby up north. Those who live up north are told that I gave birth in London. Few of them know each other or move in the same circles, which is why the deception can work. The only exception is Jules, in case she recognizes the photograph of Violet with the midwife.

Return emails are popping into my inbox. Congratulations. Compliments. There's one from Abigail at the supermarket and one from Claire, my old boss at the temp agency. I contemplate sending a message to Nicky, but he'll wonder how I managed to get pregnant after so many failures.

I leave the café and walk through Albion Street Mall. Turning left on the Headrow, I keep moving until I reach Leeds Central Library, a grand old building made of Yorkshire stone with arched windows and a marbled foyer. Stepping inside, I check the messages on my mobile phone. For the past forty-eight hours, I have kept it on silent—not wanting to be distracted. I look at the log of missed calls. Hayden arrived in London yesterday morning. I have pictured him hurrying through the airport, his duffel bag hanging off his shoulder. His parents were there to meet him. He insisted on driving straight to my flat, ringing the doorbell, wondering where I could be.

I listen to his messages. "Where are you?" he asks. "I'm at the flat but nobody is answering. Your friend upstairs says you've already gone to Leeds. I can catch a train. Call me."

The second message is more strident. "Are you all right? We're getting worried. Mum and Dad are ringing the hospitals in Leeds, but I told them you were having a home birth. Please call me as soon as you get this message."

The next one is more desperate. "I don't know what to do, Aggy. Mum is beside herself and wants to call the police. If I don't hear from you, I'll catch a train to Leeds so I'm nearby."

It's nice to hear his voice, even if he's frantic and frustrated. I knew a baby would make the difference. He's in love with me now. He'll forgive me for this because he wants to be a father.

I send him a text message saying that nobody has to call the police or worry about me.

I've had the baby—a little boy called Rory—and I'm coming home soon. I'll explain everything when I see you. Right now, I need to rest. Please let me sleep.

At midday I catch a National Express coach from Leeds to Victoria Coach Station in London, paying cash for the ticket and smiling at the CCTV camera above the driver's head.

No longer pregnant, I'm pulling the tartan trolley and carrying a baby seat with a curved plastic handle that folds down flat. Draping a blanket over the baby seat, I rest it on the seat next to me, periodically lifting the cover to whisper soothing words.

"A boy or a girl?" asks the woman sitting opposite me.

"A boy."

"Can I peek?"

"He's sleeping."

"I promise not to wake him."

"I'd rather not," I say.

She frowns and shrugs.

At Victoria Coach Station I catch a District line train to Acton Town and book into a cheap hotel with a VACANCIES sign flashing in the window. The receptionist brushes cigarette ash from her lap and stands on tiptoes to peer over the scarred wooden counter.

"Is there someone in there?" she asks, motioning to the covered baby carrier.

"Yes." I smile. "Do I pay extra for him?"

"Not unless he needs his own bed."

"No, he'll be fine."

She asks to see my driver's license. I tell her I don't have one.

"What about a passport?"

"No."

"I need proof of identity."

"I'll pay cash."

She hesitates and glances again at the baby seat. "Are you trying to hide from someone?"

"My boyfriend."

"Did he knock you around?"

"Once too often."

My room is on the second floor. I pass children's toys and bicycles in the corridor, as well as a sign reading NO COOKING ALLOWED. I can smell it anyway—cardamom, cinnamon, paprika, and cloves.

Unlocking my door, I check out the window and fire escape. An information sheet says the front desk is unmanned from 7 p.m. until 6 a.m. Guests can use their room key to open the outside door. This means I can come and go without drawing attention to myself.

I have been away from London for two nights, long enough to establish an alibi and set up half my story. Hayden and my friends think I've had a baby. They've seen the photographs and footage. In the past when I've taken a baby it has always been a spur-of-the-moment decision, which is why I failed. This time I've faked a pregnancy and a birth. I cannot turn up without a baby. Either I succeed or I die of shame.

At seven o'clock I leave the hotel through the main door and head towards Gunnersbury Park, where I catch a minicab on the North Circular. The driver drops me at the Promenade in Chiswick, on the north side of the Thames. Inhaling the icy air, I cross Barnes Bridge on the pedestrian walkway, beneath a half moon that shimmers on the water. Reaching Cleveland Gardens, I keep to the far side of the street until I see Meg's car parked in front of the house.

I don't linger. Following a familiar path, I make my way to the railway tracks, scrambling over the collapsed fence and moving gingerly over the crushed granite and quartz, listening for trains. At the back of Meg and Jack's house, I find my small clearing and fallen tree.

Climbing onto the trunk, I pull branches aside and look across the garden.

The house is dark except for a light above the stove and another upstairs in Lucy's bedroom. Fear balloons in my chest. What if Meg has gone into labor? What if she's already given birth? A shadow moves behind the curtains. Someone is putting Lucy to bed, reading her a story or fetching a glass of water. It could be Meg or Jack.

I scramble onto the capped brick wall and swing my legs over, lowering myself down the other side. Letting go, I drop into the garden and immediately crouch, trying not to create a silhouette. Looking towards the kitchen, I see a pot simmering on the cooktop. There are dishes in the sink. Finger paintings on the fridge.

Moving in a crablike run, I stay close to the fence until I reach the corner of the house, where I brace my back against the wall. A dog barks. Another answers. I'm exposed here, overlooked by windows from the neighboring house. If somebody were to look outside now they would see me. I promised myself I wouldn't take risks like this. I would follow the plan and improvise only if something went wrong.

Looking along the side of the house, I can see the sitting room, which is empty. A sleeping laptop blinks on the coffee table. It belongs to Meg. Would she take it to the hospital?

I hear voices behind me, coming from the house next door. Someone turns on a light, throwing my shadow onto the wall. I duck and scramble to the fence, knocking over something heavy that topples in slow motion. I reach out, trying to catch it. Missing. The birdbath shatters against the stone edge of the flower-bed, detonating with a sharp crack that reverberates like a gunshot.

A door slides open. The neighbors have stepped into the garden to investigate.

"It could have been a railway torpedo," says a man. "They must be working on the line."

"At this time of night?" a woman replies.

Crouched below the wall, I press my back against the damp bricks, trying to hide in the shadows. A window opens above my head. Meg's head appears.

"What was it, Bryan?" she calls.

"No idea," he replies.

Meg leans out farther, looking straight at me. "I see the problem. The birdbath has fallen over."

Bryan peers over the adjoining wall. His fingers touch my hair. "Must have been a stray cat . . . a big one. Do you need a hand cleaning it up?" He swings his legs over the wall. I duck. His shoes narrowly miss my head.

"Jack will do it tomorrow," says Meg.

"It's no bother."

"Really, Bryan, don't worry. Thanks anyway."

Bryan pauses for a moment. His trousered legs are dangling on either side of my head. One heel of his shoe touches my ear.

His weight shifts. His legs swing away. He drops back into his own garden.

"When are you off to the hospital?" the woman asks.

"Early tomorrow," replies Meg.

"Good luck."

They go back inside. Meg closes the window and draws the curtains. My heart seems to have stopped. It starts again with a rush of air into my lungs and I retch dryly, cursing my stupidity.

Recovering my breath, I retreat across the garden and squeeze my shoulders through the small door of the playhouse, where I sit on a child-sized stool with my knees against my chest. I take out my mobile and call Meg's number. She appears in the kitchen, looking for her phone. Answering.

"Hello?"

"You sound puffed?"

"Agatha?"

"Yes."

"I was upstairs putting the kids to bed."

"I hope you didn't run."

"I'm fine. Where are you? Why are you whispering?"

"The baby is asleep."

I'm watching Meg through the sliding glass doors. She's leaning against the island bench, arching her back, feeling the weight of her pregnancy.

"Congratulations," she says.

"Thank you."

"How is the new arrival?"

"Beautiful."

"Is he feeding well?"

"Uh-huh."

Her back is facing me as she flicks on the kettle and opens a new box of tea bags. Meg wants to know the nitty-gritty details of my labor and the home birth. I tell her what Jules told me about Violet's arrival and make up the rest.

"I love the name Rory," she says. "Did Hayden make it back in time?"

"No, he arrived at Heathrow this morning."

"Shame. Is he coming to Leeds?"

"No. Mum has no room for him here and I'll be back in London in a day or two."

Steam curls from the spout of the kettle. She fills a mug with boiling water, jiggles a tea bag, and adds milk. She carries her mug to the glass doors and looks into the garden. For a split second I think she's seen me, but she's studying her own reflection.

"You beat me by two days. I'm going into hospital tomorrow."

"Are you nervous?" I ask.

"A little."

A train rattles past the end of the garden. I cover the handset but it's too late.

"Are you near a train line?" she asks.

"Yes."

"It sounds like you're right outside."

"No, I'm in Leeds."

I see her yawn.

"You look tired," I say.

She laughs. "Are you spying on me?"

"I mean you sound tired."

"Exhausted."

"Go to bed and get some rest. Good luck tomorrow."

MEGHAN

To my little boy,

I've been awake since 4:30 a.m. You're not due for another few hours, but I thought I'd write you a letter and tell you what life has in store for you.

I have worried about you constantly over the past forty weeks, but I know from the scans that you're strong and healthy. A lot has happened in that time and we've had our ups and downs, but I want you to know that you're joining a wonderful family.

Your father is a man I love, admire, adore, and need. He is my rock and he will be yours too. You have a wonderful sister who is going to save the world one day and a brother who hates seeing pain or suffering. You have only one set of grandparents, but they're very active and will love you more than you will believe a person can be loved. Topping it all off, you have a very cool aunt called Grace who will try to lead you astray but that's OK because life should be an adventure.

Now I should tell you something about me—the woman who has carried you around these past nine months. Firstly, I am not crafty, so if you're looking for a mum who can decorate cakes, make Halloween costumes, or cut sandwiches into exciting shapes, you're out of luck.

I can't sing or dance, and I'm terrible at sports. No hand-eye. That's your father's domain. I'm also not very cool. I'm more the opposite of cool. I learned to play the oboe and was the goalie on my lacrosse team.

I know a lot of mums write lists of things they want for their children, or how they hope things will be, but I'm not one for lists. As you'll discover soon enough, I rely a lot on guesswork, but thankfully my guesses are pretty good.

I give you these promises:

I'm going to say some things I don't mean, raise my voice when I shouldn't, and say no when I should say yes, but I vow that when I make a mistake I will apologize.

I promise I will be there when you want and need me and sometimes when you don't, but that's my job. More importantly, I promise I will love you unconditionally, forever and ever, even if you vote Tory or support Man United or forget to ring me on my birthday.

Take care, my baby boy. I'll see you soon, OK?

Love,
Mum

P.S. If you scoot over a smidge and stop kicking me in the kidneys, I'll buy you a puppy.

By six o'clock I'm in the shower, washing my pregnant belly for the last time. Lucy, still in her pajamas, sits on the bed as I dress, asking me questions about the baby and whether it's going to hurt.

My parents arrive at seven o'clock and Jack and I

say our good-byes, which involve kisses, hugs, more
kisses, and more hugs, until I remind everyone that I'm
having a baby, not emigrating to Australia.

Jack drives me to the hospital. I keep going over
things in my head, thinking I should have made a list.
Two kids? Check. House? Check. Meals? Check.

"We should have updated our wills," I say, suddenly
remembering.

"Now you're being morbid," he replies.

"If something happens—"

"Don't worry—I'll remarry."

"That's not what I mean."

He's laughing at me.

I can't describe how I'm feeling. It's almost like a
fake sense of calm. At the hospital I fill out the various forms and get changed into surgical stockings and
a gown with an opening at the back—surely the most
unflattering garment ever designed.

As I'm wheeled along the corridor, Jack takes hold
of my hand. He's dressed in blue scrubs and wearing a
surgical mask and matching cap. I can only see his eyes.

"We're having another baby," he says, squeezing my
fingers.

"Uh-huh."

Dr. Phillips is walking ahead of us, whistling happily.
He's a chirpy morning person, which is better, I suppose, than an OB who is cranky or caffeine-deprived.

The theater is bright and white and filled with tech-
nology. A whiteboard identifies each member of the
surgical team. The anesthesiologist asks me if I'd like
him to put on some music. Jack suggests the "Hokey
Pokey" and begins singing. "You put your right arm in,
you put your right arm out, you put your right arm in
and you shake it all about . . ."

"He's joking," I say.

The anesthesiologist laughs hesitantly and begins administering the drugs.

"You don't have to stay," I say to Jack.

"I'm not going anywhere."

"But you hate the sight of blood."

"I have seen all my children born and I'm not missing this one."

AGATHA

Wearing a dark wig and a shapeless overcoat, I cross the hospital foyer pulling my tartan trolley. Ahead of me, a large family carrying helium-filled balloons and flowers has summoned a lift. The doors open. I slip inside. A pink balloon bounces against my face. IT'S A GIRL! says the message.

The maternity ward is on the fourth floor. I choose the fifth: Administration. The family get off and I ascend alone, knowing that most of the management staff will have finished for the day.

The doors open and I step out, not looking for CCTV cameras. Lights flicker above my head, triggered by sensors. A phone rings in an empty office. Turning left along the corridor, I find the ladies' toilet. Unzipping a pocket on the trolley, I pull out a yellow OUT OF ORDER sign, propping it on the carpeted floor.

After checking that the cubicles are empty, I lock the door and begin to change. Maternity support workers wear dark blue trousers and navy shirts with white piping on the sleeves and collar. My trousers are extra long to hide two-inch platform heels that will make me look taller and thinner. Leaning closer to the mirror, I pull open my upper eyelid and insert contact lenses that change the color of my irises from blue to brown. Next I adjust my wig, letting the long fringe fall across my right eye, breaking up the symmetry of my face, which will make it harder for my features to be matched by facial-recognition software.

Unzipping a small makeup bag, I use black eyeliner pencil to thicken my brows and lip liner to slenderize my lips, while adding a beauty mark low on my left cheek. Finally, I put on a pair of dark, wide-rimmed glasses, which cause me to squint slightly. Straightening up, I study myself in the mirror, amazed at how different I look. The old Agatha is gone.

The creature is unimpressed.

This isn't going to work.

Yes, it will.

You should have stolen an identity card.

How?

You could have followed a nurse home and lifted her handbag.

I'm not a pickpocket.

The front compartment of the trolley contains a six-inch knife in a leather scabbard. I debated leaving it behind, but I'm scared of what might happen if I run out of options. Strapping the knife to my ankle, I pull down the trouser cuffs, making sure it doesn't show.

I am ready. I have done all I can to prepare, but I need some luck now. Fortune favors the brave, they say. What about the desperate?

Leaving the women's room, I follow the corridor to the stairwell and descend the echoing concrete steps. Emerging into a corridor opposite the maternity ward, I glance at my watch. Visiting hours are from six to eight. People are starting to leave, queuing for the lifts, making it easier for me to go unnoticed.

A glass wall separates me from the maternity ward. The door must be unlocked from the reception desk inside. A lift arrives. A pregnant woman emerges. She's in a wheelchair, being pushed by her husband.

"Can I help you?" I ask.

"I phoned ahead," the woman says, arching her back in pain. "They told me to come straight in."

"Right. Good. What's your name?"

"Sophie Bruen."

Her husband speaks. "My car is double-parked."

"You sort that out. I'll look after Sophie."

He disappears into the lift. I buzz reception. The nurse on duty is busy on the phone. She glances up, sees my uniform, and automatically unlocks the door. I wheel Sophie into the waiting area.

"You can wait here for your husband. I'll let them know you've arrived."

I walk away, heading along the corridor, recalling the layout from my previous visit. There are ten delivery rooms to my left and two postnatal wards to my right. Two hours ago I phoned the hospital and asked if Meghan Shaughnessy could have visitors. Staff confirmed that she gave birth this morning and gave me the name of her ward.

Turning a corner, I step around a cleaner's trolley and glance into the ward. Curtains have been pulled around some of the beds, creating cubicles. One of them is open. A woman is talking to her husband. Her baby is sleeping in a small crib beside the bed. I smile at them and move inside, walking between the partitioned beds.

Almost immediately I hear Jack's voice. He's close to me, behind the next curtain, speaking to someone on the phone.

"He's the most beautiful little boy you've ever seen. . . . Right now he's sleeping. . . . You'll get to meet him tomorrow. . . . No, he doesn't talk yet, he's only a baby."

The cubicle next to them is unoccupied. I slip inside and pull the curtains closed, sealing myself off.

Jack finishes the call, sending love and kisses.

"How are they?" Meg asks.

"Excited."

"I miss them."

"It hasn't even been a day. You should take advantage of this—relax, sleep, read."

"And what are you going to do?" she asks.

"Celebrate."

"I underwent major surgery, gave you another son, and you're going to party."

"Absolutely."

Meg tries to scold him but doesn't sound serious. A phone rings. Her sister, Grace, is on the line.

Someone opens the curtain, surprising me. I jump, startled, my heart hammering. A man is looking for his wife. He apologizes. I pretend to be smoothing sheets on the bed. I close the curtains again and steady my breathing.

Meg wants to get up and take a shower. "You'll have to help me," she says to Jack.

The bedsprings shift. She groans softly. The curtains move as she brushes past me. I wait a few moments and pull the fabric aside. Jack has his arm around Meg's waist as she shuffles in her socked feet towards the bathroom.

"Are you sure you can do this?" he asks.

"I'll be fine. There's a seat in the shower."

"Do you want me to come with you?"

"I don't think we're allowed to shower together."

"I'm willing if you are."

She smiles tiredly and kisses his cheek. Taking my chance, I push through the curtains to their bedside. For a moment I think the crib might be empty because the blanket and sheet are the same color. He's swaddled in a bundle. A tiny round face with hands tucked beneath his chin.

I scoop him up and step outside, pulling the curtains closed and turning towards the corridor. Everything around me seems to have slowed down, while I have accelerated. I am faster, cleverer, and more capable than any of these plodding people.

"Excuse me, what are you doing?" asks a voice.

Jack has come back for something.

"Doing?" I ask, feeling my skin tighten across my face.

"That's our baby."

"Of course it is," I say, summoning a smile. "You must be Jack."

"Yes."

"And this little chap was born this morning. He's gorgeous. Where is your wife?"

"She's having a shower."

"Good. Well, your perfect little bundle is due to have a blood test. It won't take long."

Jack looks towards the bathroom.

"You're welcome to come with me," I say.

"Meg will need my help."

"OK. I won't be long."

I turn and walk away from him, my stomach clenching and bowels turned to water. This is a one-time operation. I cannot turn back now. I pause as I reach the reception area, aware of the glass security door. The button is beneath the reception desk. The wheelchair I pushed earlier is empty. I tuck the baby inside and steer the chair towards the doors. The nurse at reception triggers the lock mechanism. The door slides open. I wave in thanks, pushing the chair into an empty lift. I press up. The doors close. I remember to breathe. Before stepping out on the fifth floor, I light up every button, sending the empty wheelchair to each floor.

Tucking Rory under my arm like a bundle of clothing,

I carry him along the corridor to the ladies' room, stepping over the OUT OF ORDER sign. Once inside, I lay him carefully in the sink and begin swapping the nurse's uniform and platform shoes for work boots and a pair of shapeless men's overalls with a stitched logo for a plumbing company. Removing my makeup, I quickly apply another layer, using brown powder to create darker bags beneath my eyes and wrinkles across my forehead and at the edges of my mouth. My wig is replaced by a baseball cap with a graying ponytail sewn into the back. I tuck my real hair inside and pull the cap lower before putting a single silver stud in my left ear. The final touch is a smear of grease on the back of my hands and another on my neck. Glancing at myself in the mirror I see an aging tradesman who didn't escape the seventies.

Rory is still sleeping. He'll wake when he's hungry, but hopefully not yet. Most newborns sleep sixteen hours a day, so the odds are on my side.

Emptying the trolley completely, I gently place him inside, still swaddled snugly in the blanket. I have cut a hard piece of plastic to size, forming a partition that I jam halfway down the trolley, giving him room to breathe. On top I put the nurse's uniform, wig, platform shoes, and glasses.

A clock is ticking inside my head. I am taking too long. They'll raise the alarm and seal off the hospital.

The creature inside me is yelling instructions.

Hurry!

Don't panic.

They're coming.

Not yet. Unfolding a black plastic rain cover, I hook it over the tartan trolley, changing its color.

Now I'm ready. I open the door and glance down the corridor.

"Have you managed to fix it?" asks a voice.

I try to stay calm. A woman cleaner is standing in a nearby doorway clutching a wastepaper bin in her circled arms. She's Polish. Heavyset.

"Blockage is clear," I say in my gruffest voice, not making eye contact.

"Don't forget your sign," she says.

I pick up the OUT OF ORDER triangle and carry it with me as I pull the trolley towards the main lifts, consciously keeping my feet wider apart and my head angled down. I thought of giving myself a limp when I practiced my mannish walk, but a disability draws attention.

I can't risk using the foyer, and the internal stairways will have fire doors and possibly cameras. On my earlier visit, I discovered a goods lift at the eastern end of the building marked STAFF ONLY. It leads to a loading dock on the ground floor. I press the button and watch it rise slowly from the basement. 1 . . . 2 . . . 3 . . . 4 . . .

Come on! Come on!

I'm about to step inside when the alarm explodes, making my heart somersault. The raucous bell clangs through the corridors and up the lift well. I have no choice but to go on. Descending, counting down in the same slow rhythm: 4 . . . 3 . . . 2 . . . 1 . . .

I have no idea what's waiting. Armed police? Security guards? An angry father? The lift stops with a jolt. The doors slide open. I step into a darkened corridor with a concrete floor and pipes running along the ceiling. The alarm is still sounding, but the noise is muffled down here. Lights trigger above my head as I go, pulling the trolley behind me. My footsteps are too loud. The wheels of the trolley are too loud.

Around the next corner I see an exit sign above heavy fire doors with horizontal push handles. I put my weight behind the door and shoulder it open. Head down. Bracing myself for what awaits. The alarm is louder outside.

"Hold on, mate," says a voice. A security guard in a high-vis jacket is standing in the loading bay talking into a radio clipped to his shoulder. He's midthirties, Middle Eastern with a stubbled beard.

He's holding up his hand, wanting me to wait. Grateful for the shadows, I ask him what's wrong. He doesn't answer. He's still on the radio. I catch a few words: *Baby. Nurse.* I take a pack of cigarettes from my breast pocket and pull one out with my teeth before knocking it on the back of my hand. Letting it hang from the corner of my lips, I pat my lower pockets and take out a lighter, striking the wheel with my thumb and closing my eyes against the smoke. I crouch and pretend to tie the laces of my work boots, unsheathing the knife and holding it against the inside of my forearm.

The creature whispers:

Cut his throat and run!

No.

He won't be able to scream.

Not yet.

Straightening again, I lean casually against a concrete pillar, keeping my right arm behind me. The knife is in my fist, the blade facing downwards. The guard turns back to me.

"What are you doing here?"

"Blocked toilet on the fifth floor."

"You're not hospital maintenance."

"Private contractor. We work out-of-hours."

He looks at the trolley. "That's an interesting toolbox."

"Bad back," I reply.

He grabs the handle of the trolley, tipping it forward and rolling it back and forth as though feeling the weight.

"Did you see a nurse carrying a baby?"

"No. Why?"

He lets go of the trolley. The radio crackles to life. He answers. I wait. A bead of sweat rolls down my forehead and into the corner of one eye. Stinging. I try to blink it away. The guard gives me a final look and waves me away.

Pulling the trolley across the loading bay, I climb the sloping vehicle ramp, holding the knife against my stomach. The street outside is crowded with pedestrians, diners, revelers, and people heading home from work. I weave between them, moving farther from the hospital.

Run!

Act normally.

They're right behind you.

Don't turn around.

A church bell rings. Someone shouts for a taxi. I step over a smudged chalk drawing on the pavement and pass a pub with etched-glass windows. At the next corner I pause and dare to look back at the lights of the hospital. Nothing has changed. I put the knife in my pocket and continue walking. A police car speeds past me . . . then another . . . and another.

Gloucester Road station is ahead. I swipe my way through the ticket barrier and carry the trolley down the stairs. The platform is almost empty. A train has just gone. The next is due in four minutes. They are long minutes.

I stare at the electronic notice board while people seem to move in slow motion around me, turning their heads, blinking and talking. I remember seeing a TV program about a neurological condition where the brain alters the perception of time so that events appear to either slow down or pass in a blur. That's what it feels like now, as though God has pulled the handbrake and the planet is decelerating.

Slipping my hand beneath the rain cover, I unzip the trolley and work my fingers inside until I touch the blanket. I bend my wrist and reach farther until I feel Rory's head. Warm. Soft. Sleeping. I make sure nothing has fallen on his face. He has enough air.

The gust of hot wind signals an approaching train. The sound arrives and the carriages follow. Braking. Screeching. Stopping. I take a seat, holding the trolley between my knees. The doors close and we begin moving. The train enters the tunnel, but suddenly shudders to a halt. The lights blink off and on. My heart does the same.

A voice over the public address system: *Due to an earlier signal failure at Manor House, eastbound Piccadilly line services are running approximately eleven minutes late. Transport for London apologizes for any inconvenience.*

The lights blink again and the train jerks forward, slowly picking up speed, as though driven by noise rather than the live rail. At each stop I watch the carriage fill and empty with ever-changing faces, races, and mixtures— Polish, German, Pakistani, Senegalese, Bangladeshi, Russian, Chinese, Welsh, Scottish, Irish, English. I don't often feel sentimental about London, but I love being another tile in this ethnic mosaic.

At Piccadilly Circus a gaggle of teenage girls invades the carriage, shrieking with laughter and tottering on ridiculous shoes. One of them bumps into my trolley.

"Mind yourself," I say.

Her top lip curls. She pulls a face at her friends, making them laugh. Leaning forward, I press my ear to the top of the trolley, hearing a faint muffled cry. Rory has woken, but the noise of the train will keep him hidden.

At King's Cross station hundreds of people are riding the escalators and crisscrossing the concourse. I slip inside a baby-changing room, locking the door and checking it twice. Unpacking the trolley, I take Rory into my arms and rock him gently, putting my cheek against his forehead and whispering that I love him.

I lay him down on the changing table, and he watches me undress, swapping the overalls and baseball cap for my own clothes. I dispose of the disguise, dumping it beneath dirty nappies in the rubbish bin.

Taking a scarf, I drape it over my right shoulder, gathering the ends and tying them together to form a sliding knot that I can tighten or loosen as required. I push the knot back to my shoulder and slip Rory into the sling, adjusting it so that his body is snug against mine. Heart to heart.

No more wigs or disguises. We are now mother and baby. I am Agatha and this is my little boy, Rory: an Irish name—it means "red king."

Tomorrow I will take Rory home and show him to Hayden and he will see what a perfect mother I am and what a perfect wife I can be. I have my family now.

PART TWO

MEGHAN

Becoming conscious is like rising up from the depths of a dark well, swimming towards the light, my lungs empty, screaming for air. Suddenly my body arches and my eyes fly open and I draw in a breath as though screaming in reverse.

A stranger is bent over me with a hand on my chest. Not a nurse. She's wearing a police uniform—dark trousers and a long-sleeved blue shirt buttoned at her wrists. She says my name.

Snippets of memory flash into my mind as though I'm watching a frenetically edited music video. I picture myself having a shower, sitting on a plastic chair under a stream of hot water. Jack helps me get dressed. Together we return to the bed. I see an empty crib.

"Where is the baby?"

"A nurse took him for a blood test."

"What blood test?"

"She said it was routine."

Another nurse walks past us.

"Our baby was taken for a blood test," I say. "When will he come back?"

She looks at me blankly.

"Who took him?" I ask.

The shoulders of her uniform rise and fall on either side of her head.

"Why did he need a blood test? Can you find out?"

Minutes pass. The matron arrives. She asks Jack what the nurse looked like. I grow anxious. Agitated.

"Your baby wasn't scheduled for a blood test," says the matron.

"But the nurse said . . ."

"Where is our baby?" I ask, my voice rising in panic.

"I'm sure there's an explanation." A mole dances on the matron's top lip.

"What explanation?"

Something is wrong. I hear an alarm. People are shouting. Running. I wish I could remember more, but I can't hold on to the half-formed images and snatches of dialogue. I think I collapsed. I must have cried. A doctor came. He had red hair and freckles on his forehead and he slid a needle into my arm. The world grew dark, closing in to a single white point, until this last star went out.

The policewoman is still next to my bed. She is young with fleshy cheeks that give the impression she's hiding bubblegum inside them.

"Where's Jack?"

"Your husband isn't here."

"I want to see Jack."

"I'm sure he'll be back soon."

I try to get up. The pain takes my breath away.

"You're not supposed to move," she says.

"I want to go home."

"You've had surgery."

The policewoman goes to the door and talks to someone in the corridor—a nurse. They're whispering. The constable comes back to the bed.

"What did you say to her?"

"I told her to get the doctor."

"Who are you?"

"My name is PC Hipwell. You can call me Annie. Are you hungry?"

"No."

"Thirsty?"

"I need to use the toilet."

"I can help you."

Annie pulls back the sheet and I swing my legs over the side, testing the firmness of the floor. She puts an arm around my waist, supporting me on the short walk to the en-suite bathroom. When did I get a private room? I don't remember getting here. Where's Jack?

Sitting on the commode, I look at the bandages on my abdomen and recall the birth. I was conscious, but didn't feel a thing when Dr. Phillips made the incision. Jack was next to him, wearing a surgical mask and giving me commentary, pretending to call the Grand National.

"Coming to the final turn and Meg Shaughnessy is three lengths ahead of the field, making it look easy. She's approaching the last. Up and over. Kicking for home. She's five lengths clear—make that six. The crowd are on their feet. Listen to that roar!"

I wanted to kill him because he was making me laugh.

"And it's a boy," he said. "Son of Shaughnessy—a champion in the making."

I flush the toilet and Annie helps me back to the bed. There's another knock on the door—the same nurse as before. She and Annie are whispering again—talking about me. What are they hiding?

Annie comes back to the bed. "Are you sure you're not hungry?"

"I want to see Jack."

"We're trying to find him."

My voice grows more strident. "Where has he gone? What have you done to him?"

"You must stay calm, Mrs. Shaughnessy. Otherwise they'll sedate you. You don't want that, do you?"

She has an annoying, cloying voice, like a kinder-garten teacher telling a child that she's letting the class down.

"You'll feel better after a nice cup of tea."

"I don't want tea. I want Jack."

Annie holds up her hands and says she'll ask. She leaves me alone in the room. Ignoring the pain, I get out of bed and search for my clothes, opening cup-boards and drawers. I find a dressing gown and slip-pers. Where's my phone?

Edging the door open, I peer left and right along the corridor, trying to get my bearings. I need to find a tele-phone. Jack will know what to do. I turn left and shuffle towards double doors. A nurse appears. I change direc-tion and pass a maternity ward. I recognize this place.

From somewhere nearby comes the sound of a baby crying. My heart leaps. They've found him! I follow the sound and push open a curtain. A woman is holding a newborn.

"That's my baby!" I yell.

Her eyes go wide. Terrified by the sight of me.

"Give him back! He's mine!"

She hugs him tighter. I try to wrench him from her arms. Nurses come running. The constable is with them, her face flushed with anger or embarrassment.

"Let go, Mrs. Shaughnessy," says a nurse. "It's not your baby."

I'm sobbing into her shoulder. "Not mine," I say, repeating the words as the memories coalesce and I remember what happened.

My baby is missing. Stolen. Snatched away. Why? Who would do such a thing? What if he's been dumped somewhere? What if he's been left on a doorstep or in a rubbish bin? He could be buried under leaves or locked in the boot of a car. People might be walking past him and not know. They might not hear him crying.

Children get taken all the time. They wander off. They fall into swimming pools, or get into strange cars, or wander into the woods. But babies don't disappear. Babies don't follow kittens, or fall asleep in garden sheds, or get lost in shopping malls. Babies can't flag down passing cars or follow signs or knock on doors or phone home or ask strangers for help. Babies can't tell people that they're missing or find their way home like lost dogs.

Where is Jack? He should be here. I can hear myself yelling his name.

Strong hands are holding me down. The hypodermic pricks my skin and my mind slides and falls, tumbling into a chemical void.

I fight the needle. I sleep. I dream.

AGATHA

Rory had a good night. He slept beside me in the double bed. I woke every half hour and put my hand on his chest, checking to make sure. I do not feel guilt or shame. My contrition has been overtaken by love. My sense of self has been erased. Rory is all that matters. I could lie next to him for the rest of my life, staring at his beautiful face, putting my forefinger into his little fist, brushing my lips across his forehead, listening to his fluttering heart.

I whisper to him, "You are my fifth baby. Fifth time lucky. Five is my favorite number."

The sun is up. I'm cradling Rory in my arms, looking in the mirror, picturing myself in the eyes of others. His head is a funny shape—a little squished on one side like a very cute alien, but that's likely to pass in a few days.

Holding up my phone with one hand, I take photographs, selfies, smiling as though my face might break from happiness. The pictures are emailed to Jules and Hayden and Mr. Patel and my landlady and all of my friends. I tell them about the days since his birth, constructing a narrative, setting the timeline in people's minds and memories.

When I came in last night the front desk was empty. There were two teenage girls talking on the stairs, who paid little notice to a woman carrying a baby in a sling. I stepped around them and unlocked my door. Having showered and changed, I fed Rory and then turned on BBC news. There was no mention of a baby being taken. It was still too early.

This morning it's a different story. The screen shows a reporter standing outside the hospital, talking to the camera. I turn up the volume.

"At this stage details are scant, but police have confirmed that a woman posing as a nurse abducted a newborn baby from the Churchill Hospital in Central London last night. The baby boy was only ten hours old when taken from a maternity ward by a woman in a nurse's uniform who claimed the newborn needed a blood test. The alarm was raised by the baby's father and the Churchill locked down, but the woman had already left the hospital."

The footage switches to police cars parked in the street and detectives entering the doors.

"The name of the family has not been released, but police are appealing to the kidnapper to surrender the baby to police or medical services. Sources are also suggesting the newborn may need medical attention."

"Rubbish!" I say to Rory. "You're perfectly fine, aren't you? They are such worrywarts."

Letting the TV play in the background, I warm up a bottle in a sink full of hot water. Rory doesn't seem to like the baby formula, either that or he's not sucking strongly enough. When he latches onto my little finger he seems to get the idea, but he turns his face away from the bottle after one or two sucks. I try for almost half an hour, until he falls asleep. He'll be hungry later, I tell myself.

I check the messages on my phone. Hayden has left most of them. I called him last night and told him I'd be home today. I apologized for being out of touch, saying that my mobile had died and I didn't have a charger.

Now I send him another message saying that I'm on the train and should be home by midday. He tries to call me straight back but I don't answer, letting it go to voicemail.

"I can pick you up from the station," he says. "I'm staying at your flat. Your friend Jules let me in. I hope you don't mind. I can't wait to see you."

I smile to myself. Fatherhood has already transformed him. He wants to see his son. He wants to see me.

It's cold this morning. I dress Rory warmly and make sure his head is covered with a woolen hat. He opens his eyes fully when I'm changing his nappy. His arms and legs wave in the air, as though he's frightened of being naked.

The receptionist is back at the front desk. This time I put the baby carrier on the counter, letting her see Rory. She doesn't seem very interested. I make a comment about the weather, saying he'll get a shock when he goes outside.

"Who?"

"Rory."

"Oh."

"He's only three days old," I say.

"That's young to be traveling."

"We're going home."

"What about your boyfriend?"

"I've forgiven him."

I ask her to call me a minicab, and I wait in the warmth until I see the car pull up outside. The driver has to help me buckle the baby carrier into the backseat. I should have practiced. My clumsiness makes me look amateurish.

"Where to, love?" he asks in an East End accent that sounds more like an affectation than something born and bred. He's chatty and cheerful. The conversation jumps from the weather to Christmas crowds and then his own children—three of them: six, eight, and eleven. "I prefer them as babies, because they can't talk back," he says, glancing at me in the rearview mirror. "Your little one looks straight out of the oven."

"Pretty much."

"Shouldn't you still be in hospital?"

"Not really."

He asks why I was staying at the hotel.

"My parents own the place," I reply.

"Good for them."

Now he thinks I'm rich. "I mean, they manage the place—it's owned by some Russian guy."

"The Russians are buying everything," he says. "The oligarchs." He makes oligarchs sound like aardvarks.

We're circling Hammersmith roundabout and taking Fulham Palace Road. My mobile begins ringing. Hayden again.

"Where are you?"

"Almost home. I'm in a minicab."

"I'll meet you downstairs."

The driver glances in the mirror again. "Did you hear the news about that baby taken from the hospital?"

"No."

"Yeah, last night—someone snatched a little boy right out from under their noses."

"Do they know who?"

"Someone dressed up as a nurse."

"How awful. That poor mother—does she have any other children?"

"Report didn't say." Our eyes meet in the mirror. "I didn't mean to upset you, love."

I realize that I'm crying. I wipe my cheeks, apologizing.

"I'm sorry. It must be the hormones. I cried all the way through my pregnancy."

"I'm a big softy as well," he says. "Ever since I had a family I can't read stories about kiddies being abducted or abused. Chokes me up every time. If someone hurt one of mine, I'd kill him. Forget about the police or the courts, they'd never find his body—know what I'm saying?"

I don't agree or disagree. He's warming to the subject. "That's why we need the death penalty in this country. Not for everyone—for pedophiles and terrorists."

We turn onto my street. I see Hayden waiting on the steps. I'm barely out of the car when he scoops me into his arms.

"Gently," I say, flinching. "I've just had a baby."

"I'm sorry. I forgot, I'm so stupid."

He doesn't know where to put his hands. He tries his pockets first. Front. Back. Then he looks into the car. Seeing Rory, he opens his mouth in wonderment.

"Say hello to your little boy," I tell him.

Hayden reaches out and touches Rory's cheek. His hand is bigger than Rory's head.

"He won't break," I say.

"But he's so small."

"All babies are small." I laugh. "You can carry him inside."

He lifts Rory out of the car while I pay the driver and wish him a merry Christmas. Hooking a bag over my shoulder, I follow Hayden up the stairs. He's holding the carrier with both hands like it's a Ming vase. Once inside the flat, I shrug off my coat and notice the flowers—two huge bouquets are bookending the mantelpiece.

"Those arrived an hour ago," says Hayden, who

can't seem to sit still. "One lot is from Mum and Dad and the other from Jules."

"Where is Jules?" I ask. "I thought she'd be here."

"She and Kevin have gone to Glasgow to see her folks."

"When is she coming back?"

"Not for a few weeks. She tried to call you."

"I know, I'm sorry. My mobile ran out of juice. I didn't have my charger."

"Couldn't you use another phone?"

"I didn't have your number, or Jules's. Like I said, my phone died."

Rory's carrier is on the coffee table. Hayden is staring at him. "Why did you run away like that?"

"I didn't run away. I had a premonition that I was going to have the baby early. That's why I went up north. I didn't want to be caught on my own."

"But I wanted to be at the birth," he says, sounding hurt. "I came all this way."

"I know, but I got scared."

"Scared?"

"It wasn't just the thought of having a baby—but of you being there. I thought you might not want to touch me again if you saw me go through childbirth. It was pretty gross stuff. I was sitting in a paddling pool, screaming my head off."

He puts his arms around me and I lean into his chest, feeling his strength, smelling his smell.

"I know it sounds stupid," I say, "but I haven't seen you since the end of March. We've only spoken a few times on the satellite phone. I worried that you might have second thoughts if you saw me like that—perched on all fours, pushing a baby out."

"Not likely," he says, kissing my lips. Lovely.

Rory lets out a mewling squeak as though missing out on the action.

"Is he hungry?" asks Hayden.

"No, he's just waking up. Would you like to hold him?"

"I might drop him."

"No, you won't."

I unbuckle Rory and lift him out of the carrier. Hayden perches on the edge of the sofa, both feet on the floor, his back straight. "When you pick him up, you have to support his head," I say. "Right now his neck isn't strong enough to hold his head, but he'll get stronger. Now rest him in the crook of your arm with your hand under his bottom. See? That's not so hard."

Hayden looks stiff and uncomfortable, but he's smiling like he's bending bananas with his face.

"You can breathe," I say.

"Sorry. I'm a bit nervous. Maybe you should take him back."

"You're just getting to know him."

"I'll hold him later." He hands Rory back, then wipes his palms on his jeans.

"Do you like the name?" I ask.

He nods. "How did you know?"

"Your father told me. He said Rory was your grandfather's middle name and your father's and then yours."

"And now we have another Rory."

"Do you like him?"

"He's the business."

MEGHAN

"Meghan . . . Meghan . . . Are you awake?"

The voice is slowly getting closer, filling my head. I try to open my eyes but they seem to be glued shut. Wrestling my way through a haze of drugs, I try to get a hold on reality and make it solid. Images coalesce. Voices. Light. My eyes are wet. I have been crying in my sleep.

A different police constable is sitting next to my bed. She's leaning forward as though I've said something that she didn't quite catch. I open my mouth, but my lips are dry. I try again. "My baby?"

She hands me a cup with a closed lid and a straw. Water. I empty it completely.

My voice works. "Has there been any news?"

"Not yet," says the constable.

"Who are you?"

"I'm PC Soussa. Please call me Lisa-Jayne."

She has green eyes and blond hair with a fringe that keeps falling across her forehead; she brushes it back behind her left ear.

"Why are you here?" I ask.

"I'm a family liaison officer."

"A what?"

"I've been assigned to look after you."

"I want to talk to your boss."

"DCS MacAteer isn't at the hospital yet."

I try to sit up. Lisa-Jayne puts a pillow behind my

back. I'm still wearing a hospital gown and can feel the pressure on my stitches, which are bandaged beneath cotton gauze and tape.

"My mobile phone—where is it?"

"I've been minding it," says Lisa-Jayne. "We've been monitoring your messages."

"Why?"

"In case you get any calls from the kidnapper."

"Is that what happened? Did someone kidnap him? Do they want a ransom? We're not rich."

"We have to consider every possibility."

She pulls my phone from her pocket and hands it to me. I cup it in my hands, feeling the residual warmth from her body. There are dozens of missed calls, mostly from my parents and Grace and other friends, but nothing from Jack. I call his number and let it ring. It goes to messages.

"Where are you?" My voice breaks. "I need you."

I can't think of anything else to say. Ending the call, I stare at the phone. Where could he be? Why isn't he here? I want his arms wrapped around me. I want to hear him say that everything will be all right.

"Who took my baby?" I whisper.

"We don't know," says Lisa-Jayne, taking a seat next to the bed.

"She was dressed like a nurse."

"We don't believe she worked here."

"But the uniform—"

"Could have been stolen."

Someone knocks softly. Lisa-Jayne goes to the door and answers, not opening it fully. She turns. "Your parents are here. Do you want to see them?"

"Can you give me a few minutes? I need my hair-brush and a mirror."

Lisa-Jayne fetches them from the adjoining bathroom. I tilt the mirror, studying different parts of my face but not the whole. My eyes look bruised, as though I've seen too much, or slept too little. Brushing my hair into some semblance of order, I pinch my cheeks, hoping to raise some color.

My parents are ushered in, their eyes telling the story. My mother squeaks my name and hurries to my bedside, pulling me into her arms, hugging me like a child with an earache. I spy my father standing behind her, saying nothing, looking helpless. Now in his midsixties, he has always taken pride in his family, having provided for them and kept them safe. This has shaken him. This wasn't foreseen.

Letting go of my mother, I hug him in the same way, allowing myself to be enfolded in his arms, pressing my face against his chest, where I catch the scent of Old Spice and Imperial Leather. The tears come from childhood. I sob and shake. He strokes my hair and whispers my name. Now it's my mother's turn to feel left out.

"Where are the kids?" I ask, wiping my eyes.

"Grace is looking after them," says my mother.

"What have you told them?"

"Nothing. Lucy keeps asking."

"Have you seen Jack?"

"No."

"He's not answering his phone."

"I think he's helping with the search," says Dad.

As if on cue, we hear a commotion in the corridor outside. Jack appears. He's wearing the same clothes as yesterday, or perhaps the day before. Disheveled. Unshaven. Exhausted. He drops to his knees beside the bed and rests his head on my lap.

"I'm sorry! I'm sorry!" he says plaintively.

His eyes are bloodshot and he reeks of sweat and dirt and fear.

"Where have you been?" I ask.

"Driving. Walking. I thought . . . I wanted . . . I hoped . . ." He stops and starts but can't finish. "I've been looking everywhere, but it's only when you start that you realize how many streets there are in London . . . how many houses."

I stroke his unwashed hair. "You should get some sleep."

"I have to find him."

"Leave it to the police."

"It's my fault. I should have looked at her ID. I should have gone with her." He shudders. "I'm so sorry. I didn't know. I thought she . . . she said . . . she said I could go with her . . . I should have gone."

"It's not your fault," I say blankly, but inside I'm screaming: *You gave our baby to some stranger! She could be a child molester or a monster. You didn't want another child, so you gave our baby away.*

I am torn between wanting to comfort him and to punish him—to forgive or to blame. I want to play the victim, but Jack seems to have usurped that role. Everybody feels sorry for him—my mother, my father, the policewoman . . . In my head, I yell at him, *For Christ's sake, Jack, this is not about you.* Swallowing my anger, I stroke his hair and tell him to go home, to sleep.

"The police want to talk to us," he says.

Lisa-Jayne corrects him. "They've already interviewed you, Mr. Shaughnessy. They want to talk to your wife alone."

"Why?"

"It's normal procedure."

"Normal? There's nothing normal about this. I want to know what the police are doing."

I turn to Mum and Dad and ask them to take Jack

home. I tell him we'll talk later, but he's still complaining as they usher him outside.

Two detectives are waiting to see me. Chairs are found and pulled into place, one on either side of my bed. It feels more like a bedside arraignment than an interview. The man in charge hands me his card. I study it closely, giving myself time to gather my thoughts.

Detective Chief Superintendent Brendan Mac-Ateer has blue eyes, pale eyelashes, and a face so chiseled and angular that the skin looks stretched over his bones. His freckles have faded but must riot every summer across his nose and cheeks. I wonder how much he was teased in his youth—what nicknames did he suffer.

The other detective is overweight and block-headed with eyes that are too small for his skull. I don't catch his name, but he rarely speaks, preferring to take notes and occasionally exchange glances with MacAteer. The detectives sit with their shoulders canted forward. The only sounds are the creak of the chairs and the rustle of clothing.

First, they reassure me that everything that can be done is being done to find my baby. DCS MacAteer's lips barely move as he speaks, but at the same time his eyes keep darting over me with a strange intensity, as though he's putting me together like a jigsaw puzzle.

Unfolding a map of the hospital, he points out the maternity ward and the various corridors, stairwells, and lifts.

"The bogus nurse left the recovery ward through these doors, pushing a wheelchair. She took a lift to the fifth floor. A hospital cleaner saw a nurse matching the description of the abductor at about eight fifteen p.m. She was carrying something tucked under her right arm. The cleaner didn't get a good look at the woman's face, but we're hoping to talk to a plumber who was working on that floor."

He produces a grainy color photograph taken from a CCTV camera. It shows the woman from an oblique angle, slightly behind and above.

"We have enhanced the images, but none of the footage has provided a clear image of her face. Technicians are still working to see if they can make improvements. Do you recognize her?"

"No. What about facial-recognition software?"

"It only works with a good image, and if this woman has never been arrested, she won't be in our database. In the meantime, I've arranged for a police sketch artist to sit down with your husband and the cleaner. Hopefully we can come up with a good likeness. In the meantime, we've issued a description of her as white, thirty to forty-five, five foot eight to five ten, pale complexion, medium build, and dark hair.

"At this point we haven't been able to identify anyone matching this woman's description leaving the hospital, which suggests she may have had other disguises."

"Could she still be here?" I ask.

"That's unlikely. The alarm was raised within ten minutes and the hospital went into lockdown. Security guards stopped anyone leaving. Staff searched room by room. Police stopped traffic outside and talked to pedestrians."

MacAteer leans forward, resting his hands on his knees.

"It's also possible she had an accomplice, which could explain how she evaded security. Right now, we are focusing on identifying everyone who entered and left the hospital in the hours before the abduction and immediately afterwards."

"She wore a nurse's uniform."

"Which suggests a high degree of planning rather than a random, spur-of-the-moment act."

"Is that a good thing?"

"Most likely it means she really wanted a baby and will take good care of him. Equally, it could make her harder to find, because she will cover her tracks."

Over the next twenty minutes I am taken back over the events—the birth, the aftermath, going for a shower, coming back to find an empty crib.

"Have you talked to your husband about that night?" the DCS asks.

"Yes. Why?"

"Did he tell you where he went after he left the hospital?"

I falter for a moment. "He said he was looking for the nurse?"

MacAteer glances at his colleague and something unspoken seems to pass between them.

"Have you thought about a name for the baby?" he asks.

"We haven't decided."

"This is already a big news story. Public interest will be high and it would help if we had a name. It allows the media to personalize the story—to focus on an actual baby instead of a nameless one."

"You want us to name the baby now?"

"You can always change it later—come up with a new one."

I understand his reasoning, but it doesn't seem right to name a child that I cannot hold.

"We were thinking of calling him Benjamin. Ben for short."

"That's nice," says Lisa-Jayne, who has been sitting in the corner.

"So it's Baby Ben," says MacAteer. "The media will like that. What about photographs?"

"Jack took some."

"With your permission, I'd like to release one photograph immediately and hold the others back."

I scroll through images on my phone and we choose one of Ben swaddled in a cotton blanket, his face scrunched up and his eyes half-open, struggling against the unexpected brightness. I'm also in the photograph. The C-section took the hard work out of labor and I had energy left to smile.

"We're also going to need a comment from you."

"I don't want to talk to anyone," I say.

"I understand. I'll have a press officer draft something for you."

MacAteer gets to his feet.

"Is that all?" I ask.

He smiles, trying to reassure me. "Cases like this are normally solved quite quickly. A new baby doesn't go unnoticed. Somebody will contact us—a friend, family member, or neighbor—I'm confident of that."

"I don't want to stay in hospital."

"The doctors insist you should."

"I'm not taking any more sedatives."

"It will help you rest."

"It will affect my breast milk. I want to be able to feed Ben when you find him."

"Talk to your doctor. It's a medical decision."

AGATHA

Rory wakes at five in the spectral light, snuffling and gurgling. Rain streaks the window, throwing patterns on his face and across the white sheets. Leaving Hayden to sleep, I warm a bottle and sit with Rory on the sofa, stroking his cheek and looking into his eyes. I like this time of day, when I have Rory to myself.

I have everything I ever wanted, here and now under this roof, yet I alternate between anguish and euphoria, as though I'm living two different lives at once, each within earshot of the other.

So far Hayden hasn't questioned my reasons for not breast-feeding Rory in front of him. I explained about cracked nipples and mastitis and said I couldn't provide Rory with enough breast milk so a midwife suggested I supplement his feeds with formula. "I'm still expressing," I said to Hayden, showing him the breast pump. "Don't tell your mother about me having problems."

"Why not?" he asks.

"I feel guilty."

"She won't mind."

"Other mothers get quite funny about that sort of thing. Judgmental."

He looks at me sheepishly. "I might have mentioned it already. She asked how things were going."

"And you told her?"

"I said you were giving him bottles."

"Now she'll think I'm a terrible mother."

"No, she won't."

Hayden is besotted with Rory. It's amazing how men happily turn into clowns around babies, blowing raspberries into tummies, pulling faces, and making up new words, desperate to get some reaction.

More confident now, he knows how to hold Rory properly, and I've taught him how to make up bottles and test the temperature of the milk by shaking droplets onto his inner wrist. On top of all this he's been extra attentive towards me, making me cups of tea and running errands.

"You haven't changed a nappy yet," I said yesterday.

"I'll do the next one," he replied.

Later I called out, "Hey, you're up, sailor boy."

"I meant the next baby," he said with a laugh, and I felt my chest swell.

We're taking loads of photographs: Rory with Hayden, Rory with me, Rory with Mr. and Mrs. Cole, Hayden and me and Rory. I'll get the best ones framed and put on the mantelpiece.

Rory takes almost a whole bottle and I burp him on my shoulder. Hayden emerges from the bedroom, scratching his navel. I like that he's shaved off his beard. He's nicer to kiss and I can see the strong line of his jaw.

His eyes light up when he sees Rory. "Hey, watch this," he says, leaning close to Rory and poking out his tongue. A beat passes and Rory's tongue comes out, mimicking him.

"I taught him that," he says. "The kid is a genius."

He turns on the TV. The story of missing "Baby Ben" is leading every bulletin. TV reporters are crossing live from outside Churchill Hospital, interviewing patients and passersby and members of staff who say they're not allowed to comment.

"Those poor people, they must be worried sick,"

says Hayden, who is standing behind me, massaging my shoulders.

I murmur in agreement.

On the screen a detective is issuing an appeal for assistance. *"On Thursday the seventh of December at about seven fifty p.m., a woman entered the Singleton Ward of Churchill Hospital, Central London. Posing as a nurse, she took away Ben Shaughnessy, who was born earlier that day. The woman is described as being between thirty and forty-five years old, five foot eight to five foot ten inches tall, with a medium build, brown eyes, fair complexion, and dark hair, which may have been a wig."*

The scene changes and I see blurry footage of myself walking down a corridor, keeping my head down. A second clip shows me waiting at the lift. It has been enhanced, but the quality is so poor that my face looks almost pixelated.

"Do you know her?" asks the detective. *"Could she be a friend or a neighbor? Do you know anyone who has unexpectedly returned home with a baby? If you can help, please contact Crimestoppers. All information will be treated in strict confidence."*

The detective pauses and picks up a sheet of paper.

"Mr. and Mrs. Shaughnessy have asked me to thank the public for the many messages of support. They provided this comment: 'Ben was just ten hours old when he was taken. We held him only briefly, but his loss has torn out our hearts. Please give him back. Take him to a church, or a school, or leave him at a police station. Give him to someone in authority. Please, please, give him back to us.'"

A photograph appears on-screen, showing Meg propped up on pillows, holding a baby on her chest. It must have been taken immediately after the birth.

"I know her," I whisper.

Hayden hesitates. "What?"

"The mother—she goes to my yoga class. I went to her house a few weeks ago. She gave me some spare baby clothes."

Hayden walks around the sofa and sits down. "What's she like?"

"She has two other children—Lucy and Lachlan. I used to see her all the time when I worked at the supermarket."

"Why didn't you say before?"

"They didn't release her name straightaway." I pick up my mobile phone and scroll through the email messages until I find one from Meg. "There you are. I sent her a photograph of Rory and she replied."

"When was that?"

"Before she went into hospital."

"You should send her another message," Hayden says.

"And say what?"

"I don't know. Say you're praying for her."

"Isn't that being cruel? It will just remind her that my baby is safe and well and her baby is missing."

Hayden considers this. "Maybe you're right."

"She has two other children," I say. "They'll keep her busy. And I bet she sues that hospital for millions."

"That's not the point, though, is it?" says Hayden.

I lean my head against his shoulder and mesh my fingers with his, brushing my thumb over the hairs on the back of his hand. "You're right. I'll wait until she gets home from hospital and give her a call."

MEGHAN

Forty-eight hours have passed. The critical time frame. If a missing person isn't found, or a crime isn't solved, or a suspect isn't charged within two days, the chance of success begins to diminish. I'm sure I've read that somewhere or seen it on TV.

Ben has been gone for longer than that. Annie and Lisa-Jayne, my police liaison officers, are taking turns sitting with me. They're "running defense," keeping the reporters at bay, answering my phone, reading messages, and vetting visitors.

The hospital has transferred me to a different room, away from the maternity ward, so as not to upset other women who are having babies. I'm like a body that has to be removed quickly from an accident scene, or a mistake that has to be hushed up.

Pretending to be asleep, I hear the squeak of the nurses' shoes and the clatter of a trolley in the corridor outside, the singing of telephones and the droning of the intercom. My imagination projects images on my closed eyelids. I keep seeing Ben being nursed by someone else. Either that or I picture him abandoned on a mountainside like Oedipus, or set adrift like the infant Moses.

At other times I imagine that I can communicate with him telepathically. Not because we share the same DNA, but because I carried him inside me for nine months. We shared blood and nutrients. We listened to each other's hearts. He heard my voice. You cannot break a bond like that by clamping and cutting a cord or by stealing a baby from his mother.

With each new change of shift, I ask the same question: "Has there been any news?"

"No news is good news," replies Annie.

"How can no news be good news?"

"It means that whoever took your baby hasn't panicked and dumped him. She has taken him home. She'll keep him safe. She'll look after him."

I think of Madeleine McCann, the little girl who disappeared in Portugal and has never been found. What if that happens to us? What if they never find Ben? Are we going to spend the rest of our lives wondering, waiting for a knock on the door or a phone call to say that he's alive or dead?

Annie keeps reminding me that babies are resilient. The doctors say the same thing. One of them told me a story yesterday about a baby who survived in the rubble of an earthquake for ten days. *Why are you talking about earthquakes?* I wanted to say. *What does that have to do with anything?*

Annie and Lisa-Jayne are supposed to get as many details from me as possible. In practice, it means they keep asking me the same questions over and over until I get annoyed. Do I have any enemies? Did I notice anyone hanging around the corridors of the hospital?

Meanwhile, outside of these walls, Ben has become more than a name. He is a brand now—a product to sell newspapers and boost ratings. The alliteration works well in headlines:

Baby Ben—every mother's nightmare
Baby Ben—three more sightings

White van seized in hunt for Baby Ben
Baby Ben—how did he disappear?

Jack shares my uncertainty but we each pretend otherwise. He sits beside my bed or we go downstairs to the café. He's frustrated at the lack of progress, constantly asking why the police aren't busting down doors and taking down names. He wants to see posters in every shop window and to hear them shouting Ben's name from the rooftops.

I am trying so hard not to blame him. I am fighting against the idea, knowing its wrongness and irrationality, but I cannot help myself. He gave our baby to a stranger. He watched someone carry Ben away.

Annie is sitting at a nearby table, giving us some privacy. She's keeping watch for any reporters who may have sneaked into the hospital looking for an interview or photographs. They are camped outside, dozens of them, sending me letters and notes via nurses and orderlies, offering us money for an exclusive interview. One of the cleaners was caught trying to slip into my room with a disposable camera hidden in his pocket.

Jack and I are sitting at a booth, saying nothing. He has torn the top from a packet of sugar and poured the contents on the plastic table, pushing the grains into small mounds with his forefinger. I wish I could comfort him. I wish he could comfort me.

Two men approach wearing dark gray suits, white shirts, and silk ties.

"I'm Patrick Carmody," says the younger man, "director of hospital services."

"Thomas Glenelg," says the other one, handing Jack his business card.

"I cannot express how sincerely and deeply sorry

we are for what's happened," says Mr. Carmody. "I am personally shocked and saddened that a newborn baby could be taken from this hospital despite our state-of-the-art security system. Please accept my personal apology."

Neither of us answers.

Mr. Carmody glances at the other man and continues. "The Churchill is cooperating fully with the police—giving them access to our cameras, our staff, our records. If there is anything else that you feel you need, please let us know."

"You could resign," says Jack, deadpan.

Mr. Carmody laughs nervously before recovering his composure. "As well as helping the police, we are reviewing our security. The hospital board has reacted swiftly, approving identity bracelets and movement sensors to prevent this sort of thing from ever happening."

"'This sort of thing,'" says Jack, mimicking Carmody's accent. "I rather think that horse has bolted, don't you? He's thrown the jockey, kicked down the barn door, and he's out of sight."

The administrator tries again. "I understand you're upset, Mr. Shaughnessy. You have every right to be. We have a proud history at the Churchill. We have delivered thousands of babies and nothing like this has ever happened before. We have very robust security protocols, but no system is foolproof."

"You're wrong," replies Jack, interrupting him. "A maternity hospital should be completely foolproof so that no *fool* can walk out with someone else's baby."

The other man finally speaks. "The Churchill is not your enemy, Mr. Shaughnessy."

Jack glances at the business card he was given. "You're a lawyer."

"My firm represents the hospital."

"You're frightened that we're going to sue."

"That's not the reason that we've—"

"You're worried about how much money this is going to cost you."

"We wish to express our sorrow and sympathy," says Mr. Carmody.

Jack points to the lawyer. "Did he brief you beforehand—tell you what to say?"

"I don't think this is helpful—"

Jack pushes back his chair. "Get out!"

"Please don't raise your voice," says the lawyer.

"You want me to be quiet?" asks Jack, doing the opposite. "Our baby was taken from *your* hospital by someone wearing one of *your* nursing uniforms, walking past *your* guards, *your* security cameras, and you want me to stay quiet. Fuck you!"

For a moment I think Jack might punch him. Instead he flicks the business card onto the floor. "Don't come near us again. From now on, you talk to our lawyer."

DCS MacAteer has come back to see me. I'm out of bed and moving without pain and the doctor says I can go home tomorrow. We're talking in the patient lounge, which has a TV, several sofas, and a wall of vending machines selling snacks and soft drinks.

MacAteer counts out his loose change and buys me a can of lemonade that clatters into the metal tray.

"I'm sorry I don't have a glass."

"That's OK."

We sit. I sip. The detective speaks.

"We have been over the CCTV footage and believe we have identified how the kidnapper got in and out of the hospital." He opens the flap of an envelope and produces a photograph showing a woman in an over-sized coat pulling a wheel-along tartan trolley across the foyer.

"We know this woman entered the hospital wheeling a tartan trolley. We believe she disguised herself as a nurse and kidnapped your son, but we haven't discovered how she smuggled Ben out of the Churchill."

MacAteer produces a second photograph. This one shows a man with a long gray ponytail wearing overalls and a baseball cap, pulling a dark-colored trolley.

"Earlier, I mentioned a plumber who was seen working the fifth floor at about the time Ben was taken?"

I nod.

"We haven't managed to find this man, or any reason for him being at the hospital that night."

"Are you saying she had an accomplice?"

"No." MacAteer puts the photographs side by side. "Based on the security camera footage, we have a woman kidnapper who didn't *leave* the hospital and an unidentified plumber who didn't *arrive*. This strongly suggests we're dealing with the same person dressed in different disguises."

I look again at the images. At first glance—at any glance—they look like completely different people.

"The genius is in the detail," says MacAteer. "We found traces of makeup in a washbasin on the fifth floor and a single contact lens on the floor."

"But where is Ben?"

"We believe he was placed in the trolley."

My hand finds my mouth. "He'll suffocate."

"No, there's plenty of air."

MacAteer shows me another photograph taken by a CCTV camera at the hospital's loading dock. It shows the plumber walking away from the camera, heading towards the street, pulling the dark-colored trolley.

"We've enhanced the footage, but this is the best we can do."

"They're unrecognizable."

"Yes, but now that we know about the second disguise, we can look for clearer images from cameras in the area and reinterview witnesses. In the meantime, there's something you can do for me. I want to arrange a media conference for you and Jack. We need you to make a further appeal."

"What does Jack say?"

"He's agreed."

I nod.

"Before then, I'd like you to talk to a psychologist who has worked with the police before. I've asked him to draw up a psychological profile to give us a better idea of who we're dealing with."

"A profile?"

"He can help understand what might be going through this woman's mind, or how she'll react to the media coverage. His name is Cyrus Haven and he's the very best."

AGATHA

"Let's go out," says Hayden.

"Where?"

"We'll take Rory for a walk."

"But it's cold outside."

"The fresh air will do him good. Come on. I'm getting cabin fever in here."

"You're a sailor."

"You know what I mean."

I strap Rory into his pram and tuck a snuggly blanket around him before we push him along New King's Road to Parsons Green. Hayden orders a pint from the White Horse and we sit outside at a table, enjoying the weak winter sunshine.

Hayden sees someone he knows and introduces me as his fiancée. I feel warm and tingly inside, as though I've downed a double vodka and cranberry, even though I haven't touched a drop.

Someone has left a copy of the *Metro* on the table. Hayden spreads it beneath his pint glass. Baby Ben has filled the first four pages and newspapers are competing to see who can whip up the most interest. The *Daily Express* offered a reward of £50,000, only to be topped by the *Daily Mirror*'s £100,000, until the *Sun* trumped them both with £250,000.

"They're wasting their money," says Hayden.

"Why do you say that?"

"Baby Ben is long gone."

"You think he's dead?"

"I didn't say that."

"What then?"

"I reckon he was probably stolen to order. Some rich couple or Arab sheikh wanted a baby boy, so he had one stolen."

"Why wouldn't they just buy one?"

"You can't just *buy* a baby," scoffs Hayden, sounding like an expert. "I bet whoever took Ben has already smuggled him out of the country—probably bribed someone at Immigration, or flew him out on a private jet." He looks back at the *Metro*, whistling at the reward. "We could do with that sort of money."

"We're OK."

"We could buy a house."

"My flat is big enough."

"Not for long." He pinches my bum. "What about the other babies?"

I laugh. "One at a time, sailor boy."

Across the road on Parsons Green, mothers or nannies are sitting on park benches, watching toddlers toddle and babies crawl and children ride scooters along the asphalt paths. Many of the women are wearing matching sweatshirts. I look more closely. Each top features the photograph of a baby, beneath the words "Where is Baby Ben?" Across the back is the sponsor's name—*The Daily Mail*.

"Have you noticed how people are staring at us?" I say.

Hayden puts down his pint glass. "What do you mean?"

"They look at Rory and I can see them thinking, you know . . . wondering if we've stolen him."

"But we didn't steal him."

"I know, but you look at the mother over there—the

one under the tree. Who's to say if that's her baby? It
could be Baby Ben."

"I told you, Baby Ben is long gone—he's out of the
country by now."

"What if he's not?"

"Think about it," he says. "He was taken, what—
three days ago? If he were still in this country, someone
would have noticed. You can't just bring a strange baby
home. Neighbors would hear him crying, or notice her
buying nappies. It can't be easy to hide a baby." He
reaches into the pram and puts his entire hand over
Rory's chest. "But we should keep a close eye on our
little fella in case somebody tries to steal him."

"You don't think they would."

"I'm kidding." He drains his glass and belches. "One
more for the road."

He goes to the bar. Reaching into the pram, I
stroke Rory's cheek. With each passing day, I feel more
assured of his place in the world. He has taken root in
my heart, anchoring himself to me. I am his mother
now. He reaches out for me. He longs for my touch.

I'm sure Hayden feels the same way. Some men
get funny about babies because they think a woman
only has a finite amount of love to give, but it's not
about dividing or subtracting or making do with less.
Our hearts expand. We have double the love, maybe
more.

Hayden is back, nursing a fresh pint. Making conversation, he asks me where I was born and raised,
wanting to know about my mother. I should be flattered
by his interest, but I don't want him turning over rocks
and peering underneath. At the same time, I don't want
to appear evasive or secretive. I have to give him something, so I mention Elijah being killed on his way to

school. Hayden wants all the details. Did I see it happen? Did I blame myself?

"Why should I blame myself?" I snap. "It wasn't my fault."

"OK, OK," says Hayden, holding up his hands. "Jesus! I was only making conversation."

I apologize. He goes quiet. I ask him if he always wanted to join the navy.

"Hell, no! I was keeping a promise."

"How?"

"I had a mate called Michael Murray and one day we each cut our right thumbs, mixed the blood, and made a promise that when we grew up we'd join the navy."

"Like blood brothers."

"Yeah."

"Did he do it?"

"'Course not. He sells vacuum cleaners for his old man."

"But you kept your promise."

"I sort of had to."

"Why?"

"I had a few problems with the police when I was sixteen and finished up in court. My solicitor told the magistrates that I was hoping to join the Royal Navy. A criminal conviction would make it difficult. The magistrates gave me a caution and let me go. After that, I felt obliged to follow through."

"What were you charged with?"

"Criminal damage."

"What did you damage?"

"I set fire to a teacher's car. He was an arsehole."

"I'm shocked."

Hayden looks at me sheepishly. "You must have done something terrible when you were younger."

"Never."

"I bet you did. I bet you're keeping it a secret. I'm going to get in touch with your mum and find out exactly what you were like."

That statement rattles something inside me and I feel the creature begin stirring, pushing aside my organs.

"I've upset you," says Hayden. "What did I say?"

"It doesn't matter."

"Is it the questions? I'm interested."

"Rory needs to be fed."

"You could breast-feed him."

"I'm still too sore."

Buttoning my coat and releasing the brake, I steer the pram between tables and onto the pavement. Hayden hurriedly finishes his pint and jogs to catch up with me. We walk in silence.

"You should get one of those sweatshirts," he says.

"Huh?"

"The Baby Ben tops. Nobody will stare at you then."

MEGHAN

The psychologist is younger than I expect, in his midthirties, dressed in a long-sleeve cotton shirt, buttoned at the throat, and loose-fitting jeans. Tall and lean with prominent cheekbones and eyelashes that most women would kill for, he looks like a college student trying to save on haircuts.

Cyrus Haven shakes my hand, holding it a second longer than is comfortable while he seems to study me. I've heard it said that a person's eyes are the only things on the face that do not age. They are no less bright on the first day than their last day. The doctor's eyes are pale blue with pupils blacker than charcoal.

"May I sit here?" he asks.

"It's the only chair," I say.

He laughs and agrees. I wonder if he's nervous too.

We're in my private room at the hospital, where the curtains are open on a gray London day. My suitcase is half-packed, lying open on the bed. Jack is coming to take me home in a few hours.

Cyrus takes a yellow legal pad from a satchel that has been hanging off his shoulder. He searches for a pen, opening the many pockets until he finds one and holds it up triumphantly. He scribbles something on the page, but the pen doesn't work. He shakes it a few times and tries again. Nothing.

"I can ask a nurse."

"No, it's fine," he says, putting the pad away. He

takes out a folded white handkerchief, shakes it open, and begins cleaning his wire-framed glasses. I wonder if this whole routine is part of a performance. He's pretending to be forgetful and preoccupied so that my defenses will be lowered.

The silence expands.

"Would you like a cup of tea?" I ask.

"No, thank you."

Cyrus places his glasses on his nose and adjusts them. He's handsome in a disheveled, obviously English way and reminds me of a tutor that I had at university. He was Cyrus's age and I was a lot younger, but like a lot of students, boys and girls, I had a crush on him. For some reason, the tutor seemed to call on me more than the others. I was flattered. I even fantasized about him because he was clever and accomplished, with ungovernable dark hair and a small cleft in the center of his chin that I wanted to touch with my tongue to see how deep it went.

One day he invited me to his rooms. I accepted. I thought he might make a pass at me, a notion that terrified and excited me, but instead he handed me an unbound proof of his latest novel, asking if I would read it for him because I had "a good eye."

"A good eye?" I asked.

"You're strong on grammar and spelling."

The memory makes me cringe with embarrassment.

Cyrus has been watching me. "How are you sleeping?"

"They give me pills."

"Are you eating?"

"You've been talking to the nurses."

"They're worried about you."

He notices a framed photograph of Lucy and Lachlan in my open suitcase and asks me their names. Half an hour later I realize that I'm still talking. Imperceptibly, he has drawn me into a one-sided conversation, learning where I was born and went to school, about my parents and sister and Jack. Soon I'm telling him about buying the house in Barnes and falling pregnant again. I don't mention the arguments or the doubts or the one-night stand with Simon.

He has a soft voice that washes through our discussion, nudging it in different directions or exploring new corners. I can't remember the last time I revealed so much to a man like this—a stranger.

Eventually we reach the present. Cyrus knows the general details of the abduction and has seen the CCTV footage, but he wants me to recount the story again. He explains the nature of cognitive interviewing; how it can help people recall more of what they've been through.

"There's no pressure. Relax. Lie back. Close your eyes. Tell me about the birth. Imagine you're a film director trying to re-create the moment, telling people where to stand and what to say."

I do as he says, describing the cesarean. How Jack made me laugh. "For a long while he didn't want a third child, but he took one look at Ben and melted."

By eleven o'clock, I told Cyrus, we were back in the shared ward. I slept for a few hours, woke, ate lunch, and slept again. Jack called my parents and Grace, telling them the good news. My parents came to see me during visiting hours. Grace was looking after Lucy and Lachlan.

"When you went for a shower, did you notice anyone in the ward?"

"No."

"Picture the scene."

"Jack helped me walk to the bathroom. He had his arm around me. We walked between the beds."

"Did you hear any voices?"

"The woman in the next bed was talking to her husband."

"Anyone else?"

"A nurse."

"Where?"

"Beside one of the beds. I didn't see her face. She was straightening the sheets."

"What about her hair?"

"Dark. Long."

"How was it styled?"

"It was tied back."

"Look beyond her, what do you see?"

"A curtain."

"Open or closed?"

"Partially open."

"What else?"

"A woman. I think she'd just had a baby. Her family had come to visit, bringing flowers and balloons. They might have been Italian. Noisy."

"Were any of them facing the nurse you saw by the empty bed?"

I concentrate, trying to think back.

"The grandmother! She was looking in my direction. She apologized about the noise."

My eyes flash open. "She must have seen the nurse."

"Perhaps," says Cyrus. "It's worth talking to her."

"Could I remember more if you hypnotized me?" I ask.

"There might not *be* any more."

In the same breath I remember Simon and suddenly change my mind. Cyrus seems to register the U-turn, but says nothing. I hate the way he uses silence like a lever and fulcrum, moving me to speak.

"Are you married?" I ask, wanting to change the subject.

"No." He smiles ruefully.

"Why did you make that face?"

"I don't think I'm the marrying kind."

"Are you saying . . . ?"

"I'm not gay, if that's what you're asking. I live with my girlfriend. She's a lawyer."

"But you don't think you'll marry her?"

"My parents weren't a great advertisement for marriage."

"Are they divorced?"

"They're dead."

"I'm sorry."

"It happened a long time ago."

Cyrus gets up and goes to the window, staring at the sky as though something has scratched at the edge of his memory.

"Why did she take Ben?" I ask.

He runs his finger down the glass. "It could be any number of reasons. Pedophiles are very age specific and they don't usually target babies. More likely we're looking for a woman who cannot conceive or who has miscarried or lost a child. She may be trying to hold a marriage together or to stop a relationship falling apart. A baby is her solution—something to paper over the cracks and keep a man from leaving her."

"A lot of women have miscarriages."

"You're right. And most of them learn to cope with their distress. Sometimes a person like this has a history of parental neglect. It could be a broken home or abuse. She may have been starved of love and is seeking a baby who will love her unconditionally."

"You sound like you sympathize with her."

"I understand her. She's vulnerable and damaged."

"Will she hurt Ben?"

"Not unless she's backed into a corner."

"So what now?"

"I draw up a profile and a media strategy."

"What do you mean by 'strategy'?"

"Whoever took Ben will be watching the news and reading the newspapers. She's listening. This means we can communicate. We can send her messages. We can keep her calm."

"How?"

"By not treating her like a criminal or demeaning her or making her frightened."

"How does that help get Ben back?"

"We show her your pain. If she's lost a child, she knows what you're going through. We can use that."

Cyrus picks up his satchel, swinging it onto his shoulder. He looks around the chair as though he might have dropped something and then seems unsure whether he should shake my hand.

"Try to stay positive," he says, without sounding patronizing.

I want to tell him the same thing, but don't know why. Then it dawns on me. Cyrus reminds me of the Tin Man in *The Wizard of Oz*. He's not so much broken as in need of oil. Something has happened in his life that weighs down his steps and makes his movements creak and groan. Maybe that's the fate of someone who spends his life delving into other people's minds— listening to their worst fears, unmasking their flaws, and discovering their motives. Maybe a man like that begins to rust or seize up—haunted by too many ghosts in the machine.

AGATHA

I'm learning to cook. Up until now poaching eggs and warming baked beans was the frontier of my culinary capabilities, but I want to show Hayden that I can be a good wife and look after him. Tonight we're having chicken Kiev with green beans and honeyed carrots.

"Where are the chips?" he asks.

"The recipe doesn't have chips."

"I like chips."

"Not everything has to be served with potatoes."

He prods the chicken Kiev with his fork, but once he takes a mouthful he scarfs the lot and asks for seconds.

After I've cleaned up the kitchen, we cuddle on the sofa, flicking between channels on the TV. Rory is asleep, but he'll wake before midnight.

"Shouldn't you be expressing?" Hayden asks, stroking my hair.

"Since when did you become the breast-feeding police?" I reply, poking him in the ribs.

"Can I watch you expressing?"

"I get embarrassed."

"Why?"

"It makes me feel like a cow on a milking machine."

"I want to see."

"Maybe later."

I take the remote control, mute the sound, and straddle Hayden's thighs, kissing him on the lips and moving my hips in tiny circles until I feel him grow hard. I lead him to the bedroom, whispering that we have to be quiet. Rory is asleep in his crib.

"What if he sees us?" asks Hayden.

"He's a baby." I kiss him again and slide my hand into his jeans. "I love it when you stand to attention."

We make love for the first time since he went away to sea. He braces himself on his arms, not wanting to lower his weight on me.

"Are you sure we should be doing this?" he asks.

"It's fine."

"I don't want to hurt you."

"You won't hurt me."

He's much more gentle than when we first met. Back then he was like a rutting bull, pinning me to the mattress as though trying to punish me for the wrongs of other women—girls who wouldn't sleep with him, or who dumped him, or who were out of his reach.

"Shouldn't we be using a condom?" he asked.

"Shhhhhhh."

He begins moving, showing his urgency yet trying to hold himself back, but I raise my hips to meet each thrust until I feel him surrender. He shudders and sighs, kissing my earlobe and whispering, "I love you." My heart expands to fill every corner of my body, leaving no room for the creature or the doubts that it feeds upon.

I fall asleep with Hayden's arms wrapped around me. Truly happy.

I know motherhood is hard, but I love this new gig. I don't mind waking at 4 a.m. to feed Rory or getting hosed down while I'm changing his nappy. I don't care that he cries so often or that he vomits on my clothes.

Nothing is too big of a chore. I did three loads of washing yesterday. I folded, ironed, vacuumed, sterilized bottles, and made formula. Between times I locked myself in the bathroom and pretended to use my breast pump.

Fatherhood has changed Hayden. He's softer and more caring. He does chores around the flat and volunteers to do the shopping, often taking Rory with him strapped in a sling against his chest. There is nothing sexier than a man with a baby. It doesn't feminize or weaken him—it makes him look like a good provider and a role model, someone who will stick around.

The navy has given him two weeks' paternity leave on full pay. After that he's taking holidays, so we'll be together until mid-January, when he's due to rejoin his ship in Portsmouth.

I wish he could stay longer. Part of me wants to hold on to this feeling forever—the newness and excitement—but another part is fearful of exposing myself and trusting too much. I am not used to people staying with me. Normally I prepare myself for disappointment, expect rejection, or assume the worst.

I'm still cautious around Hayden's parents. I know that Mr. Cole likes me and Mrs. Cole is a besotted grandmother who hovers around Rory, making any excuse to pick him up and show him off. She's already planning a christening for the spring, when Hayden is next home on leave. She wants to invite aunties, uncles, and cousins. I've never had a big extended family that gets together at Christmas or for anniversaries, and sometimes this feels like I've stumbled into a Disney movie or one of those family sitcoms where the worst thing to happen is when someone burns the turkey or spikes the punch.

We're visiting Mr. and Mrs. Cole for Sunday lunch,

which is proper roast beef with all the trimmings. Yorkshire pudding. Horseradish. Baked spuds. Gravy. Hayden's sister, Nigella, has come down from Norfolk, leaving her husband behind but bringing a strange antagonism towards me. Every time I say something about pregnancy or childbirth she makes a sniffing sound, as though she disagrees, but she doesn't follow up with a comment.

When I try to chat with her about babies she makes a snide remark about new parents being boring because all they can talk about is their children. I pull Hayden aside in the kitchen, muttering, "What's her story?"

"It's not your fault," he whispers. "She's been trying to have a baby and has miscarried twice."

"Why didn't you tell me?"

"Nobody is supposed to know. Mum only just told me."

"What about your dad?"

"Totally in the dark, so don't say anything."

Over lunch, Mrs. Cole asks Hayden when he's going to make me "an honest woman."

"Agatha is honest."

"I mean, when are you going to marry her? A baby needs a proper name."

"He has a name," says Hayden.

"Not in the eyes of God," says Mrs. Cole. "Otherwise, people might think he's a . . ."

She doesn't finish the statement.

"People don't care about stuff like that anymore," says Hayden, looking uncomfortable.

I interrupt. "If we get married too soon, people will think it's only because of Rory. By waiting, we show them that we're really in love." I squeeze Hayden's hand.

Nigella makes a gagging sound like she might throw up. I feel my hackles rising.

When the table has been cleared, we retire to the parlor. Hayden turns on the TV to watch football. The news is showing—another story about Baby Ben.

"Oh, I didn't tell you," says Hayden. "Agatha knows Meg Shaughnessy."

Mrs. Cole is pouring tea. "Who?"

"Baby Ben's mother."

The whole family looks at me.

"We did yoga together when I was pregnant," I explain.

"And you visited her house," adds Hayden.

"What's she like?" asks Mr. Cole.

"She's really nice."

"Her husband's a bit handsome," says Nigella, picking polish from her fingernails.

"They have two children—Lucy and Lachlan. They're six and four, I think."

"That poor woman," says Mrs. Cole. "Is their house nice?"

"What difference does that make?" sniffs Mr. Cole.

This puts her back up. "Well, him being on TV, I expect they have a very nice house."

"Very nice. Four bedrooms. It's in Barnes, not far from the river," I say. "It's close to where I used to work."

"Where did you work?" asks Nigella.

"In a supermarket."

"A supermarket!" She makes it sound like a leper colony.

The TV is showing closed-circuit footage from the hospital. A grainy figure in a nurse's uniform is walking away from the camera, turning and entering a lift. The frame freezes and the camera switches to a close-up.

"She looks like you, Agatha," says Nigella.

"Me?"

"Yeah."

"She looks nothing like her," says Hayden defensively.

Mr. Cole leans closer from his armchair. "She does a bit."

I feel my chest tighten, but manage to laugh. "You're right."

"Your hair is shorter," says Hayden.

"I could have been wearing a wig," I say.

"You have the same shaped face," says Nigella.

"It wasn't always this round. Pregnancy bloated me."

"You're not bloated," says Hayden.

"No, but I could lose a few pounds."

I sense Nigella smirking from the other sofa.

The TV is showing a picture of Meg and Jack leaving the hospital.

"So who do you think took Baby Ben?" asks Mr. Cole.

"Probably someone who couldn't have her own baby," I say, watching Nigella stiffen. "Sometimes when a woman miscarries or can't get pregnant, she loses the plot."

"Maybe we should change the subject," says Mrs. Cole.

"I'm not saying all women—just some of them. They grow bitter and jealous. I feel sorry for them."

Nigella excuses herself and leaves the room, holding her hand over her mouth.

"Is she all right?" I ask. "Did I say something to upset her?"

MEGHAN

Dozens of reporters are milling outside the house, blocking the pavement and taking up parking spots with their broadcast vans and satellite trucks. Our rubbish bin is overflowing with their coffee cups and fast-food wrappings.

Jack has to park around the corner and we run the gauntlet of the TV cameras, flash guns, and boom microphones. Lisa-Jayne tries to force a path through the scrum, yelling at reporters to stand back.

"Mr. and Mrs. Shaughnessy have nothing to say. If you don't get out of our way, I'll have you arrested . . . I'm not going to ask again."

Recording devices are thrust into my face. Questions are shouted. Someone touches my arm. I pull away as though scalded. A female reporter forces a letter into my hand. Without thinking, I take it from her.

"We can offer you more," yells someone else.

"Don't trust her," a third person replies.

Lisa-Jayne is calling for backup on her shoulder radio. We're nearing the front gate. Jack has his arm around me. I can feel that he wants to lash out at someone, or scream abuse, calling them ghouls and pariahs, but he works on TV; he knows how the media operates.

We reach the front door and the sanctuary of the hallway. A final letter is thrust through the letterbox and the noise abates. Lisa-Jayne promises it won't happen again. Jack grunts in disgust and disappears into the back garden.

I go upstairs and unpack my bag from the hospital. Among the nightdresses and pajamas I discover the baby clothes that Ben was supposed to wear home. I lay the tiny outfit on the bed, trying to imagine my Ben is here with me, watching me unpack. It has been four days, but feels like years. Lucy and Lachlan are staying with my parents. I miss them . . . their voices, their mess, their arguments, and their hugs. I walk from room to room, all of them familiar, yet somehow they're not the same. They're darker and colder and devoid of color.

In the newly painted baby's room I run my fingers over the nursery-rhyme stencils and spin the mobile above the cot, watching the hand-painted African animals circle above the mattress.

The rocking chair in the corner was a gift from my parents when Lucy was born. Lachlan's favorite blankie is washed and ironed on the polished wooden seat. He donated it to the new baby when I told him he was too old for such things. Picking it up, I hold the frayed blanket against my cheek, remembering how Lachlan carried it everywhere with him. Moments later, without realizing how, I am kneeling on the floor, pressing my face into the blanket and sobbing like a child.

Lisa-Jayne yells up the stairs. "I've made a cup of tea."

"I'll be down in a minute," I say, wiping my cheeks.

I wash my face in the bathroom. In the mirror above the basin I see a stranger with red-rimmed eyes and lank hair. I try to find physical signs of my bereavement—an extra line on my forehead, or scarring on my skin, or a missing limb. Losing a baby is so fundamental and shocking, surely there must be tangible evidence. I can *feel* the hole inside me.

In the mirror I notice the edge of the bathtub, where a menagerie of animals is lined up as though waiting for Noah to arrive. Cows. Ducks. Sheep. Horses. One of Lachlan's trucks is resting in the plughole. The shelf above is stacked with baby shampoo, bubble bath, bath bombs, and more toys.

There is a tap on the door. Lisa-Jayne. "Are you all right?"

"Fine."

She's listening at the door. I can hear her breathing. After a while she leaves and I'm alone again. Sitting on the edge of the bath, I try to count the minutes since Ben was taken. How long did I spend with him? How long has he been missing? Would I recognize his cry, or his smell? Would I recognize him at all? I can't remember the color of his eyes, or the size of his feet, or the length of his eyelashes.

Jack is gone by the time I get downstairs.

"He said he had something to do," says Lisa-Jayne, who has pinned back her blond hair like a gymnast. "Is everything OK between you two?"

"We're fine."

In truth, I feel less anxious when Jack isn't around. We have barely spoken in the past few days and I cannot look at his face without seeing my own fear reflected in his eyes.

Lisa-Jayne is going to stay to make sure we're not bothered by reporters or strangers knocking on the door. She'll sleep in Lachlan's room. DCS MacAteer suggested we book into a hotel, away from the media, but I want to be home, lying awake in my own bed. I know it's ridiculous, but I imagine that Ben is going to call me, or find his way home by himself, which is why I have to be here just in case.

Opening my laptop, I begin reading the dozens of

emails in my inbox. There are messages of support and sympathy, offering prayers and best wishes. Many of the names I recognize. There are teachers from Lucy's school and Lachlan's preschool; mothers from my mothers' group and old friends from university and my magazine days.

I read a selection of them. Nobody seems to know what to write. Agatha's name is on the list.

> *Hi Meg,*
>
> *I heard the news. I'm shocked. Horrified. I can't believe this has happened. I feel guilty about my own happiness because I know how difficult this must be for you. If there's anything I can do. If you need a shoulder . . . or a friendly face . . .*
>
> > *Thinking of you,*
> > *Agatha xx*

Almost immediately she sent a second message.

> *Meg, it's me again. I just wanted to say that I'm sure Ben will be fine. Whoever took him will be looking after him. This will all work out.*
>
> > *xx*

I want to be charitable about all these messages of support, the offered prayers and heartfelt sympathy, but instead I find them irritating and self-serving, as though the authors feel better about themselves for having been in touch. I know that's unfair. What would I do in their situation? The same.

I look at my mummy blog. One of the newspapers revealed my blogging career, quoting some of my posts.

Now my followers know that "Cleopatra" is Meghan Shaughnessy and Jack is "Hail Caesar." The news has triggered hundreds of comments, most of them expressing sympathy and shock.

Who are these people? They don't even know me. They've read a few blog pieces about my family foibles and daily tribulations and now they feel invested in me, but instead of being comforted or encouraged, I feel angry. They have no right to claim ownership of my feelings or my ordeal.

A woman from Norfolk claims she saw Ben in a dream and that he's alive and living with a family of gypsies in Dorset. A different woman, a clairvoyant called Carla, says that if I send her a sample of Ben's placental blood she'll conduct a séance to find him. A man called Peter from Brighton writes about a vision. Ben is somewhere near water, he says, next to an old barn. His vision also contained pigs, a Citroën, and a milk tanker.

I begin deleting their messages, but stop myself. I don't believe in ESP or tarot cards or any sort of psychic phenomena, but I cannot bring myself to close off any possible lead.

The doorbell rings. Lisa-Jayne answers it. She's talking to someone, telling them to leave. It's most likely a reporter. Moments later she appears at the bedroom door.

"Someone called Simon insists on talking to you. He says he's a friend."

My stomach flips over. "I don't want to see him."

"OK."

She is halfway down the stairs when I change my mind. I want to know why he's here and what he's planning. I call after her. "Let him in. I'll be down in a few minutes."

I brush my hair and put drops in my eyes to take away the redness. I don't know why that's important, but I refuse to crumble in front of Simon or show him any weakness.

He's in the sitting room, standing at the window, looking through the curtains at the reporters outside. He's dressed in a crumpled linen jacket and tight jeans, and his two-day growth is flecked with the first traces of gray, but he's not self-conscious about it yet.

"What do you want?" I ask, not hiding the chill in my voice.

"I was worried about you." He glances back to the window. "It's a zoo out there."

"Are you one of the animals?"

"Give me some credit, Megs."

"So you're not working?"

"No." He runs his finger along the mantelpiece. "Where's Jack?"

"Out."

"You didn't have to put him through this."

"What?"

"Jack—he doesn't deserve to suffer like this. Neither of us do."

My look of puzzlement seems to confirm his suspicions.

"You're very good, Meg. Quite the actress."

"What are you talking about?"

"You could end this right now—the whole circus— simply tell the police what you did with the baby."

I stare at him in disbelief, aware my mouth is open because my tongue has gone dry.

"I remember what you told me when we last spoke," he says, picking up a framed photograph of Lucy and Lachlan. "You swore on your baby's life that I would never see the child. Never hold him in my arms."

"You think I did this?"

"Convince me you didn't."

I'm so angry my eyes are swimming. "You think I orchestrated the abduction of my own baby."

"You could be arrested for wasting police time," says Simon. "Children's Services will take away Lucy and Lachlan. You'll lose everything."

"Simon, Simon, Simon," I say, sighing and shaking my head. "Tell me how I managed to smuggle my own baby out of a hospital when I'd just had surgery?"

"Maybe you cooked it up with your sister. Grace came to see me, by the way. She threatened to expose me as a drug dealer."

"That's wrong—I'm sorry—but if you think I did this, you're crazy."

"Am I? Maybe you hired someone—you paid them to take the baby and keep it safe."

"Really! Who did I pay?"

He shrugs his shoulders as though it doesn't matter.

"You think I paid someone to dress up as a nurse and take Ben. How long are they supposed to look after him—a week, a month, a year? Don't be an idiot."

Simon's resolve is wavering.

"You can't wish me away, Meg, and you can't hide your baby forever."

"Get out!"

"You're giving me no option. I'm going to take my concerns to the police."

"They'll laugh at you."

"Jack won't be laughing."

I slap him hard across the face. That's the second time. Clearly, Simon has a face that deserves to be slapped. I want to do it again. I want to claw at his eyes. I want to wipe the smug look off his face.

"Get out! Get out!"

Lisa-Jayne has come to the door, drawn by our raised voices.

"Is everything OK?"

"I want him out of my house!" I scream.

"I was just leaving," says Simon, pushing past Lisa-Jayne. He's in the hallway and out the door, which I lock behind him, latching the security chain. Afterwards, I sit at the kitchen bench. Lisa-Jayne fetches me a glass of water. My hands are shaking. Water spills. She's waiting for an explanation.

"I want you to keep that man away from me . . . away from my family."

"Why?"

"He . . . he . . . he's trying to blackmail me."

"What? How?"

"It doesn't matter."

"How is he trying to blackmail you?"

"Forget it. Just keep him away."

AGATHA

Rory had a difficult night, crying and whimpering. He wasn't hungry or wet or running a temperature, although I think he should be feeding more. I weighed him this morning using the bathroom scale. I know it won't be very accurate but I'll do it again tomorrow and the next day until I get some idea if he's putting on weight.

I look a mess. I have bags under my eyes and my face is fat for no reason. I hate it when that happens. I hardly ate anything yesterday. I didn't pig out on cakes or chocolate biscuits. On days like this I look in the mirror and see my true self, a monstrous creature who belongs in a freak show. Instead of smooth skin, I see scars, wounds, and runnels that are carved or bulging in my flesh.

Hayden also didn't sleep, which puts him in a foul mood. He complains when I boil his eggs for too long and burn the toast. Later he criticizes how I iron his shirt. I knew the honeymoon couldn't last. Already he's growing tired of me. Once the novelty wears off, he'll realize that he could have done better. We'll begin fighting over little things and I will test the bonds of his love because I doubt their strength. I will demand more of him—daily proof—and this will drive him away.

Why do I do that? I am my own worst enemy. Every time I risk being happy, I find a way to fuck things up because, deep inside, the creature twists and slithers, gnawing away at my self-belief, reminding me of my past failures, my other babies, the bodies in the glade; deep inside, I know that I don't deserve to be loved.

My phone is ringing. I don't recognize the number.

"Hello?"

"Agatha?"

"Yes."

"It's Nicky."

It takes me a moment to put the name and voice together. I haven't talked to my ex-husband in three years. Every Christmas he sends me a group letter telling me his news, which is how I know that he married a divorcée from Newcastle and became stepdad to two boys.

"Nicky—what a surprise—how are you?"

"I'm good. And you?"

"The same." An alarm is sounding in my head. Why is he calling me now?

We both pause and then start talking at the same time.

"You first," I say.

"I'm down in London for a conference and yesterday I bumped into Sara Derry. You remember her— she worked at your temp agency."

"Of course."

Where is he going with this?

"We were chatting away and she suddenly dropped a bombshell. She said you'd had a baby. Congratulations."

"Thank you."

"A little boy. I was amazed. I mean, I thought there must have been a mistake."

"Mistake?"

He hesitates and changes direction. "It's brilliant. You must be so happy."

"Yes."

Another long pause, even more uncomfortable this time.

"Can I take you to lunch?" he asks.

"I'm pretty busy right now."

"Of course. How about a coffee? I can drop round. I'd love to see the baby."

I don't want him coming here. Hayden doesn't know about Nicky. He doesn't know that I've been married and divorced or spent years trying to have a family.

I hear a sound behind me. Hayden is standing in the kitchen doorway. He mouths the words "Who is it?"

"Nobody," I whisper.

Nicky is still talking. "I want to hear how you managed to get pregnant after all those attempts. Remember that last fertility specialist—he said you couldn't conceive."

"He was wrong."

"Obviously."

He doesn't believe me.

"I'm free now. I could come around. I have your address."

"I've moved."

"Really? Your mother said you were at the same place."

My heart skips. "When did you talk to my mother?"

"In August—on her birthday. Are you still in Fulham?"

"No. Yes."

Hayden is watching me.

"I've changed my mind," I say. "Let's meet somewhere."

"Great. I have a meeting in South Kensington. I can meet you afterwards. Is that OK?" Nicky names a place and we agree on a time. "Make sure you bring Rory. I want to meet this miracle baby."

"How do you know his name?"

"Sara told me, of course." He laughs.

I end the call quickly. Hayden is standing over me.

"Who was that?"

"An old friend."

"A boyfriend?"

"No, not really."

"What does that mean?"

"He's a friend of the family—a pseudo uncle. I haven't seen him in years."

"So you're meeting him."

"For coffee."

"Can I come?"

"You'll be bored. How about you take Rory to your mum's? She'll like that."

The restaurant is one of those hole-in-the-wall places in South Kensington that defy physics by being bigger on the inside than the outside. There is a bar along one wall, opposite a series of booths. Farther from the front, the restaurant opens out into a large dining area overlooked by a mezzanine level. By day it serves coffee and cream teas. At night it becomes a tapas bar.

Nicky hasn't changed much. He's a little grayer around the temples and has put on a few pounds. The extra weight makes him look more feminine because it sits on his hips.

"You didn't bring the baby," he says, sounding disappointed.

"No. He didn't sleep well last night."

"Shame."

Nicky takes my coat and hangs it up for me before summoning a waitress to take our order. It's strange, sitting opposite my ex-husband after all this time—

hearing his voice again, which sounds so intensely familiar, but also foreign because it belongs to a past life. Unlike Hayden, who is quiet and moody, Nicky is cheerful and expressive, wearing his heart on his sleeve.

We're not far from the Victoria and Albert Museum and tourist coaches are parked along the road outside. Workmen are putting up Christmas lights, stringing them from overhead wires that are threaded between lampposts and trees. Come nightfall, the wires will disappear in the darkness and the lights will make everything look festive and bright.

"So how did you do it?" asks Nicky, not dropping his gaze.

"Do it?"

"Get pregnant."

"It just happened."

"Really?"

His eyes are so intense it's like he's wearing makeup.

"If you must know, I used a donor," I say angrily, before apologizing. "Sorry. I don't want people knowing."

"Why not?"

I shrug. "It's simpler."

"Your mother didn't mention you were pregnant."

"I didn't tell her until the third trimester. I didn't want to get her hopes up—not after what happened the last time."

Nicky's eyes cloud over with sadness and he takes a moment to compose himself. Our coffees have arrived.

"Are you with someone?" he asks.

"Engaged."

"Good for you."

I tell him about Hayden, playing up the navy angle, making it sound like he's destined to captain his own frigate or be vice admiral of the fleet.

"We're going to get married in the summer and honeymoon in Tahiti."

"Tahiti? Wow! So he's the biological father?"

"Yes," I reply.

Nicky folds and unfolds his napkin. "That story about the stolen baby—such a terrible business."

"I haven't been following it closely."

His eyebrows lift. "It's hard to avoid."

"I have been rather busy of late." I laugh, not meeting his gaze.

"Yes, of course."

Nicky begins talking about how he drove past our old house in Highgate. "I think they've done an attic conversion," he says. "We always talked about doing that . . . when we had children." He looks at me apologetically, wishing he could take the statement back. "Do you ever wonder what would have happened if our Chloe had lived? She would have been four this year."

I don't answer.

"I wonder all the time," he says. "I see a little girl in the street, or the park, and I imagine that she might be our Chloe—alive and well, being raised by someone else."

"If I thought that, I'd go crazy."

"You're right. We both went a little dippy, didn't we? I remember you talking about stealing a baby. You were kidding, I know, but you said we should find a couple who already had children and take a baby from them."

"I was grieving."

"Of course."

I manage to hold Nicky's gaze when all I want to do is look away. The creature inside me uncoils.

He knows! He knows!

"So where did you have your baby?" Nicky asks.

"In London."

"Oh, Sara said it was in Leeds."

"What I mean is, I gave birth in Leeds but came straight back to London. Hayden had just flown in from Cape Town. He's been fighting pirates in the Indian Ocean."

Nicky tilts his head. "I was in Leeds a few weeks ago. I knocked on your mother's door. The place looked closed up. A neighbor said she'd gone to Spain for the winter."

"She came back for the birth."

"And then went back to Spain?"

"Yes."

He knows! He knows!

I look at my watch. I'm not wearing one. I glance at my phone. "I really have to go. Rory has to be fed."

"Sure. Absolutely." Nicky gets up and holds out my coat while I slip my arms into the sleeves.

"It was lovely seeing you again, Aggy. Look after that baby."

"I will."

We separate on the pavement outside. I walk two dozen steps and look back. Nicky is still watching me.

He knows! He knows!

He returns my wave before crossing the road, heading for the nearest Underground station. When he's far enough ahead of me, I turn and follow, keeping my head down and weaving between pedestrians. Nicky is tall enough to spot in a crowd.

He knows! He knows!

He won't say anything.

He'll tell the police.

He has no proof.

It doesn't matter.

South Kensington station is always busy. There are multiple walkways and passages leading to different

platforms. Keeping Nicky in view, I pull up the hood
of my coat, shielding my face from the cameras. At one
point Nicky pauses to give money to a busker playing
the violin. I stop suddenly and turn, walking against the
flow. After a few seconds, I spin back and follow him
again.

He has reached the eastbound platform of the District and Circle lines, which is crowded with sightseers
leaving the museums. Murmuring apologies, I brush
past shoulders and weave between bodies, following
Nicky to the far end of the platform.

I glance at the information board. The next train is a
minute away. Nicky is looking at his phone.

He's calling the police.

He could be reading emails.

Or sending a message.

It's nothing.

He's jealous because you couldn't give him a child.

Nicky loves me.

He knows! He knows!

The train is approaching, beating out a rhythm on
the rails. Images flash against my closed lids. I see the
police arriving at the flat. I see them taking my baby
away. I'm fighting at their arms, begging them to give
him back . . . to let me hold him.

Nicky has shuffled forward, standing close to the
edge. I'm right behind him, close enough to see the
fine downy hair on the nape of his neck and the dandruff on his shoulders. People are pressed around us.

He knows! He knows!

What can he do?

He can tell the police.

No.

The wind lifts the hair from Nicky's forehead as the
train appears, rushing towards us. The front carriage is

forty feet away, thirty feet, twenty feet . . . I glimpse the driver behind the windshield. A man. Looking bored.

He knows! He knows!

What can I do?

Stop him!

How?

My hands touch the middle of Nicky's back. His head begins to turn, but I push harder, feeling his weight. Giddy for a moment, I muffle a laugh as he pitches forward, fighting for balance, waving his arms in tiny circles. For a moment he seems to defy gravity, but then he falls, disappearing beneath the train with a soft *whump*—a sound repeated with every passing wheel.

A woman screams. Then another. I join them. People are shouting as carriages flash past us, slowing to a halt. Passengers are standing inside, waiting to get off, unaware of what's happened beneath them. A young pudgy girl of five or six is staring at me. She's holding a doll in the crook of her arm and tugging at her mother's sleeve.

Her mother covers her eyes, telling her not to look.

"What happened to the man?" asks the girl.

"Shhhhh."

"Where did he go?"

The girl pulls her mother's hand from her face and stares at me accusingly. I cannot meet her gaze. I turn away and move through the crowd. People are pressing forward, hoping for a closer look. Others want to escape. I push past them, weaving between the forest of shoulders, keeping my head down, listening to their conversations.

"Someone jumped?"

"He collapsed."

"Shit! Are we going to be late?"

It seems to take an age to reach the exit, the stairs. My hands are shaking. My mind numb. I must think clearly. If I leave the station it will look suspicious. I should catch a train. Choose a different platform. Get away. Cover my tracks.

The creature inside me has gone quiet, but I know what he's thinking.

He knew! He knew! He knew!

MEGHAN

Lucy and Lachlan race each other through the front gate and down the path, hurling themselves into my outstretched arms. Flash guns are firing and TV cameras capture the moment. Our private family reunion has become public fodder, to be shown and reshown on every news channel. We are the stars of our own reality TV show: *Meet the Shaughnessys*.

Jack follows them down the path, carrying their twin suitcases. The photographers are yelling instructions, wanting us to pose for more shots, but I shoo the children inside and we shut the door.

I hug the children again, properly this time. Lucy talks a mile a minute, trying to tell me all her news before Lachlan has time to construct a sentence.

"I think I have nits. My head is all itchy. Grandma gave me a special shampoo, but it hurt my eyes and I had to wear conditioner on my head for ages. I cried when she combed it out, but she didn't find any nits. So how come my head is so itchy?"

"I'm hungry," says Lachlan.

"I'm making a snack now," I say.

Lucy crawls up onto Jack's lap. Lachlan comes to me.

"Did you have the baby?" Lucy asks.

"Yes—a little boy."

Lucy frowns. "I was hoping for a girl."

"But you knew we were having a boy."

"Yeah, but I thought maybe you made a mistake or changed your mind—like that time we ordered that lamp from IKEA and picked up the wrong one and we decided that the wrong one looked better than the right one so we didn't take it back."

"Babies aren't like lamps from IKEA," I say.

"So where is he?" asks Lachlan. "Can we see him?"

"Not just yet."

"Why?"

I look at Jack. We've already discussed how to handle this.

"Ben has gone missing," I say.

"I knew it," says Lucy triumphantly. "I heard Granddad and Grandma talking. They said someone stole him."

"That's right," says Jack. "But we're going to get him back."

Lachlan frowns. "Why did they steal him?"

"They must have wanted a baby," replies Lucy, making it sound so logical.

"But you can't just steal one," says Lachlan. He looks at me for corroboration.

"The police are looking for him," I say. "That's why all those people are outside the house. They're reporters."

Lachlan's eyes have gone wide. His hand goes to his mouth. "What if the Child Catcher got him?"

"It's not the Child Catcher," Jack says. Ever since Lachlan watched *Chitty Chitty Bang Bang* he's been terrified of the Child Catcher—a villain who lures children into a cage by offering them lollipops and sweets.

There are lots more questions about the police and the reporters outside.

I can see that Lachlan is struggling the most. "Does that mean he's gone forever?"

"No."

"So where is he?"

"He's staying with some other family."

"Like a sleepover," says Lucy.

"No, not quite." My heart wants to break. "Ben has a new home and he's being looked after by someone else."

"But why?" asks Lachlan.

I don't know how to answer him.

"Won't he miss us?" Lucy asks.

Jack comes to my rescue. "The person who took Ben is sad. She is so sad that she thought a baby might make her happy—even if it is someone else's baby."

"Why can't she have her own baby?" Lachlan asks.

"We don't know," says Jack, "but we're going to get Ben back."

"When?"

"Soon."

"Tomorrow?"

"Maybe not tomorrow."

"Snack time!" I announce, clapping my hands. "Who wants oven chips?"

"Yeah," they chorus.

Jack carries Lucy to the kitchen, which he doesn't do much anymore because she's grown so big. I carry Lachlan, sniffing his hair, drawing his smell deep into my lungs, wanting to remind myself that these two are safe and belong to me.

It's strange having Jack at home during the day. His boss has given him indefinite leave from work, but Jack doesn't know what to do with himself. I can manage to fill each hour with chores—cooking, cleaning, and sewing buttons—while Jack wanders through the house,

looking out the window, checking his email, looking out
the window again.

Normally he'd play tennis or go for a run, but
everything we do is being monitored, recorded, and
broadcast. The reporters outside are knocking on our
neighbors' doors, asking to use their bathrooms or looking for quotes. At the same time, photographers and
cameramen have set up stepladders so they can shoot
over our box hedge at the bay window and front door.
Our house is the backdrop for hourly updates, delivered breathlessly by journalists, while the bright lights
blast through our front curtains, casting shadows on the
walls.

We're trapped in here. We're like rats in a cage, or
goldfish in a bowl. Last night Jack and I lay in bed like
strangers, staring at the ceiling. At one point his knee
touched my thigh and I slid another few inches away
from him. He uttered a gentle snore and I resented
him even more.

Eventually I slept. Ben appeared in my dreams. I
heard him crying and my milk came in and I wondered
how my heart could keep beating of its own accord
when it felt so broken and mangled. Every four hours
I have been expressing and putting the milk in the
freezer, adding to my growing supply, hoping it will be
necessary.

I woke to the sound of reporters laughing outside.
Making jokes. I know from Jack how journalists find
humor in the darkest stories because it inoculates them
against tragedy or overcomes the boredom. They make
jokes about Julian Assange, Chelsea Manning, Boris
Johnson, and Donald Trump. Nothing is off limits or
"too soon."

The TV is a constant soundtrack as I follow every
bulletin, listening to the endless parade of child-care

experts, doctors, hostage negotiators, and bereaved parents who are asked to comment on the investigation and how Jack and I might be feeling. Our friends are also asked to comment, ambushed as they step out of their cars or front doors. Startled by the cameras, they mouth sympathetic platitudes, adding nothing, filling airtime.

There have been dozens of unconfirmed sightings up and down the country. New mothers are complaining about being stopped by strangers in the street who peer into their prams and quiz them suspiciously.

Occasionally something new emerges. A hospital blanket was discovered in a toilet cubicle at King's Cross station. The tartan shopping trolley turned up on a train that arrived in Edinburgh. A cleaner took it home, thinking it was abandoned, but saw the trolley mentioned on the news and handed it over to police.

"So Ben is in Scotland," I said to Annie.

"We don't know that."

"But the trolley?"

"It might have been left on the train. There are seven stops between King's Cross and Edinburgh."

"So he could be anywhere?"

"We're checking the CCTV footage and ticket purchases from those stations."

I am trying to stay positive, modulating my voice to sound low and reasonable whenever I talk to the police, but inside I'm yelling, *Just find him, for God's sake!*

In the meantime, the cards and letters keep arriving. The postman came twice today, delivering three sacks each time. Annie has suggested she read everything first in case one of the messages is from the kidnapper, but I think she's trying to protect us from the trolls. Already there are conspiracy theories appearing on the Internet. Someone has suggested the kidnapping is a hoax to raise Jack's profile. Others say that an organized crime syndicate was behind the abduction, trafficking white children to slave traders in the Middle East. I shouldn't read the crazies. My imagination has enough material.

Annie suggests we go stay with my parents.

"You said the kidnapper might try to make contact?"

"We could put a transfer on your numbers."

"What if they try to bring Ben home?"

Annie doesn't answer, but I know she thinks I'm clutching at straws. I don't care. I'm allowed to be irrational or insanely optimistic. What I refuse to do is lose hope.

Lucy has gone to school today, but Lachlan is staying home because I need the distraction. Neither of them has mentioned Baby Ben since yesterday. I don't think they're unmoved, or uncaring. That's the difference between children and adults—children don't put as much energy into being sad.

I have my laptop open on the kitchen bench and have been searching the Internet for other stories of missing children. When Madeleine McCann disappeared, the circus ran for months and then years. Jack gets angry when I mention facts like this. "It's not the same," he says. "We're going to find Ben."

Right now he's upstairs, sitting in an airless study, watching football or playing computer solitaire. Or maybe he's also searching the Internet, looking for solace or reassurance or a clue.

"Dr. Haven wants to come over," says Annie, cupping her mobile phone in her hands. "He's finished the psychological profile."

"When?"

"He can be here in fifteen minutes."

"OK," I say, desperate for any news. It's not boredom

I feel so much as ineffectiveness. I want to be doing something useful or positive that might make a difference.

Annie is brushing her hair and applying lip gloss in the hallway mirror. I wonder if it has anything to do with Cyrus Haven.

"How well do you know him?" I ask.

"Who?"

"Dr. Haven."

"Not very well."

"Oh. I thought you might be friends."

Annie colors slightly and I know that I'm on the right track. Either she carries a torch for Cyrus or there has been a past relationship.

"How did you meet him?" I ask.

"He interviews officers who are involved in shootings or who are injured in the line of duty."

"Did that happen to you?"

She nods. "I'm not supposed to talk about it."

Her reluctance makes me even more curious. "He's a very interesting man, Dr. Haven. A good listener. I guess he has to be. But he also strikes me as being very sad."

"That's understandable," says Annie.

"Why?"

"After what he went through."

"What happened to him?"

"It's not really my place."

I open my laptop and call up Google, typing in the name Cyrus Haven.

"You won't find anything," says Annie.

"Why not?"

She chews the inside of her cheek. "You didn't hear this from me, OK?"

I nod.

"Look up the name Elias Haven-Sykes."

Dozens of links appear on-screen with dramatic shout-lines:

Family Hacked to Death
Youngest Son Discovers Family Massacre
Haven-Sykes Committed to Mental Hospital

Opening some of the links, I read them in silence.

Elias Haven-Sykes, aged eighteen, used a machete to murder his parents and two younger sisters in Manchester in 1995. One member of the family survived—Cyrus Haven-Sykes, aged thirteen, who came home from football practice and discovered his brother watching TV while resting his feet on their father's body. Their mother lay dead on the kitchen floor. His sisters had tried to barricade themselves in a bedroom, but were dragged from beneath their beds and hacked to death.

Annie has been watching me read.

"Why?" I whisper.

"Elias was a diagnosed schizophrenic. He'd been in and out of psychiatric hospitals since he was sixteen."

"Where is he now?"

"Rampton, as far as I know. Maximum security."

"Does Cyrus ever talk about him?"

"No."

I close the computer, not wanting to read any more. I remember the case now, but not the names of those involved. One image in particular flashes into my mind—the photograph of a teenage boy dressed in a black suit, standing alone amid the coffins of his family. The caption called him "the loneliest boy in the world."

        ✧   ✧   ✧

Cyrus arrives at midday. He is so unprepossessing and unremarkable that the reporters ignore him until the last moment, when he's nearing the front door. One of them calls his name. The others are soon scrambling out of cars and vans, but the door has closed by then and Cyrus is shrugging off his leather jacket. Annie hangs it up for him. Their hands touch and a look passes between them.

I make a pot of tea, which Cyrus doesn't drink. He seems to enjoy the ritual of tea, but not the taste.

"Where's Jack?" he asks.

"Upstairs."

"How is he?"

What does he want me to say? Jack is struggling and I can't help him and I don't know if I want to. I know it's not fair or rational to blame Jack, but since when is life fair? I say none of this out loud, but sense that Cyrus hears it anyway.

As if summoned, Jack arrives in the kitchen. He takes a seat and accepts a cup of tea, staring at the milky brown liquid as though trying to remember what it's called.

Cyrus takes a single sheet of paper from his satchel. He puts it on the table and centers it between his elbows. A forefinger pushes his reading glasses higher on the bridge of his nose.

"This is what I've told the police," he says. "They're looking for a woman in her thirties or early forties who was comfortable in a hospital setting, blending in and interacting with patients and visitors without attracting attention or being deterred. She was also familiar with the layout of the Churchill—the stairwells, lifts, and cameras—which suggests that she has worked at the hospital or visited it previously. The police are checking employment records and older CCTV tapes."

Cyrus moves his finger down the page.

"She is an accomplished liar, which might sound obvious, but it's not easy to lie when the stakes are this high. Most people will show evidence of the stress— they will blush, or stammer, or perspire, or fidget, but this woman was very cool under pressure.

"I think she has a high degree of intelligence that might not be reflected in her level of education."

"What do you mean?" asks Jack, who is folding a paper towel into smaller and smaller squares.

"High intelligence doesn't always equate to academic achievement. She may not have had the opportunity or the application necessary to go beyond secondary school. But she's clearly very clever. Look at the planning involved—the different disguises, the precautions, the verbal and nonverbal behavior, and her interactions with people like you."

"So we're dealing with a criminal mastermind?" Jack says sarcastically.

Cyrus doesn't react. "Not a mastermind, but a clever woman who didn't appear lost or nervous or frightened. One who has spent months planning this crime."

"You're making excuses for the hospital—giving them a way out."

I interject. "That's not what Cyrus is saying."

"He's calling her a genius."

"I'm giving you a psychological profile," says Cyrus. "I don't make excuses for people. I try to understand them. Normally, when I look at a crime scene, I see the limitations of the perpetrator. Almost always they fail because of their inability to plan ahead. They concentrate on the crime, but not their exit strategy. They get impatient and stop short of working out what happens next. In this case, the woman planned everything in meticulous detail—how to secure a baby and how to get away. She didn't improvise or say, "Oh well, if I get that far, I'll wing it." She had an extra disguise. She had the trolley. She must have heard the alarm go off. She knew they were looking for her. The hospital was a labyrinth. The exits were being sealed off, but she didn't panic, or run, or draw attention to herself. It took police days to discover how she smuggled Baby Ben out of the hospital."

He pauses, waiting for Jack to respond or comment. When there's no reply, he continues.

"The perpetrator is likely to be married or in a relationship, but not a stable one. This is one of the reasons she wants a baby—to cement a relationship; to make a man stay with her who she fears might leave.

"She is willing to take risks. Through each step of the abduction the chance of discovery increased, but she carried on—changing her clothes, walking the corridor, penetrating the heart of the hospital. At any point, a member of staff could have questioned her credentials or raised the alarm.

"I believe she acted alone, but she will have prepared a place for the baby and created a credible story."

"What story?" I ask.

"Most likely she faked a pregnancy—convincing her friends and family that she was due any day."

"So she stuffed a pillow up her dress," says Jack.

"I think she would have been a little more sophisticated than that," says Cyrus. "Pregnancy prosthetics can be bought online. Other sites sell fake pregnancy tests and ultrasound pictures."

"Why didn't she have her own baby?" asks Jack.

"Maybe she can't. IVF is expensive and has a one-in-four chance of success. Adoption might also be difficult, depending upon her age and background. In my work I've come across a number of childless women who have contemplated taking a baby. Some had trouble with relationships; others were delusional, or infertile, or so desperate for love that a child had become their holy grail."

"Will she hurt Ben?" I ask.

"Under normal circumstances, no."

"What are the *other* circumstances?"

"If she's frightened, or backed into a corner, or desperate to avoid detection, she might panic, but if we send her the right messages, if we keep her calm, she will love Ben and keep him safe."

"Do you really think she's listening?" asks Jack. "Where's the evidence? The police are treating her like a victim, not a criminal. Everybody is supposed to feel sorry for her—but what about us?"

"He's right," I say. "Treating her like a victim hasn't worked."

"She isn't a criminal or a victim," says Cyrus. "Not in her mind. By now she's convinced that Ben is *her* baby and we are the people who want to take him away from her. We are the criminals."

"That's ridiculous," I say, my voice shaking. "He's *our* baby."

"Of course he is," says Cyrus. "And we'll get him back." He takes off his glasses and rubs the bridge of his nose. "More than sixty babies have been abducted in Britain over the past thirty years, and all but four have been recovered safely. I know that's a very thin numerical base, but I hope you can take comfort from figures like that."

The answer is no. The opposite is true. There is no comfort in being a statistical exception. It's like having a rare disease or being the victim of outrageous misfortune—you keep asking yourself, *Why me? Why not someone else?*

Cyrus looks again at the page on the table. "Having studied the abduction—particularly the detailed planning and the confident execution—I'm starting to suspect this woman might have done this before."

"Taken a baby?" asks Jack.

"Either as a trial run or a failed earlier attempt."

"When? Where?"

"I've asked DCS MacAteer to go back over the files of past abductions as well as missing children and security breaches at hospitals and schools."

I look at Jack, wondering if he's getting the same message.

"There's something else," says Cyrus, choosing his words carefully. "I think we should consider the possibility that Ben was chosen."

"What do you mean, *chosen*?" I ask.

"There were eighteen babies in the maternity ward that night. This woman walked past at least six mothers with newborn babies. Why didn't she choose one of them?"

I am struggling with the notion. "So you think . . . ?"

"I'm trying to explain the inconsistencies."

"Why would she choose Ben?" asks Jack.

"She may have seen Meg arriving at the hospital, or she may have recognized you from the TV; or she could have identified you earlier. Did you notice anyone following you in the weeks leading up to the birth? Any strange cars, or phone calls?"

I shake my head, less certain than before.

"How many other people knew when and where you were having your baby?"

I try to think. My mothers' group, my hairdresser, my yoga instructress, the girls in the class, Lucy's teacher, the staff from Lachlan's preschool . . . My doctor knew, of course. My mother . . .

"What about your blog?" Jack asks.

Cyrus raises his eyes from the page. "What blog?"

"I write a mummy blog," I explain. "It's a hobby, I guess."

"What do you write about?"

I shrug, feeling embarrassed. "About my life, the kids, Jack . . . but I never use our real names."

"She has six thousand followers," says Jack, trying to be helpful.

"Did you tell people when you were having your baby?"

My heart sinks. "I might have mentioned . . ."

"Did you give the date?"

I nod.

"Did you mention the hospital?"

"Maybe."

"Have you corresponded with any of these women?"

"They comment on my posts or send me messages."

"And you reply?"

"Not all the time."

I know what he's thinking. Some of these readers will be pregnant, or have young families, or might have lost babies.

"Any haters or trolls?" he asks.

"Maybe. Some. Very rarely. Hardly any. I have never posted where I live or mentioned the names of streets or schools." I know I sound defensive.

"How do we get all that free stuff?" asks Jack.

"Companies know who writes these blogs," I say. "And my friends know."

I am digging myself into a hole, but this is not about protecting me. I try to think. Could someone have been stalking me? I rack my brain. A few weeks ago a BMW followed me through a changing light at Hammersmith. What about that creepy woman who hangs around the pond when I'm feeding the ducks with Lachlan? She's always scratching at her arms and talking to herself. Once I start, I can't stop. There's a homeless man who sleeps in the doorway of the church. He sometimes knocks on people's doors, asking for odd jobs. And a man at the library who tries to look up women's skirts when they sit on beanbags to read stories to their children.

"Has anyone taken a special interest in your pregnancy?" asks Cyrus.

"I don't think so. I know lots of pregnant women. I've been doing prenatal yoga classes at the fitness center and my blog gets lots of comments from new mums."

"Has anyone stood out? They might have been particularly intense, or asked a lot of personal questions."

"Not really."

Jack interrupts. "What about the one whose husband is in the navy?"

"Agatha," I say. "She's not intense."

"Who's Agatha?" asks Cyrus.

"She does my yoga class."

"How long have you known her?"

"A month or so. She works locally."

"And she's pregnant?"

"She had her baby before me."

Cyrus is taking notes. "Do you have an address for Agatha?"

"I have her phone number and an email address."

From outside I hear a commotion. Shouts. Scuffling. Annie opens the front door. Reporters are besieging DCS MacAteer as he steps from a police car. Chaperoned by his driver and another detective, he pushes his way through the media scrum, ignoring their questions.

I meet them in the hallway, which is suddenly very

crowded. MacAteer glances at Cyrus, nods, no hand-shake.

He addresses me. "A newborn baby has been left outside a church in Little Drayton in Shropshire. It's a baby boy, but we don't know if it's Ben," he says.

I step back, swaying and reaching for the wall.

"The baby has been taken to the nearest hospital. I want to stress: we don't know if it's related to this case, but I thought you should hear about this from me and not from the rabble outside."

A question gets stuck in my throat.

Jack speaks. "What do we know?"

"From the initial reports, the baby might only be a few hours old. He's being examined by doctors."

"It's Ben!" I blurt. "It's him."

"We don't know that," says MacAteer. "We may have to do a DNA test."

"Please let me see him. I could feed him. I'm still expressing."

MacAteer exchanges a glance with Cyrus. They think I'm being irrational. I start to argue. Cyrus cuts me off. "Please, Mrs. Shaughnessy. Meghan. Don't make this any harder."

MacAteer takes out a small plastic test tube. "We want to take a DNA sample—a simple mouth swab."

"Of course," says Jack, reaching for the test tube.

"No, it should be me," I blurt, aware of the dangers of DNA and the sins it could reveal.

"Mother or father, it makes no difference," says MacAteer.

I take the tube from Jack and run the cotton swab around my cheek before dropping it into the tube. MacAteer seals the top and tucks it into his inner pocket. "I'll let you know as soon as we have news," he says. "In the meantime, PC Hipwell will stay here and handle the media. Until we know more, I recommend that you don't make any public statements."

The detectives leave the house, triggering another barrage of questions. Annie and Cyrus remain behind. He asks whether Jack or I have ever been to Little Drayton, or if we know anyone who lives there. We shake our heads.

Jack turns on the TV. We're watching a female reporter outside the hospital in Stoke, struggling to hold down her hair in the wind.

"The infant boy, who weighs seven pounds, was found lying inside a cardboard box left next to the main doors of the hall. Paramedics transported him to Royal Stoke University Hospital, where a spokesman issued a brief update in the last half hour describing the baby as being dehydrated but generally in good condition.

"The discovery has triggered intense speculation that the infant could be Ben Shaughnessy, the newborn baby taken from a London hospital seven days ago. Police are refusing to comment, but a short time ago the detective in charge of that investigation visited Baby Ben's parents, Jack and Meghan Shaughnessy, at their house in London."

The footage changes to an image of DCS MacAteer and his colleagues walking into our house. The entire scene happened less than twenty minutes ago and already it's on the news.

"It's Ben," I whisper.

"We don't know that," says Jack.

"Who else could it be?"

"Babies get abandoned all the time."

I shake my head. "Not *all* the time . . ."

AGATHA

The intercom buzzes. I'm dreaming about Rory's first birthday party. The guests are arriving with presents and balloons. I've made a teddy bear cake and set out plates of mini sausage rolls and finger sandwiches. The buzzer sounds again and the scene dissolves in my head.

I hear voices. Hayden is talking to someone on the intercom. He meets them at the top of the stairs—two police officers. I'm watching through a crack in the bedroom door.

"I'm sorry to disturb you," says the detective. "We were hoping to speak to Agatha Fyfle."

"She's sleeping," says Hayden.

"I'm awake," I say, calling from the bedroom. "I need a few minutes."

Listening at the door, I straighten my dress and fix my hair, telling myself to breathe normally and stay calm. Are they here about Nicky or the baby? Does it matter?

You went too far.

It was an accident.

You killed him.

No!

You pushed him.

I loved Nicky.

The police officers are sitting at either end of the sofa—one in uniform and the other wearing an ugly blue suit worn shiny at the elbows. They stand, politely. The uniformed officer is in his late twenties with short-cropped hair and a round face that hides a future double chin. The detective is two decades older with a boozer's nose and thinning hair. I offer to make them tea or coffee. They decline. I take the armchair. Hayden perches on the roll of the armrest.

"Can I call you Agatha?" the older one asks.

I nod.

"I'm not sure if you've heard the news," he says. "There was an incident at South Kensington Tube station the day before yesterday. A man fell under a train."

"How awful!"

"We believe you may know the victim," says the detective. "Nicholas David Fyfle."

I let out a squeak of alarm, covering my mouth. "It must be a mistake."

"What makes you say that?"

"I saw Nicky yesterday—or was it the day before? No, yesterday. We had coffee together."

"Where was that?"

"At a restaurant near the V&A."

The two officers exchange a look. The detective speaks. "Am I right in thinking you were married to Mr. Fyfle?"

"That's not true," says Hayden. "He's her uncle."

I grab his hand and address the detective. "We divorced three years ago."

Hayden pulls away. "You didn't tell me you were married." He makes it sound like an accusation.

"We weren't together long," I explain.

"Huh? But you said he was your uncle."

Hayden is making too much of this—embarrassing me in front of strangers. I knew he'd be the jealous type, which is why I didn't tell him in the first place.

The two officers look at each other uncomfortably,

neither wanting to be caught up in a domestic dispute. The senior one clears his throat. "When you had coffee with Mr. Fyfle—how did he seem?"

"Fine. Good. He was down in London for a conference." I blow my nose on a tissue and sniffle.

"How would you describe his state of mind?"

"I'm not sure I understand the question."

"Did he seem upset or depressed about anything?"

"Depressed? No, not really. He was talking about his wife and stepsons. I think he was a little homesick."

"Did he tell you that?"

"No. I mean, he intimated as much."

"Did he mention any marital problems?"

"Not exactly."

"What then?"

"He said he wasn't living up to 'expectations.'" I use my fingers to make the quotation marks.

"Whose expectations?"

"I assumed he meant his wife's."

"Money issues?"

"He's a writer," I reply, as though that should explain everything.

The uniformed officer speaks. "So your divorce was amicable?"

"Absolutely."

"And you kept his name?"

"Yes."

"Why was that?"

"I don't know, really. I couldn't be bothered doing all that paperwork, changing my driver's license, my passport, my credit cards . . ."

Hayden is pacing at the window, pretending to look out, but his eyes are darting from side to side.

"Where did you say good-bye?" asks the detective.

My mind reaches back.

"On the street—outside the café."

"And that was the last time you saw Mr. Fyfle?"

I hesitate, not wanting to be caught out. I replay the scene. My face was hidden. If the cameras had picked me out they wouldn't be asking these questions.

"I thought I might see Nicky again at the station, but he was ahead of me."

"What were you doing at the station?"

"I was catching a train to Earl's Court. Nicky said he was going to Victoria."

"Did you see him on the platform?"

"No. I took the Piccadilly line."

"Why didn't you walk to the station together?" asks the detective.

"I only realized after Nicky had gone."

Hayden interrupts. "So did this guy jump or was he pushed?"

"Why would you think he was pushed?" asks the older detective, swiveling his whole body to study Hayden, who grows nervous at the scrutiny.

"No reason," he says. "But you seem to be asking a lot of questions. If the guy topped himself, why bother?"

I flinch and glance at the officers apologetically.

The detective looks at me. "We have spoken to several eyewitnesses who suggest Mr. Fyfle may have been pushed or bumped from behind. The CCTV images also indicate possible contact, which could have been accidental."

"Who was it?" asks Hayden.

"We haven't managed to identify the individual. We believe that he or she was wearing a long, hooded overcoat." The detective tilts his head. "Do you own a coat like that, Mrs. Fyfle?"

"Miss," I say, correcting him.

"Miss Fyfle."

"I didn't push Nicky!"

"I asked if you had a hooded overcoat."

"What did it look like?"

"Black or perhaps navy—with a looping cowl that becomes a hood."

I glance at Hayden, who is waiting for me to say something.

"I used to have a coat like that, but I gave it away to charity."

"When was that?" asks the uniformed officer.

I pause as though straining to remember. "Weeks ago now—I put it in one of those charity clothing bins."

I can see Hayden's reflection in the glass. He's staring at me.

"Well," says the detective, wiping his hands down the front of his trousers, "I think that covers most of it. If you do remember anything more . . ."

"I'll be in touch," I say.

They're almost at the door. The detective turns. "Out of interest, did Mr. Fyfle contact you, or did you call him?"

"He called me."

"How long had it been since you'd spoken to each other?"

"Years."

"So why did he call?"

"He had heard about the baby."

"Baby?"

"I had a baby boy ten days ago." I point at the cards on the mantelpiece, some from friends and others that I posted to myself.

"Congratulations."

"Thank you," I say. "Nicky and I didn't manage to have children. We tried. I think it's why we broke up in the end—the stress and disappointment."

"I see," says the detective, but I don't like the tone of his voice. I don't know if he does *see* or how much he's *seen* or if he believes me.

"Good-bye, Mr. Cole," he says to Hayden, who doesn't respond. I stand on the landing and watch them descend the stairs, bracing myself for what's to come.

Hayden paces back and forth behind the sofa, tugging at his ear, something he does when he's thinking. Having taken a seat, I keep turning my head to maintain eye contact.

"Why did you lie? You said he was an old friend—an uncle."

"I thought you might be jealous."

"Me? Why?"

"Men can get funny about that sort of thing."

"Is that right? Who told you that—your *other* husbands?"

"There was only one. Please don't be like this."

"Why did you divorce?"

"We couldn't have a baby. Nicky had a low sperm count. We tried everything, but it didn't work out. That's what we talked about over coffee."

"Does Jules know you were married?"

"No! Yes. I might have told her."

"So everyone knows except me?"

"No, not everyone."

"What else aren't you telling me?"

"Nothing."

"What about your coat? You told those coppers you gave it to charity when it's right this minute hanging in your wardrobe."

"That's not the one I meant."

"What?"

"That's a different coat."

"It looks the same."

"I like the style. The old one was getting worn at the elbows and had lost two buttons."

"When did you buy a new coat? You've barely left the flat."

"I bought it online."

Hayden wants to believe me, but I can see that he's struggling. He hates secrets and doesn't like being surprised. At the same time, he's enjoyed being a father and playing happy families. I can see it in his eyes and hear it in his voice when he talks about Rory.

I put my arms around him from behind and hug him, pressing my head to his back. He turns around and we kiss. I open my eyes and discover that he's watching me. The creature slides between my organs and coils around my heart, slowly tightening.

Stupid! Stupid! Stupid!

MEGHAN

The baby isn't Ben. According to the hospital, he was barely six hours old when abandoned. The mother, all of sixteen, gave birth in her bedroom and smuggled him outside in her schoolbag, leaving him on the steps of the hall. Mother and unwanted child have since been reunited. How touching.

My first reaction was denial. I said the mother was lying and demanded a DNA test. *How ironic.* In the same breath, my shoulders shook and I knew I was being irrational. It's someone else's child, but that doesn't make it fair. She doesn't *want* a baby. She doesn't deserve one.

Annie broke the news to us. My strength disappeared and I took myself to bed clutching a box of tissues. Jack came in later and sat beside me. I knew he wanted to talk but I pretended to be asleep. Call me a coward, but I know how any discussion will end. I will accuse Jack of never wanting Ben in the first place, of suggesting a termination, of wishing for something like this. And he will look at me like a fur seal about to be clubbed and beg me for forgiveness, which I will give him because I know it's not his fault, but the absolution will be phony because it doesn't come from the heart.

The longer this goes on, the worse it becomes. At first I was swept along by the support and public goodwill, but now that's not enough. My life has stopped. The planet does not turn for me. I keep reminding

myself of Annie's words that no news is good news, but
is that true? I don't know anymore. In the meantime,
I hope for a miracle while fearing that God is punishing me for being unfaithful to Jack or for not believing
in Him. When it comes to religion, I am one of those
doubters who keeps demanding proof, who is awe-
struck and horrified by turns at the beauty and the cruelty that believers claim in the name of their God.

I try to pray but I struggle to recall the hymns and
psalms from my days at Sunday school. The only prayer
I can remember is from our weekly assemblies, when
we stood in class groups promising to love one another,
saying that "as many hands build a house, so many
hearts make a school." I close my eyes and summon my
own words. Listening. Hoping for an answer.

Nothing.

God is on another call.

We have the media conference this afternoon. DCS
MacAteer requested we arrive early to rehearse what
we're going to say. We leave the house just after two
o'clock. I'm wearing makeup for the first time in ages
and I've dressed in a pre-pregnancy skirt with the top
button undone, hidden beneath a sweater.

The police station is shabbier than I expect. Apart
from the computers and printers, it doesn't look very
high-tech or cutting edge or *CSI*. The incident room
is cluttered and noisy, full of functional furniture that
must have been fashionable in the nineties. Detectives
in plainclothes are answering phones and tapping on
keyboards. How is that going to find Ben? I want to ask.
They should be knocking on doors and shaking trees.

Cyrus Haven is already seated at the table in the
conference room, dressed in his familiar loose-fitting

jeans and a buttoned-up shirt. Immediately I relax. I don't know why, but he makes me feel as though I can get through this.

MacAteer takes a stick of gum from his pocket. Unwrapping the foil, he folds the strip onto his tongue and chews noisily, sucking out the flavor.

"I've asked Dr. Haven to run through a new strategy."

"Why do we need a new strategy?" asks Jack, who seems to be spoiling for an argument.

MacAteer pushes back. "Because the current one hasn't worked."

"Circumstances have changed," adds Cyrus, whose voice exudes calm. "When Ben was first taken we adopted a strategy of appealing directly to the woman who took him. We wanted to show her the enormity of the anguish she had caused to you—and encourage her to give him up willingly. We have moved past that now. The longer she has had Ben, the stronger the bond will be between them. If we haven't reached her by now, one of two things must have happened. Either she's stopped listening, or she's decided not to respond."

"What you're saying is that she doesn't care," I say.

"I'm saying that you don't figure in her calculations. All she cares about is Ben."

I feel sick.

"That's why I want to change the focus of our message. Instead of appealing directly to the abductor, we talk to those around her—friends, family, and neighbors. We give them reasons why they should ask questions. We help them see that whoever has Ben is misguided and has lost sight of what is right and wrong. And if they truly want to help this person, they should get in touch with us."

"You think someone will turn her in," says Jack.

"If we give them the right reasons."

"Why haven't they done it already?" I ask.

"They could be frightened or confused or unwilling to get involved. We can change that by taking a very soft tone and avoiding confrontation. We must help the public understand that whoever took Ben is not being viewed as a criminal who must be caught and punished. She is a victim. Something dreadful has happened that prompted her into making some terrible decisions. Perhaps she lost a baby or was denied one. She has suffered enormously, which is why we have to show her compassion and understanding. We must urge others to do the same and intervene on our behalf and hers."

Jack grunts. "So it's not enough that we've lost a child—she's the one who deserves sympathy?"

"If we find her, we find Ben," says MacAteer, who seems to be tiring of Jack's petulance.

Cyrus continues. "Right now the media is controlling the message—finding new people to interview every day, reporting rumors instead of facts. They are setting the agenda—not us. We have to change that. From now on we speak with one voice and set clearly defined goals. And the first step is to have a single person associated with the message."

"OK, I'm up for that," says MacAteer.

"No, not you," says Cyrus. "You're a police officer. You represent the punitive side of this equation."

"Who then?"

Cyrus looks at me.

"No, no, not me." I'm shaking my head, not because I'm shy but because I'm scared. "What if I make a mistake? I could push her over the edge."

"I've written you a script. All you have to do is read it out."

"Why can't Jack do it? He's used to being on camera."

"It's more powerful coming from you."

Jack touches my arm. "You can do this. I can help you."

Flash guns strobe and shutters click and TV lights blast whiteness against my downcast face. It feels more like a show trial than a media conference. The TV cameras are arranged in a crescent shape around the front of a stage that has a long table and chairs. The press photographers are on either side, yelling our names, wanting us to turn this way and that.

I blink into the lights with watery eyes, lowering my head to make sure I don't trip up the stairs. Jack is next to me, yet I have a strange hollow feeling that I'm alone, a sensation of missing someone who is right beside me. I want to reach out and take his hand, but something stops me.

MacAteer pulls out a chair. I tuck my dress under my thighs and sit upright, knees together, staring straight ahead while the flash guns create white dots behind my eyelids.

Once the noise has died down, it is my turn. I try to remember what Jack told me—to look directly into the cameras and forget how many people are watching. My first few words are shaky, but they grow more solid as I continue.

"This has been a very emotional nine days and we have been overwhelmed by the messages of support, the letters of sympathy, and the prayers that have been offered by so many people." I pause, looking up from the page. "It seems as though Ben has been adopted by the whole country and belongs to all of us, which is enormously gratifying.

"Saying that, I am going to speak very personally

today because I don't think anyone can begin to imagine what Ben means to us. We are a strong family, but we're not whole at the moment. We have a little boy and girl at home who haven't met their brother yet. They're heartbroken and we can't explain to them what has happened. I can't explain it to myself.

"I know that somebody out there must know where Ben is. Maybe you don't realize, or you're unsure, or you're frightened. You might suspect someone you love, which is why it's so hard to come forward. I understand loyalty and love. I know the strength of families."

I promised myself I wouldn't cry, but I can feel the tears hovering at the edges of my eyelids. I steel myself, remembering Dr. Haven's words: *The kidnapper might have stopped watching, but her friends and family will hear you.* I picture them now.

"If you do have suspicions, you are not helping anyone by remaining silent. Come forward. Call. Leave a message. At the very least, let us know that Ben is safe. That's all I want—some sign that he's OK."

The last words get stuck in my throat and come out in a whisper. Jack puts his arm around me. I lean my head into his neck and dissolve into his embrace.

The reporters begin yelling questions. One shouts loudest.

"Why aren't you DNA-testing every baby born around that time?"

MacAteer has taken the microphone.

"More than two thousand babies are born every day in Britain. We couldn't force parents to give us DNA samples. And even if we could, the cost would run to millions of pounds."

Someone else yells, "Have any of the alleged sightings been confirmed?"

"We continue to follow up hundreds of leads."

Another hand goes up. "Why haven't you released more of the CCTV footage from the hospital?"

"The footage is of such poor quality that we believe it could hamper the investigation by muddying the waters and making our task even harder."

"How?"

"The only person likely to recognize the kidnapper from the footage is the kidnapper herself. Rather than help anyone identify her, the footage could make her fearful and agitated. We are not here to punish anyone. Whoever took Ben Shaughnessy needs help and support. We can offer that. We can get her treatment. We can provide counseling."

AGATHA

"Turn the TV off," I say.

Hayden looks at me, surprised. "Aren't you interested?"

"No."

"Why not?"

"It makes me too sad."

It's true, but I can't explain it to Hayden. I know what it's like to lose a baby. I have felt what Meg is feeling, but she has Jack and Lachlan and Lucy. She should be thinking about them.

Hayden mutes the sound and picks up the TV guide, flicking through the pages. "So who do *you* think took him?" he asks.

"Who?"

"Baby Ben."

I shrug, wanting to change the subject.

"I've changed my mind," he says.

"What do you mean?"

"I thought it was some rich person who wanted a baby, but now I think it's probably some nutter."

"What makes you think she's a nutter?"

"Stands to reason," he says. "You said it yourself—she likely couldn't have her own kid, or lost a baby, and it sent her a bit gaga."

"A lot of women lose babies."

"You know what I mean." He props his feet on the coffee table, which I hate. "They're making out she needs help, but if someone took our Rory I'd want to kill her. I'd track her down, get him back, and do it with my bare hands."

"You'd strangle her."

"Yeah. I'm trained, you know—hand-to-hand combat." He holds up his palms. "These are lethal weapons."

"You'd kill a defenseless woman?"

"If she took our baby, yeah."

He scratches at his crotch and examines a scab on his elbow. "She's not going to get away with it."

"Why not?"

"Someone's going to turn her in. Stands to reason. She comes home with a baby that she can't breast-feed or who wakes the neighbors with his crying. What happens when the baby gets sick or needs a jab? What happens when he starts school?"

"That's years from now."

He waves at me dismissively. "What about a National Insurance number, or a birth certificate, or a driver's license, or if he applies for a passport?"

"People will have forgotten by then."

"You sound like you want her to get away with it."

"No. I'm just saying that she might."

Hayden makes a scoffing sound and I wonder if he's talking like this to goad me or because he suspects. The creature slowly uncoils, slithering through my intestines, turning my bowels to mush.

He knows! He knows!

"Shhhhhh!"

He knows! He knows!

"Who are you shushing?" asks Hayden.

"No one."

I start making up a bottle for Rory. Hayden watches as I measure each spoonful of powdered formula and tip it into bottles of boiled water.

"I thought you were still expressing."

"This is just for backup."

"Why don't you let him suckle on you?"

"My nipples are still sore."

"When are they going to be better?"

"I don't know."

"That woman who stole the baby—what would she be doing?" he asks.

"What do you mean?"

"How would she be feeding Baby Ben?"

"Using baby formula, I suppose."

He knows! He knows!

"How do you think she got away with it?" he asks.

"I don't know."

"Maybe she faked a pregnancy—convinced everyone that she was having a baby," says Hayden.

"It's not likely though, is it? I mean—nine months of faking it."

He picks at the dirt beneath his fingernails. "I thought that's why the police came here."

"What do you mean?"

"Those two coppers—I thought they were looking at everyone who had a baby in the past two weeks."

"I had Rory before Ben was taken."

"Yeah, you're right," he says, sounding noncommittal.

He lights a cigarette and cracks open the sitting-room window, kneeling on the floor to blow smoke outside. I can still smell it. I want to tell him to go downstairs, but I don't say anything. Instead I wonder if the police are checking up on me. I haven't registered Rory's birth, but the law gives me a month. He doesn't need a birth certificate, so I can put it off for longer without anyone knowing.

"You should call that woman," says Hayden, who stubs the cigarette out on the window ledge.

"Who?"

"Baby Ben's mum—you should find out how she's doing."

"I don't want to bother her."

"But she's your mate." His face lights up. "Fuck!"

"What?"

He gets to his feet. "We should call the newspapers!"

"Why?"

"You could sell your story."

"I don't have a story."

"Sure you do. Your best friend has had her baby stolen. They'll love it—one new mother talking about another, her mate. The heartbreak. It could be worth a fortune—I mean, at least ten grand, maybe more."

"She's not my best friend."

"They don't know that."

"No!"

He's not listening. "You could do TV interviews. What's that show—"

"I'm not going on TV. Meg isn't that good a friend."

"But you said—"

"We did yoga together."

"You've been to her house."

"Once."

"Have you talked to her since it happened?"

"No. I sent her a message saying I was praying for her baby. I was thinking of sending a card, but I don't know if that's appropriate."

Hayden slumps on the sofa, angry that I won't agree.

"We could use that money."

"We're fine."

He spends the next fifteen minutes in a bad mood. Finally he says, "I bet they're making money out of this. They'll be suing the hospital and selling their story to the highest bidder. Can you imagine—the perfect couple, a TV star and his hot-looking wife and a stolen kid. They'll be milking this for all it's worth."

"They're not so perfect," I say.

"What does that mean?"

"Nothing. Forget it."

MEGHAN

Jack left the house hours ago without giving me a reason. I watched him from the upstairs window as he marched past reporters, ignoring their questions, and got into his car. He did the same thing yesterday, not coming home until after I'd gone to bed.

"What were you doing?" I asked him this morning.

"Walking," he said, making it seem like a stupid question.

I know that he's under pressure. With each passing day he looks more dazed, like a polar bear kept in captivity too long, rocking from side to side. He keeps asking why the police haven't found Ben. He knows I can't answer the question, but he asks it anyway because it improves on the silence between us.

We don't have a police officer in the house full-time anymore, but Lisa-Jayne or Annie visits every day, keeping us informed. It has been two days since the media conference and the public response has swamped the police hotline with thousands of calls, including dozens of fresh sightings, none of them confirmed. Amid the tsunami of new information are the time wasters, trolls, psychics, seers, and conspiracy theorists. I closed down my blog today because some of the messages were so toxic.

In the meantime, I go through the motions of motherhood. I make supper and turn down beds and kiss foreheads and sing lullabies. I hope someone is doing the same for Ben.

Cyrus says the woman who took him is probably childless, or has lost a baby, or is trying to hold a relationship together. I have known marriages like that. I'm pretty certain that two of my best friends had babies to make their boyfriends commit—men who were hovering on the threshold. Is that so wrong? Their marriages have lasted. They have more children and mortgages and all the trappings. If I had the courage to ask, I'm sure neither of those women would regret what they did to "close the deal."

The police call me at nine. A station sergeant at Fulham police station tells me Jack has been arrested for assault and trying to take a woman's baby.

"Oh my God! Is the woman all right?"

"She's fine," the sergeant says, "but she's insisting that we press charges. I did explain the situation, but couldn't dissuade her."

"Where's Jack?"

"We're holding him in one of the cells."

"Do I have to post bail?"

"That won't be necessary, but someone will have to come and pick him up."

"Can you put him in a cab?"

"I'd feel better if somebody came and collected him."

I hang up and wonder if I should call my parents, but I don't want them knowing about this. Waking Lachlan and Lucy, I put them in their dressing gowns and slippers.

"Where are we going?" asks Lucy.

"To get Daddy."

"Where is he?"

"He's been talking to the police."

The temperature has fallen and it's too cold for the reporters and photographers to be standing outside. Most are sitting in cars, occasionally running the engine to stay warm. Moving quickly, I have the kids buckled up in their seats before the assembled media can react.

"Is there any news?" one of them shouts as I reach the driver's door.

"No news."

"Do you think Baby Ben is still alive?"

I flinch and turn. "That's a horrible thing to say."

He's waiting for an answer. I slide into the driver's seat and shut the door, fumbling for my keys. More reporters are shouting questions. Ignoring them, I pull out and almost hit a TV cameraman, who leaps out of the way.

"Why did he ask if Ben was alive?" asks Lucy.

"He didn't say that."

"Could Ben be dead?"

"No."

"Who's dead?" asks Lachlan.

"Nobody."

I put on a storybook recording and open the window a crack, wanting the cold air to help me stay alert. I'm not supposed to be driving so soon after having a cesarean. Bloody Jack!

The station sergeant is lanky and slope-shouldered with scrubbing-brush hair. He lets us wait in his office, away from prying eyes, while Jack is brought up from the holding cells.

The police have managed to piece together his movements. He started off at the Kings Arms on Fulham Road drinking pints and whiskey chasers. From there he went to Duke on the Green and the White Horse. At some point he finished up at the Trafalgar on King's Road, where the publican refused to serve him after he abused a barman. Less than a block away, Jack confronted a woman who was walking her dog and pushing a baby in a pram. She screamed for help. Two men came to her aid. Jack threw a punch, but they wrestled him to the ground. After calling the police, the bystanders told the woman she couldn't leave until she verified her story, which made her even more upset.

"Where is she now?" I ask the sergeant.

"We sent her home."

"I want to apologize to her."

"Maybe it's best if you leave her alone."

Jack shuffles past the door, escorted by two constables. He has buttons missing from his shirt and a graze on his forehead that is weeping blood. I don't know what the stain is on his trousers. I hope it's not urine. He doesn't acknowledge us as he signs for his wallet and mobile phone.

Lucy and Lachlan are quiet as we walk to the car. Neither of them takes Jack's hand, as though sensing that he's wounded. I want to say something. I want to berate him for his miserable self-absorption and his self-pitying macho bullshit. At the same time, I picture him walking the streets, lost in his own madness.

We drive home in silence. Jack tucks in his shirt and combs his hair before we face the firing squad of cameras outside the house. Once inside, he goes upstairs and I hear the shower running. Meanwhile I put the children to bed and make myself a hot chocolate. I take it to the front room, curling my legs beneath me on the sofa, nursing the mug.

I hear the stairs creaking. Jack looks for me in the kitchen and the laundry room and eventually finds me sitting in the dark.

"What are you doing?"

"Thinking."

He sits on the floor and leans his head against my thigh. My hand hovers above his head but I cannot bring myself to stroke his hair.

"You have to forgive me, Megs," he whispers.

"There's nothing to forgive you for."

He sits up. "Stop. Stop. Please. You're breaking my heart. Look at me."

I can't.

"I know you blame me."

"I don't blame you."

"Yes you do." He lets out a muffled sob. "You think I didn't want another baby. And you think this was my fault, but it's not fair."

"I know."

"I miss him too."

"Yes."

I reach out and push back his fringe, running my fingers through his wet hair. His body shudders.

"I know it's not fair, but I don't know who else to blame," I say.

"I can't live like this, Megs. You can't keep pushing me away."

"I'm sorry."

"I want us to go back to the way we were."

"So do I."

His eyes are shining. "I keep wondering what we did to deserve this."

"Nobody *deserves* this."

"It's me," he says. "I have a bad smell about me. Even Simon isn't talking to me."

Every muscle tightens. "When did you see Simon?"

"I went round to his place today. He accused me of wallowing in self-pity. I told him he had no idea what it was like to be a father and to have a child go missing."

"What did he say?"

"He said I was talking out of my arse and he knew exactly how it felt. He said if I took better care of things at home, this might not have happened. I asked him what he meant and he said, 'Ask Megs.'"

"Me?"

"Yeah."

"I don't know what he's talking about."

"Did something happen? I mean, you and Simon used to get on, but now you don't want him in the house. Did he say something or do something? Did he touch you?"

"We've been through this."

"Because if he did—"

"He didn't touch me."

Jack sighs and presses his fingertips to the cut on his forehead. "I'm sorry about today."

"You should go to bed."

"I can't sleep."

"Take one of my pills."

He kisses me on the cheek and I hear him climb the stairs. Twenty minutes later, I follow him and find him snoring gently in our bed. I check that Lucy and Lachlan are also asleep before pulling on a warm jumper and lacing my sneakers.

Bundled up against the cold, I open the French doors and cross the back garden by torchlight. Dew glistens on the grass ahead of me. Reaching the shed, I use the trellis to pull myself up onto the wall and swing my legs over the side, dropping down into a pile of dead leaves and lawn clippings.

I'm not supposed to be climbing or lifting anything

heavy until my stitches have healed. The torch throws shadows on a fallen tree and I notice a small clearing with signs of previous occupation. There are empty cans of soft drink and chocolate wrappers. Maybe this is a teenage love nest, uncomfortable but well hidden.

I glance back at the darkened house. Anyone sitting on the log could look across our garden to the kitchen and dining areas and see shadows against the curtains upstairs.

Turning away, I negotiate an overgrown path through blackberry bushes until I reach the railway tracks and turn east towards Barnes station. At the nearest level crossing, I follow the footpath, hearing the rattle of distant trains.

On the South Circular I hail a passing cab and give the driver Simon's address. Twice on the journey, I almost ask him to turn back. I'm angry, which is not a good start.

We're here. The lights are on. I ring the doorbell and listen for the footsteps. Gina answers—Simon's girlfriend—I didn't expect . . .

"Megs! What are you doing here?"

"I need to speak to Simon."

"Of course. Come in. Your hands are freezing."

She takes my coat and yells up the stairs for Simon. The house is overheated and smells of curry.

"Do you want a glass of wine?" asks Gina. "The bottle is open. Or a cup of tea?"

"No."

"Have you eaten?"

"I'm fine."

"I'm so sorry about . . . everything. I wanted to call you, but I figured you were probably overwhelmed with calls and messages."

"I really need to speak to Simon."

"Oh, right, of course." She yells for him again.

Simon appears on the stairs, dressed in baggy jeans and a sweatshirt.

"Look who it is," says Gina.

"I need to talk to him alone," I say.

Gina's smile fades. "Of course, I'll . . . I'll just pop upstairs." She and Simon exchange a glance as they pass each other.

Remaining in the hallway, I look up the stairs and make sure she's gone. Simon follows me into the kitchen.

"What did you say to Jack?" I ask.

"Nothing."

"He knows something happened between us."

"He knows shit."

"I told you to leave us alone."

Simon matches my anger. "Is that why you sent the police around here—asking me questions?"

"What?"

"Two detectives came to see me. They wanted to know where I was when Ben was stolen. They asked me about my relationship with you. The word 'blackmail' was mentioned."

"Did you tell them anything?"

"No. What did you say about me?"

"Nothing."

"Bullshit!"

"I was angry. Something slipped out. I told them to forget what I said."

"Clearly they didn't get your instructions," he says sarcastically. "Thanks to you, I'm a suspect. They know about my priors—the drug possession and dealing. Gina has started asking questions. If any of this gets back to the network, I'll lose my job."

"It was a mistake. I'm sorry."

"That makes me feel much better."

"You promised not to tell Jack."

"That was before you dumped me in the shit. Now all bets are off."

"You can't do that."

"Why not? You don't care about me. I think Jack deserves to know who he married."

"No. Please. I'll do the DNA test as soon as we find Ben." Even as I utter the words, I want to take them back, but it's too late.

Simon cocks his head, looking at me dubiously. "What if he's mine?"

"I'll tell Jack. But if the test shows that you're not the father, I want you to leave us alone. This stops once and for all. Is that agreed?"

Simon nods, no longer jacked up and tense. His voice softens. "I'm sorry I accused you of arranging the kidnapping."

I don't want to forgive him. I want to be home in bed with Jack.

Simon moves closer. "Is there any news?"

"No."

"What can I do to help?"

"Nothing."

My body is shaking. Simon puts his arms around me and for the briefest moment I sink against him, accepting his embrace, enjoying the physical contact. I push him away. Hating myself. Hating him.

"Remember what I said."

AGATHA

Rory had a difficult night. He screamed for hours and wouldn't feed. I tried everything. I rocked, jiggled, soothed, and patted his back. I carried him in a sling, held him against my heart, and walked him up and down stairs. I tried white noise—the dishwasher, washing machine, running water, music videos, and the radio. He finally fell asleep at 3 a.m., curled up on my chest on the sofa.

I weighed him again this morning—stepping on and off the bathroom scale and calculating the difference between my weight when I hold him and when I don't. As far as I can tell, he's not growing. "Failure to thrive" is how they describe it on the Internet.

So far I've tried three different types of formula but Rory won't take more than thirty milliliters at a sitting, which he sometimes throws up. He has to start growing soon. He can't be like the others. My dearest babies have all died young. I tell myself there is a purity in that because only the young are completely innocent. My babies didn't have time to grow up and become adults; to be disappointed or disappoint others. They will always shine brightly and be forever good.

Emily was the last one. I lost her three years ago. Nicky and I were separated, but not yet divorced. I went to Brighton for a week, hoping to find companionship among the summer crowds, but I found no comfort. I exhaled loneliness. It followed me around like a raincloud or a smell.

On my last night—a Saturday—the pubs were full of drunken revelers listening to doof-doof music and smokers spilling onto the pavements. I bought a can of soft drink and sat on a bench on the pier, watching courting couples snog in the shadows or paddle at the water's edge. It had been a hot day and everybody seemed to be waiting for the mercury to fall.

I contemplated catching a late train back to London rather than spending another night in my cheap hotel. A young mother passed by pushing a pram. I don't know what made me follow her home. I didn't plan to steal her baby. I only wanted to look.

The woman lived in a garden flat on a quiet street with an alleyway at the back and a rear garage with a sign saying PLEASE KEEP ACCESS CLEAR. A small spiral staircase climbed to the back door. I waited and watched until the lights went off.

A net curtain billowed from a window that had been hinged open to catch the breeze. I reached inside, unhooked the latch, and lifted the window high enough to crawl through. The baby girl was sleeping in a Moses basket. She looked to be about three months old. A baby monitor blinked above her head. I turned it off. The red light died.

I picked her up and put her in a pillowcase and carried her out the window like a burglar stealing silverware from a country house. By the time anyone knew Emily was missing I was back in London. Nicky had moved out of the house and we had plans to sell, but in the meantime I had the place to myself.

Emily lived for twelve days. It was my fault. She fell asleep while I was feeding her and I put her straight into her crib, laying her on her back, when I should have kept her upright on my shoulder. If I had burped her properly she wouldn't have vomited and aspirated milk into her lungs.

I woke at five and found her. She wasn't breathing. Her skin was blue. The vomit had dried on her cheek and on the back of her head. I washed her little body and wrapped it in a sheet and took it to my special place. I laid her to rest alongside Chloe and Lizzie, the ones who never grew up—forever innocent and untainted. Set free.

It's still early when I put Rory in his pram and push him through the streets, hoping the fresh air might make him hungry. I catch a bus to Hammersmith and another along Kensington High Street as far as the Tube station.

I have to wait until nine thirty before a young librarian opens the doors of Kensington Central Library. By then the queue consists mainly of homeless people who are looking for somewhere warm to spend a few hours.

"If you fall asleep I'm kicking you out," says the librarian. "This is a library, not a shelter."

Sitting at a computer, I create a username and password before beginning a search. Rory watches me from his pram. Periodically, I pause and stroke his forehead, explaining what I'm doing.

I type in a search for breast milk and come across dozens of classified ads:

Healthy Mother Ready to Sell Extra Milk ASAP
Breast Milk for Sale, Excess Amounts (no drugs
    or alcohol)

> High Quality breast milk London SW1—organic
> diet only!

At the same time there are government warnings
about sourcing breast milk from the Internet, saying it
could be tainted or diseased. I wonder if they'd ask for
identification. Would they care?

I contemplate sending an email, but wonder if the
police might be monitoring sites like these looking for
me. I can't take the risk.

Deleting the search, I clear the browser history and
take Rory across the road to the pharmacy, where I look
at treatments for colic and brands of baby formula that
I haven't yet tried.

Hayden is waiting for me when I get home. Rory
has fallen asleep. "I left the pram downstairs," I say as I
put him in his cot. "I picked up a few things for supper.
Can you pop the groceries in the kitchen?"

Hayden hasn't moved. I smell cigarette smoke. He
promised not to do that.

I begin putting groceries away, sorting out the cold
items for the fridge. Opening cupboards. Hayden is
staring at me from the doorway. Something is wrong.

"Your mother phoned," he says.

I don't respond.

"When did she go back to Spain?"

"I'm not sure," I say, continuing to unpack. Hayden
picks up a can of tomatoes and seems to weigh it in his
fist.

"She was pretty fucking surprised when I mentioned Rory. Do you know what she said?"

I don't answer.

"She said, 'Who's Rory?' And I said, 'Your grandson.' And she laughed like I was joking. 'But you were
at the birth,' I said. And she laughed again."

Still I say nothing. Hayden slams the can of tomatoes down on the counter, which sounds like a gunshot in the small kitchen. He holds it up again. I hear Rory start to cry.

"I can explain."

"OK."

"First tell me what you told her."

"I told her about Rory. I said you had him in Leeds—a home birth. Is any of that true?"

"Yes."

"Who was with you?"

"A midwife." I fill the electric kettle. "Do you want a cup of tea?"

"Fuck the tea! Why did you lie to me?"

"I don't get on with my mother. I knew she'd try to take control. She belittles me. She bosses me around. She manages to poison everything good in my life."

"Why go to Leeds? You could have stayed in London and had the baby. I could have been there."

"I got scared."

"Scared of what?"

"I've never told you this before—but Nicky and I lost a baby. I was five months pregnant. She died inside me. I was terrified it might happen again. That's why I didn't want you there. I didn't want anyone with me—not friends or family."

Hayden doesn't seem to know how to react. He wants to believe me, I can see that, but his faith has been shaken. He asks about the miscarriage. He wants the details—who, where, what, and why? I find myself telling him the truth.

"I saw what it did to Nicky—losing a baby. That's why we divorced. The marriage couldn't survive the heartbreak." Rory is still crying, growing more and more distressed. "That's why Nicky contacted me. He heard about me having a baby. He was happy for me, but also a little sad."

"Is that why he topped himself?" asks Hayden.

"I don't know. Maybe."

I move towards the bedroom, wanting to comfort Rory. Hayden grabs me by the wrist, twisting it painfully.

"Why lie to your mother?"

"I didn't lie to her. I just didn't tell her. It's none of her business."

"Why do you hate her so much?"

"You wouldn't understand."

"Try me."

"She's crazy. Manipulative. Cunning. She has a thousand clichés in her head and when she opens her mouth it's like they're all trying to escape . . . I bet she said she loved me."

Hayden nods.

"Did she say I broke her heart?"

"Yeah."

"Was she drunk?"

"She sounded sober."

"She's very good at hiding it."

I peel Hayden's fingers away from my wrist. He hasn't finished. "What else have you lied about?"

"Nothing."

"You lied to Jules, to me, to my family . . . It's not right. You made me feel like an idiot."

"I'm sorry." I put my head against his chest.

He pushes me away, holding me at arm's length. "Your mother didn't even know about me."

"Because I don't talk to her."

Hayden doesn't answer. Stepping around him, I fetch Rory from the bedroom, jiggling him in my arms until he stops crying.

Hayden hasn't given up. "I want to know the name of the midwife—the one who delivered the baby."

"Why?"

"I want to talk to her."

"What can she tell you?"

"The truth."

"I'm telling the truth. Why would I lie about her?"

"Call her."

He knows! He knows!

I pick up my handbag and take out my mobile, flicking through the contacts list. Hayden waits.

"I can't find it."

"You don't have her number?"

"I do. I'm trying to think . . . My phone was dead, remember? I have her number written down somewhere."

"What about paperwork? There must be something."

"Of course, lots of paperwork," I say, getting flustered. "I can't remember where I put it."

He knows! He knows!

"So you have no phone number and no paperwork—this is bollocks!" He grabs his jacket.

"Where are you going?"

"I'm taking Rory for a walk."

"No!" I say it too urgently. "I mean, where?"

"Maybe we'll go to the zoo. He's never been to the zoo."

"Can I come?"

"No!"

"Why?"

"I don't want to see you for a while."

I make up a bottle for Rory and help Hayden get him ready. I'm still reaching for excuses, not wanting them to go. I tell him that I'm desperately in love with him and that I've never seen a father as wonderful as he is and that I couldn't do this without him. I say that I would marry him tomorrow at Fulham Registry Office and I would go anywhere in the world with him, as long as we were together.

Hayden says nothing. He's not listening to promises or platitudes. He doesn't love me anymore.

"Don't tell anyone," I say, pleading with him.

"Tell anyone what?"

"I mean, don't tell your parents about my mother. They might not understand."

"You're right," he replies. "I *don't* understand. You tell me lies and you don't do anything to help us."

"What does that mean?"

"You could have sold your story to the papers—the one about knowing Baby Ben's mum. We could have made some money."

"I don't want to talk to reporters."

"Mrs. Shaughnessy is doing plenty of talking. She's always on the news, crying for the cameras. I'm sick of hearing her voice."

"Don't say that."

"Why?"

"You don't know her."

"I know her type—perfect hair, perfect teeth, perfect marriage—and now the perfect sob story. She gives me the shits."

Hayden used to feel sorry for Meg, but now he's attacking her because he's angry with me, or testing me. I have to show him I can be honest. I have to win back his trust.

"They're not perfect," I whisper.

"You said that before, but what does it mean?"

"Jack Shaughnessy had an affair."

"How do you know?"

"I saw him with another woman. He was buying condoms at the supermarket. She was parked outside. He jumped in her car. They were kissing."

"Who was she?"

"An estate agent. She sold them their house."

Hayden whistles through his teeth. "Dirty bugger!"

I shouldn't have told him. I should have kept my mouth shut.

"Please don't tell anyone," I say. "It ended weeks ago . . ."

Hayden doesn't answer. He carries Rory down the stairs and straps him in the pram, tilting it backwards as he lowers it down each step to the street.

I watch them from the front window, resting my forehead against the glass, following their progress until they reach the corner and disappear. I want to go after them. I want to snatch Rory back.

I know that Hayden wants to believe me because he loves our little boy, but I'm giving him too many reasons to doubt. He hasn't accused me of faking my pregnancy and stealing a baby, but has it crossed his mind? No. He doesn't think I'm clever enough to do something like that.

But from now on he's going to watch me more closely and check up on everything I've said and done. Even if I forge the paperwork for the birth, I can't conjure a midwife out of thin air.

Why couldn't my mother leave me alone?

MEGHAN

The police arrive before 6 a.m., in a convoy of cars blocking the street outside. Doors open in unison and officers march past the reporters and cameramen. Jack answers the doorbell still in his pajamas. DCS Mac-Ateer hands him a search warrant.

"Who is it?" I ask from the top of the stairs.

Officers are moving past Jack. They're dressed in overalls and wearing latex gloves.

"We have authority to search this property," Mac-Ateer announces, no longer sounding avuncular or sympathetic. "I will allow you to stay here so long as you don't interfere. Police personnel will accompany you while you get dressed. I suggest you then assemble in the kitchen."

"What about the children?"

"Them too."

Jack keeps asking what's happened. Do they have information? Is there some reason why they're here? He looks at me, hoping for an explanation. I shake my head. Lisa-Jayne accompanies me to the bedroom and watches me dress. I move towards the bathroom. She follows.

"Can't I do that alone?"

She shakes her head.

"Why are you here?"

She doesn't answer.

For the next two hours we sit in the kitchen as police search everywhere from the attic to the cupboard below the stairs. Our computers and iPads are confiscated. We're told we'll get them back once the hard drives have been copied. Belongings are picked up, opened, and examined; books are feathered, furniture is moved, and carpets are peeled back to reveal bare floors. I wonder what they imagine they might find: Hidden rooms? Secret stashes? This is crazy.

Our questions are ignored. Officers are polite, but adamant that we don't interfere. First names are no longer used.

Jack is incensed. "What have we done? Where is the justification? They're trying to deflect attention. They can't find Ben, so now they're going to blame us."

"That's ridiculous. Why would they think that?"

"I don't know—but look at what they're doing."

He confronts MacAteer, demanding an explanation, refusing to be fobbed off. The detective unbuttons his suit jacket and pushes his hand into his pocket.

"We have received information."

"What information?"

"Someone called the hotline."

"Who? What did they say?"

"On the night Ben went missing, you left the hospital before the police arrived."

"I was looking for Ben."

"You were missing for almost two hours."

"I knew what the nurse looked like. I thought she might be nearby . . . I've told you this already."

"Did you come back here?"

"What? No!"

"You were seen carrying something from the house that night."

"That's ridiculous. Whoever told you that is lying."

"By leaving the scene, you compromised the investigation. You weren't available to give us a detailed description. There could have been fibers on your clothes. DNA trace material."

"I didn't think."

"Where did you go?"

"I told you."

I'm looking at Jack, as though I'm part of the interrogation, suddenly wanting the same answers. Jack meets my gaze, his eyes pleading with me, no longer angry. I see another emotion there: fear.

"Do we need a lawyer?" he asks.

"That's completely up to you, Mr. Shaughnessy."

DCS MacAteer turns to me. "I wish to speak to you in private."

I want to tell him that Jack and I have no secrets from each other, but that's not true . . . not since I slept with Simon. Not after this.

Leaving Jack with the children, I follow the detective to the sitting room. He closes the door. I notice signs of the search. Officers have tried to put everything back in place, but it's not the same. The photographs on the mantelpiece are in the wrong order and the DVDs are mixed up. It's like a robbery where nothing has been taken except my peace of mind.

MacAteer motions to the sofa. I choose to remain standing. The room feels too small for the both of us.

"I'm going to ask you several questions," he says. "I would appreciate you answering them truthfully."

"When have I not been truthful?" I say, trying to sound annoyed.

"Did your husband want this baby?"

I hesitate a moment too long.

"Don't treat me like an idiot, Mrs. Shaughnessy. I have men and women working around the clock on this case. Thousands of hours of overtime. Resources. Expertise. Answer the question."

"He wasn't happy at first, but he came round," I say.

"Has he ever hurt you or your children?"

"Never."

"Your daughter was taken to hospital at the age of two with a cut above her eye."

"She tripped over Jack's legs and hit her head against the window seat."

"Does he view online pornography?"

"No. Never. I mean, I don't think so."

"We're going to search his computer. We're going to search yours as well."

"I have nothing to hide."

Even as I utter the statement I realize how trite it sounds—like a line from a crappy movie. A great actress could deliver a line of dialogue like that, but I'm not a great actress and I'm a worse liar.

MacAteer is getting to the point. "Two days ago you left the house at ten o'clock at night."

"I went for a walk."

"Why?"

"I needed some time alone."

"Where did you go?"

"Nowhere in particular."

"How did you get out of the house?"

I waver, wondering how much he knows. "I climbed over the back fence and walked along a railway line."

"You crawled through undergrowth?"

"I didn't crawl."

"You've recently had a baby. You're supposed to be resting. Yet you snuck out of the house, climbed a wall, and illegally trespassed on a railway line."

"I didn't sneak. I would have gone out the front door, but in case you hadn't noticed, there are reporters outside."

MacAteer isn't buying any of this. "You had a visitor when you came home from hospital. Simon Kidd. Who is he?"

"An old family friend. He was best man at our wedding and is also Lucy's godfather. He works with Jack."

"You were upset afterwards."

"It was nothing."

"You told PC Lisa-Jayne Soussa that Simon Kidd was trying to blackmail you."

"It was a misunderstanding."

MacAteer gives me a fierce, tight-lipped smile.

"Mrs. Shaughnessy, have you or anyone close to you been contacted privately by any third party claiming to have your baby?"

"No."

"Because if you have been contacted and you were considering paying a ransom to a blackmailer, you would be breaking the law."

"I understand. I promise you, we haven't been contacted by anyone." An odd feeling of relief floods through me. I'm going to get away with this.

MacAteer picks up his hat and walks to the door. He has one hand on the doorknob.

"Just one more thing—is Ben your husband's baby?"

"I beg your pardon?"

"Is he Jack's?"

There is a momentary pause—a gap in time—that might only last a heartbeat, but it feels much longer.

"How dare you suggest . . . I love my husband." My anger sounds forced and absurdly formal. "That's an outrageous thing to say."

MacAteer nods but doesn't apologize. He places his

hat upon his head and tilts the brim as a tiny gesture of farewell.

"Take care, Mrs. Shaughnessy. The value of a secret depends upon whom you're trying to keep it from. You may think it's worth a lot. I may think it's worthless. Someone always has to pay."

AGATHA

I always knew there was a risk that my mother would find out about Rory. I hoped it would be months from now, when people had forgotten details of his birth and he was fully established in my life.

Now she keeps phoning and leaving messages, asking when she can come and see her grandson. I've ignored every call, letting them go to voicemail, but I can't keep putting her off.

I punch out her number and listen to the ringtone.

She picks up. "Agatha? I've been sitting here, hoping you'd call."

Her voice has a quivering frailty, which I don't remember. An affectation, maybe, trying to gain sympathy.

"A baby," she says excitedly. "I couldn't believe it when Jayden told me."

"Hayden," I say.

"Oh, sorry, Hayden, yes."

"We're engaged."

"That's wonderful. I'm happy for you. How is Rory?"

"Fine."

"Is he a good baby?"

"Yes."

"Are you breast-feeding him? They say it's the best thing. I know I didn't breast-feed you, but we didn't know as much about breast-feeding back then."

"And you wanted to keep your figure?" I mutter.

"What's that, dear?"

"Nothing. Why did you call me?"

"A mother doesn't need a reason to call her daughter."

"How did you get my number?"

"I called your old temp agency."

"So what do you want?"

"I want to come and visit . . . to see my grandson."

"No."

"Please, Aggy, don't be cruel. I know I made mistakes. I know I wasn't always there for you, but I've said I'm sorry, and those things happened a long time ago."

"Why did you call me yesterday?"

"What?"

"You spoke to Hayden. You must have had a reason to call."

"Yes, I did. It was about Nicky. It was in the papers. I get them delivered from London. A story, only a few paragraphs, saying he fell under a train. You did know, didn't you? About Nicky, I mean."

"Yes."

"I wasn't sure. They think it might be suicide."

There is a pause.

"I always liked Nicky," she says.

"You barely knew him."

"He used to call me every week when you were married."

"Liar!"

"He did! I promise. Even after your divorce, he sent Christmas letters and would telephone on my birthday, which is more than you ever did."

"He didn't know you like I did."

She ignores the comment. "Poor Nicky. Such a nice man. It must be horrible for his poor wife."

I don't respond.

"You and Nicky were really good together. It's a shame you couldn't have children. I know you tried."

Another silence, this one painfully long.

"How did you manage to get pregnant?" she asks.

"Normal way."

"Nicky always said . . . I mean . . . I thought . . ." She doesn't finish the statement. The pauses are making her stutter.

"Well, if that's all," I say, preparing to hang up.

"But you haven't said."

"Said what?"

"When I can come and see Rory."

"Never."

"Please, Aggy." Her voice is breaking. "I have no one else. I want to be a grandmother. I want to make amends."

"It's too late."

"Don't be cruel."

I listen to her hiccuping sobs and try to hang up, but the phone is still in my hand. "When are you back in Leeds?" I ask.

"At the end of March."

"Maybe you can see him then."

MEGHAN

The police are here again today. This time they're scouring the trees and bushes behind the garden wall, next to the railway tracks, because I told them about the hiding place I discovered when I snuck out to visit Simon.

Initially, DCS MacAteer dismissed the idea of someone watching the house, but Cyrus Haven convinced him to take it seriously. Now forensic technicians in white overalls are hammering stakes into the damp earth to set up a grid.

I can hear Jack coming before he reaches the kitchen. Ever since the police searched the house and seized his computer, he has gone quiet. At first he railed against their incompetence, accusing them of trying to shift the blame or "covering their arses." At the same time, he's trying to figure out which of our neighbors called the police and claimed to have seen him carrying something out of the house on the night Ben was taken. His suspicions have settled on the Pringles, who live two doors away and have a teenage son who was arrested for vandalism last year after Jack caught him damaging cars in the street.

I'm standing at the French doors watching the technicians at work beyond the garden. Jack appears at my shoulder.

"Did the police ask you about Simon?"

"Yes."

"Why do you think they wanted to know so much about him? Surely he can't be a suspect?"

"I don't know."

Jack pauses and chews at the inside of his cheek. "The other night—when I was arrested—you went to see Simon."

It is not a question.

"Yes."

"Why?"

"I was worried about you."

"Me?"

"You'd just been arrested. You accosted some poor woman. You were drunk. I thought you were losing it."

"Why visit Simon?"

"You told me that you'd been to see him earlier that day and he made some reference to me."

Jack presses his thumb against his wrist as though taking his pulse. He lifts it and watches the white thumb-shaped outline slowly turn pink. I feel him framing another question.

"Why did you climb the back wall?"

"Because of the reporters."

"You could have called Simon."

"I wanted to see him face-to-face."

Jack looks past me into the garden. Some of the technicians are on their hands and knees, scraping, sampling, and dusting—putting food wrappers and soft-drink cans into plastic bags.

"At least you've given them something to do," he says.

The front doorbell chimes. I answer it. Our local priest, Father George, has come to visit. Since the kidnapping, he has dropped around every few days, sitting in the front room, drinking tea, and offering me sympathy and a shoulder to cry upon. I haven't used the shoulder, but I appreciate the sentiments.

Jack makes an excuse and flees, leaving me to handle our spiritual well-being. Father George is in his sixties with one of those deep, sonorous voices that you normally hear on motivational tapes or late-night radio. His visits are beginning to irritate me because he treats me like I'm Lucy's age and I've lost a pet rather than my baby. At the same time, I feel guilty every time I see him.

When we set our hearts on sending Lucy to St. Osmund's Catholic Primary School, we knew it wouldn't be easy. There were usually ninety applications for only thirty positions in the reception class. Part of the application was a declaration from the parish priest saying that Lucy had been baptized and that we attended church regularly. For six months we trooped off to mass every Sunday, making sure to say hello to Father George as he greeted people at the doors. It seemed quite exotic for a while, dabbling in the religiosity of it all, the supernatural and otherworldliness, to pray and praise and give thanks. Of course, once Father George signed the form and Lucy was accepted, our weekly visits to mass began to dwindle.

I apologized to Father George for having used him.

"You didn't use me." He laughed.

"We tricked you."

"As did most of the other parents."

"Is that frustrating?"

He smiled wryly. "They're good people with busy lives. I'm sure that one day they'll return to the fold—just as you will."

Father George and the parish council have organized a candlelight vigil for tomorrow evening, which I've insisted be nondenominational. I haven't agreed to attend, but I know it's expected. As if reading my thoughts, Father George reaches across from his armchair and clasps my hands.

"We want you to know that you're not alone. We're all praying, you know. I daresay the whole country."

"Not everyone," I reply, anger flushing into my eyes. "The person who took Ben isn't praying for his safe return."

He smiles serenely, unshaken by my animosity, which makes me want to rage, *What sort of God does this? What sort of God creates a world where there's so much misery and injustice and pain?*

I say nothing. Father George opens his Bible. "Would you like to pray with me now?"

"I'm not very good at praying."

"I can start."

I sit quietly as he makes the sign of the cross and conducts a one-sided conversation with God, asking Him for strength and guidance and love on my behalf.

"Help Meghan not to blame herself or those close to her," he says. "And help her never to give up hope. You know what it's like to lose a son. You sent Jesus down to earth and he paid the ultimate price for our sins. Please, help Meghan overcome this test with your love and guidance; help her heart to heal."

After Father George has gone, I discover that he's left the Bible on the coffee table. Pages have been marked with red ribbons. Opening to one of the passages, I read a few lines about God healing the brokenhearted and binding up their wounds, but I see nothing about finding missing children.

Saint Anthony is the patron saint of lost things. Does that include children? Probably. There's a saint for most things—sailors, scholars, brides, and prostitutes. There's even a patron saint of drug dealers—Jesús Malverde. I saw that once on an episode of *Breaking Bad*.

AGATHA

Rory vomited both feeds last night. I had to change his sheets twice and dress him in clean clothes. This morning I weighed him again and there's been no change in the past week. I know bathroom scales aren't very accurate, but I don't need a machine to tell me that he's sickly and struggling.

There are no gassy smiles or happy sighs, yet when he looks at me with his enormous eyes, he seems to be saying, *Please, Mummy, don't give up on me. I'll get better*.

He's asleep now, lying next to Hayden on the bed.

Turning on the TV with muted sound, I catch a glimpse of a reporter standing beside a railway line. The camera pans to the left and zooms between trees to reveal a familiar-looking house. Then it pulls back to show men and women in white overalls searching the undergrowth and shrubbery beside the tracks.

I press the volume button.

"Forensic teams have been out since early this morning, searching the back garden and surrounds, taking away samples and measuring footprints. Police aren't saying exactly what they're looking for, but through those trees and over that wall is the house belonging to Jack and Meghan Shaughnessy, the parents of Baby Ben."

I recognize my fallen tree . . . my clearing . . . my hiding place. What could I have left behind? There were some soft-drink cans and chocolate wrappers. A few times I peed when I couldn't hold my bladder any longer. They don't have my fingerprints on file, or my DNA.

You were seen.

Nobody saw me.

What about the neighbors?

I was careful.

They'll trace your phone.

There are hundreds of phones passing that place every day.

I turn off the TV and tell myself to relax. I have to stay calm and look after Rory. He needs all of my focus if I'm to make him healthy and strong.

It helps to stay busy. Two bags of rubbish need to go out. Hayden should have done it last night. I carry them to the ground floor and down the front steps, turning towards the bins. Two people step from a car. One of them is a woman, squeezed into high-waisted slacks and a matching navy jacket. The man is younger, but pretending to be world-weary and experienced.

"Is your name Agatha?" the woman asks in a neutral way, neither friendly nor hostile.

I nod, aware of the door behind me.

"We're detectives investigating the disappearance of Ben Shaughnessy."

A voice fills my head, telling me to drop the rubbish and run, lock the doors.

"We were hoping we could have a word?"

Do they have a warrant?

"What's this about?"

"I believe you are acquainted with Meghan Shaughnessy."

"We're friends."

Ask for the warrant.

I force myself to move, carrying the bags to the bins and putting them inside. I wipe my hands on my jeans.

"Have you found Baby Ben?" I ask.

"Not yet."

"Poor Meg," I say, brushing a strand of hair from my eyes. "She must be devastated. I sent her a message, but it's hard to know what to say."

"You've just had a baby yourself," says the man.

"That's right."

"It's cold out here. Maybe you could invite us inside."

"I don't really want to wake the baby."

"We'll be very quiet."

I lead them up to the flat, where I've left the door propped open. "Can I get you a cup of tea or coffee? I only have instant."

"We're fine," says the woman detective, who gives me her card. I study it for a moment, buying time, reading her name out loud. "Detective Sergeant Alison McGuire."

"And this is Detective Constable Paulson," she says, studying the array of "best wishes" cards on the mantelpiece. "You had a boy."

"Yes."

"What's his name?"

"Rory."

The woman has thick eyebrows and olive skin and might possibly look attractive if she let her hair down and smiled more. She takes a seat. Hayden chooses that moment to make an appearance. He's wearing only boxer shorts, scratching at the dark strip of hair beneath his navel. He blinks at the detectives but doesn't act surprised. Crossing to the kitchen, he turns on the tap and fills a large glass of water, drinking it too quickly so that droplets fall onto his chest. He wipes his mouth.

"We're investigating the disappearance of Baby Ben," explains DC Paulson.

Hayden sits on the edge of my armchair. Beads of water are clinging to his chest hair.

"You might want to put some clothes on," says the DS.

"Last I checked, this was my place," replies Hayden.

She nods as though accepting his ground rules. "Your wife was telling us about your new baby."

"We're not married."

"I see."

Hayden doesn't seem to like the fact that she's a woman.

"We're engaged," I say.

"Are you Rory's father?"

"Yeah," replies Hayden.

DC Paulson has taken out a notebook. Pencil poised.

"When was your baby born?" he asks.

"Almost three weeks ago." I give him the exact date.

"Where did you have him?"

"In Leeds—that's where I'm from. My mother lives there."

I'm volunteering too much information. I should wait for their questions.

DS McGuire toys with a loose thread on the cuff of her jacket. A man would tear or bite it off. A woman will wait for scissors.

"I've spent some time up north," she says. "What hospital did you choose?"

"I had a home birth. I wanted familiar surroundings."

A trick question, deflected easily, but now she's unsure how to follow up.

Hayden has put his hand on my shoulder, as though offering support.

"Were you present at the birth?" she asks him.

"No, I just missed it," Hayden explains. "I'm Royal Navy. I flew in from Joburg. Arrived a day too late."

"I went into labor early," I say.

"So who was with you for the birth?"

"A midwife," I say, trying to sound calm.

"And your mother," adds Hayden, lying for me.

Why would he do that?

"I emailed photographs to Meghan," I say. "She was so excited for me. Now I feel guilty."

"Guilty?"

"Given what happened. There I was, celebrating and feeling so clever, and two days later Meg had her baby stolen."

"You couldn't have known," says Hayden.

"I know, but still . . ."

"Do you have photographs of the birth?" asks DC Paulson.

"Of course." I pick up my phone and scroll through the pictures until I find the ones that I took upstairs in Leo's bedroom. "I didn't take many. My mother isn't much of a photographer."

I hand him the phone. He passes it to his colleague.

"How long have you known Mrs. Shaughnessy?" asks DS McGuire.

"Not that long. We do yoga together. I used to see her when I worked at the supermarket in Barnes. She gave me some baby clothes."

Again, I'm talking too much. The detective glances slowly around the room, as though noting the general shabbiness and cheapness of my furniture.

"When did you see her last?"

"A few weeks ago—before I went up to Leeds."

"You knew she was having her baby on December seventh?"

"Yes, she told me."

"Have you met her husband, Jack?"

"No. I've seen him on TV. He's a sports reporter."

Stop talking, Agatha!

DS McGuire returns my phone. "When you were at yoga classes, did you ever notice anyone hanging around, or asking questions? Someone who might have taken a special interest in the fact that Mrs. Shaughnessy was pregnant?"

"Special interest?"

"More than usual."

I think about this. Begin a sentence. Stop. Shake my head.

"What is it?" asks DC Paulson.

"It's probably nothing," I say.

"Let us decide."

"Well, there was this one woman . . . Meg and I were having coffee in Barnes. As I was leaving, she came up to me and asked where I was having my baby."

"Did she talk to Mrs. Shaughnessy?"

"I'm not sure."

"What did this woman look like?"

"My height, dark hair, heavyset, but not fat," I say, pausing to concentrate. "She looked like she'd just had her hair done—maybe at one of the local hairdressers."

"How do you know that?"

"You can tell when it's been cut and blow-dried."

"How old was she?"

"Late thirties or early forties."

"Was she pregnant?"

"Not obviously. I guess her clothes were baggy."

A pencil scratches on the page.

"Why does it matter whether she was pregnant?" I ask.

"We think whoever took Ben might have faked a pregnancy to hide their crime."

"Really?"

"You don't sound convinced."

"Is that even possible? What about all the scans and tests? Surely somebody would find out."

DS McGuire wants to get back to talking about the woman. "Had you ever seen this particular woman before?"

"No."

She opens a folder and takes out an identikit picture from the hospital. "Could this be her?"

"It's hard to tell."

The next image is a still photograph from the CCTV cameras at the hospital. I am being presented with a photograph of myself as a brunette with long hair. The grainy image shows the top of my head. A second image is from behind. *That uniform made me look huge.*

"It could be her," I say. "I can't be certain."

There is a squawk from the baby monitor resting on the kitchen bench. Rory is awake. He grumbles and lets out a louder cry.

"He's hungry," I say, getting to my feet. I cup my breasts. "I still can't get over how he does that—one little cry and my milk starts flowing."

Hayden has gone to get Rory. He emerges from the bedroom, holding him in the folds of a blanket. Rory is wide-awake, watching the detectives, neither of whom look particularly paternal or maternal.

"You're welcome to stay," I say, "but I'm getting my boobs out." The younger detective wants to be somewhere else. I walk them to the door.

"If you see Megs, tell her . . . tell her . . . I'm thinking of her. And if there's anything I can do to help . . ."

I wait on the landing, watching them leave, listening

to the creature. *What if they look for a record of Rory's birth? What if they call your mother? What if they look for the midwife?*

Hayden is sitting on the sofa, jiggling Rory in his arms. "They weren't very friendly."

"They were OK."

"I don't like cops."

"Why?"

He shrugs. "A lot of them have mini Hitler complexes, you know. They enjoy pushing people around."

I want to ask him why he lied for me, but I'm afraid of the answer. I'm hoping he's still on my side. Nobody could fake a pregnancy as well as I did. The police should ask Meghan. She'll tell them. She doesn't doubt me.

MEGHAN

Lachlan and Lucy have been bathed and dressed in their best clothes, hair washed and brushed, shoes polished. They're under instructions to stay clean while I get ready. I keep changing my mind about whether I want to go to the candlelight vigil, but Jack says we should thank people and acknowledge their support.

I have nothing to wear. I don't want to dress in maternity clothes and I can't fit into most of my pre-pregnancy dresses, apart from one clingy woolen number that makes me look lumpy.

Jack is polishing his shoes on the landing. I've told him not to do it there because he'll get bootblack on the carpet, but he never listens. I turn back and forth in front of the mirror, not liking anything about myself, but also not caring. I just want to get this over with.

Downstairs, I put on my coat and call the others. Lachlan runs down the hallway. His trouser cuffs are too short. I swear I took them down only a few days ago. I want to put a brick on his head to stop him growing.

Lucy looks pretty in a tartan dress with red tights and black patent leather shoes. She has matching red gloves to wear because it's cold outside.

"Are you ready?" asks Jack.

"I guess."

"We can do this."

I try to give him a smile.

The security lights trigger as we leave the house and reach the front gate. Two police officers are waiting to escort us to St. Osmund's, which is about half a mile from here. They offered to drive us, but we're going to walk in a kind of candlelight procession, collecting people as we pass. TV cameras and photographers are being kept behind barricades. The bright lights whiten every face and turn every breath into a pale fog.

Hooking my arm into Jack's, we each take a child's hand. Neighbors appear, holding lamps, torches, and candles flickering in paper cones. They nod as we pass and fall into step behind us as our procession wends its way through the narrow streets, across Barnes Green and along Church Road where it turns left into Castelnau and heads towards Hammersmith Bridge.

Soon it's clear the church isn't big enough. People are standing in the aisles, along the walls, and spilling outside onto the steps. Seats have been reserved for us at the front. Lucy and Lachlan sit between us, both too small for their feet to touch the floor. My parents and Grace are next to me. Jack's brother and sister-in-law have come down from Scotland.

Around us there are mothers, friends, neighbors, workmates, babysitters, and people I'm only on nodding terms with, like the butcher and the Korean woman who does my nails. My yoga teacher has had her baby and looks impossibly thin. The headmistress from Lucy's school is directing people into pews, making sure they make room for more. Two of my oldest friends from university have made the journey from Leicester and Newcastle.

A woman with a lovely voice leads a choir, which entreats everyone to lift their hearts to God. Most people move their mouths silently, pretending to sing. After the hymn, Father George gives a nice sermon about those times when God seems absent and how we must hold on to faith, or risk falling into fear.

He calls on Jack to say a few words. My heart lurches. I had no idea he had planned this. Jack climbs several steps to the lectern, where he pauses and adjusts the microphone, tapping it with his finger. Apologizing.

"Since Ben was taken, I have asked myself countless times: Why? Why him? Why us? There is no answer, but that doesn't stop me searching for one. A child is reported missing every three minutes in the UK. Across Europe that number rises to one child every two minutes. In America it is close to one child every minute. I know figures like this sound shocking, but we only hear about a fraction of these cases because most of the children come home or are found quickly. We have all sorts of safeguards. Amber Alerts. Digital billboards. Child-rescue organizations. Facebook. Twitter. Stranger Danger campaigns. CCTV cameras. Yet still children disappear. Until two weeks ago, I thought I understood what it would be like to have a child go missing. I had watched other parents on TV. I had put myself in their shoes. I was mistaken. To lose a child is beyond comprehension. It defies biology. It derails common sense. It violates the natural order.

"Like a lot of people, I sometimes fail to appreciate how lucky I am to have such a wonderful wife and family, a good career, great friends, and, as this evening shows, a very close-knit community. Often I forget to give thanks and I take things for granted. Not anymore. To the woman I love, sitting in the front row: I cannot give you what you desire the most—a chance to hold your baby boy. I have seen your selfless devotion to Lucy and Lachlan and I know how deeply you feel Ben's absence because there is no loss quite like a mother's loss.

"On every occasion over the past fortnight when I have wondered how I can get through this—I have looked at you. Your strength of character, fortitude, and resolve are truly inspirational. I love you, Meghan Shaughnessy. I love you, Lucy and Lachlan. And Ben, wherever you are, I love you too."

That's when I dissolve, collapsing into sobs. The rest of the vigil passes in a blur. I find myself standing and moving through the crowd. Thanking people. Shaking hands.

I notice Agatha. That must be her fiancé, Hayden. He's carrying their baby in a pouch against his chest.

"I didn't know if I should bring him," Agatha says, unsure of whether to hug me or shake my hand. I kiss her cheeks. "I thought it might be insensitive."

"No, it's OK."

"This is Hayden."

"It's nice to meet you," I say. He nods and looks uncomfortable, as though sadness might be infectious.

Stepping closer, I look at their baby, whose face is partially hidden in the folds of Hayden's shirt.

"He's beautiful," I say, struggling to get the words out.

"I'm sorry about Ben," says Hayden. "I hope they find him."

I don't answer. I'm being moved on.

I turn to Agatha. "Look after him."

She doesn't understand.

"Your baby," I explain. "Never let him go."

AGATHA

There are reporters, photographers, and cameramen everywhere. Surely there must be bigger stories to report. What about the wars, terror attacks, home-grown jihadists, or drowning refugees? Public attention should have moved on by now. Something newer and fresher should have captured the headlines.

Reporters are mingling with the crowd, asking the same questions: "How do you feel? Are you shocked? Fearful?"

What do they expect people to say? Clichéd questions get clichéd answers. "Nothing like this has ever happened around here," someone says. "What's the world coming to?" says another. "It makes you wonder, doesn't it?" adds someone else.

Wonder what? I want to scream. *Wonder why bad things happen to good people? Wonder if we'll be home in time to watch* Dancing with the Stars?

Why won't people accept that Ben is gone? Rory is the one who matters. It would be cruel to send him back. The interests of the child must always come first—that's what judges always consider in child custody cases. Rory *has* a mother. He *has* a family. Ben doesn't exist anymore.

Meg was fine until Jack made that speech and now her mascara is smeared on her cheeks and she has panda eyes. Lucy and Lachlan look like they're handling it well. People often forget about other siblings in situations like this. It's like what happened to me when Elijah died. I was forgotten. Unloved. Less important. That's what I want to say to Megs. "Love your other children. Focus on them."

People linger outside the church, hugging and handing out tissues. Random strangers touch Rory's head and smile, as though reassured that the world goes on. The priest draws a small sign of the cross on Rory's forehead and says a blessing.

I turn and almost bump into Megs. She looks at Rory and I feel a rush of fear.

What if she can tell? Some animals can smell their own children or recognize their cries. I don't know if Megs spent long enough with Rory to know these things, but she carried him for nine months inside her womb.

"He's beautiful," says Meg.

"I wasn't sure I should bring him," I stammer.

"Of course you should. Is he a good baby?"

"They're all good babies," I reply, before realizing how that sounds. "I'm sorry. I shouldn't have said that."

She hugs me and looks at Hayden.

"It's nice to finally meet you."

"And you," he says.

"Did you make it home for the birth?"

"Not quite."

"Well, you're here now."

"I'm sure they'll find your little boy," says Hayden.

"Thank you."

Megs is ushered away by a police constable, who is keeping reporters at bay.

"Let's go," says Hayden, who seems to share my unease.

A photographer steps between us. Without asking, she begins taking pictures of Rory and Hayden.

"Can we get a shot with you?" she asks. "We're doing a story on the candlelight vigil. Do you know the Shaughnessys?"

"Yes."

"Can you lift him out of the sling? That's it. Hold him a little higher. Next to your cheek."

The flash keeps firing. A recording device is thrust under my chin.

"Are you frightened for your own baby?" asks a reporter.

"No. Why?"

"It's shocking, isn't it? You don't expect babies to be stolen."

"No. I guess not."

"Do you have a message for the person who took Baby Ben?"

"No, not really, I think everything has been said."

MEGHAN

Morning, 6:15. Red digits glow on the radio clock. My hand slides across the cool sheets, but the bed is empty. Jack must have woken early and decided to get up. We made love last night after the vigil. He didn't penetrate me (my stitches) but we found other ways to get close and it did more to heal us than a dozen counseling sessions.

Yet even as he moved against my hand and lips, I felt Jack slowly running down like the mainspring of a clock. I pulled his face close to mine and saw the tears. He squeezed his eyes shut, trying to hide them as he moved faster and moaned my name.

I doze again. When I wake the second time, I turn on my mobile. There are dozens of messages—questions about a story in the newspaper. I open a link but the doorbell chimes downstairs. I hear Annie's voice and DCS MacAteer's. I jump out of bed and shrug on a dressing gown, pulling my hair into a band.

They're in the kitchen—Annie, Jack, and MacAteer. Lucy and Lachlan are watching cartoons in the sitting room. Newspapers are spread across the bench. Jack is poring over them, looking shocked and pale.

I join them and glance at the pages, noticing a photograph of Jack and me. A second picture shows a glamorous-looking woman with tousled hair, white teeth, and a low-cut blouse. I recognize her: the estate agent who sold us the house.

The headline screams: I DIDN'T STEAL BABY BEN.
And the one below it: *But I'm in love with his dad.*
Jack tries to close the pages. I put down my hand
and push him away, reading the opening paragraphs.

A London estate agent has denied any involve-
ment in the abduction of Baby Ben Shaughnessy,
but admitted to having an affair with his father,
well-known sports presenter Jack Shaughnessy.

Rhea Bowden claims she and Jack "shook the
house down" when they had sex in dozens of different properties she was selling in South London. Those houses include the one in Barnes
that she sold to Jack and Meghan Shaughnessy
last December, three months before she and
Jack began their affair.

Jack is trying to force my fingers off the page. "Please,
Megs," he says, his voice thick with . . . what . . . ? Guilt?
Shame? Remorse?
I keep reading.

"We bumped into each other at a trivia night
at a local pub, the Sun Inn, and Jack offered to
buy me a drink. He bought a bottle of champagne," Rhea Bowden told the *Daily Mirror*.

"We flirted and laughed and were both pretty
drunk by the second bottle. We finished up kissing in a doorway and making love in my office.
I knew he was married, of course, but I didn't
realize his wife was pregnant.

"After that, Jack would call me when he had
an afternoon off. We'd either meet at my place
or go to one of the houses I was showing. I know
it was wrong, but whatever people think or say

about me, I didn't take Baby Ben. I love Jack. I
would never harm his family."

The newspaper rips as Jack wrenches it away from
beneath my balled fists. My eyes are swimming but I
refuse to cry. I look at the other front pages. They all
have the same story, writ large in bold headlines. I picture the entire country sniggering over their cornflakes
or muesli, gossiping around the photocopier, or over
garden fences, or at checkouts. We are no longer that
poor family who lost a child. We are tabloid fodder. We
are a soap opera. Jack hasn't just cheated on me, he has
humiliated me; he has made a mockery of our marriage
and every statement we've made about being a loving
family. We don't deserve sympathy. We don't deserve
to get Ben back.

I go upstairs. Jack tries to follow. MacAteer stops
him. He has questions to answer.

"Can't it wait?" asks Jack, pleading with him.

"No."

I pull an overnight bag from the cupboard and randomly fill it with clothes. I get dressed. I zip up my
boots. I walk downstairs, out the front door, along the
path. My keys fall out of my hand. I bend to pick them
up. The circus is all around me—the cameras and
reporters—shouting questions.

"Did you know about the affair?" someone yells.

"Are you leaving him?" asks another.

I can't answer. I lock the car doors and push the
ignition, sideswiping a police car and shattering the
side mirror as I pull away. I don't care. I'll run them all
down. They can lock me up and throw away the key, as
long as they leave me alone.

AGATHA

My little boy is dying. I have known it for days, but have told myself that he'll bounce back and grow stronger. Yes, he's struggling, but all babies feel poorly sometimes. They go off their food, or run a temperature, or cry for no reason.

I have never feared anything for myself, not since I was a child, but I fear for Rory. What if I cannot protect him the way he should have been protected? What if I fail?

Last night I fell asleep next to his Moses basket. Waking stiff and cold, I reached out and touched Rory's forehead. His tiny body was radiating heat. I wiped him down. I gave him medicine. I waited until he fell asleep before I shook uncontrollably, knowing it was happening again. I am losing someone I love. He is fading away, disappearing by degrees, ounce by ounce.

I come awake. It's light outside. I'm alone in bed. Hayden must have risen earlier and left me sleeping. I go to Rory's bed. His body is so pale and bloodless I catch my breath. Terrified, I extend my hand and brush my fingers over his chest. His lungs fill. His heart beats. He lives. Just.

The fever is still gripping him. I give him paracetamol and wipe him down. I let him hold my finger in his fist as I try to breathe for him, inhaling and exhaling.

He's dying.

Not yet.

He needs a doctor.

I can't.

Shrugging off my nightdress, I open my wardrobe and notice something different. My clothes have been moved—pushed aside at each end, exposing the rear shelves. The middle one has a blue box made of coated metal with a hinged lid and padlock. It contains a few scant mementos from the past—the bits worth keeping: a second-place prize certificate for handwriting, a spelling trophy, my birth certificate, an out-of-date passport, a handful of wedding photographs, and a strip of photo-booth prints showing me at age sixteen, sitting on the lap of a boy I liked, whose name I can't remember.

The box is facing the wrong way. I look more closely and notice scratch marks in the paint where the hinges have been unscrewed and reattached.

I carry the box to the kitchen, where Hayden is eating a bowl of cereal.

"Have you been going through my stuff?"

"What stuff?"

"My box."

"Why would I do that?"

"That box is private."

"Why?"

"It just is."

"I don't like secrets."

"It's not secret, it's private. Don't you trust me?"

"You lied about being married, about your mother, about giving your coat to charity. You even lied about your age." He points to the box. "I saw your birth certificate. You told me you were twenty-nine. You're thirty-eight."

"A woman is allowed to lie about her age," I say, trying to sound lighthearted.

Hayden's face is blank. He doesn't find me funny anymore.

"I called that number you gave me for the midwife. It was a recorded message. She's away until January."

"That's not my fault."

I feel relieved but don't let it show. It took me a day to think up that plan—buying a SIM card and recording a message using a voice-disguising app: *"You have called the voicemail of Belinda Wallace of the Yorkshire Home Birth Service. I am out of the office until January seventh. Have a wonderful Christmas and New Year."*

Hayden hasn't finished. "So I called your doctor—I found his number in your phone—but he didn't know you were pregnant."

"I stopped using him. Jules helped me register with her GP."

"Right, that explains everything," he says cynically.

I pretend he's joking. "What is this, the Spanish Inquisition?"

"I'm not sure yet," says Hayden, softening a little. "I want to believe you, Aggy, but I'm frightened of what you might have done . . . and who you've hurt."

Standing barefoot on the floorboards, I begin to shake and I swallow a coppery taste that could be blood. Every sound is amplified. I hear the soft swish of traffic on the wet road outside and a District line train pulling into Putney Bridge station.

I glance around the kitchen at the teapot and the breakfast cereal and the milky bowl on the pine table. I have to tell him. I have to beg him to forgive me. We both love Rory. Neither of us wants to lose him. It can be *our* secret.

I begin talking but my mind doesn't work because I've barely slept. What if he disagrees? What if he calls the police?

"I'm worried about Rory," I say. "He's not feeding. He's hardly had anything since yesterday."

Hayden doesn't hesitate. His questions can wait. He goes to the bedroom, where Rory is lying on our bed, wedged between two pillows. His legs are forced apart by the size of his nappy and his weight loss looks even more severe.

Hayden touches his forehead. "He's on fire."

"But feel his hands and feet—they're cold."

"Wake up, baby," he says, gently shaking Rory. His eyes flicker.

Hayden picks him up. Rory sags in his hands, his head rolling to one side.

"He's gone all floppy."

"He's just tired."

"No. He needs a doctor."

"Or I could give him some more Calpol."

"How much did he have to eat yesterday?"

"I give him what he wants. Sometimes he falls asleep before he finishes."

"What's the name of your new GP?"

"Let's wait a little longer."

"No, I want you to call the doctor."

My mobile is on the kitchen table. I scroll through the contacts list and pretend to call a number.

"Is that Dr. Kneeble's surgery?" I say, talking to nobody. "This is Agatha Fyfle . . . Yes, that's right. Merry Christmas to you too. I had the baby a few weeks ago and he's running a temperature."

Hayden whispers loudly, "Tell him it's serious."

I cover the phone. "I'm talking to his receptionist."

"You're making it sound like nothing."

I go back to the fake call. "He's off his food and slept badly. Yes, I've done that . . . every four hours . . . I see. So you have nothing until then? OK. Put him down.

His name is Rory Fyfle, no, I mean, Rory Cole. He's sixteen days old."

"When?" asks Hayden, as I hang up.

"Tomorrow."

"What!"

"It's the first available."

"That's too long."

Hayden picks up his phone.

"What are you doing?"

"Calling Mum. She'll know what to do."

"No. He'll be fine." I grab at his arm. He shrugs me away.

"I don't care what you've done, Aggy, but Rory is sick. We're not going to wait."

Ten minutes later we're dressing Rory in socks, mittens, and a woollen hat. Mrs. Cole called her GP and managed to get us an appointment. I know the risks, but Hayden refuses to do nothing. He carries the pram downstairs and pushes it ahead of me.

"Come on, come on."

"I'm hurrying."

The doctor's surgery is in Brent Cross on the Northern line. We have to catch three different trains to get there. As we wait on the platform, I keep checking Rory, praying for him to spark up or cry or do something energetic. Instead he looks sluggish and barely conscious. I offer him a sip of boiled water in a bottle, but it dribbles down his chin.

I have to prepare myself. I have to be confident. The doctor is going to ask questions. I need to have the answers tripping off my tongue as though everything is normal. I'm a new mother with a sick baby. Breathe. Relax. I can do this.

Mrs. Cole fusses over Rory when we arrive at the surgery. Her whole demeanor changes around him.

She lights up. Having a grandchild seems to have given her energy and dynamism, as though she's fulfilling her destiny.

The waiting room looks like a United Colors of Benetton advertisement. Indians. Pakistanis. Africans. An Ethiopian woman has a toddler clinging to her colorful dress. She can't speak English. I envy her. I wish I could pretend to be foreign and not understand the questions.

I'm asked to fill out a form detailing my medical history.

"Where was Rory born?" the receptionist asks.

"In Leeds."

"Did you bring along his personal health record?"

"I left it at home. Sorry."

"What's the name of your home health aide?"

I make up a name.

"Is her number in your phone?"

"No, she gave me her card. I stuck it on the fridge. I'm sorry. I'm not being very helpful. I can't think straight at the moment." I summon tears. The receptionist tells me not to worry. We can complete the form later.

"Are you breast-feeding?" she asks.

"I did for a while, but I struggled."

"But you're still lactating?"

"Ah, yes."

"What was Rory's birth weight?"

"Six pounds and three ounces."

"Was it a vaginal delivery?"

"Yes."

"Any problems?"

"No."

Each new lie seems to wrap me in another cable that gets tighter around my chest. The creature inside me twists and turns, calling me names, hissing at me to run.

I go back to my chair and wait. Ten minutes later we're summoned inside.

"You don't have to stay," I tell Mrs. Cole, but it sounds ungrateful. "I mean—I don't want to keep you if you're busy."

"I'm not busy," she says. "I've brought my knitting." She holds up a tiny half-finished cardigan threaded on her needles.

Dr. Schur is in his sixties with a full head of gray hair sculpted into a wave that looks almost aerodynamic. He's particularly pleased to see Hayden.

"The amount of times I stitched you up, I didn't think you'd survive this long," he says, laughing.

"Put the little fellow up here," he says, pointing to the examination table. "And get him undressed."

For the next few minutes he says nothing as he does the usual checks—eyes, ears, nose, heart, and lungs. He takes each of Rory's little limbs and bends them back and forth. He rotates his hips. He looks in his mouth. He feels his skull.

"He's very dehydrated. Has he been vomiting?"

"No. I've been giving him boiled water."

"Are you breast-feeding?"

"Not all the time. My home health aide told me I should put him on the bottle for a few days and he seemed to take to it."

"But you're still lactating?"

I half nod.

"We have a nurse here who is very good with breast-feeding problems, but I'm more concerned about his weight and his persistent fever."

"I've been giving him paracetamol," I say.

"For how long?" asks Dr. Schur.

"Since yesterday morning . . . every four hours."

The doctor continues to examine Rory, turning his arms and legs, looking at his elbows and behind his knees.

"Purely as a precaution, I want you to take Rory to hospital," he says.

"Why?" I hear the panic in my voice.

"It's extremely unlikely, but I tend to err on the side of caution."

"What's unlikely?" asks Hayden.

"Meningitis is very rare, particularly in babies who are only a few weeks old, but he does have a fever and a rash on the inside of his right thigh, which are some of the symptoms. I want to start him on broad-spectrum antibiotics immediately—just in case—but the hospital can test him properly. I'll phone ahead. You won't have to wait."

Dr. Schur goes to his desk and types on his computer, humming to himself. He unlocks a cabinet and takes out several sealed packets of medicine, making a note of the serial numbers. He administers the first dose to Rory.

"You can get him dressed," he says to Hayden before turning to me.

"Now you, young lady, how about I check you out?"

I step away. "No!"

"I want to make sure your uterus has shrunk back into your pelvis."

"I'm fine."

"Are you getting any contractions or after-pains?"

"No."

Hayden has stopped dressing Rory and is staring at me.

"Just pop off your trousers and sit up on the table. It will only take a few minutes."

He knows! He knows!

"I don't want you looking down there. It's not you . . . I . . . I have a problem with male doctors. Something happened when I was young . . . I only let women doctors touch me."

"I can get Nurse Hazelwood to come in. She can examine you and talk about the breast-feeding."

He knows! He knows!

"No, thank you," I say, pulling my coat around me. "You've been very helpful, but I don't want to be examined."

Dr. Schur looks at the form I filled out earlier. "You haven't given us the name of your home health aide."

"I left her card at home."

"Or your GP—what's her name?"

"I'm seeing her later."

He knows! He knows!

"Where did you have your baby?"

"In Leeds," I say, sounding annoyed. "I told your receptionist. She wrote it down."

"Where in Leeds?"

My tongue seems to have swollen, blocking my throat.

"You're upset, Agatha. I think we should calm down," says the doctor.

"I am calm."

"Take a seat. I'm sure we can sort this out."

"No! I'm leaving." I pick up Rory and push past Hayden.

Dr. Schur steps in front of the door. "We need to discuss this."

"There's nothing to discuss."

He touches my shoulder. The creature inside me is out, unchained, filling my throat.

"GET YOUR FUCKING HANDS OFF ME!"

I don't recognize the voice. It's as though an entirely different person, an imposter, has momentarily taken my place. Dr. Schur takes a half step back and I reach the door. It opens outward and I keep moving, through the waiting room. Mrs. Cole is on her feet.

"GET AWAY FROM ME, BITCH, OR I'LL CUT YOUR EYES OUT."

She reels backwards, her mouth gaping.

Hayden is yelling at me to stop. I turn my head and see Dr. Schur talking to the receptionist. She picks up the phone.

I keep moving. Running.

They know! They know! They know!

MEGHAN

The bastard! The fucking bastard!

Jack had an affair. He took another woman into our bed, into many beds, or on the floor, or sofa, or kitchen bench. I cannot help but picture him fucking Rhea Bowden in all those houses in South London with a FOR SALE sign out front. It makes me feel physically sick.

Every time I push the images away, they come back again. Of all the women he could have slept with he chose a blowsy, painted, bleached estate agent who looks like a cougar. She's older than I am. The fucking bastard!

He's been calling constantly, leaving messages, which I delete without listening to. I tell my parents not to answer their phones. Later, I hear Jack knock on the door and my father tells him to "give her some space." Jack jams his shoe in the closing door and my father raises his voice.

I hate him. I hate him so much that I never want to see or speak to him again. That's what I tell myself and that's what I believe. I am not hysterical. I am completely calm. I am rehearsing what I'm going to say when I tell him our marriage is over and I want a divorce. Jack will be numb. He will be distraught. He will beg for one more chance.

At the same time, I'm torn between anger and relief, loving and hating—a perilous dichotomy—because I am not innocent. I slept with Simon. A one-night stand that will always stand. Five minutes of drunken passion, a moment of weakness, my act of infidelity. Jack has been seeing Rhea Bowden for months. Surely his betrayal is bigger than mine. Worse.

The newspapers say the affair ended after someone shoved a note beneath the wiper blades on Jack's car, warning him to stop fooling around. Clearly one person knew that he was married. It could have been one of my girlfriends. I cringe at that thought. My friends are notorious gossips, incapable of keeping a confidence, particularly a scandalous piece of news like this one. One would have told the others, who would have passed it on, until everyone in Barnes knew except me.

How they must have whispered behind my back, pointing me out and smiling conspiratorially. Real friends tell each other. Real friends help you bury bodies. Real friends bring their own shovel and don't ask questions.

Maybe I deserve this, but I didn't mean to sleep with Simon or get pregnant again. Jack made a conscious choice to cheat on me. The stupid, weak, pathetic bastard deserves to be lonely. These are the thoughts that keep bouncing around my head as though I'm forewoman of a jury, considering the evidence, trying to reach a verdict.

I'm alone in my childhood bedroom, which has been redecorated since those days, but I remember which posters once covered the walls and where I positioned my bed so I could lie awake at night looking at the rooftops on the far side of the road. I had a desk in the corner, which had a secret shelf behind the second drawer where I used to hide my cigarettes and my first joint, which I was too scared to smoke.

My mind drifts forward. I remember falling pregnant with Lucy, how excited Jack and I were. How we spent long hours talking about all the things we were going to do. On the night before she was born (she was ten days overdue) we shared a curry and made love to see if we could bring on my labor.

After the birth, I slept for hours. I remember waking up and seeing Jack holding Lucy in his arms, staring at this perfect little model of a person we had just made. He had taken her to the window of my private room and was pointing things out. "That's a double-decker bus," he said. "I'll take you on a bus one day. You'll love London."

Next I remember when Jack's father died. We went to the hospice and sat beside his bed and watched the end approach with each breath. That was the day I realized that life is a series of good-byes and I had to make sure that I didn't waste my days or use them up too soon.

Two nights ago, Jack delivered a speech in the church that had me in tears. He said he loved me and that I made him stronger. I must believe that's still true. I'm angry with him. I want to punish him. I want to pinch his skin until he yells. I want him to know what he's done, but I don't want to say good-bye, I don't want to lose him.

The doorbell chimes. My father answers and I hear his footsteps on the stairs. A gentle knock.

"The police are here," he says, his voice full of concern. "They've been trying to call you."

DCS MacAteer is standing in the hallway alongside Cyrus Haven. They haven't bothered taking off their overcoats. My heart skips. MacAteer suggests I sit down.

"No, tell me."

"There's been a development," he says. "We may know the identity of the kidnapper."

"Is it Rhea Bowden?"

Has she been arrested? I hope they marched her into the station in front of the cameras. Where's Ben?

MacAteer asks, "Do you know a woman by the name of Agatha Fyfle?"

"What? Yes."

He begins explaining, but I interrupt. "It can't be Agatha. She had her baby before me."

Neither man responds.

"How did you meet her?" asks the detective.

"She worked at a local supermarket—the one opposite the Green. We did yoga classes."

"She was pregnant?"

"Yes."

"Did she ever come to your house?"

"Once. I gave her some baby clothes."

"Could she have been faking her pregnancy?" asks Cyrus.

"No. She had her baby before me. I saw the photographs."

"Do you still have them?" asks MacAteer.

"They're on my phone."

I scroll through my emails and show them the images of Agatha holding her baby. Cyrus studies them closely.

"These could have been taken anywhere."

"She had a home birth," I say.

"These could have been staged," says MacAteer.

"How? She's holding a baby."

"Her upstairs neighbor gave birth a month ago. She had a baby girl."

I shake my head, trying to think clearly. Agatha came to my house. Both of us got drenched in the rain. She used my bathroom, borrowed my clothes. I didn't see her get undressed.

MacAteer continues. "Agatha Fyfle visited a doctor in North London this morning. She didn't have any of the relevant paperwork for her baby and couldn't give the doctor the details of her health visitor, or her midwife."

"She said her mother was with her."

"Agatha's mother has been in Spain since early October," says Cyrus. "I spoke to her an hour ago. The first she knew of Agatha's baby was when she spoke to her daughter's fiancé, Hayden Cole, a week ago."

How could her mother not know?

I go back over the details. Agatha came to the candlelight vigil. She had a baby with her. I touched his head. Surely I would have known if it was Ben. I would have recognized him. In the same breath I hear myself saying, "You have to arrest her."

"We have to be certain," says MacAteer.

"But if you arrest her, she'll have to bring the baby. You can do a DNA test."

"Not without a warrant. We need proof."

My voice rises in fear. "You said she took him to a doctor. Is he sick?"

"He was running a temperature," says Cyrus. "The GP put him on antibiotics and recommended further tests. Agatha fled before he could raise the alarm."

"How sick? What's wrong with him?"

"There is a small chance that he has meningitis."

I raise my fist to my mouth and bite down hard on the knuckles, wanting to draw blood.

"We're watching Agatha's flat," says MacAteer. "If she comes home, we'll interview her."

"What if she doesn't go home?"

"We are watching the train stations, airports, and ferry terminals, as well as contacting friends or acquaintances who might put her up."

"What about her mother's house in Leeds?" Cyrus asks.

"That too," says MacAteer.

"Ben won't survive outside on a night like tonight," I say.

"I'm aware of that, but if we broadcast Agatha's name and photograph, we risk putting Ben in even greater danger. Remember our strategy. We have to keep her calm."

Fuck the strategy! I want to yell. *My baby is sick.*

Cyrus has more questions for me, wanting details of how much Agatha revealed about herself. I know what he's doing—trying to determine her state of mind. He wants to know if Agatha is the sort of person who would panic under pressure. I don't know if I'm the best person to ask. I thought Agatha was a friend. I invited her into my house. I gave her baby clothes. We sat in my kitchen and talked about pregnancy and babies and the future.

What sort of monster steals another woman's child?

AGATHA

They will be coming for us now. They will surround the flat and break down the front door, splintering wood and bending hinges. They will storm up the stairs and go from room to room, searching for us.

I should have known it would come to this. I should have taken Rory overseas when I had the chance. Packed my things and smuggled him out past Customs and Immigration. I could have taken him to . . . to . . . Where? I have no money or contacts or experience of being on the run.

The creature is blaming me—listing my mistakes, my stupidity. I'm useless. Pathetic. I have failed again. What did I expect? I am going to lose it all— my baby, my fiancé, my freedom . . . I have no right to happiness. Like wealth, or beauty, it is given to others, not to someone like me.

Foolish! Foolish! Stupid girl!

I glance down at Rory, asleep in my arms, and my chest heaves with suppressed sobs. These past few weeks have been the happiest of my life. I have lived my dream. It was my turn . . . my time. I have been loved. I have been whole.

I should have known it wouldn't last, but I will not cry. Not here. Not now.

The cab ride from Brent Cross is slowed by traffic on the North Circular. I'm almost at Chiswick when I discover I only have twenty quid in my purse. The meter is gone past that already.

"Can you pull over just here?" I ask the driver.

"What about Fulham?"

"No. Here will be fine."

I take out all my notes and coins, counting them while the driver waits impatiently.

"I'm terribly sorry, but I don't have enough. I'm five pounds short." I look at him, hopefully.

"Have you been crying?" he asks.

The words get stuck in my throat.

He looks at my baby. "Give me twenty. I don't want the shrapnel. We'll call it even."

The cab pulls away. I risk looking at my phone. Hayden has been calling, leaving voice and text messages. Maybe I should call him back. I could tell him the truth and ask for help. He loves Rory as much as I do. Together we could come up with a plan. Escape. Start again somewhere new.

In the same instant I remember that the police can trace mobile phones. I turn mine off and take out the SIM card, throwing it into the gutter. I'm standing at the side of Chiswick Roundabout smelling exhaust fumes and watching the blur of traffic. Kew Bridge station is just down the road. I can catch a train. Where? I can't go back to the flat. I have no credit or debit cards. I left them in Rory's changing bag, which was hanging on the back of his pram. I didn't think. I had no time.

I hold my hand against Rory's forehead. His fever has broken and he has more color in his cheeks. I still have the antibiotics the doctor gave me. I can give him another dose in a few hours. How will I feed him? Change him?

At the railway station, I find a public phone box and call Hayden's number. He answers on the first ring.

"Agatha! Where are you? I've been worried sick."

"Are you at the flat?"

"Yeah."

"Are the police there?"

"Who? No."

"Look out of the window."

"What's going on? Where are you?"

More urgently. "Look out of the window."

"OK, OK. What am I looking for?"

"Can you see anyone?"

"No."

In the background I hear the intercom buzzing. "Hold on," says Hayden.

"Is it them?"

He doesn't answer, but I hear him talking to someone on the intercom. "She's not here. Who wants to know?"

I don't hear the answer. By then I've hung up.

I glance around me, certain that I'm being watched. Trying not to make eye contact with anyone, I walk down the station steps to the platform. A uniformed transport officer is at the bottom of the stairs, reading a free newspaper, waiting for the train. A sports bag is nestled between his feet. He looks up from the paper and notices Rory in my arms.

I keep walking to the far end of the platform and hide behind a painted concrete pillar. Opposite me, on the westbound platform, a workman is picking up rubbish with a clawed stick. He's listening to music from earbuds that dangle from beneath his dreadlocks. He could be part of a surveillance team. I glance farther along the platform. Two Asian women are chatting. Neither of them looks my way. They wouldn't, would they? They'd deliberately avoid me.

Rory whimpers. He's hungry. I have nothing for

him except boiled water. Why couldn't they leave us alone? Why did they have to keep searching for Baby Ben? They portrayed him as some sort of fairy-tale infant stolen by wolves or left to perish in the wilderness. He was always safe, always loved. If they had just let him go, we would have been fine. Happy.

I have tried not to think of a moment like this. Failure has shadowed me, but I refuse to look over my shoulder. I have been here before. It feels like I'm leaning out of a burning building, fearing the fall as much as the flames, knowing I cannot survive either, yet I must choose one.

The creature whispers to me, telling me I've lost. He is a brutal beast, determined to undermine and demoralize, to never forgive or forget. What did I expect? I kill babies. I only have to touch them and they die. Chloe. Lizzie. Emily. Elijah. All dead because of me. Now I'll lose Rory.

The next train is coming. How easy it would be to step out now. What is there to live for if they take Rory from me? I will not see color, or taste sweetness, or feel warmth. I will be nobody. I will be worse.

My toes are on the edge of the platform. I rock forward and back on my heels, hearing the rails vibrate. Feeling the rushing air.

You're a coward.

I'm not a coward.

Do it, then!

Images flash through my mind. My funeral. Who would be there? Nobody—not after what I've done, unless my mother shows up, dressed like a Spanish widow and wailing over the casket, beating at the polished lid with her bony fists.

My life has been forgettable, but my death could make amends. It could shock and horrify. It will be written about. It will make the news. The train driver will never forget. Meghan and Jack, they will have nightmares, waking in a cold sweat with my name on their lips, my face in their heads.

I rock back and forth, leaning out farther each time. Look how easily Nicky died. He had no time to regret. Nothing flashed before his eyes except the train that crushed his body. My life could be over just as quickly. My pain. My doubts.

Do it! Go now!

What about Rory?

Take him with you.

He doesn't deserve that.

You'll have him forever.

How? He deserves more.

Suicide is the ultimate act of selfishness, but surely it becomes more so if we take another life. It's like saying, "I cannot handle this world so I choose to die, but I cannot handle death so I choose to take someone with me." How cowardly. How self-obsessed. A cry for help becomes a wicked act. Unforgivable. The grounds for eternal damnation.

The platform trembles. A train horn blasts. I reel away, as though blown backwards by the noise, clutching Rory to my chest. The train brakes. Slows. Stops. The doors open.

The transport officer is beside me. "Are you all right?" he asks.

"I'm fine."

"Did you fall?"

"No. Thank you. It's nothing."

"Your baby is crying."

He points at Rory, whose little face is a picture of misery, his features bunched up and reddened.

I carry him onto the train. The transport officer

takes a seat, watching me. I stay beside the doors, waiting for the beeping sound that signals they're going to close. At the last possible moment, I step back onto the platform and the doors shut behind me. The officer gets to his feet. He walks down the moving carriage, trying to keep me in view, but the train carries him away.

Rory has gone quiet. He's watching me expectantly. It will be dark soon. We need shelter. Food. The supermarket! I know where Mr. Patel leaves the spare keys. I know the code for the alarm—unless he changed it after I left. The place closes at nine o'clock. I'll be able to get nappies and formula. We can sleep there tonight, as long as we're gone by six in the morning.

I sit on the metal bench and hold Rory on my lap. "We're going to be all right," I whisper, kissing his cheek. "Today was not ours, but there's always tomorrow."

MEGHAN

A dark-skinned Hawaiian girl in a coconut bikini and hula skirt jiggles back and forth on the dashboard. Jack stuck the doll there, thinking her funny in a retro-sexist way, and now she reminds me of Rhea Bowden, shimmying her hips and acting slutty. I hit the girl with the back of my hand. She bends and bounces back, shimmying even harder.

"Is there anything you want to talk about?" asks Cyrus, who insisted that he drive.

I don't answer.

"I saw the newspapers."

"Everybody saw the newspapers. The whole world is laughing at me."

"They feel sorry for you."

"Even worse."

"Can I just say—"

"No! I don't want to talk about it."

We drive in silence, crossing Putney Bridge and turning onto Lower Richmond Road.

"I'll say one thing," says Cyrus. "Then I'll shut up."

He pauses, as though expecting me to argue. I don't.

"I have cheated on someone—a one-night stand that meant nothing, but it cost me a relationship with a woman I cared deeply about."

"She wouldn't forgive you?"

"I couldn't make it up to her."

Pain is etched around his eyes. His voice drops. "I tried

to make her understand that resentment towards me was punishing both of us. It may not be fair that you forgive Jack, but forgiveness by its very nature isn't fair. Someone must make a greater sacrifice. Someone has to start."

"You're saying that it should be me? Why is it always the woman?"

"It's not, I promise you. I talked to Jack. He's devastated."

"Good!"

"He thinks he's lost you."

"Even better."

I wrap my arms around my chest and look out the window.

"Do you still love him?" asks Cyrus.

"That's not a fair question."

"You're right. I should ask if you can forgive him."

"How do I do that?"

"Talk to him. Let him explain."

I don't want to hear the details. I don't want to imagine him and Rhea Bowden together. I can't bear the thought of touching him, after what he's done—where he's been. I want to cut his penis off.

Cyrus is still talking. "It's not easy. First you have to look behind you at what you've shared, then you look ahead. You focus on rebuilding, not blaming."

"Is that what happened to you?" I ask.

"Almost," he replies, steering the car onto our street. "I didn't try hard enough."

Jack meets us in the hallway, unsure whether to hug me or stay back. He reaches for my bag. I turn my head at the last moment and press my lips against his, holding the back of his head. His body shudders and melts against mine. I can taste coffee on his lips.

"I'm sorry," he whispers.

"I know."

"It will never happen again."

"No, it won't . . ."

I kiss him again because I don't want to talk about Rhea Bowden or think about Simon Kidd. The fate of my marriage can wait. All my energy has to go into getting Ben back. After that I will decide if I still want Jack.

PC Soussa has been reassigned as our family liaison officer. She's in touch with MacAteer, who is back at the station, commanding the task force. Agatha hasn't returned to her flat in Fulham and her mobile phone stopped transmitting in Chiswick in West London shortly before 2 p.m. Twenty minutes later she used a pay phone at Kew Bridge station to call her fiancé, Hayden Cole, who has denied knowing anything about Baby Ben or the abduction. He claims to have been duped by Agatha, who faked her pregnancy while he was away at sea.

Agatha's phone records and email accounts are being searched, looking for clues to where she might go. In the meantime, DCS MacAteer has decided not to release her name or photograph in case he pushes her to do something desperate. I can understand the logic, but the maternal part of me wants to plaster her image on every lamppost and yell her name from the rooftops.

The phone rings. Jack answers and puts MacAteer on the speakerphone. The DCS sounds energized, as though the previous weeks have been a warm-up. Now we're into the main game.

"We know Agatha Fyfle traveled to Leeds by train on December fourth, but have found no evidence of her giving birth," he says, his voice sounding hollow and metallic through the speakerphone. "At midday on December sixth, she caught a bus from Central Leeds to London Victoria. CCTV footage shows her holding a baby carrier, but doesn't show an actual baby. According to her fiancé, she didn't spend that night at her flat in Fulham, which means she may have somewhere else to go—a friend's house or accommodation, perhaps a hostel or a hotel. This puts her in London before you went into hospital."

"She called me that night," I say. "She said she was in Leeds."

"That was seven fifty-five p.m. Technicians have triangulated Agatha's mobile signal. The call came from London—somewhere quite close to you."

"How close?" asks Cyrus.

"Best estimate—the back garden."

Something seems to shake loose and drop into my stomach. I glance out the French doors and remember the conversation. I was in the kitchen, making a cup of tea. Agatha told me all about her baby and the birth. I pictured her in her mother's house in Leeds, but in reality she was outside, looking at me through the glass doors. We both heard the same train.

"Why us?" I whisper.

"She couldn't have her own child," says the DCS. "Her mother confirmed it."

"But why us?" I ask, louder this time. "I only met her two months ago."

"I think she saw you a lot earlier," says Cyrus. "I suspect Agatha thought very carefully about what baby she wanted. It helped her to rationalize what she planned to do."

"There is nothing rational about any of this," says Jack, who is scornful of giving Agatha any motive or justification.

"She idolized you," says Cyrus. "You were success-ful, wealthy, well liked. You have two children already—a boy and a girl. Agatha would have seen you as having the ideal life."

If only she knew the truth.

MacAteer's call has been interrupted. He apolo-gizes and makes us wait while he's briefed. We can't hear the other side of his conversation.

"Are you sure? How many? . . . OK. . . . Get foren-sics. I want the scene locked down and sealed off."

He comes back on the speakerphone, but I hear something new in his voice, an added gravity that makes me frightened.

"Our technicians have been tracing Agatha Fyfle's movements in the days leading up to the abduction. She traveled by train to Leeds on December fourth and went to her mother's house. The following day, she woke early and traveled to the outskirts of the city where she walked along a canal into the woods. The technicians have identified where she stopped by tri-angulating signals from her mobile phone. A team of police reached the location twenty minutes ago—a ruined farmhouse in a clearing above a weir." The detective hesitates. "They discovered three stone cairns arranged around the clearing."

My hand flies to my mouth as my mind collapses inwards like a house of cards accosted by an open door.

"Graves," I whisper.

"It's too early to speculate," says MacAteer. "Foren-sic teams are on their way."

"She's taken other babies," I say, looking at Cyrus. "You predicted this."

"We shouldn't jump to conclusions."

My mouth has gone dry. "Is she going to kill Ben?"

"They may be miscarriages."

"Three of them?"

"Christ!" says Jack, leaning his head against the wall.

My mood has been swinging wildly between elation and despair. Suddenly it plunges again. We must find her. We have to get Ben back.

At the same time, I'm torn between two opposing desires. One part of me wants to force Agatha to run, giving her nowhere to hide. Another part of me knows that she needs to find somewhere warm and safe to shelter my baby for another night.

I am trapped between these two thoughts—willing her onwards, yet hoping she fails.

AGATHA

December cold, I shiver through the last hour, hugging Rory tightly to my chest, keeping him warm. Crouching behind rubbish bins, I watch Mr. Patel lock up the supermarket and leave through the rear door, twirling his keys on his forefinger as he walks down the alleyway to his Mercedes.

A dark-colored cat streaks out from behind the bins, chasing something smaller and equally dark. I almost scream and drop Rory, whose eyes pop open. He doesn't cry. Such a good boy. I've given him another dose of antibiotics, squirting the medicine in the back of his mouth so he didn't cough it up. He's hungry, but I have nothing to feed him unless I get inside.

Keeping to the shadows, I reach the dead-bolted door and lift a loose brick at the base of the wall. The key is attached to a plastic fob and is meant for whichever employee is tasked with opening up each morning.

Feeling for the lock, I stab at it blindly, knowing that once inside I will have about twenty seconds to get to the control panel and punch in the code to deactivate the alarm.

The key slides into place and turns. The door opens and I hear the first shrill pre-alarm beeps, getting louder as I approach the panel. My hands are so cold I hit the wrong code. I cancel the attempt and try again. How long do I have left? Ten seconds? Five? Unless the code has been changed?

I'm halfway through the sequence of numbers when sound explodes around me and the lights begin flashing, illuminating every aisle of the supermarket. I hit the last number. *Enter.* Silence. I must have woken half of Barnes.

I look down an aisle through the front windows at the street beyond. A red bus passes. An elderly couple, out walking their dog, glance into the supermarket and keep going.

Rory lets out a muffled sob from beneath my coat. I carry him inside and lock the door. The heating has gone off but there's enough residual warmth in the supermarket to shrug off my coat. Lifting Rory out of the sling, I rock him back and forth, making shushing sounds, telling him it's all right. He settles by sucking on my little finger.

The aisles of the supermarket are lit by low-watt security lights, which give everything a yellow-green tinge. I'm going to be visible to anyone passing outside. I get changed into a smock left behind by one of the staff and move along the aisles, collecting nappies, wipes, baby powder, formula, and bottles. It's not until I see the shelves full of crisps, biscuits, and chocolate bars that I realize my own hunger.

Using the staff kettle to boil water, I sterilize two bottles and make up formula, wedging a bottle in the freezer between the frozen peas and oven chips, trying to cool it down. I check on it every few minutes, testing the temperature.

In the meantime, I clean and change Rory, checking for any signs of a rash. Dr. Schur said he was underweight and malnourished, but that's not my fault. I've tried to feed him. I did everything they said in the books.

Sitting on sacks of rice, I feed Rory, who finishes a

whole bottle, sucking on air to get the last drops. I burp him against my shoulder, praying that the milk stays down. He doesn't fall asleep immediately. He watches me as I make another two bottles in case we have to leave in a hurry.

I find a steak-and-mushroom pie in the freezer cabinet and use the microwave in the storeroom to thaw it out. I cook it up with a packet of frozen vegetables and serve my feast on a paper plate with plastic cutlery. Scanning the shelves, I find the most expensive bottle of red wine and open that as well, raising a glass to Mr. Patel and toasting his generosity.

"This is the life, isn't it?" I say to Rory, who watches me eat. "Wouldn't it be nice to stay here forever?"

I know that's impossible. At six in the morning someone will show up to open the supermarket and the deliveries will begin—the bread and milk and newspapers. At six thirty the doors will open and the early risers will drift in, picking up supplies on their way to work.

"I feel like something sweet," I say to Rory, whose eyes are growing heavy. I walk to the freezer chest and open the sliding lid, perusing the tubs of premium ice cream.

"Will it be Ben & Jerry's, Häagen-Dazs, or Bessant & Drury's? Why not try them all?"

I start with three tubs, tasting each one. I'm opening a fourth when someone knocks on the front doors. A young couple, teenagers, are signaling me. They're both drunk and holding each other up.

"We're closed," I yell.

"We need cigarettes," says the boy, waving a twenty-quid note.

"Try the pub."

"They kicked us out."

"Not my problem."

The girl twists up her face. "Don't be such a cow. You can open for one minute."

"Can't do it. Register's closed."

The boy slams his hand against the doors, making them vibrate. He does it again and I have to warn him that I'll call the police.

He steps back and looks around until he spies a plastic milk crate. Picking it up, he hurls it against the glass, but it bounces off and hits him in the shin. It must hurt, because he's hopping around. His girlfriend kicks at the door.

"I'm calling the police," I say, holding up my phone.

"Fat cow!" she replies.

The girl drags her boyfriend away, weaving across the road to the bus stop, flipping off a passing driver who toots his horn.

Pouring another glass of wine, I glance at the magazine covers featuring beautiful women with airbrushed bodies and celebrity couples with varnished lives, who will grow old gracelessly and cling to fame. One of them shows a woman in a bikini and sarong on a white-sand beach, where the azure water matches her eyes. A little boy is playing with a bucket and spade at her feet. I once asked Hayden if he would take me to Tahiti, but he laughed and said I'd get seasick. That was before Rory.

I want to go home. I want to sleep in my bed. I want Hayden's arms around me and to hear him say that he loves me. We were so happy together. We could have been a great couple, envied by others, like Jack and Meghan. Not perfect, I realize that now, but worth preserving. A marriage should have children. It's hard enough to keep one together even with a child. Without them, I don't know if it's possible. I saw that with

Nicky—how the joy and spontaneity and laughter went out of our marriage when he was forced to wank into a cup while I was prodded, poked, and inseminated with my legs in stirrups and a stranger's hands touching me.

Rory is asleep. I run my finger down his cheek and across his parted lips, knowing how little time we have left. There's nowhere we can hide. I don't have the money or the anonymity. I don't have the energy.

Curling up on the floor next to Rory, using my coat as a blanket, I try to sleep and dream of Tahiti—the warm water and soft breeze and my little boy playing in the sand. Everything scares me—the traffic outside, the creaking of the roof, and the silence. The creature has won. He knows that. He is feasting on my inner organs, enjoying his last supper.

MEGHAN

Trapped between wakefulness and terrible dreams, I toss and turn, occasionally opening my eyes, hoping for morning to appear beyond the window. The curtains remain dark and the city sleeps.

At some point I get out of bed and walk through the quiet house. Jack is sleeping in an undersized bed in the newly decorated nursery.

"Are you awake?" I whisper.

"Uh-huh," Jack says, mumbling into his pillow.

I sit next to him. The bed sags. "What are you thinking about?"

"Same as you."

"Do you think he's all right?"

"I hope so."

The curtains are open and the branches cast shadows on the wall.

"Are you sure we can survive this?" I ask. "Maybe we're not meant to stay together."

"Don't say that."

"Why did you sleep with Rhea Bowden?"

"Because I am monumentally stupid."

"That's not an answer."

He takes a deep breath. I feel his chest expand and contract. "I wish I could tell you."

"I can make it a multiple-choice question. Was it a midlife crisis? Boredom? Did you stop loving me?"

"No, no, never that."

"She's not younger than me. She's not prettier." My voice is growing strident. "Explain it to me?"

"She was there," he whispers.

"What?"

"Rhea Bowden. She was there."

"Mount Everest is there. You could have mounted that."

"I don't love her. I never did."

"Oh, so it was just sex." My sarcasm stings him. He shifts uncomfortably. I catch the scent of his deodorant and the warm fug of his body. "I'm giving you a chance to explain."

He turns to face me, propping his head on his hand. "It was exciting at first. Frightening. Different. You and I had stopped talking to each other."

"We talk all the time."

"We talk about bills and expenses and kids, but not about each other. We don't share our intimate thoughts anymore. We don't talk about the future or laugh about the past. I used to believe that life was leading somewhere, but it's not, is it? This is it! We're simply existing."

"And Rhea Bowden changed that?"

"No. I thought she might, but I was being stupid." He reaches across the bedspread and touches my hand. I pull it away.

"Every time I think of you with that woman . . ."

"Don't, then."

"How do we get beyond this?"

"We start again. We do it for Lucy and Lachlan and Ben. We owe it to them."

He reaches for my hand. I let him take it. "Every word I said at the church was true. I think you're truly remarkable. And whatever happens—whether we're together or apart—I will always love you."

I pull back the covers and slide onto the narrow bed next to him. His arms close around me and we spoon as though trying to mold our bodies into one.

"This doesn't mean you're forgiven."

"I know."

I notice a suitcase on the floor and a pile of Jack's clothes.

"Are you leaving me?"

"I didn't know if you wanted me to stay."

"I thought maybe you had already gone."

"No."

"Are you sure?"

"Positive."

AGATHA

I wake with a start, frightened that I might have overslept. The clock on the microwave says 5:14. I touch Rory's forehead. He doesn't stir. The fever has gone. Getting stiffly to my feet, I put on my coat and warm a bottle in the microwave.

Rory's mouth opens at the touch of the teat and he sucks automatically, taking the whole bottle. I change his nappy again and pack a few spares. The clock says 5:40. I have another fifteen minutes.

Mr. Patel's secret place is a drawer beneath the cash register. It's where he stores the mobile SIM cards and lottery scratch cards and the cash float for the registers. He keeps a spare key in the broom cupboard so that whoever opens up each morning has cash for the register.

Unlocking the drawer, I take a handful of SIM cards and the bundle of banknotes, leaving the coins behind. Reaching farther into the drawer, my fingers search for something heavy, wrapped in an oily cloth. The gun. The one Mr. Patel boasts about and shows to new employees, hoping to impress them. The gun he doesn't like to use. My fingers close around the handle. I draw it out, unwrapping the cloth, weighing the pistol in my hand. I spend a few moments identifying the safety catch and how to remove the magazine. The knot inside my chest seems to loosen. I have options now. I won't be bullied or rushed. I will decide how this ends.

Tucking the pistol into my bag, I cover it with nappies and wet wipes and two bottles of formula. The clock says 5:55—time to go.

Where?

Away from here.

Foolish. Foolish.

Shut up!

You could have ended this yesterday if you weren't such a coward.

I have a plan.

Tahiti! Is that your plan? Foolish girl!

Slipping Rory into the sling, I adjust the knot, securing him snugly against my chest, then button my coat around him. I leave through the rear door, along the lane, passing Lucy's school before cutting across the edge of Barnes Common to the railway station. I buy a coffee from a man with a van who wears fingerless gloves and sells homemade muffins. He banters, chirpy for the hour, but I'm not in the mood for small talk.

Bundles of free newspapers are stacked beside the station entrance. I look at the front page and find no mention of Baby Ben or of me. I look at pages two and three. Nothing. I expected my picture to be all over the papers by now—the woman who stole Baby Ben. Instead they're still fixated on Rhea Bowden and her affair with Jack. Poor Meg. It's bad enough being cheated on without it becoming public. I blame Hayden. He must have thought he was so clever, selling that story to the papers, but all he's done is jeopardize a marriage.

You should hate her.

Why?

She has what you want. She's rubbing your nose in it.

That's not her fault.

Fuck her up! Show her how it feels.

What feels?

Losing someone you love.

Waiting on the eastbound platform I am joined by a handful of early-morning commuters, breathing in clouds and stamping their feet against the cold. The train rounds a distant bend, appearing from the mist and slowing to a halt. The doors open. I take a seat in a quiet corner before retrieving my phone and inserting a new SIM card.

Hayden will probably be asleep or under arrest or both. Whatever the case, they'll be listening to his calls.

He answers groggily.

"It's me," I say.

"Aggy?"

"Yeah."

There is a long pause. He has covered the phone as though he's talking to someone. Another voice comes onto the line.

"Agatha, this is Brendan MacAteer of the Metropolitan Police."

"I want to speak to Hayden."

"You can speak to him, but first I have to ask if Baby Ben is with you and if he's all right."

The question irritates me. Why is he asking about Ben? It's always been about Ben, never about Rory. I want to scream at him. How dare he ignore my child!

"Put Hayden on," I say through gritted teeth.

"Listen to me, Agatha. I know you're scared, but I can help you. We all want to see that nobody gets hurt."

"Put Hayden on the phone right now or I'm going to hang up. I won't be calling back. You have three seconds."

"Agatha, please listen to me."

"Two seconds."

"I want to help you."

"One."

"Here's Hayden."

The phone is handed over.

"It's me again," he says. I hear someone in the background mention the word "train." They'll be looking for me.

My voice falters. "I guess you've worked it out by now."

"A while ago."

"I'm sorry that Rory isn't your baby."

"That doesn't matter now. How is Rory? Does he still have a fever?"

"No. He's better."

"He could have meningitis."

"I don't think so. He's hungry again."

"That's good."

Someone in the background is feeding Hayden lines, trying to keep me talking while they search.

"What about you?" Hayden asks.

"I'm OK." Tears are splintering my vision and my nose has started to run. "I didn't mean to trick you. I thought that if you spent time with me and Rory you might fall in love with both of us."

"You were right," Hayden says, his voice breaking. "When you first told me you were pregnant I didn't want to be a father. I wasn't ready. Even when I came home for the birth, I told myself that I wouldn't change my mind, but I was wrong. From the moment I set eyes on Rory, I knew my life would never be the same."

"Do you mean that?"

"Uh-huh. There's something I haven't told you. It was going to be my Christmas present to you. I wrote to the navy last week and resigned my commission. I planned to get a job closer to home. Nearer to you and Rory."

"I'm sorry," I sob, feeling even more miserable.

Glancing out the window at the factories and warehouses, I picture the police trying to find me. How long will it take to trace the call? Do they have satellites trained on me now? You see that in all the spy films—satellite cameras that can zoom down and pick out a car license plate or a face in a crowd. The train is pulling into Clapham Junction. There are no police on the platform.

"Did you tell the papers about Jack and Rhea Bowden?" I ask.

"No, I swear. She must have sold the story herself," says Hayden.

I want to believe him.

"Give yourself up, Aggy. Tell us where you are. I'll come and get you."

"I can't do that."

"Rory isn't ours."

"I know."

"What are you going to do?"

"I'll give him to Meghan," I whisper, wiping my nose on my sleeve.

Hayden doesn't answer straightaway.

"I know the police are listening. Tell them I'll give the baby to Meghan. Nobody else. Understand?"

"I don't think they'll go for that idea."

"Remember that place you took me to on our first weekend together? You wanted me to learn things about the navy."

"Yeah."

"That's the place."

"What time?"

"This morning. I don't know what time. Remember what I said. It has to be Meghan. Not the police. Tell them I have a gun. If I see a copper, I'll shoot Rory."

"You wouldn't hurt Rory."

"How would you know? I've killed babies before."

"Don't say that, Aggy. Just come in."

"Not this time." I muffle a sob with my fist. "Hayden?"

"Yeah."

"These past weeks—with you and Rory—have been the happiest of my life."

"Mine too," he says, and I believe him.

MEGHAN

Arriving at Chiswick police station, we're taken directly to MacAteer's office on the second floor and told to wait. Through slatted blinds, I view the incident room where dozens of detectives are on the phones or poring over train timetables and CCTV footage. The helter-skelter of activity should bolster me, but I'm beyond reassurance.

MacAteer's voice echoes across the room.

"There are three million fucking cameras in this city and you're telling me not one of them has picked her up?" He kicks at a chair, which rolls into a bin. Detectives keep their heads down, not wanting to make eye contact.

The DCS is issuing orders. "Tell the Imperial War Museum we want full access to their control room and security cameras. Front office staff will be replaced by undercover officers and the public have to be kept away from the foyer."

"How do we do that without alerting her?" asks a detective.

"I don't care—just do it."

MacAteer is walking and talking. "We need eyes on her as soon as possible, which means putting plain-clothes officers at the nearest train stations and bus stops. They're to follow from a distance. Nobody, I repeat nobody, approaches her until we have the SWAT teams in place. Is that understood?"

Nods all round.

MacAteer has reached the office. He shakes Jack's hand and smiles at me, trying to be reassuring.

"Thank you for coming." *As though we had a choice.* "How much have you been told?"

"Agatha called her fiancé," says Jack.

"We've traced the signal to a South West train traveling between Wandsworth station and Clapham Junction at six twenty-four this morning. By the time we intercepted the train, it had reached Waterloo station. She wasn't on board."

"What about Ben?" I ask.

"We believe he's with her."

"Is she going to give him back?"

"She says she'll hand Ben over to you. She wasn't clear on the time, but we think she's heading to the Imperial War Museum."

"Why there?" I ask.

"It's where Hayden Cole took her on their first date."

MacAteer glances at a message on his phone. "We're going to put a female officer in your clothes—someone with the same build and hair color."

"But Agatha knows what I look like," I say.

"I'm not putting you in danger."

"Won't she get angry if someone else shows up?"

"It won't be an issue."

"How can you say that?"

I look at Jack, hoping he might back me up. *Come on!* He remains silent.

MacAteer continues. "We believe Agatha Fyfle spent last night at a supermarket in Barnes. She entered after hours and disabled the alarm system. An employee reported the break-in at six this morning, when he arrived for work. Somebody stole nappies, baby formula, and food. The manager had a handgun locked in a drawer below the cash register. The gun is now missing, which is why I won't risk putting you anywhere near this woman."

"Agatha wouldn't shoot me."

"You don't know that."

I begin to argue, but MacAteer cuts me off. "Five years ago, Agatha was interviewed about the abduction of a baby girl in Brighton. Although never considered to be a serious suspect, she was traced by officers using accommodation records to locate any visitors to Brighton that weekend."

"The baby was never found," I say, the words like cotton in my mouth.

"How do you know that?" asks Jack.

"I heard the mother being interviewed on the radio. Emily. That was the baby's name."

Anxiety expands in my chest like a balloon. I picture the stone markers found beside the canal near Leeds. What did Agatha do? Did she panic and hide the evidence? What will she do if I don't show up?

MacAteer answers a knock on the door. A car is waiting to take him to the Imperial War Museum.

"Please let me come," I beg. "Ben is going to need me."

"It's safer if you stay here," he says.

"You either take me or you arrest me."

The detective looks at Jack, hoping for a supporter.

Jack raises his palms, as though opting out of the debate. "If I were you, I wouldn't argue with my wife."

AGATHA

At Clapham Junction, I catch a train to Three Bridges in West Sussex before changing platforms and taking a London-bound service to Victoria. The city passes the window—railway workshops, besmirched brick walls, and pitted asphalt car parks that give way to terraced houses and blocks of flats. A blur of blue, white, and yellow rushes past in the opposite direction, making the windows rattle and the air pressure change.

Unwrapping a new SIM card, I slide it into my phone, pressing it on. The screen lights up. I call another number. There are phantom clicks on the line. A woman answers.

"I'd like to speak to Meghan Shaughnessy," I say.

"Are you a reporter?"

"No."

"Are you a friend of hers?"

"She knows me."

"Mrs. Shaughnessy is busy at the moment. I can take a message."

"Tell her it's Agatha."

The woman on the phone seems to choke on her own saliva.

"Please hold," she says, covering the phone. I can still hear what she's saying. "It's her! Trace the signal. Let the boss know."

She uncovers the handset. "She's coming now."

"You're lying. Put her on or I'll hang up."

"She's upstairs."

"No she's not."

The phone is covered again. I hear muffled voices. Instructions.

"Here she is," says the woman.

Meg is breathing hard. "It's me."

"Are they listening?"

"No."

"Don't lie to me."

"Yes. I'm sorry. Is Ben all right?"

"He's fine."

"They said he was sick."

"He's better now."

There is a pause. The silence weighs more heavily on Meg. "The police say you're going to give him up."

"Only to you."

"Can it be someone else?"

"No."

"They say you have a gun."

"I'm not going to shoot you."

"The police don't know that."

Another silence. I take a deep breath and begin to explain. Meg interrupts.

"You're on a train. You could leave Ben at the ticket office or give him to a conductor."

"No."

"But if you did that—"

"You're not listening," I say sharply.

She apologizes. I begin again, unsure where to start. Perhaps it doesn't matter. Maybe Meg will never understand what it's like to be me. She grew up in a loving family and went to the best schools and then to university. She got a dream job, working for a women's magazine, where she got to flirt with Jude Law over lunch. She married a handsome, successful man, and fell pregnant at the drop of a hat. How can she ever understand my life? What it's like to live in a cramped, claustrophobic tunnel that gets smaller and darker as each year passes. There is no light at the end—no paradise, no rest. I am stuck in this squalid, fetid hole with a creature that slithers in my guts, telling me I don't deserve the light, that I am not a real woman because I cannot have a baby.

I don't know if I've said any of this out loud but I realize that I'm still talking as the train crosses the Thames and the water below me swirls and eddies around the pylons of Chelsea Bridge, foaming and bubbling on the outgoing tide.

A clipped female voice comes over the intercom: "We are now approaching London Victoria." The train brakes—the metal wheels squealing.

Meg will have heard it. So will the police. I feel as though I'm trapped between two worlds—the past and the present. I cannot see beyond today, because others, luckier than me, have taken my future and left me no room.

"If you want your baby—you have to come and get him. I'm not giving him to anyone else."

MEGHAN

By the time the police reached Victoria Station, Agatha had slipped away into the maze of crowded walkways, corridors, and exits that lead to other lines or onto the street. Now they're studying the CCTV footage from dozens of cameras, hoping to discover which way she went. Three Tube lines intersect at Victoria, as well as an overland service that brings tens of thousands of people into the West End every day.

Wipers thrash and sirens wail. From inside the police car the noise sounds strangely muted and it takes me a moment to realize that we are the source of the sound, making heads turn and cars pull aside.

Traffic is stretched back for more than half a mile along Westminster Bridge Road on the approach to the Imperial War Museum. Motorcycle outriders have joined us, ahead and behind, unblocking intersections and finding a route through the bottlenecks.

Lisa-Jayne is behind the wheel with Cyrus in the front passenger seat. Jack and I sit in the rear. He reaches out and takes my hand, lacing his fingers through mine.

I keep remembering my conversation with Agatha, replaying it in my mind, looking for some new detail that might help. She said she was sorry, which is a good sign.

"Did she sound rational?" asks Jack, as though reading my thoughts.

"I don't think she's crazy."

"Of course she is—she faked a pregnancy and stole a baby."

"And fooled everyone."

"Clever people can be crazy."

Cyrus doesn't comment, but I suspect he agrees with me. In all of our dealings, he has never used words like "crazy" or "deranged" or "delusional" when referring to Ben's kidnapper. Agatha has always been a victim in Cyrus's mind, something Jack will never accept. He's forever denouncing psychologists and psychiatrists for creating the "age of victimhood" where everyone finds someone else to blame for their problems rather than take any personal responsibility.

"We need to talk about what happens next," says Cyrus, turning in his seat. "DCS MacAteer won't put you in danger—it's more than his job is worth—but Agatha may insist on speaking to you. If that happens, you need to have answers ready."

"What sort of answers?"

"She may want to test you. She may change her mind. You have to be ready to convince her."

I nod.

"First and foremost—you ask to see Ben. It's called proof of life. You have to be sure that she has him."

"OK."

"Agatha is likely to be anxious and frightened. She may seem calm but have conflicting emotions, particularly at the hand-over. When she sees someone pick up the baby, she'll likely realize that she won't see him again. That's when she could change her mind."

"What do I do then?"

"Keep her calm. Engage with her. Listen when she's talking. Show that you understand. Agatha will want to dictate the terms, but you can start to move her."

"How?"

"By winning her trust," says Cyrus. "It may help if you refer to the baby as Rory rather than Ben, because that's who he is to Agatha. She has looked after him ever since he was born. Giving him up will be hard."

"Do I ask her about the gun?"

"No."

"What if she doesn't want to give him up?"

"Encourage her, gently. Ask about the baby—how is he sleeping and feeding? Tell her she's done a great job."

I nod.

"The police will have marksmen training their weapons on Agatha. If they get a clear shot and they see her become agitated, they may decide to take her down. You cannot interfere with this."

"I don't want anyone getting shot."

"Which is why you have to keep her calm."

"What if she won't give him to the policewoman? What if it has to be me?"

"DCS MacAteer will have to make that call. At some point, Ben has to be handed over. That's the most crucial moment. Either Agatha's resolve will crumble or she'll fight back."

"Will she hurt him?" asks Jack.

Cyrus shakes his head. "But she will die for him."

The police car pulls up on Lambeth Road. A constable opens the door for me and holds an umbrella over my head. A police helicopter is hovering above us, visible between the bare branches of the trees. I hear a megaphone telling people that the museum is closed and to move away from the area.

We are taken along a path and up a short set of

stairs, between two enormous guns that are pointing north towards the Thames. DCS MacAteer is waiting in the marbled foyer. I look past him into a vast room where old-fashioned warplanes are suspended from the ceiling as though frozen in midflight. I recognize the V-1 and V-2 rockets, as well as a Spitfire, which swoops overhead as though ready to strafe unwanted visitors. The interconnecting halls rise a hundred feet to a domed ceiling that is flanked by staircases that turn back and forth up to the higher levels.

I am taken into an anteroom and then an administration office, which has become the control room. Cyrus is talking to a woman with hair similar to mine who has been dressed in a skirt, blouse, and overcoat. She is about my size with the same complexion, but nobody would ever mistake us.

"She's not going to fool anyone," I tell MacAteer when he breaks from a huddle of plainclothes detectives.

"The officer is a trained negotiator."

"What if you make her angry?"

"I know what I'm doing."

MacAteer reaches into a box and produces a bulletproof vest.

"Is that necessary?"

"Everyone has to wear one."

The vest is lighter than I expect. I pull it over my blouse and he clips the straps, pulling them tight.

"Can you breathe?"

I nod. "Won't Agatha see all the police cars and the helicopter?"

"I can't risk putting people in danger."

"What if she runs?"

"We're sealing off the area."

A man approaches. Dressed in black overalls, he's

so laden with body armor that I doubt he can swing his arms. Through an open doorway, I notice at least eight more men in identical clothes. They are moving out, some taking the stairs, which zigzag back and forth as they climb to the higher levels of the museum. Others take up positions behind pillars or against walls.

The SWAT leader briefs MacAteer.

"I have one team covering the main doors from the cloakroom. Another is covering the foyer and main hall."

"What about outside?"

"We have firearms officers on the roof and others deployed in the grounds, dressed as gardeners and council workers. Their default aiming position is the upper torso—center of mass—but we can go for a head shot if she's carrying the baby across her chest."

Without thinking, I cry, "Please don't shoot anyone!"

The men turn. "Go back to your husband, Mrs. Shaughnessy," says MacAteer.

"Let me talk to her," I plead. "Nobody has to get hurt."

"We have this under control."

Lisa-Jayne is told to escort me back to the anteroom office, where I argue with Jack. He doesn't seem to care what happens to Agatha.

Before any of this happened, before Ben was taken and the harsh media spotlight lit up our small corner of the world, my life had been comfortable and untroubled; a well-worn middle-class progression that felt like a dream run but could have been a rut. How dare I complain. I was born in the right time and right place to the right family. I met a man and we built a life together. Yet sometimes even the most charmed existence can change in the blink of an eye, or turn on the length of an eyelash. One moment of indecision. A cancer cell. A rogue gene. A wrong turn. A red light. A drunk driver. A cruel piece of misfortune.

Each time I close my eyes, I picture Agatha walking towards the museum, aware that she's being watched. She is carrying my baby in a sling across her chest. The foyer is empty. She sees a woman who looks a little like me from a distance but soon becomes someone else. They argue. My surrogate tells Agatha to calm down. Agatha calls my name. She wraps her arms tightly around Ben. A red dot appears on her cheek and moves up her nose and onto her forehead.

In a fleeting puff of blood and vapor she spins and falls, carried down by gravity, striking her head on the marble floor. I see the blood covering Ben's face. I don't hear him crying.

My eyes open. The clock doesn't seem to have moved. I am sweating beneath the bulletproof vest. Lisa-Jayne brings me a glass of water, but I cannot swallow.

Minutes pass slowly: 11:04 . . . 11:05 . . . 11:06. Where is she? There have been no sightings of Agatha from the officers outside.

MacAteer has spoken twice to the police commissioner, who wants to know how long the operation is going to last. He takes another call. I only hear one side of the conversation, which involves a lot of cursing and threats. "What's happened?" asks Jack when the call ends.

"Hayden Cole jumped out of the police car on Fulham Palace Road forty-five minutes ago."

AGATHA

The carriage is full of men in suits and women in dark overcoats and winter boots. Day shifts and night shifts are blended together. Fresh faces and tired faces. The showered and the soiled. A boy opposite me is wearing an England shirt and paint-speckled jeans. He slouches lower with man-spread knees, his head rocking from side to side as he gently snores.

I look out the window, aware of how drab the world has become, how gray and turgid and run-of-the-mill. It carries on blithely ignoring my plight because I have no weight or consequence. How do people do it—keep going—why do they make the effort?

I hold Rory on my lap, letting him sleep in the crook of my left arm. My right hand is in the pocket of my coat, where I've put the gun. I'm sweating in the over-heated carriage but I will not take off my coat because I do not trust the police to do as I've asked.

The creature is awake.

Foolish girl, foolish girl, foolish girl.

I'm doing the right thing.

By giving up.

I'm not his mother.

You're the only mother he's ever known.

He's not mine.

He could be. Turn around. Run.

Where?

Most of the commuters get off at Canary Wharf and

Heron Quays. Only the tourists and sightseers remain by the time we cross under the Thames. The train slows again. Stops. I loop the colorful cotton sling around my neck and hold Rory close to my chest as I step onto a crowded platform and ride the long escalator up into the daylight.

Rain is falling. I don't have an umbrella. Tilting my face, I feel a thousand tiny spines of raindrops melting on my cheeks, clinging to my hair and eyelashes. I wrap one side of my overcoat around Rory and keep moving, weaving between shoulders, head down, hood up.

As I walk along the avenue of trees, I notice how the branches almost meet in the middle of the road. Across the gravel forecourt, I glimpse the Maritime Museum through the railing fence. The cream-and-pink stucco façade has been darkened by the day, looking gloomy rather than grand. Just visible through the colonnades, the Royal Observatory is etched sharply against the gray. Hayden once took a photograph of me straddling the Prime Meridian line, the meeting point of east and west. He told me I was standing at the center of time.

Where are the police, I wonder. I expected them to be waiting. Maybe they're hiding. I imagine SWAT teams behind the darkened windows and sharpshooters on the rooftops.

Shortly after eleven I walk through the main doors, past the information desk and the cloakroom. There are parties of schoolchildren queuing up, dressed in blazers and boater hats and brightly polished shoes. Heads must be counted. Names must be crossed off. The officious-looking head teacher is a sour-faced woman in a black flared skirt and thick stockings. She treats them like prisoners instead of students.

I stop and look around me. Nobody seems to

be watching me. I glance at Rory, who is sucking his thumb.

"Why am I giving you back?" I whisper. "They're not even here."

Exhausted, I take a seat on one of the island benches and turn on my phone, calling Meghan's number.

She answers nervously.

"Where are you?" I ask.

"Waiting."

"So am I."

There is a pause. She asks me to hold on. I can hear her walking and opening a door. Closing it. Whispering.

"Are you at the Imperial War Museum?"

"No. I'm in Greenwich . . . at the National Maritime Museum."

Meghan is flustered now. "We thought . . . you were supposed . . . we've been waiting . . ."

Why would Hayden send them to the wrong place?

"I've been here all along," I tell her.

"Please, please, I'm coming," she says. "Don't go anywhere. Where will you be?"

"There's a painting I love. It's in the Special Exhibitions Gallery."

At that moment I hear a voice behind me and I end the call.

"Hello, Aggy."

I turn slowly, reaching into my pocket for the gun.

"What are you doing here?"

Nerves are sparking in Hayden's eyes. He's dressed in jeans, a leather jacket, and a baseball cap with the price tag still attached. Unshaven and red-eyed, he looks as though he hasn't slept. Glancing down, he sees the top of Rory's head, just visible behind the folds of my coat.

"How is he?"

"Getting better."

"That's good."

"Why are you here?"

"Can we go for a walk?" he asks.

"Why? I don't understand."

"Please, Aggy, I'll explain outside. You go first."

Doing as he asks, I retrace my steps up the stairs and out the main doors, and turn left along the asphalt path. Glancing over my shoulder, I see him walking twenty yards behind me, his hands deep in his pockets and collar turned up.

I wait for him under a canopy of bare branches. Hayden steps closer and cups my head in his hands. I flinch, thinking he might be angry, but he leans closer and kisses me gently, holding his lips on mine until I breathe in his sigh. His arms slip around me and I press my head against his chest.

"What are you doing here?"

"I came to help."

Stepping back, he unbuttons my coat, reaching inside until he brushes his thumb over Rory's cheek. His fingers are cold. Rory's eyes open momentarily and close again.

"I'm going to miss him," says Hayden, his voice thick with emotion.

"Are the police going to charge you?"

He shrugs.

"I'll tell them it wasn't your fault."

"It doesn't matter."

"Please tell your parents that I'm sorry."

"You gave them a grandchild. You gave me a son."

"And now I'm giving him back."

"That's why I'm here."

"I don't understand."

He looks nervously over his shoulder, studying the

entrance to the park and the surrounding streets. "We don't have much time. I sent the police to the wrong museum, but it won't take them long to realize."

He slides his hands behind my neck and loosens the knot on the sling.

"What are you doing?"

"I'm taking Rory."

"Why would you do that?"

"So you can run."

"Run where?"

"You can get away." He pulls a bundle of cash out of his pocket. "This is five thousand pounds. It's all I have." He holds out the money, wanting me to take it.

"I can't run. My face will be on every TV screen and newspaper. They'll be watching the ports and airports."

"I have a navy mate who's on the same ship as me but won't be home until mid-January. I have the keys to his flat in Portsmouth. You can hide there for a few weeks. I can bring you food."

"A few weeks isn't long enough."

"It'll give us time to think of another plan."

"They'll find me eventually."

Hayden's face twists. "I'm trying to help you, Aggy. I know what you did was wrong—but you're giving Rory back. He's fine. You don't deserve to be punished for this."

"But I do."

"No, no. You were hurting. Lonely. The police told me about your teenage pregnancy and the adoption. That wasn't your fault."

"I've done other things."

Hayden raises his face to the rain and groans, as though wanting to scream in frustration.

"I took another woman's baby," I whisper. "You weren't to blame. I tricked you. I'm sorry. Now I'm giving him back."

"OK, but let me do it for you," he says, pleading with me.

"This is not your mistake."

"I love you, Aggy. I didn't *want* to fall in love, but I couldn't help myself. I know you think it was just because of Rory and becoming a father, but that's only part of it. I fell in love with *you*."

I try to say something, but he doesn't give me the chance.

"Why do you think I kept quiet about your mother not being at the birth when the police asked? When I couldn't contact the midwife, I knew what you'd done. I knew that Rory wasn't ours, but I didn't want to give him up. I wish you'd told me earlier, but then he got sick and we didn't have a choice. When you ran off from the surgery, I tried to stop Dr. Schur calling the police. I vouched for you. I said that I'd seen you breast-feeding . . . and that we had a proper birth certificate. I lied for you. I lied for us. But I couldn't stop him."

His voice cracks. "They're going to send you to prison, Aggy. You don't deserve that. Take the money. Run. Go to my mate's place. In a few weeks, I'll find somewhere else for you to go."

"I can't run," I whisper.

"Of course you can. People run all the time. They disappear. I can keep you hidden. We're going to lose your little boy, Aggy, but we don't have to lose each other."

Hayden pauses, searching for the right words. Reaching for them. Coming up empty. He tries again. "This doesn't have to be the end. We'll give the baby back. You can plead guilty; tell the jury you were obsessed, mad with desire for a baby. The judge will show mercy. At most you'll serve two, maybe three years, and then you'll be free. We're still young. We can get married and have our own baby."

I reach out and brush his unshaven cheek, calling him a silly boy. "I can't have children."

"Right. OK. But we could adopt a baby. I don't mind. Rory isn't mine, but I still love him."

"Nobody will ever let me adopt a baby—not after what I've done."

Hayden rocks from side to side, pulling at his ears, desperately searching for answers. I'm the cause of his pain.

"Go home, my love. They'll be here soon."

"But nobody knows where you are."

"I told them."

"What?"

"I called Meg. I told her they were at the wrong place."

Hayden looks over his shoulder again, with more urgency now.

"Quick! Give me Rory. We can still do this."

"No."

Ignoring me, he takes his right arm from the sleeve of his jacket and holds Rory against his chest before refastening the buttons, concealing the baby completely.

"They'll think you were involved," I say, trying to stop him. "The police will lay charges. You'll lose your commission. Your career . . . I've hurt you enough already."

"I don't care. I'm leaving the navy. None of it matters."

"Yes, it does."

Hayden's eyes are swimming. "Please, Aggy, why won't you run?"

"This is my mistake, not yours. I won't let you risk everything for me."

He isn't listening. He doesn't understand what I've

done—what happened to the other babies, or what I did to Nicky. The lives I've ruined. I grab his arm, clasping the empty leather sleeve of his jacket. He flicks me away. I reach out again, calling Rory's name.

"Give him back!" I yell.

"Let me help you."

"Nobody can help me."

The creature uncoils.

Stupid, stupid, stupid girl! He's stealing him.

He'd never do that.

He wants Rory for himself.

He loves me.

He's lying.

My fingers have found the pistol. I pull it free. My vision is fractured by tears and I can barely recognize my own voice, which rises from the depths of my chest, shaking with disappointment or grief.

"GIVE HIM BACK TO ME!"

Hayden hesitates, staring at the gun. "Don't do this, Aggy."

Shoot him!

He loves me.

Nobody could ever love you.

You're wrong.

Hayden hands Rory over without saying another word. He turns and walks away, wiping something from his eyes.

MEGHAN

The rain has turned to sleet, angling across the windows of the cab like windblown gobs of spit. Tires swish beneath me and classical music plays on the cab radio, Vivaldi's *Four Seasons*: "Winter." A different storm rages within me. We were sent to the wrong place. Did Hayden Cole do it on purpose or was it a mistake?

I am alone in the cab but it won't take them long to realize I'm missing. They'll send someone to the bathroom to search for me or Jack will raise the alarm. I told nobody about Agatha's phone call. Instead I excused myself and managed to shake Lisa-Jayne as MacAteer stood his men down.

Hayden Cole was in the backseat of a police car being driven to the Imperial War Museum when he told police he was going to be sick. The escorting officers lowered a rear window. Hayden squeezed out before they could react. The police gave chase, but lost him in Fulham Palace Road Cemetery. I don't know why Hayden ran, but he's become a fugitive just like Agatha.

Right now, I'm certain of only one thing—my baby is in Greenwich. I promised Agatha I'd come alone. I am keeping this promise because I don't want anyone to get hurt, but the doubts are creeping in. What if I'm wrong? What if Agatha and Hayden had this planned all along?

The cab is passing through South London. Outside, I see drab gray shopfronts and blocks of flats that no amount of Christmas decorations and colored lights can make cheerful. I used to love this city—the plane trees and bridges and cathedrals and monuments. I loved its narrow streets and quaint shops and grand gardens. That hasn't changed, but I could leave London tomorrow and not miss it as long as I had my family with me. People, not places, make a life whole.

I roll my head against the glass.

"Are you all right, love?" asks the cabbie.

"Yes, thank you."

"You look familiar."

"I'm nobody."

The cab drops me on Romney Road and I step over puddles to reach the footpath. Despite the rain, crowds of tourists are queuing to visit the *Cutty Sark*. A Japanese tour group marches past me carrying matching umbrellas, following a guide into Greenwich Park.

My mobile is ringing.

"Where the hell are you?" asks Jack.

"I'm getting Ben."

"Are you crazy?"

He's yelling to someone—MacAteer, most likely, whose blood pressure will be stratospheric. "Where are you? Tell me!"

"I'll be fine. Agatha wants to give him back."

"She has a gun, for God's sake!"

"Nobody has to get hurt."

"Listen to me, Meg, don't do this. Tell me where you are."

"I'll call you when it's over."

I hang up and turn off my phone.

The woman at the ticket desk offers me a visitor's map of the museum, but I ask for directions to the Special Exhibitions Gallery.

"It's on the lower ground floor," she says, before interrupting herself. "You're that woman from the TV—the one whose baby got taken."

"No, that's not me."

My knees are shaking as I take the stairs and cross the marble floor, looking between pillars and display cases of naval uniforms and artifacts. A lone figure sits on an island bench in the middle of a cavernous room. My shoes squeak on the polished floor. Agatha raises her eyes and blinks back tears. I notice the sling across her chest, but can't see Ben.

"What took you so long?" she asks, looking behind me, as though expecting to see the police.

"There was a misunderstanding."

"Hayden sent you to the wrong place."

"Why?"

"It doesn't matter now."

I feel the weight of the silence, but not the sadness, because I have eyes only for the sling around Agatha's chest. She reaches across her body and pulls it aside. I see a small pale face with enormous eyes that seem to open at the sound of my voice. They trap us like that—babies—with one look they can take hold of our hearts because our hearts have no defenses against such beauty and fragility.

Ben utters a weak squawk and as if by magic my breasts begin to ache and my milk comes in. I forget everything Cyrus told me about keeping my distance and stumble forward, kneeling beside Agatha.

"He's hungry," she says. "I don't have another bottle."

"I could feed him," I say hopefully.

She ponders this and nods.

Getting up, I begin to unbutton my coat. Agatha sees the Kevlar vest but doesn't say anything.

"Can you help?" I ask.

She loosens the straps and I pull the vest over my head, dropping it on the floor. At that moment, I glimpse the handgun tucked into the pocket of her coat.

I look at Agatha, waiting for a sign.

She unties the knot behind her neck and lowers Ben into her lap. "You can take him."

Unbuttoning my blouse and unclipping my nursing bra, I slide my hands across her thighs and lift Ben to my breast, watching his lips part. He doesn't latch on. I brush the nipple against his top lip, encouraging him to open his mouth wider.

"It might take him a while," says Agatha, who is now holding the gun on her lap.

At the fourth attempt, Ben locks on and sucks hard. His lips barely seem to move, but I can see him swallowing. Filled with joy and relief, my eyes brim over. I did not think, I dared not hope, I prayed, I wished, I did not give up, but now the emotion of the moment overwhelms me.

Agatha reaches into her bag and finds me a tissue.

"I want to say I'm sorry for what I did," she says. "I don't expect you to forgive me, but you should know that I've loved him as much as any mother could. It wasn't personal, by the way. I didn't take him because I wanted to hurt you or Jack. I idolized you. I wanted a life like yours."

"Our life isn't so perfect."

"It was to me."

"Jack and I let each other down all the time."

"Have you forgiven him for Rhea Bowden?"

"I'm trying to," I say. "Did you put the note on his windscreen?"

Agatha nods and gazes down at Ben. "When I was growing up, I used to sit around with my girlfriends and talk about who we'd like to marry. We decided how many children we wanted and gave them preppy names like Jacinta and Rocco. All of us took it for granted that we'd get married and have babies. It was an automatic progression—school, a career, boyfriends, marriage, a mortgage, and children.

"I would even draw sketches of myself and my perfect family, or cut out pictures from magazines and stick them in a scrapbook. I gave myself a chic haircut and self-satisfied look, a handsome husband, a boy and a girl, a nice house in London or the home counties."

She could be describing *my* life.

"That was my fairy tale and I didn't doubt it would come true, but I was wrong and there's no one to blame. It wasn't my fault, or Nicky's."

Agatha toys with the gun, turning it in her hands. "It's not just the absence of a child, but everything that goes with it. The rites of parenthood—the mothers' groups, school-gate chats, Saturday sports on the sidelines, class dinners, school fund-raisers, and speech days. For you, these things are so commonplace you don't give them a second thought. For me they are everything I'll never have. I am an outlier. I am the incredible disappearing woman. I am childless. Less of a person. Not in the club. You take those things for granted."

"No, I don't."

"I've heard you complaining to the other wives. You're all the same. You tell each other about daily dramas, sleepless nights, lazy husbands, fussy eaters, messy rooms, and food allergies. I used to hate you for that." She pauses. "No, I'm sorry—'hate' is too strong a word. I thought you were ungrateful."

"They're just stories," I say. "Everybody complains. I know I'm lucky. And I know I shouldn't take my life for granted."

"But you do. I bet when you see a woman my age without children you automatically wonder if she left it too long, or put her career first. You think maybe she was too selfish or too choosy."

"I don't think that," I say, but in my heart I know she's right.

Feeling lightheaded, I swap Ben between breasts. He belches quietly, leaving a thin trail of milk on my skin.

"I didn't have children to make you feel bad, Agatha. And it's not my fault that you couldn't have a baby, or you lost one. I know it's painful. I know you feel cheated. But you're not the first woman who couldn't fall pregnant, and infertility isn't the worst thing in the world. I'll tell you what's worse. Having a child go missing is worse. Lying awake at night, not knowing if he's alive or dead. You have an empty womb. I had an empty cradle. Mine is worse."

Agatha's eyes flash. "Would you swap your life for mine?"

I shake my head.

"I thought so."

My thumb brushes over Ben's forehead. His eyes are open and he's gazing at me, already falling in love.

Agatha is right. Up until a few weeks ago I had no idea what it was like to be infertile, or to lose a child. I understand that now.

"What are you going to do?" I ask.

Agatha looks at the gun in her lap. "I haven't decided."

"You could give that to me."

She shakes her head.

"Please, don't do anything foolish, Agatha."

She sighs tiredly. "I've been doing foolish things my entire life."

AGATHA

Meg rearranges her bra and buttons her blouse. Rory has fallen asleep on her lap, his belly full.

"You should go," I tell her.

"What about you?"

"I'm going to stay here for a little while."

"You could come with me."

"No."

Meg hesitates, wanting to argue, but she has what she came for. She says she understands how I feel, but I know that's not possible. She can sympathize, but not empathize. Few people can truly appreciate what it's like to give up a child. I was fifteen when it happened to me and I didn't just give up my newborn. I gave up the one-year-old and the two-year-old and the three-year-old and every other year-old that she became. I surrendered every Christmas morning, every visit from the tooth fairy and school concert, every Mother's Day, birthday, and kiss good night.

How can Meg comprehend that? Maybe if she had miscarried, or woken next to the cold, marble-cold body of a baby girl, or lived with a cruel creature twisting inside her, she'd understand.

Why should she have three children when you have none?

That's her good fortune.

She's one of them—part of the chorus.

Meg isn't like that.

She's everything you hate. A smug mummy blogger who is pandered to by advertisers and politicians.

No!

She said an empty cradle was worse than an empty womb. What she meant was "You wouldn't understand because you're not a mother." Arrogant bitch!

Meg is sliding her arms into her coat.

She thinks her experience invalidates yours. She thinks she's better than you are.

No!

Stop her!

It's too late.

"I'm going to leave now," Meg says, holding Ben against her chest. "Thank you for bringing him back."

I nod. She's staring at the gun.

"Do you want to say good-bye?"

I shake my head. A single tear rolls down my cheek and falls onto my knuckles where I'm gripping the gun. The small clear teardrop looks like a jeweled bead, magnifying the skin beneath, creating a tiny curved reflection of the ceiling.

Each step takes Meg farther away.

She doesn't love Rory like you do. She doesn't know him. Take him back!

I can't.

Yes, you can. Raise the gun. Pull the trigger. It's easy.

She reaches the pillar and changes direction, heading towards the stairs.

I look down at the gun. The single tear has rolled along my forefinger and brushed against the trigger.

It is so strange, this life we lead. We search for happiness, but so much is about survival. Existence. We try to manage expectations, but really we're treading water, wasting time, or contemplating lives we might have led. Pretty soon we're like every other godless, money-hungry, backstabbing, jaded, jealous human being, wishing we were richer, prettier, younger, luckier, or could do it all over again.

For me there is no such thing as forgetting. I used to see a psychotherapist every week—Nicky's idea—who told me that I had to take all my negative thoughts and low self-esteem and lock them in a metal box like a pirate's chest with multiple chains and padlocks. I had to bury this box deep in a desert so big that I could dig for ten thousand years and never find it. I tried to do that, but the memories seeped out like nuclear waste with a half-life that lasts millennia.

No matter how hard I try, the creature will always be with me, skulking at the edges of every clearing, waiting for the fire to burn down or the lights to go off before creeping towards me. I can't even be sure whether these are my thoughts or if the creature is thinking for me. I don't know how much of *me* there is left.

Lowering the gun to my side, I walk slowly across the gallery until I'm standing in front of my favorite painting, *Tahiti Revisited*, looking at the palm trees and the warm river and the rocky peaks. I remember asking Hayden if one day he might take me there, but that won't happen now.

Staring into the painting, I imagine myself dissolving into the canvas, appearing on the other side. Three Polynesian women are bathing in the river. Friends or sisters. One is swimming in the water, staring at the sky, while the others dry themselves on the shore, draping towels over a stone carving. The nearest woman has her back to me; her buttocks are heavy, her breasts hidden, her skin tattooed. Slowly, gradually, I imagine my way into her body. I feel the water drying on my skin and the warmth of the sunshine on my shoulders. I glance at the thatched hut in the middle distance and raise my eyes to the rocky peak bathed in light.

A little way off, just out of view, my babies are playing in the crushed coral sand, collecting shells and floating sticks on the tide. All of them are here: Lizzie, Emily, Chloe, and Rory—living in paradise, growing up and growing old, never being cold or hungry or lonely or scared. What is love if not a trick of the light?

Behind me I hear heavy boots on the stairs, but I will not leave my island. I want to smell the tropical flowers, taste the fruit, and feel the sand between my toes. I wade into the warm water, feeling it creep above my knees and thighs . . .

"DROP YOUR WEAPON!" says an amplified voice.

. . . above my chest, up to my shoulders, caressing my skin . . .

"DROP YOUR WEAPON!"

"You mean this old thing?" I say, raising the gun to my temple. "I would never—"

· MEGHAN

We went to mass on Christmas morning, walking across Barnes Green to St. Osmund's. It's not that we've suddenly become religious or undergone any sort of spiritual conversion, but I wanted to thank Father George and the community for all their prayers and good wishes.

Maybe that's what Agatha has done for me—she's given me a reason to believe. I once dismissed faith because I viewed it from an intellectual standpoint, but faith has nothing to do with intellect. Equally, none of the kneeling and muttering of creeds provides any guarantee of contact with God. We can't register our prayers like a parcel and get a signature on delivery.

After the Christmas service, we walk home, following the same path that we took on the evening of the candlelight vigil, along Church Road to Barnes Green. Jack pushes the pram with Ben while Lachlan and Lucy run ahead.

We're having Christmas at our place and the house is already full of laughter and torn wrapping paper. My parents are here, along with Grace and her new boyfriend. Simon and Gina have also arrived, laden with presents for the kids.

I'm cooking turkey with all the trimmings: cranberry sauce, roasted chestnuts, brussels sprouts, orange-glazed carrots, pigs in blankets, and roasted potatoes. Brushing a damp hair from my forehead, I smile at Ben, who is sitting in a bassinet on the work-bench, watching me make the bread sauce.

They're playing charades in the sitting room. It's Lucy's turn and I know she's doing *Frozen* because she does it every time, and Lachlan guesses it first go. He comes running into the kitchen. "Mummy, Mummy, I guessed it, I guessed it!"

"Good for you." I wipe my hands on my apron. "Come here, sweetie. I want you to open your mouth really wide."

"Why?"

"I'm just going to rub this cotton swab around your cheek. It won't hurt."

He shows me all his teeth and I run the small cotton stick twice across the inside of his cheek before popping it into a plastic tube and screwing on the lid.

"What's that for?" he asks.

"Good luck," I say, ruffling his hair. "Do you want some crisps?" I hand him a bowl. "Make sure you share them."

Later, Simon comes in to see me. I know what he wants to ask. He leans over the bassinet, holding out a finger, which Ben reaches up and clasps tightly.

"That's some grip," he says, staring at the baby, try-ing to see some semblance of self or evidence of pater-nity.

I take another cotton swab and place it against Ben's rosebud lips. He opens his mouth automatically and I rub the stick around his cheek. Turning my back on Simon, I palm the swab and hand him the sample I col-lected earlier from Lachlan.

"Here it is," I say. "Remember our deal. If he's yours, I tell Jack the truth. If he's not yours, you leave us alone. So think carefully before you go ahead and risk my marriage and your friendship."

"I have thought about it," says Simon, holding the sample up to the light, as though amazed that something so small and ordinary could wield such power.

"What have you decided to do?" I ask.

"I'm going to try to get Gina pregnant, but I might hold on to this."

"Well, I don't know how long that sample is good for, but this is a one-off opportunity."

Simon looks at me with a sparkle in his eyes, which could be the champagne. "Do *you* know?"

"I've always known."

"So he's not mine?"

"No."

Simon slips the test tube into his pocket as Jack arrives wearing a Santa hat that is too small for his head. He puts his hand against the small of my back. In the old days, he would have hugged me, but now he is feeling his way back into my affections, always asking permission before crossing any threshold. "What are you two whispering about?" he asks.

"Babies," I say, leaning my head back to kiss his cheek.

"We're not having any more," he says in mock horror.

"Not us," I say, nodding towards Simon.

"Really? Is Gina . . . ?"

"No," says Simon.

"But you're . . . ?"

"Having fun trying."

"Good for you," says Jack. "What took you so long?"

"I've been waiting for the right woman to come along," says Simon, giving me a sad, sweet smile.

Shooing them both out of the kitchen, I check the turkey and turn the potatoes. Ben makes a cooing sound and gives me a beautiful smile, his first, lighting up his eyes. He is a precious gift, an oops baby who stumbled into the world and captivated a nation, which shone a spotlight onto our small, humdrum lives for a brief period. I don't know what they discovered, but certainly not a perfect marriage. That would be boring. We need the darkness to appreciate the light, and the bumps along the road to stop us falling asleep at the wheel.

Will Jack and I last? I have no idea. We're together and we're still in love and we have three beautiful children, so I'm putting my money on silver if not gold. Anniversaries, I mean.

Whatever happens, we will always have Lucy and Lachlan and Ben. Children are like time capsules that we shoot into the future, hoping there will still be a world for them to inherit. I don't know if they are chips off the same block, or if one apple has fallen farther from the tree, but what does it matter?

They are loved. Longed for. Ours.

AGATHA

The morning after I killed myself, I opened my eyes and saw the light angling through the blinds and felt the sheets against my skin and the cool air being drawn through my nostrils.

Someone knocked on the door and pushed it open.

"Good morning, Agatha, my name is Colin." He carried a breakfast tray and his white uniform seemed to glow against his black skin. The tray had toast and scrambled eggs made with lots of parsley and a dollop of cream.

"Where am I?" I asked.

"You're in hospital."

"Am I sick?"

"Your mind needs fixing."

Later they let me go to the lounge, where the staff had put up a Christmas tree with brightly colored baubles and twinkling lights and an angel perched at the very top. I looked out the window, which had vertical bars, and I saw the winter outside.

In the afternoon I had a visitor—a nice man named Cyrus who let me hold his hand as I told him about my life. Nobody has ever listened to me like that—not my mother, or my stepfather, or Mr. Bowler, or Nicky, or Hayden, or the fertility doctors, or random men I took home and fucked, hoping to fall pregnant.

"Have you ever been to Tahiti?" I asked him.

"No. Have you?"

"Yes."

"When?"

"I go there all the time."

"Tell me about your other babies."

"You'll never understand."

"I'd like to try."

That evening I sat in a wheelchair in front of the TV, listening to a choir sing Christmas carols, and I was glad that I didn't die.

"What would you like to do tomorrow, Agatha?" asked Colin. "We have yoga and Pilates, or you could do some planting in the greenhouse."

"Oh, I can't do that," I said. "My daughter is coming to visit. She's driving all the way from Leeds."

"What's her name?"

"I don't know, but she's very pretty and clever and she'll tell me her name when she gets here."

On the morning after I killed myself . . . and the next morning . . . and the one after that, which was Christmas Day . . . I learned how to wait.

ACKNOWLEDGMENTS

Having penned twelve novels, it is a wonderful thing to come to the blank page with all the same excitement and wonder as when I wrote the first lines of *The Suspect* in 2002. Often readers ask me if I have a favorite book among those I've written, and I always answer that choosing one would be like disclosing that I have a favorite child. (They each have their moments.)

What I will say is that I strive to push myself as a writer, never falling back on a formula or writing the same story twice. This is particularly true of *The Secrets She Keeps*, a novel whose structure, substance, and twin voices are the most ambitious I've ever tackled. If I have succeeded it is because of some wonderful editors, most notably Mark Lucas, Lucy Malagoni, Rebecca Saunders, Ursula Mackenzie, Colin Harrison, and Richard Pine.

I am indebted to my wonderful publishing teams at Little, Brown Book Group UK, Hachette Australia, Goldmann in Germany, and the renowned Scribner in the United States, who are publishing me for the first time. I hope this is the start of a beautiful partnership.

A special thanks to Lisa Soussa, who generously donated to the wonderful charity Dreams2live4 and won the right to have a character named after her in the novel.

Saving the best until last, I acknowledge my beautiful and talented daughters, Alex, Charlotte, and Bella, and the woman they most take after, their mother, Vivien, my wife, the one. She knows she's the favorite.

ABOUT THE AUTHOR

Michael Robotham is a former investigative journalist whose psychological thrillers have been translated into twenty-three languages. In 2015, he won the prestigious Gold Dagger from the UK's Crime Writers' Association for his novel *Life or Death*, which was also shortlisted for the 2016 Edgar Award for Best Novel. Michael has twice won a Ned Kelly Award for Australia's best crime novel, for *Lost* in 2005 and *Shatter* in 2008. He has also twice been shortlisted for the CWA Ian Fleming Steel Dagger, in 2007 for *The Night Ferry* and in 2008 for *Shatter*. Michael lives in Sydney with his wife and three daughters, who are growing up and leaving home.

Turn the page for a sneak peek at
Michael Robotham's next book
featuring Cyrus Haven,

GOOD GIRL, BAD GIRL

"*Good Girl, Bad Girl* is a gripping read. You won't
be able to look away."

—Karin Slaughter, #1 internationally
bestselling author

"Stellar . . . Robotham is a master plotter at the top
of his form, and readers will surely hope to see
more of his complicated new characters."

—*Kirkus Reviews* (starred review)

Available from Scribner

1

CYRUS

"Which one is she?" I ask, leaning closer to the observation window.

"Blonde. Baggy sweater. Sitting on her own."

"And you're not going to tell me why I'm here?"

"I don't want to influence your decision."

"What am I deciding?"

"Just watch her."

I look again at the group of teenagers, girls and boys. Most are wearing jeans and long tops with the sleeves pulled down to hide whatever self-inflicted damage has been done. Some are cutters, some are burners or scratchers or bulimics or anorexics or obsessive compulsives or pyromaniacs or sociopaths or narcissists or suffering from ADHD. Some abuse food or drugs, others swallow foreign objects or run into walls on purpose or take outrageous risks.

Evie Cormac has her knees drawn up, almost as though she doesn't trust the floor. Sullen mouthed and pretty, she could be eighteen or she could be fourteen. Not quite a woman or a girl about to bid good-bye to childhood, yet there is something ageless and changeless about her, as if she has seen the worst and survived it. With brown eyes framed by thickened eyelashes and bleached hair cut in a ragged bob, she's holding the sleeves of her sweater in her bunched fists, stretching the neckline, revealing a pattern of red blotches below her jawline that could be hickeys or finger marks.

Adam Guthrie is standing alongside me, regarding Evie like she is the latest arrival at Twycross Zoo.

"Why is she here?" I ask.

"Currently, her primary offense is for aggravated assault. She broke someone's jaw with a half brick."

"Currently?"

"She's had a few."

"How many?"

"Too few to mention."

He's attempting to be funny or deliberately obtuse. We're at Langford Hall, a high-security children's home in Nottingham, where Guthrie is a resident social worker. He's dressed in baggy jeans, combat boots, and a rugby sweater, trying too hard to look like "one of them"; someone who can relate to teenage delinquency and strife rather than an underpaid, low-level public servant with a wife, a mortgage, and two kids. He and I were at university together and lived in the same college. I wouldn't say we were friends, more like passing acquaintances, although I went to his wedding a few years ago and slept with one of the bridesmaids. I didn't know she was Guthrie's youngest sister. Would it have made a difference? I'm not sure. He hasn't held it against me.

"You ready?"

I nod.

We enter the room and take two chairs, joining the circle of teenagers, who watch us with a mixture of suspicion and boredom.

"We have a visitor today," says Guthrie. "This is Cyrus Haven."

"Who is he?" asks one of the girls.

"I'm a psychologist," I reply.

"Another one!" says the same girl, screwing up her face.

"Cyrus is here to observe."

"Us or you?"

"Both."

I look for Evie's reaction. She's watching me blankly.

Guthrie crosses his legs, revealing a hairless pale ankle where his trouser cuff has ridden up his shin. He's a jolly, fat sort of bloke who rubs his hands together at the start of something, presupposing the fun that awaits.

"Let's begin with some introductions, shall we? I want you to each tell Cyrus your name, where you're from, and why you're here. Who wants to go first?"

Nobody answers.

"How about you, Alana?"

She shakes her head. I'm sitting directly opposite Evie. She knows I'm looking at her.

"Holly?" asks Guthrie.

"Nah."

"Evie?"

She doesn't respond.

"It's nice to see you're wearing more clothes today," says Guthrie. "You too, Holly."

Evie snorts.

"That was a legitimate protest," argues Holly, growing more animated. "We were protesting against the outdated assumptions of class and gender inherent in this white-male-dominated gulag."

"Thank you, comrade," says Guthrie, sarcastically. "Will you get us started, Nathan?"

"Don't call me Nathan," says a beanpole of a boy with pimples on his forehead.

"What should I call you?"

"Nat."

"You mean like a bug?" asks Evie.

He spells it out: "N . . . A . . . T."

Guthrie takes a small knitted teddy bear from his pocket and tosses it to Nat. "You're up first. Remember, whoever has the bear has the right to speak. Nobody else can interrupt."

Nat bounces the teddy bear on his thigh.

"I'm from Sheffield and I'm here 'cos I took a dump in my neighbor's VW when he left it unlocked."

Titters all round. Evie doesn't join in.

"Why did you do that?" asks Guthrie.

Nat shrugs nonchalantly. "It were a laugh."

"On the driver's seat?" asks Holly.

"Yeah. Course. Where else? The dickhead complained to the police, so me and my mates gave him a kicking."

"Do you feel bad about that?" asks Guthrie.

"Not really."

"He had to have metal plates put in his head."

"Yeah, but he had insurance and he got compensation. My ma had to pay a fine. Way I see it, the dickhead *made* money."

Guthrie starts to argue but changes his mind, perhaps recognizing the futility.

The teddy bear is passed on to Reebah from Nottingham, who is painfully thin and who sewed her lips together because her father tried to make her eat.

"What did he make you eat?" asks another of the girls, who is so fat that her thighs are forcing her knees apart.

"Food."

"What sort of food?"

"Birthday cake."

"You're an idiot."

Guthrie interrupts, "Please don't make critical comments, Cordelia. You can only speak if you have the bear."

"Give it to me, then," she says, snatching the bear from Reebah's lap.

"Hey! I wasn't finished."

The girls wrestle for a moment until Guthrie intervenes, but Reebah has forgotten what she wanted to say.

The bear is in a new lap. "My name is Cordelia and I'm from Leeds and when someone pisses me off, I fight them, you know. I make 'em pay."

"You get angry?" asks Guthrie.

"Yeah."

"What sort of things make you angry?"

"When people call me fat."

"You are fat," says Evie.

"Shut the fuck up!" yells Cordelia, jumping to her feet. She's twice Evie's size. "Say that again and I'll fuckin' batter you."

Guthrie has put himself between them. "Apologies, Evie."

Evie smiles sweetly. "I'm sorry for calling you *fat*, Cordelia. I think you've lost weight. You look positively svelte."

"What's that mean?" she asks.

"Skinny."

"Fuck off!"

"OK, let's all settle down," says Guthrie. "Cordelia, why are you here?"

"I grew up too soon," she replies. "I lost my virginity at, like, eleven. I slept with guys and slept with girls and smoked a lot of pot. I tried heroin at twelve and ice when I was thirteen."

Evie rolls her eyes.

Cordelia glares at her. "My mum called the police on me, so I tried to poison her with floor cleaner."

"To punish her?" asks Guthrie.

"Maybe," says Cordelia. "It was like an experiment, you know. I wanted to, like, see what would happen."

"Did it work?" asks Nat.

"Nah," replies Cordelia. "She said the soup tasted funny and didn't finish the bowl. Made her vomit, that's all."

"You should have used wolfsbane," says Nat.

"What's that?"

"It's a plant. I heard about this gardener who died when he touched the leaves."

"My mum doesn't like gardening," says Cordelia, missing the point.

Guthrie passes the teddy bear to Evie. "Your turn."

"Nope."

"Why not?"

"The details of my life are inconsequential."

"That's not true."

Evie sighs and leans forward, resting her forearms on her knees, squeezing the bear with both hands. Her accent changes.

"My father was a relentlessly self-improving boulangerie owner from Belgium with low-grade narcolepsy and a penchant for buggery. My mother was a fifteen-year-old French prostitute named Chloe with webbed feet . . ."

I laugh. Everybody looks at me.

"It's from *Austin Powers*," I explain.

More blank stares.

"The movie . . . Mike Myers . . . Dr. Evil."

Still nothing.

Evie puts on a gruff Scottish accent. "First things first. Where's your shitter? I've got a turtle head poking out."

"Fat Bastard," I say.

Evie smiles. Guthrie is annoyed with me, as though I'm fomenting unrest.

He calls on another teenager, who has a blue streak in her hair and piercings in her ears, eyebrows, and nose.

"What brings you here, Serena?"

"Well, it's a long story."

Groans all round.

Serena recounts an episode from her life when she went to America as an exchange student at sixteen and lived with a family in Ohio, whose son was in prison for murder. Every fortnight they insisted Serena visit him, making her wear her sexiest clothes. Short dresses. Low-cut tops.

"He was on the other side of the glass and his father kept telling me to lean closer and show him my tits."

Evie sneezes into the crook of her arm in a short, sharp exhalation that sounds a lot like "Bullshit!"

Serena glares at her but goes on with her story. "That night, when I was sleeping, the father came into my room and raped me. I was too frightened to tell my parents or call the police. I was alone in a foreign country, thousands of miles from home." She looks around the group, hoping for sympathy.

Evie sneezes again—making the same sound.

Serena tries to ignore her.

"Back home, I started having problems—drinking and cutting myself. My parents sent me to see a therapist, who seemed really nice at the beginning until he tried to rape me."

"For fuck's sake!" says Evie, sighing in disgust.

"We're not here to pass judgment," Guthrie warns her.

"But she's making shit up. What's the point of sharing if people are gonna tell lies?"

"Fuck you!" shouts Serena, flipping Evie the finger.

"Bite me," says Evie.

Serena leaps to her feet. "You're a freak! Everybody knows it."

"Please sit down," says Guthrie, trying to keep the girls apart.

"She called me a fucking liar," whines Serena.

"No, I didn't," says Evie. "I called you a *psycho* fucking liar."

Serena ducks under Guthrie's arm and launches herself across the space, knocking Evie off her chair. The two of them are wrestling on the floor, but Evie seems to be laughing as she wards off the blows.

An alarm has been raised and a security team bursts into the group therapy room, dragging Serena away. The rest of the teenagers are ordered back to their bedrooms, all except for Evie. Dusting herself off, she touches the corner of her lip, then rubs a smudge of blood between her thumb and forefinger.

I give her a tissue. "Are you all right?"

"I'm fine. She punches like a girl."

"What happened to your neck?"

"Someone tried to strangle me."

"Why?"

"I have that sort of face."

I pull up a chair and motion for Evie to sit down. She complies, crossing her legs, revealing an electronic tag on her ankle.

"Why are you wearing that?"

"They think I'm trying to escape."

"Are you?"

Evie raises her forefinger to her lips and makes a shushing sound.

"First chance I get."

2

CYRUS

Guthrie meets me in a pub called Man of Iron, named after the nearby Stanton Ironworks, which closed down years ago. He's perched on a stool with an empty pint glass resting between his elbows, watching a fresh beer being pulled.

"Your regular boozer?" I ask, sitting next to him.

"My escape," he replies. His fingers are pudgy and pale, decorated with a tri-band wedding ring.

The barman asks if I want something. I shake my head and Guthrie looks disappointed to be drinking alone. Over his shoulder I see a lounge area with a pool table and slot machines that ping and blink like a fairground ride.

"You're looking good," I say. Lying. "How's married life?"

"Terrific. Great. Making me fat." He pats his stomach. "You should try it."

"Getting fat?"

"Marriage."

"How are the kids?"

"Growing like weeds. We have two now, a boy and a girl, eight and five."

I can't remember his wife's name but recall her being

eastern European, with a thick accent and a wedding dress that looked like a craft project that had gone horribly wrong. Guthrie had met her when he was teaching part-time at an English-language school in London.

"What did you think of Evie?" he asks.

"She's a real charmer."

"She's one of them."

"One of who?"

"The lie detectors."

I suppress a laugh. He looks aggrieved.

"You saw her. She knew you were lying. She's a truth wizard—just like you wrote about in your thesis."

"You *read* my thesis?"

"Every word."

I make a face. "That was eight years ago."

"It was published."

"And I concluded that truth wizards didn't exist."

"No, you said they represented a tiny percentage of the population—maybe one in five hundred—and the best of them were accurate eighty percent of the time. You also wrote that someone could develop even greater skills, a person who wasn't disrupted by emotions or lack of familiarity with the subject; someone who functioned at a higher level."

Christ, he did read it!

I want to stop the conversation and tell Guthrie he's wrong. I spent two years writing my thesis on truth wizards, reading the literature, exploring the history, and conducting experiments on more than three thousand volunteers. Evie Cormac is too young to be a truth wizard. Usually, they're middle-aged or older, able to draw on their experiences in certain professions, such as detectives, judges, lawyers, psychologists, and secret service agents. Teenagers are too busy looking in the mirror or studying their phones to be reading the subtle, almost imperceptible, changes in people's facial expressions or the nuances of their body language or their tones of voice.

Guthrie is waiting for me to respond.

"I think you're mistaken," I say.

"But you *saw* her do it."

"She's a very clever, manipulative teenager."

The social worker sighs and peers into his half-empty glass. "She's driven me to this."

"What?"

"Drinking. According to my doctor I have the body of a sixty-year-old; I have high blood pressure, fatty tissue around my heart, and borderline cirrhosis."

"How is that Evie's fault?"

"Every time I talk to her, I want to curl up in a ball and sob. I took two months off earlier in the year—stress leave, but it didn't help. Now my wife is threatening to leave me unless I agree to see a marriage counselor. I haven't told a soul that information, but somehow Evie knew."

"How?"

"How do you think?" Guthrie doesn't wait for me to respond. "Believe me, Cyrus. She can tell when people are lying."

"Even if that were true, I don't see why I'm here."

"You could help her."

"How?"

"Evie has made an application to the court to be released, but she's not ready to leave Langford Hall. She's dyslexic. Antisocial. Aggressive. She has no friends. Nobody ever visits her. She's a danger to herself and others."

"If she's eighteen, she *has* the right to move on."

Guthrie hesitates and tugs at his collar, pulling it away from his neck.

"Nobody knows her true age."

"What do you mean?"

"There's no record of her birth."

I blink at him. "There must be something—a hospital file, a midwife's report, school enrollments . . ."

"There are no records."

"That's impossible."

Guthrie takes a moment to finish his beer and signal the barman for another. He drops his voice to a whisper. "What I'm about to tell you is highly classified. I'm talking top secret. You can't breathe a word of this to anyone."

I want to laugh. Guthrie is the least likely spy in history.

"I'm serious, Cyrus."

"OK. OK."

His beer arrives. He centers it on a cardboard coaster and waits for the barman to wander out of earshot. A shaft of sunlight is slanting through a window. Full of floating specks, it gives the pub the ambience of a church and that I'm hearing Guthrie's confession.

"Evie is the girl in the box."

"Who?"

"Angel Face."

Immediately, I understand the reference but want to argue. "That can't be right."

"It's her."

"But that was . . ."

"Six years ago."

I remember the story. A girl found living in a secret room in a house in north London. Thought to be eleven or twelve, she weighed less than a child of half that age. A mop-headed, wild-eyed, feral-looking creature, more animal than human, she could have been raised by wolves.

Her hiding spot was only feet away from where the police had discovered the decomposing body of a man who had been tortured to death, sitting upright in a chair. The girl had lived with the corpse for months, sneaking out to steal food and sharing it with the two dogs that were kenneled in the garden.

Those first images were flashed around the world. They showed an off-duty special constable carrying a small child through the doors of a hospital. The girl wouldn't let anyone else touch her, and her only words were to ask for food and whether the dogs were all right.

The nurses dubbed her Angel Face because they had to call her something. The details of her captivity dominated the news for weeks. Everybody had a question. Who was she? Where had she come from? How had she survived?

Guthrie has been waiting for me to catch up.

"She was never identified," he explains. "The police tried everything—missing persons files, DNA, bone X-rays, stable isotopes . . . Her photograph went around the world, but nothing came back."

How could a child appear out of nowhere—with no record of her birth or her passage through life?

Guthrie continues. "She became a ward of the court and was given a new name—Evie Cormac. The Home Secretary added a Section 39 Order, which forbids anybody from revealing her identity or location or taking any pictures or footage of her."

"Who knows?" I ask.

"At Langford Hall—only me."

"Why is she here?"

"There's nowhere else."

"I don't understand."

"She was placed in a dozen different homes, but each time she either ran away or they sent her back.

She's also had four caseworkers, three psychologists, and God-knows-how-many social workers. I'm the last one standing."

"What's her mental health status?"

"She passed every psych test from Balthazar to Winslow."

"I still don't understand why I'm here."

Guthrie sucks an inch off his pint and looks along the bar.

"Like I said, Evie is a ward of the court, meaning the High Court makes all the important decisions about her welfare while the local authority controls her day-to-day care. Two months ago, she petitioned to be classed as an adult."

"If she's deemed to be eighteen, she has every right."

Guthrie looks at me plaintively. "She's a danger to herself and others. If she succeeds . . ." He shudders, unable to finish. "Imagine having her ability."

"You make it sound like a superpower."

"It is," he says earnestly.

"I think you're exaggerating."

"She clocked you straightaway."

"Being perceptive doesn't make someone a truth wizard."

He lifts his eyebrows, as though he expected more of me.

"I think you're trying to fob her off," I say.

"Gladly," he says, "but that's not the reason. I honestly thought you could help her. Everybody else has failed."

"Has she ever talked about what happened to her—in the house, I mean."

"No. According to Evie, she has no past, no family, and no memories."

"She's blocked them out."

"Maybe. At the same time, she lies, she obfuscates, she casts shade and misdirects. She's a nightmare."

"I don't think she's a truth wizard," I say.

"OK."

"What files can you show me?"

"I'll get them to you. Some of the early details have been redacted to protect her new identity."

"You said Evie broke someone's jaw. Who was it?" I ask.

"A member of staff found two thousand pounds in her room. He figured Evie must have stolen the money and took it from her, saying he was going to hand it over to the police."

"What happened?"

"Evie knew he was lying."

"Where did she get the money?" I ask.

"She said she won it playing poker."

"Is that possible?"

"I wouldn't bet against her."